**A LOVELY YOUNG AMERICAN GIRL,
HER BEAUTIFUL SOCIALITE MOTHER,
AND THE PROUD EUROPEAN ARISTOCRAT
WHOM THEY BOTH LOVE...**

Against the dazzling background of an international pleasure resort on the golden coast of Spain, these three people, with their friends, enemies, lovers and acquaintances, play out a drama of pride, passion, courage and betrayal that will have you hanging from page to page until the final stunning climax . . .

"The glittering seductive skin of this novel contains the dance of a group of people who are full of mystery."—Muriel Rukeyser

"The plotting is expert . . . it gets hold of you and your interest never flags."

—*Saturday Review Syndicate*

"An absorbing work of fiction, powerfully written and superbly plotted."

—*Book-of-the-Month Club News*

(please turn page)

THE
COLUMBUS
TREE

Peter S. Feibleman

A SIGNET BOOK
NEW AMERICAN LIBRARY
TIMES MIRROR

Library of Congress Catalog Card Number: 72-90511

SIGNET TRADEMARK REG. U.S. PAT. OFF. AND FOREIGN COUNTRIES
REGISTERED TRADEMARK—MARCA REGISTRADA
HECHO EN CHICAGO, U.S.A.

SIGNET, SIGNET CLASSICS, SIGNETTE, MENTOR AND PLUME BOOKS
are published by The New American Library, Inc.,
1301 Avenue of the Americas, New York, New York 10019

FIRST PRINTING, FEBRUARY, 1974

1 2 3 4 5 6 7 8 9

PRINTED IN THE UNITED STATES OF AMERICA

For Lillian Hellman

"Goe, and catche a falling starre,
Get with child a mandrake roote,
Tell me, where all past yeares are,
Or who cleft the Divel's foot,
Teach me to heare Mermaides singing,
Or to keep off envies stinging,
And finde
What winde
Serves to advance an honest minde."

JOHN DONNE

Cloven ppl. a. ME [pa. pple. of CLEAVE v.] Divided lengthwise; split.

C. *hoof* or *foot,* the divided hoof of ruminant quadrupeds; ascribed in pagan mythology to the god Pan, and thence to the Devil, and often used allusively as the indication of Satan, or Satanic agency. Hence c.-hoofed, -footed, *adjs.*

THE SHORTER OXFORD ENGLISH DICTIONARY

Contents

THE
COLUMBUS
TREE

ALONG the coast there's a town called Suelo, and west of Gibraltar you can see it from the water. There are other towns that follow the Spanish coast there that you cannot see. Suelo is a fishing village that stretches from the water's edge up into a small range of hills and almost makes it, as if it were trying to join the sea with the land. The last house is three quarters of the way up. All of the houses look like they are burning, so white you can't stare at them at noon, and always in the afternoon there are nets drying in the late shattered light. In the summer the white sky is fierce and hazy with a deep burning glow like silver and the air is cool off the sea. But sometimes a shaft of dry wind from the African desert crosses the thin stretch of water separating the two continents here and runs like a hot breath above the land. In December it rains and there are two months of winter with little ugly cold winds that ruffle the tops of trees and flatten the grass. But very soon it's hot again and over the blinding textured houses the white dust-ball sun makes the town shimmer. By three o'clock on a summer's day you think the place is crowding out of the sea, shaking itself off in the light. The fishing village couldn't exist farther up the hills than it does, but you sometimes have the feeling that it tried.

There are not many things to know about Suelo; but it was once destroyed. There was an earthquake somewhere in Africa that caused a seismic sea wave. The big wave came in the night at seven and a half minutes past eleven and left four hours later taking the town with it. There are those now living who remember that their great-grandfathers knew about it. They say that it was not expected because the earthquake that caused it had not been felt in Suelo, not even a tremor. There was another kind of warning more difficult to recognize. At fifteen minutes to seven in the evening the surf stopped. It was an omen of disaster —a kind of foreshadowing of death—but in the whole village only two people screamed. One of them was a child. The

1

other, they say, was a deaf-mute who had never made a sound before. Andalusian superstitions are as deep as they are outlandish; the story of the deaf-mute was believed because it meant something. Along the coast the surf is a part of the way of things, and those who live by the rhythm are used to it and never listen to it—as people who are accustomed to living never listen to their hearts. The cessation of surf was like a heart attack in the town, and people stood still no matter what they were doing and listened to the silence. They cocked their heads and stood frowning. Then they went back to talking or cooking or cutting up fish or whatever they had been doing before. Several times during the three hours of silence a few of them quit work and turned again to listen. After a while for no known reason people began to whisper. The child was calmed by its parents. But the deaf-mute, they say, went on screaming.

The September night was thick and it wasn't till late that a rip came in the clouds and let enough light in to see the ribs of sand stretching out endlessly, glistening, where the water had been. The small ribs of sand were uniform, like the roof of a gigantic open mouth. Word spread slowly up into the hills from the houses closest to the beach that the sea was gone. Nearly everyone went down for a look. They knew then what they had been hearing was the absence of the surf and they had just time to know it before the sea came back. What had happened was only an enlargement of the ordinary. As the water is sucked out a few feet from shore for each small wave it had been sucked out several miles for this big wave. Death often comes in waves, and this wave came in like death. It creased in the distance, but before it did, before they even saw it—at the first sharp hissing out of the blackness, no louder than the crumpling of dry tissue paper—it was at that first moment, they say, that the deaf-mute stopped screaming. Some of the fishermen tried to run up inland and others saw that there was no use running and stood, quiet, and waited. When the swollen water came it was so loud they couldn't hear it. It didn't look like a wave. It was just there. When they heard it as a single long pouring, it rose. It lifted like a sigh into the earth far above the town, just rising and rising, and it took away everything.

The town of Suelo is a scattered nest of limestone-white houses like eggs in the sun at the meeting between the flanks of two long hills. The hills are like thighs, smooth and rounded, from the hip to a point just below the knee. The suggestive shape of the hills is a matter of interest only to the pilots who fly past Suelo from Tangiers or Marrakesh on their way to Lisbon; the pilots grin down and leer at the nestling houses. They wink sometimes. The fishermen's white dwellings are caught there in the heaving of the gentle soil lying back into the low uplands, and when the pilots see the two long surging thighs of the earth, they reach down and feel their testicles. They tilt their wings and flirt with the town.

That is a short history of Suelo, which is like any other Andalusian fishing village on the water. Only seen from the air it is small and obscene and tender. Or it was until the second big wave came. The wave from the land.

For a long time there had been visitors. They came singly and in couples and sometimes in groups of three. They came mostly from Madrid. One or two a year were from farther north than that—Bilbao or Valladolid. The visitors came and went and after a while they were like the low steady surf, no one noticed them. There was one small hotel called the Pez Espada that was more of a boarding house, and they either stayed there overnight or did not stay. Those who came were not rich so they didn't seem to mind the one drawback, the stickiness of the beach. It was caused by tar inside the sand from the bottoms of the fishing boats and the visitors either brought turpentine with them or wore rubber sandals. Tourists with money to spend preferred the northern Spanish towns along the Basque coast on the Bay of Biscay where it was colder and the sand was clean and white. Suelo attracted only the people who couldn't afford the expensive places and some came every year. As often as four or five times a month the town had guests.

Then without warning they stopped coming.

The fishermen of Suelo should have known what this new silence was going to mean but they did not. They only noticed that something in the usual rhythm of things was missing, and they listened for the missing sound and again heard nothing. The occasional laughter of two or three people running into the water was gone. There was only an ominous peaceful silence; but this time no one screamed. What had happened was soon known. A man from the neighboring province of Málaga, not a Castilian but an Andalusian businessman, had come one morning and bought a lot of property along the coast at Suelo. The businessman had ordered a machine, a bulldozer, to clean the sand of tar. It took a long time and every day the bulldozer

3

could be seen running up and down the beach. The local people smiled at first and then they ignored it. The bulldozer was enormous and it had been freshly painted. It was of a reddish purple hue, the color of a deep blush. The fishermen got used to seeing the big bashful machine working. It did not disturb them much, but it disturbed the bathers, and they stopped coming. When the machine finished its work the beach was not clean—it still retained a gray color—but the tar no longer stuck to everything that touched it. The machine had broken it up into minute particles like the sand. Then the machine went away and there was the silence. For months there was nothing but the quiet lapping of the waves and the sound of the fishermen's own voices and they listened painfully, craning their necks and holding their breaths until finally, in the distance—in the far north from the direction of Madrid and of Paris and of London—they heard the faint first edge of a buzz in the air.

ONE

Americans

WILL stood at the northwest side of the highest hill and listened to the plane that was circling to land. He squinted. From the sound he knew it was a seaplane, a small two-seater that had been chartered, and he thought he knew who had chartered it. It was going to land soon, he could tell from the noise of the motors. He could not see it. The buzzing of the plane and the pearl-white stillness of the September sky burned into his ears and eyes at the same time and met somewhere under his stomach. The air was singed; it smelled of the surrounding bushes of dark green thyme. With his eyes shut Will could feel the dry dust in the webs between his fingers, and the odor of thyme was as strong in his mouth as a taste. A wave of sleep came over him and he blinked into the air. He stopped trying to see the plane, and looked down at himself, letting his eyes swing in a kind of zigzag path over his own body. He was a spindly boy of twelve who would be thirteen years old tomorrow and he looked it, he thought. He was ashamed of his size—he was small for his age—and he hated the way his ribs stuck out one by one like shelves through his T-shirt. His body embarrassed him. He had left his mother with her preparations for his birthday party that would take place tomorrow in the Hotel Malage. She was using the birth-day as an excuse to have one of the society parties that she had taken to giving more and more lately. She had told Will to run along and take a swim. He had come up here in-stead.

He lay back between two low bushes and moved his back-bone like a snake for a place his body would fit into. After a while he found one—except for a rise that stuck into his left shoulder blade. He sat up and took a flat stone and scraped the piece of earth away. He was lying at a seesaw angle with his feet against a rock and he could see easily down into the town. He cast his eyes like beams below him and let them splay softly over the different kinds of hotels. There were a lot of them. Except for the part in back, most

7

of the Spanish fishing village had been destroyed by the long endless wave of visitors that grew each year. People traveled from all over Europe and from America to Suelo —along the beach there were twenty-two hotels of different classes and still others being built. Looking down Will counted five more before his eyes began to water. He could feel the sun on his knees; the heat licked up just under his crotch. It made him hot there and he felt his piece twitch against his bluejeans. He considered about taking it out for a while. For a year he had known how to do it in fast long jerks until the new feeling, the life-feeling, came. It was a way to let something inside him out of a cage; but he needed to keep it caged now and think. He had a bad problem that kept twisting in his mind. It was about his half-sister.

Her name was Alice Littlejohn, only she had always hated the name of Alice. She preferred to be called just Little-john. The odd part was that neither one of them was much like their mother, Helen. Littlejohn was nine and a half years older than Will—going on twenty-three. She lived in New York. Her father was a minister who had inherited a lot of money. He preferred to live simply and practice his faith; he had given most of the money to Littlejohn. She came to see Will twice a year wherever he was and Will waited for the visits. She had always been the person in the world he was most connected with. He could not explain that.

Littlejohn's father had divorced their mother and Will's father had been her second husband: he had not had time to divorce her—he had been killed in the Second World War. Now, in 1957, he had been dead thirteen years and one month. Since his death Will had lived alone with Helen, but for the last couple of years he had lived in boarding schools and had stayed with her only on vacations. (Helen traveled a lot, visiting friends and going to this or that resort.) This year he had gone to the Lycée Français in Madrid where classes were taught in French, though many of the students were Spanish; Helen had decided a European upbringing would be good for him. So far Will's Spanish and French were both good and he could understand some Italian too and a little German. Just over three months ago he and Helen had come down to Suelo for the summer; Littlejohn had joined them here in June.

Now on the hill he opened his eyelids enough that the light swam around in two loose pools. He could see two of his eyelashes like black thorns stuck into the flesh. His life had been confused ever since the day last June that Little-john came.

Now she was gone—Will didn't know where—and that was the last of the rattling facts of the summer, and the worst; it wasn't possible, but there it was.

He could see the plane now coming in below to land on the water. Through the heat waves it looked like a long slant of silver that flashed like a knife over the sea. Then he remembered what Littlejohn had said to him when she left this last time. It was a blunt fact, a thing that didn't fit inside his train of livingness at all without mashing all the other facts to pieces. She hadn't told it to anybody else. She had turned from the boat that was waiting for her, and walked back to Will and put her head close on the left side where the six freckles were, so close the freckles stood out from her skin like little maps in front of his eyes, and said, "I'm going to have one, Will." Just that—no more. Then she had turned quickly and left, so that when Will watched the motor launch through the spray that rose behind it like a fan opening out of the sea he had seen not the fan but only the six freckles. Six maps. Six words. *I'm going to have one, Will.* That made so much sense they made no sense at all. When the freckles had faded from his eyes she was already gone in the water.

Hunching back in the dust he thought now that in just three months there had been so many new happenings in his life he had had no time to get used to any of them. There was the fact of life and the fact of death. There was even the fact of murder. Besides that, a Spanish child had died: two people had been killed, two were starting to be born, in this one summer. . . .

The seaplane had landed now. He watched it below him cutting channels behind it like white burns in the water. It waddled in the sea toward the Hotel Malage. Then watching the sky he could hear the singing of crickets in the bushes around his head. He belonged in the green smell growing out of the dust. If he could catch up with the last three months, things would be easier; if he could start back at June, he could get used to the new pieces of living. Like that first morning—the day Littlejohn had come to Suelo —June the Fifth. Though not so much had happened to him that day, still he knew it had all started then.

It had begun when they were driving in her convertible under a streaky gray sky darker than this one. It had been just the two of them. Him and Littlejohn.

On the morning of June the Fifth.

THEY drove that day watching the big black shadows wheel in the sky. Will could see them clearly—they were birds of some kind. Looking back from the convertible he could almost make out the separate feathers. He asked what they were but Littlejohn didn't hear him, for thinking, or else because the top was down and the wind was too loud. South of Seville the air from the hot fields of alfalfa was so thick you could feel it, sick-sweet and heavy on the tongue. Will dipped his jaw and took a mouthful of air and pushed it back out. He decided to ask the question again. He could still see the black shapes turning, like shadows on the sky, as if they were caught in the air. "What are they?" he said.

"Vultures," Littlejohn said without looking. "Dirty birds."

"Why dirty?"

"Because they are. They wait up there watching an animal die till it's dead, and the animal dies watching them wait. They're horrible."

Will looked back again to see what it was the birds were circling over, but they were too far away now. They looked like smoke over the low gray hills. Littlejohn turned a curve and they were gone. Ahead was the smudged sky with long ash-clouds running across it and then he saw a gas station and some people standing outside next to a station wagon: sailors from the American naval base farther on at Rota. The two men were in uniform. The women were dressed in bright colors and one of them had high-combed hard hair like painted tin, shiny—the dead color of yellow that comes from hair dye. "Navy ladies," Littlejohn said. "More dirty birds."

Will could tell she was in a bad mood; she was trying to sound too hard. He turned his head and looked at her.

Littlejohn was dressed like a man, with boots halfway up to the knees over bluejeans and a white shirt and no cap. She never wore any makeup and the sun had burned her hair white and gold on top, different colors—not like the

women at the gas station. Littlejohn's hair was short; it
looked like long pieces of flame, like she was burning.

Will dropped his gaze to where the hard sunlight gave
Littlejohn's light blue eyes a kind of feverish glitter. You
couldn't tell from her profile, but from time to time she
was just the smallest bit cross-eyed—it was nearly unnoticeable, but it was one of the features he loved best about
her looks. It didn't happen unless she was angry or something; then her eyes would flash, and then you saw that the
right one listed a fraction of a degree toward the center.
The defect made Littlejohn look off balance and strangely
vulnerable right at the times when she most wanted to look
the opposite. Sometimes it gave her whole face—at times almost too stark to be considered pretty—an odd sexual quality. She was pretty, though. Not as beautiful looking as
Helen, but then nobody was as beautiful as Helen. Right
now the wind was molding Littlejohn's shirt against her
right breast, and Will could feel the curve of it more that
way than if he had reached out and touched her. The look
of her breast made a sort of ache in him. The more she
tried dressing like a man the more she looked like a woman,
he knew. She wasn't all that much taller than he was, and
trim, but everything was there, the full curve of it, and
sometimes the little nipple at the end.

Littlejohn saw him looking and put a hand up through
her hair and then back on the wheel. "Will, don't stare at
me," she said, "I'm driving."

He sat back and looked ahead again. A car was coming
in the opposite direction; it wasn't an American car and
the man behind the wheel didn't have American eyes. The
strange man's face lit up in the half-second when he saw
Littlejohn, just as the two cars passed. His eyes glowed out
as if they had a light of their own. Will thought they were
Spanish eyes, but he wasn't sure. He had this theory all eyes
have countries. Except dead eyes; they must be like photographs of eyes, homeless. Only that was a guess—Will had
never seen a dead person. He turned around but the strange
man in the car had already disappeared down a side road
behind them. The road was at a turnoff that was marked
"Sanlúcar." Will could still make out the dust from his car.
"I didn't like the way he looked at you," he said.

"Who?"

"That man."

". . . What man?"

"He's gone now," Will said. For no reason he added, "I
ought to marry you."

"You can't," Littlejohn said.

"We didn't inherit all the same genes. It's a question of genes. A half-brother isn't really a brother."

"Look, Will," Littlejohn said, "shut up for a while. I'm thinking."

"You don't sound like you," Will said. "You're talking like somebody else."

"Like who?"

"Somebody tough. You're not like that."

He put his hands on the seat next to him. For a second he was word-proud, as if all the thoughts in his brain were swelling—he could feel them in his head and in his pants. The thoughts were getting bigger and he sat there listening to the swelling of the words.

"It's going to be a hot day," he said. "Where'll we go?"

Littlejohn didn't answer right away. "I'd like to see Jerez, and I'd like to take a look at the coast around Cádiz," she said finally. "We can stop and have lunch somewhere. There's . . . I have a thing I want to talk to you about. We needn't hurry, as long as we make Suelo while it's daylight."

"It doesn't get dark now till nine," Will said.

They drove a while in silence.

"I've never been to Puerto de Santa María," he said. "It's a port town between the American base and Cádiz. Mother's never been there either. She talks about a lot of places she's never been to. She just talks a lot."

"That she does," Littlejohn said. "So do you. That you inherited."

Will crossed his arms and looked to the right. They were passing soft rolling fields now, yellow and green and studded with white houses. It wasn't just the way she was talking. He had known all morning that Littlejohn had something special to tell him. She had phoned the day before from Madrid to ask Will to take the bus up from Suelo and meet her in Seville; even Helen had found it suspicious. Littlejohn wouldn't have wanted to spend the day driving around in a car unless there was something she needed to say to Will privately without their mother anywhere near. Helen hadn't much liked the idea but there was nothing really wrong with it; Will had taken the first bus, the early one, and got off at the last stop outside Seville just before ten o'clock that morning. He had waited an hour drinking an orangeade at a white wicker table in a dusty outdoor restaurant under a tin canopy on the main highway. Then he had seen her.

Littlejohn had come in a silly way, driving too fast, rising over the gray hills as if the sun were chasing her. She had skidded to a stop at the restaurant where they had arranged to meet, and she hadn't talked. She had just picked Will up in the rented car and looked at him once, long and hard, the way she always did after a six months' separation, and touched his face with the flat of her hand and then started the car up again and they drove together silently on the road south from Seville through the alfalfa fields in the white sunlight with the death-gray hills behind them. Littlejohn was like that—she didn't say a thing until she got good and ready. Even though she had arranged it, she wouldn't tell him what it was that she had come to tell him until the time was right. It was an old habit, her private sense of timing—Helen always claimed it came from Littlejohn's father, the Reverend John Littlejohn. It was unnatural for a girl to be so quiet, Helen had said when Littlejohn was younger. It was unnatural for a girl to be so full of a minister's silences.

She braked now behind a hay truck and waited for a chance to pass it and Will put his head back on the seat and thought for maybe the millionth time in his life about his own father. He hadn't known his father but he had seen a picture of him. William Charles Locke, a war hero. You couldn't tell much from the picture but he looked perfectly nice. Nobody ever told Will much about it so he sometimes dreamed about it. He didn't miss his father—he never had; but he dreamed of wars and all the ways his father's plane had chewed into the soft earth. He didn't mind thinking about the men killed instantly; he only didn't like the ones left dying slowly and screaming. Maybe it wasn't like that but he thought it was like that. Maybe war wasn't the way he dreamed it was either.

"Here we are," Littlejohn said. He sat up and looked.

It was true whenever he thought about his father he stopped noticing things. They were coming into the city of Jerez. Littlejohn pulled up in front of a small white-fronted bar that had two tables outside. They went in and sat down and she ordered a glass of wine, and Will ordered a *caña* —a small glass of draft beer. "The beer is weak in Spain," he said, "all the kids take a little." Littlejohn nodded and the waiter went to make their drinks. The waiter had almond-shaped Moorish eyes. The little room was dark and tile-cool. It buzzed with flies. The waiter brought their drinks with a plate of sour-smelling olives and set it down between them. His eyes inched over Littlejohn's body as he straightened. Most men looked at her that way. Will raised his glass when Littlejohn raised hers. They touched glasses, and Littlejohn looked at him. Her eyes were sea-colored over the light yellow wine. She didn't look cross-eyed at all today. She watched Will while she tasted it. "It's sherry."

"Sure."

". . . Why sure?"

"It's what Jerez is," Will said. "The story is that none of the Englishmen who came here to make wine could say Jerez, so they pronounced it sherry."

"Why did they come here to make wine?"

"The Spaniards were making it," Will said. He had learned all this at school.

"Oh," Littlejohn said. She put her glass down on the tin-topped table and stroked it. Will watched her hand. The ends of her fingers were shaking. "Do you like Spain, Will?"

He lifted his shoulders.

"You're not unhappy?"

"No."

Littlejohn usually asked him the same question. When she came they went places together and talked to each other. Will could explain things that were on his mind to her in a way that he could not talk to anybody else. Only today she looked edgy, he thought. More than edgy.

"What are you scared about?"

Littlejohn kept her eyes on her glass. "What makes you think I'm scared?"

"You looked funny when you came this morning."

"I haven't had much rest," Littlejohn said, "that's all. . . . I threw a few things in a bag and flew from New York to Madrid. I rented the car in Madrid. . . . I spent last night in Córdoba. I just need some sleep. That's all it is."

Will took a gulp of his beer and swallowed it. He didn't believe her. The beer was salty and not very bubbly but it had a nice bitter flavor.

"You hungry?" Littlejohn asked, "or should we have lunch later?"

"Later."

They got back in the car and drove south through the dusty city of Jerez. It smelled of olive oil and black tobacco and in some places there was the odor of carnations. The heat swam up from the streets in hard baking waves and he was glad when they could see the open road again. As they came out of the choked buildings they passed white-walled *bodegas*, wineries where the sherry was aged and bottled, but by then you couldn't smell anything but dust again with the sun in it.

Will swiveled his eyes in the burning-hot air. The fields

on either side of the road had turned a sulky brown. There were splotches of some kind of grain that stuck up, low motionless and shining, in the windless heat. The sun poured down over the car and after a while Littlejohn pulled over to the dirt at the side of the road and put the top up. When she started along the highway again she drove more slowly. Then in the silence she said it:

"I'm going to be married, Will."

He had been watching the dust that rose like a sheen in the air ahead of them and he had been thinking about drinking an ice-cold Coke.

"You hear me?"

For a while Will didn't move. He considered the new fact, but it didn't knife into his stomach like it normally would have—it came more in a fuzzy feeling around his skin, as though he had put his finger in a weak electric plug. He knew Littlejohn was expecting him to have a re-action to it but he only sat there.

The new fact didn't sound at all like her, he thought. It was their mother Helen who was always getting engaged. As a rule Helen decided to marry somebody on the average of once a year; a Christmas when she wasn't planning on it wasn't really a celebration. Littlejohn had decided years ago that she herself would never get married. Back when she was fifteen and Will was six she had told him about it. She wasn't going to look at men seriously. It wasn't in her. She was going to become an anthropologist and study bones.

"I have to. It's time," she said now as if he had asked her why, "it's like this, Will . . . the French have the right idea—you don't necessarily get married because you're dying of love. That kind doesn't always last."

The whole thing sounded like she had been practicing it in a tape recorder.

"Why then?"

Littlejohn said, "You just need a reason to stay alive." It was a funny answer, but she meant it, he could tell. It didn't sound rehearsed.

"Mother will want to know if he has money," she added.

"Does he have money?" Will said. It was the game they used to play when they were younger—getting each other ready for Helen's questions.

"No," Littlejohn said. "I have."

Will yawned, hard.

"My getting married won't change us. I'll come to see you just as often."

"It doesn't bother me," Will said. "I'm fine."

". . . You only yawn like that when you're nervous."

"It's you," Will said. "You're nervous. I watched when you came to pick me up. You were driving away from the sun."

Littlejohn stared at the road in front of them without speaking for a minute or so.

"What's he look like?" Will said.

". . . Oh, he's good-looking, I think," she said slowly. She laughed. "I must have thought so, anyway."

"Where did you first meet him?"

There was a pause. "I can't remember," Littlejohn said.

". . . You what?"

"It's a problem I've always had," she said. "Not remembering."

"How can you marry a man if you don't remember what he looks like?"

"I'll remember him when I see him."

"Okay," Will said.

He couldn't explain the feeling that was inside him now. The electricity in his brain was making side roads down through his body—it was like there was a short circuit in his thinking. On any other day, the idea that Littlejohn might belong to some stranger would have made him sick to his stomach. Will's father was dead but his mother was another kind of silence. Littlejohn had always been his life-line person. His biggest fear every six months was that something might happen to stop her from coming to visit—it hadn't entered his head she might make a private life for herself that far away. Only now that she had, he felt only this long loose buzzing like a person separated. He couldn't make it out.

The car went over a bump and for an instant Will's brain went weird and floaty. Then he realized what it was. It wasn't the news about Littlejohn that was making him dizzy. It was the beer. A *caña* was only a few swallows; it was safe as long as you'd had something to eat first—but he had forgot to eat breakfast that morning before he took the bus, and the olives in the bar hadn't been enough to stop the effects of the alcohol. I'm drunk, he thought, this is what it feels like to be drunk. You don't care about anything—you just sit there and tingle.

"I'd better get some food into you," Littlejohn said from the driver's seat. She had been eyeing him.

"I'm fine," Will said aloud. "I feel fine."

They were within a few kilometers of the port now—you could begin to smell the sea. On their right was a high wicker fence made of steel and beyond it the American naval base. All you saw of the base was mile after mile of wide flat green.

"How far is Suelo from here?"

"Not so far," Will said.

"You can ask me anything else you want."

". . . About what?"

"You know what."

Will kept his head turned away and let the focus of his eyes swim along the steel wicker evenly without catching on the metal. He didn't want to talk about it any more. Ahead the road curved sharp to the left. After a few kilometers more, they came to the coast town called Puerto de Santa María. Littlejohn turned right and drove into it over a dusty road that passed the small bull ring; then she followed the piers along the sea until they came to a square and a little park and what looked like the main street of the town.

She and Will got out and stood looking up and down. The town was so dry in the white summer sun it looked hazy. There was a layer of dust like a dirty pink stocking in the air.

Littlejohn led the way and they sat at a table outside a seafood bar overlooking the park. Will ordered a ration of clams *a la plancha* and one of boiled shrimp and two grilled fresh sardines. They sat and watched the townspeople mill through the streets into bars to have wine or beer with a food appetizer of any kind, hot or cold, for in Spain people rarely drink without eating. There were boys on bikes and people walking. When the *tapas* came Will showed Littlejohn how the clams had burst open on a hot griddle and then been sprinkled with lemon juice. She ate the way Will told her but he could tell she was somewhere off in her mind. She still had the driven look as if something was chasing her. After some of the shrimp and one of the sardines the fuzziness in his own brain began to disappear.

"What else will Mother ask?"

Littlejohn shrugged. "Whether I'm pregnant."

". . . Are you?"

"No," she said. She was staring at the cobblestone street in front of her and her face was quiet as stone.

"What else?"

"Nothing else . . . she may not even ask that. She'll probably just clam up. I'd like another glass of wine," Littlejohn said.

Will ordered it and they finished the shrimp, breaking

the pink heads off and sucking them and then peeling the slim bodies. Littlejohn wiped her mouth. "Let's walk," she said.

They strolled through the park that was only a wide paved road with benches on either side, where cars couldn't go. There were old women dressed in solid black with heavy black stockings. Their skin was creased and dry and they watched Littlejohn's boots and hair with the look of the very old or the very young who stare as if their eyes could wipe away the mystery of the object and reveal its true nature.

Will walked a little faster, still waiting for the panic-pain that would come from the fact of her marrying some stranger. He expected it to hit him now that the effects of the beer had worn off but the pain didn't come. He decided to test it. "Where will you live after you're married?"

"Long Island," Littlejohn said. "We . . ."

Someone yelled behind her and they stopped and watched. A red Thunderbird convertible was driving too fast along the main street of the town. There were three American sailors in it, two sitting up on top of the backs of their seats. The sailors were drinking beer out of bottles. The huge car looked like an angry whale in the little town. The sailor who was driving had a bottle too, and they were all three laughing in a loud way. The car floated from side to side over the thin street, not slowing or honking for corners. A couple of fishermen yelled and made filthy gestures as it turned up another street. A skirt of dust flared up and flirted behind it in the noon light.

"There's our navy now," Littlejohn said. "Our brave boys overseas. My God, how can we do it?"

"Do what?"

"We wouldn't support the Republic in the Spanish Civil War. Now we come in and back up the Fascists. Look at the town . . . our sailors don't even know what they're here for. How could they know, when we can't tell them? The plain stupidity of it. The poor bastards . . ."

"Who?"

Littlejohn kept silent for a moment. "Oh, everybody," she said slowly.

Will watched her. "You *are* scared of something."

They walked past an old Spanish woman who had been watching them. The woman pointed in an accusing way with a finger at the dust left by the American Thunderbird. She nodded her head reproachfully at Littlejohn, as if Littlejohn might have been responsible for the behavior of the car.

"She must think every American knows every other American."

"No," Will said. "She doesn't know what an American is. She just thinks all foreigners know each other."

"How can you tell?"

"It wouldn't matter if they were Spanish sailors from Madrid. A foreigner in Spain is just a person who doesn't come from your home town."

They walked out of the park across the square onto the water-logged docks that reeked sweetly of tar and rotting fish in the sun.

"Tell me about Suelo. What's it like?"

"Mother likes the owner of the hotel. Holtz. He's a German. The Hotel Malage's all done in colors. Everything has to match."

". . . Match how?"

"Everybody has a different color bungalow. It you live in the blue bungalow then your tablecloth in the dining room is blue and your beach umbrella is blue, and all your towels, and your barstool . . ."

"Jesus," Littlejohn said.

". . . you can even get blue sun glasses at the desk."

"I'm sorry I asked."

"There's a green bungalow and a red one and an orange one. They have forty bungalows—forty different combinations of colors. Everything in the main building is divided up and . . ."

"Will, forget it. Please . . . I'll see it soon enough. Let's plain walk," Littlejohn said.

They turned and went back again to the town square and then back into the park. Will raised his right hand and fingered his body under the ribs around the stomach as if the ache he was waiting for was hiding there. He thought purposely, *Littlejohn is getting married.* He mouthed the words over, but the stubborn pain refused to come. He was completely sober now and he felt only a sort of dreamy disbelief in the news. He tried to think of Littlejohn standing stiff in front of an altar next to a blank-faced groom in a wedding costume but the picture in his mind was not real.

He walked a little behind her, watching her profile against the light. The light had turned a soft blue, endless, the color you think of when they talk about atmosphere. Her face against it was like something torn out of the sky.

Then, watching her, he could tell that something was about to happen. Not from her expression—her nostrils flared for an instant, but otherwise her face didn't change. He could just tell.

He wasn't sure when he first heard the brakes behind them screeching, but right away he could hear the dog. The shouts of the men came later; the first was the noise a dog makes when it's hit hard, a high long yelling with throbs of sound in it. The screams of the men and the dog were like the noise in his dream when the plane chewed into the earth. Turning, Will saw the red Thunderbird again. It had hit a dog and skidded into a building.

Littlejohn said, "Wait . . ." but Will had already started to run; it was four blocks down the street on the other side of the park. There was a crowd gathering and people shouting. A woman had joined the screaming now; you couldn't tell when she had started. She had pitched herself alongside one of the shop owners on the street. There were two bodies, both men and both of them still alive. There was a child who lay in a broken way, and there was a donkey caught and half crushed between the right fender of the car and the building. There was a lot of blood and the donkey was braying very loud. There was nothing for Will to do. People were helping the men on the ground. Somebody was calling for a doctor. Two of the American sailors sitting in the car looked hurt; one held a red hand to his face. The driver had stepped out of the wreck and stood now to one side of it. He was holding onto his empty beer bottle as though it meant something to him, looking at the mess on the street and shaking his head. He couldn't seem to take in what had happened or what he had done. He scanned the crowd and all at once, without any warning, he looked at Will. Their eyes locked and Will found himself looking back at the face of a man he had never seen. Years later he thought there were many things that he could have known if he had only read the real meaning of the dazed hopeless expression on the face of the drunken American sailor who had crashed into the building.

A bunch of curious townfolk were pushing from behind, and Will turned from the sailor and walked out of the accident against the tide of people. He couldn't find Littlejohn. His insides had spread at the sight of the blood, and he could feel his stomach fluttering weakly in two parts like broken wings. He passed a bar they hadn't seen from the park; it looked like an imitation American hard-liquor bar, and it had been full of American sailors out of uniform and girls. The sailors were joining the Spanish people at the edge of the accident; the girls stood alone grouped together in the dark entrance of the bar. Will passed it and turned the corner. Then he saw the dog.

It was the size of a terrier, short, with greasy brown hair and the lean look of a stray, and it had flies around it. It was making the throbbing sound Will had heard before. It was sitting in its own blood, and one of its eyes were hanging out. Will stuck his hand out open but there was no place to touch the dog, and it went on yelling. Then Littlejohn found him.

When she saw Will's face she swept past him and bent down and got the dog. She straightened and held it in a certain way. The dog was still making the sound, but after a while it grew softer in her arms. There was a grease mark on Littlejohn's right wrist. She took the dog across the street to a man who had turned away from the accident. The man looked bored.

"Ask him if there's a vet," Littlejohn said.

Will did.

"*Veterinario?*" The man lifted his shoulders.

"*Se muere ya,*" another man near him said. "*Déjalo ya.*"

"No," Will said fast in Spanish, "where is the animal doctor?"

"*No hay,*" the first man said. He watched Littlejohn. "*Señorita . . . sangre.*" He pointed to the blood on the dog.

Littlejohn turned and walked to a woman she had seen standing in a curtained doorway on the corner. It was another entrance to the bar they hadn't been able to see from the park. It was dark inside. "Talk to her in Spanish," Littlejohn said to Will over her shoulder.

"She's not Spanish," a voice behind the woman in the bar said. "She's Dutch. There isn't any veterinary. There's a *practicante* lives two streets over . . . he's only a kind of practical nurse, but he might be willing to bandage the dog for you. He might even be sober," the soft-throated voice in the dark said.

Littlejohn asked, "Is there an American hospital at the navy base?"

"Yes," the woman in the dark said. "That's an idea. You never know about that hospital. They might take dogs . . . they won't take people."

"I'll take him to the *practicante.*"

"That's what I would do," the woman said. "Were I a dog lover."

Littlejohn crossed the street fast and they walked where the woman had pointed. She stumbled once. The dog started yelling again and she held it closer till it stopped. Will beat on the door; a heavy woman with a mop opened it. She stared at the dog. Then she started to close the door.

"Take some money out of my purse," Littlejohn said. "Tell her I'll pay double."

"I speak English," the *practicante*'s woman said. "Double?"

"Five hundred pesetas. It was hurt in the crash. You must have heard the sound of the crash."

The woman didn't move.

"All right," Littlejohn said. "Twice double . . . open the door."

They followed her into a patio and the woman put the mop down. *"Jaime,"* she called loud to the back, *"levántate ya, jo'er."* There wasn't any answer. *"Hijo puta, ya 'stá bien, no?* Sons bitch asleep from wine," she said. *"Jaime?"*

"I'll go back and find him," Littlejohn said. "I'd like my brother to wait with you. . . . Accidents make him sick." She went across the patio and knocked on the door.

"You no pay to my husband. You pay me."

"Do it," Littlejohn said. She threw her purse across the patio to Will. Then she went into the back room with the dog.

Will reached in the purse and held a thousand peseta note out to the woman. It was a crisp new bill and she took it from him and held it like a live bird. She folded it as if she were breaking its neck.

"Nervioso?"

". . . No."

"Why you get sick to see accident?"

"My father was killed," Will said, "like that." It wasn't that simple, but he couldn't explain that the sick tightness at seeing accidents was like a birthmark on his brain. He was surprised at the way his voice came out—steady and even. He was breathing hard but he hadn't expected he could speak clearly.

"How?"

"A plane."

". . . You want one drink water?"

He nodded and the woman gave him a clay *botijo* from the corner. It was heavy and beaded with cold drops on the outside and he lifted it high. He spilled water out of the smaller hole into his mouth and drank, letting it collect first in gulps at the back of his tongue. He let some of it trickle from the *botijo* over his face. The water was musty and cool and he could taste the clay.

"Which was the airplane of your father?"

"*La guerra*," Will said.

"Which war?"

"The one of the world."

"The second? I speak English," the woman said, "my sister teach me as follows. I am, you are, he is, Seven Up, side car V O, they will be. Every part of grammar. . . . . This my sister is very intelligent teach. She? More what I, oh she much more. She no listen this fucky fucky to sailors. All she got, this whole English grammar perfect. . . . You feel better now?"

"Yes."

"You think I speak English very well?"

"Yes."

"You should talk to my sister," the woman said.

After a while Littlejohn came out alone. She had washed her arms and cleaned the blood off the front of her shirt. She took her purse and lit a cigarette, watching Will. "I remember not so long ago a thing like this would have sent you into a screaming fit for hours," she said, slow. "Why didn't you tell me you'd grown up?"

Will didn't answer.

"Oh well," Littlejohn said. "Why don't you get your dog; I'll wait here."

He crossed the patio to the practitioner's room. It smelled of wine but the table looked clean and there was a bottle of alcohol. There were bandages on it and an empty syringe. The *practicante* was sitting on a cot in the corner smoking black tobacco. You could smell it and wine and old sweat and the alcohol. Will wondered if they found his father's body and tried to save his life and if the foreign room had smelled this way. He never wondered how he lived, but he sometimes wondered how he died. He couldn't help that. The dog was bandaged, but it wasn't asleep. It was lying on a table. Its remaining eye followed Will across the room.

"He lost blood," the *practicante* said drunkenly in Spanish. "He is lucky, this dog. He has an injection. Be careful how you pick him up."

"Thank you."

"Nothing. *Con Dios*," the man said.

"*Adiós*," Will told him.

The dog rested against him like a rag.

There were three children staring at Littlejohn in the patio when he went back, the oldest about eight. Two of them were standing against the *practicante*'s wife and the other one was hiding behind her. When Will came out all three children turned from Littlejohn and watched the dog. They looked thin and sickly, with the confused dreamy eyes that come from hunger, and the *practicante*'s wife had to push them away from her body to open the door.

Will and Littlejohn went out into the light and Littlejohn looked up and blinked. "There isn't any sky," she said, ". . . is there? Like any Spanish sky?"

"No," he said.

The blue was wild now. The dog lay still and Will followed Littlejohn back to the car. The day had been breathless in the last blast of heat but now you could feel the first slice of a breeze from the sea; it came between the buildings and the bars.

"Nobody was killed. I tried to help before, but the people wouldn't let me." Littlejohn touched the grease mark on her wrist. "I went back again and asked. They took the ones who were hurt to a hospital. The sailors in the bars just went back to their whores. It's all forgotten now. What an awful thing we've done to this town."

Will didn't answer.

"I asked about the dog too. It doesn't belong to anybody. You can keep it," Littlejohn said.

They walked up behind her rented blue car and Will saw it. There was something off balance. Somebody had taken the radio antenna and bent it double. It was hanging down like a long broken bone. Littlejohn reached out and touched it.

"The Spanish kids sometimes do that," Will said. "In little towns. They do it to foreign cars."

"I don't blame them. It doesn't matter. I don't use the radio."

"It's cooling off . . . you can put the top down if you want."

"No," Littlejohn said. "I wouldn't drive through this town in an open convertible after the way those sailors drove . . . I'd be ashamed. . . ."

She got in the car and Will sat next to her and set the dog in his lap. It was drugged enough to let him do what he wanted. Littlejohn put the car into gear and started off. The streets were thin and crowded and she drove slowly. She braked and honked at every corner. Toward the back of town the people were living in the streets after the heat. They sat on wooden chairs outside watching the car pass. You could see the flat hatred in some of their eyes. The car Littlejohn had rented in Madrid wasn't as big as the Thunderbird but it was American-designed and twice as big as most

Spanish cars. It was bulky in the narrow streets and they both felt embarrassed in it. A woman dressed in black, toothless, watched them, blinded by the sun on the fender. You could smell the sour wine and hot oil in the white houses. Will kept his eyes on the town as they drove. The air was fresh but the buildings belched out at him, hot and rotten and gorgeous. There were sights and smells, flowers and flies. There was sun into horse manure and donkey dung in jasmine. The whole town was quiet.

Littlejohn drove out of the town to the rutted road that led to the highway. After that she turned and followed a sign that pointed the way to Suelo. She crossed some railroad tracks and started driving out of the sun. The day was ending.

"Did you see her children?" Littlejohn said.

"Yes."

"What must she think? . . . we spent a thousand pesetas on a dog. Did you see her children?"

"The town is already angry."

"Why not?" Littlejohn said, "why wouldn't it be?"

The earth was cooling faster and they drove a while more. The light had changed again. The sun was low and bloated like an orange disk, big and watery over the gray and the green. The yellow Andalusian summer twilight was beginning. Will felt his hand grow wet and he looked down. The dog was slobbering quietly on the insides of his fingers.

"You were right, Will," Littlejohn said. "I am afraid."

Will looked at her. Her eyes were on the rear-view mirror. She was staring straight at the sun. He looked back at the road.

"It's every place I go. It's like something is waiting out there. I don't know what it is."

Will kept still and listened and Littlejohn cleared her throat.

"It's why I'm getting married. I've been scared a long time. I don't know what it is. I hate not knowing what it is."

She stopped talking and Will thought about it. The facts of the day altered in his mind, and he could feel a flush of something extra inside him as if his heart had squeezed one more beat.

Then in the dizzy sun it happened again. The words swelled in his mind and he could feel the sun and the heat all through him. The heat was in his pants and in his brain and at the base of his throat. She had recognized something in him without being told. The words swelled up bigger and spilled out of his mouth.

"I'll stay with you," he said. "Till you're married."

Littlejohn watched the sun in the mirror and the road ahead of them.

She blinked a few times.

"I will," he said.

"Fine."

He turned back and they both faced the road. Will sat still with the swelling of himself as if nothing had happened. The dog on his legs was licking his hand again. The road ahead was straight now. There was a herd of smooth brown goats next to the road on the right and an old man tending them, his skin cracked and brown, stung and red from the weather. When the car passed, the man followed it with his sun-broken face and for a crazy second Will wanted to lean out the window and shout to him. He didn't, because it wouldn't have made any sense—but he wanted to. He wished he could have told the old man of this change that had come about in him. He wished he could have touched the goats. He wished he could sing.

LITTLEJOHN lay down in the blue canvas chair under the mid-morning sun and squinted through the sharp blinding rays at her mother. The terrace of the main building was full of people but at this end it was more private. Helen was sitting at a white table under a multicolored umbrella with three other women. They were playing bridge. The umbrella over them had a stripe for every bungalow of the hotel to indicate it was not the property of one guest in particular. Everything in the Hotel Malage that didn't pertain to a given bungalow had forty colors on it to show that any guest could use it. The terrace was tiled that way in a forty-color-combination mosaic and even the waiters had mosaic shirts with forty little colored squares sewn into them. It was enough to drive you crazy, Littlejohn thought. She lay quiet under the trellis of jasmine and studied her mother's face.

The four women playing bridge at the table were protected by the umbrella and by a canvas canopy. They were playing like converging birds in silhouette against the beach and the sea. They sat around the table attacking the cards; it was painful to watch them against the light.

The beach beyond the terrace was both gray and harder white than the jasmine and the sea was dull green. The sun on the grains of sand was vicious. The sound of bees buzzing in the jasmine was as loud behind Littlejohn's head as the low waves.

Through her dark glasses and across the blast of white harsh light Littlejohn traced with her eyes down Helen's profile. It was exquisite; Helen's loveliness was always startling to look at. In her way the woman herself was perfect, Littlejohn thought. Perfectly something. Born and bred in New Orleans, Helen always explained, of impoverished ex-aristocracy, French Louisiana-style—or just another poor New Orleans family. ("Part Creole," Helen said.) Orphaned early; married rich; divorced and remarried and widowed. Soft elegant hair like wheat. The thin grace of a greeting-card

27

heart; forty-four and won't ever look it, Littlejohn thought. She described her mother in her mind. Arched eyebrows and a wide brow. One or two gold bangles—diamonds only after dark. Never any vulgar jewelry. A classic beauty. Yes, she's a beauty, Littlejohn thought. Lost what little feeling she had, but still has all her teeth. Excellent taste and pearly teeth. Like a mouthful of shells. Doesn't smile too often not to waste the effect. Long neck. Delicate nostrils and sloping bones. No blood, but nobody's perfect.

Helen set a card down with her elegant fingers and touched her left cheek with one crimson fingernail. The game was for high stakes and she was playing carefully. Almost too carefully. Something was odd about the determination on her face. She knows I'm looking at her, Littlejohn decided; she knows if anybody's looking at her. It's one of the things she most cares about—it has to be. Otherwise what kind of woman would keep a twelve-year-old boy in Spain, on the pretext of educating him and improving his languages, just out of her own boredom and desire? She must see herself, she must. Only how does she sleep with herself, let alone everybody else?

But there it was—Helen slept every night, all night. And Littlejohn couldn't sleep at all. It was a week since she had come to Suelo. She hadn't been able to sleep for a long time before that and she hadn't slept last night. She had lain awake in bed and the nightmare-thing, the sun-thing, the thing that was like the shape of emptiness, had come at her every time she closed her eyes. She had had to keep her eyes open until dawn when the sun itself came up, and then she shut her eyes in the sun's face. She had dozed maybe two hours. Then the sounds of people from other bungalows running down to the beach woke her. Now she was stretched out in the canvas chair having another go at it but it wasn't going to work now either, she could tell. It was getting worse and worse every day.

In the stinging light her mind grew bright and lazy. She could hear the bees and the bidding of the bridge players and the sea. Here I am, she thought, here is my morning prayer. In the great American search for identity let me get lost. God help me to try to think one ugly thought every day. God help me.

On the other side of the bridge table the center of the terrace was filling with other guests from the hotel. Littlejohn scanned them without moving her body. Two of the men were waiting for her to get up and go for a swim. The hotel lifeguard and a blond Texan from the American base who was six feet four. Smeared with suntan oil they both looked like ads for muscles. The lifeguard was Spanish with dark shining skin and the Texan was married and had the biggest feet she had ever seen. Both of them had been flirting with her for the week since she had arrived and both of them bored her. They had been flirting with her mother too; her mother didn't want them either. Funny, she thought, how most people get what they don't want. Very funny. She stretched her body in the canvas and blinked at the sky. The silence was heavier. The heat was oppressive—you could feel it in your lungs when you breathed—the solid white glaze overhead was like glass.

The droning of the voices from the bridge table and the noise of the bees in the flowers were getting confused now in her ears. In the silence, it sounded like the bees were playing bridge and the women were sucking honey out of the flowers. She opened her eyes and looked at the players. There was something vaguely threatening about them. As if an unspeakable game was being put into play by some crazy god high above the table. She couldn't sleep here.

Then with her eyes closed even behind her dark glasses she could see the awful blasting disk of the sun.

She opened her eyes again quickly and blinked. The light was like acid on her pupils.

She could not think when the real problem had started. It had always been true of her, she knew, but it was only recently that it had begun to bother her. The problem was that she could remember almost nothing about her life. Most people have memories, or say they have. But except for a few isolated times that appeared to her as short pictures, she couldn't remember a thing. In the last few months she had begun to think that it was as if her growing up had happened to somebody else. School and college, summers and travel and winters had dissolved into one big edgeless dream that she herself seemed to have taken no part in, and the single times that protruded out of it as memories were pitifully few.

There was a boy at a school dance who had pressed against her until he had made her feel the hardness between his legs. There was the day she fell off a bicycle and broke her arm. There was her father, who called himself a Christian socialist minister, guilt-ridden about the fortune his own father had sweated out of people; she remembered his face, gray and expressionless, the day in the lawyer's office when he had signed over the bulk of the money to her. There was a man in college she remembered, a radical named Sowetsky;

he had made a casual pass at her and she had said no. Then there was E. J. Williams, the campus stud, whom she had agreed to marry because she was afraid of being alone too much longer. She remembered his breathing in the back of his car the first night. He had held her so hard she could feel his chest pounding through his sweater. If E. J. Williams had tried, he could easily have taken her that night. He didn't try. Instead, he asked her to perform the same service she had performed before for other boys. The second she touched the swollen knob of his penis with her mouth, she heard him groan. There was a single sticky drop at the end of the knob and she held the big penis at the base and began to put it on like lipstick. She had only tasted it once with the tip of her tongue when he grabbed the back of her head with his hand and thrust forward. The hard muscle filled her mouth. It kept pumping at her until she couldn't breathe or hold any more, and the next day her jaw ached.

Finally she remembered one or two faces in the liberal organization she had worked for in New York after her graduation. She had done social work for them in Harlem. She remembered a black man, a heroin addict she had seen lying on the floor of a Harlem tenement; the black man had said a strange thing. She had come to ask him to sign a petition to get rid of the tenements. He had looked up at her from the basement floor in soft and dreamy disbelief. His eyes had filled slowly with a gentle liquidlike sleep, and he was smiling. He seemed to see something inside her. "You and me got poverty in us," he said. She had watched him.

"Lady," he said. "I don't need your poverty on top of my poverty."

That was the day she had agreed to marry E. J. Williams. It was the last thing in her life that she could clearly remember. It all summed up to bewilderment, and anger at nothing.

Now on the terrace she listened again to the voices: *Two hearts. Pass. Two spades. Two no trump. . . .* She opened her eyes for a third time and looked at the bridge players. Then she looked past the table and a little swoop of cheer ran through her like a warm flush. Will had come onto the terrace. He was standing on the other side of the table by the ledge watching her; he was holding the dog they had taken to the *practicante* in Puerto de Santa María. He had named it Sneakers from the bandages on its front paws. Littlejohn raised her dark glasses a fraction of an inch with one finger and dropped them again to let Will know she had seen him. They didn't bother talking; they only swapped eyes.

Then she listened to the bridge game droning on.

"It's the heat," the one called Mrs. Lawson was saying to Helen, "they don't tell you about it in the guide books."

Helen sipped her sherry.

"And the flies," Mrs. Lawson said. "The flies."

"Three hearts," the English one said. Thin hooked voice, hard as a parrot's beak. Cold face.

"How is called *bastos?*" the painted Spanish one said.

"Clubs."

"Ah. Pass," the Spanish one said.

"Not on a two bid," Mrs. Lawson said. "Say three no trump."

"Three no trump," the Spanish one said.

"Pass," Helen said. The way she said it, the one word was a lecture on boredom.

You have to give her credit, Littlejohn thought—she has the voice when she wants to use it. Helen was out to knife the English one. You could tell from her mouth. The English one knew it too. You could tell that from hers.

The Spanish one held up the score pad and Littlejohn glanced at it. She could not remember ever having seen her mother or anyone else play for such high stakes. Or maybe, she thought, she had just never bothered to notice the stakes her mother played for.

The gray beach beyond the terrace was whiter now that the sun was almost at zenith; under its slightly gray surface it looked at least twice as white as the jasmine. You could hardly see the four women in the light.

Will wandered over to Littlejohn, circling around the table and holding the dog away from Helen. He was in his bathing suit. He sat next to Littlejohn, leaning against the outside of her left leg and facing the sun. He didn't seem to mind looking into the glare. Littlejohn watched his thin back and felt a queer flood of tenderness well up in her. Will's body was just beginning to break the mold. The bones were cracking. It was the strange time when a boy's body looks as if it will always be a boy's body. He would be a man before another summer.

The card game had turned to gossip now; it was strange the way the sense of a threat still floated over the table like a big invisible hand. . . .

"Listen," the one called Mrs. Lawson said, "did you see the countess arrive last night?"

"*La Condesa*," the Spanish one said. "*Sí . . . La Condesa de Guzmán.*"

Helen swirled her sherry glass between two red-tipped fingers and pretended she didn't know she was being spoken to. She was looking at her cards.

"I heard," Mrs. Lawson said, "the Countess came to leave their sons with him. Only she doesn't need to come with them, they're grown; I heard she wants him back. You can't get a divorce in Spain."

"Divorce, no," the Spanish one said. "Separation."

"That's what I heard," Mrs. Lawson said. "He's very political. Wrote this article or something got published in France, the only reason Franco didn't put him in jail is how old the family tree is. They say it was this family of dukes and counts for a long time. I mean it goes back centuries."

"Odd if it didn't," the English one said.

"Odd?"

"They haven't been making counts on the continent *too* frightfully recently," the English one said. "Have they in America?"

Mrs. Lawson said, "So anyway, they say he's not here yet, but she is. Was, up to last night anyway. In the gold villa with her sons. They're all talking about it."

"They?" the English one said.

"What?" Helen said. Eyes just a fraction over the cards.

"It's so hard to know what Americans mean by *they*," the English one said. "Does it mean *every*body?" She was looking straight at Helen. She's asking for it, Littlejohn thought. She'll get it, too. She doesn't know Helen.

"I just meant the whole hotel," Mrs. Lawson said.

"I say," the English one said, "the American language *is* confusing. *They* think this . . . *they* say that. For a while I thought it meant all the psychoanalysts or something. . . ."

Helen smiled. Eyes back on the cards. Holding her guns for some reason. Littlejohn wondered why.

"Perhaps I can find someone to give me lessons in the American language," the English one said.

"Why don't you find your husband?" Mrs. Lawson said.

The other three looked at Mrs. Lawson with surprise. The delivery wasn't good but the line was—the English one's husband was the six-foot-four Texan from the American naval base. He had given up waiting for Littlejohn and during the last few minutes he had been staring at Helen.

"I say," the English one said, laughing. "What a smashing idea."

"Won't he teach you?" Mrs. Lawson was beaming, pleased

by her success. You can't trust women like Mrs. Lawson, Littlejohn thought; when they hit it home it's an accident and they generally run after it and fall on their asses.

"I suppose my husband might help me," the English one said. "Yours does . . . he was terribly helpful, all last night."

"Whose bid is it?" Mrs. Lawson said.

"Yours," the English one said.

"May we have a review of the bidding?" Mrs. Lawson said.

"I know what you mean," the English bird said. "One begins to talk, and one forgets to play."

"One," Helen said. Not even smiling. Like a sleepy hawk. She was still holding off—there had to be a reason, Littlejohn knew. Normally Helen would have eviscerated the English bird by now with one fingernail. It was curious; Helen only behaved that way when she smelled danger. But what could the danger possibly be with those three birds?

Littlejohn glanced over at the score pad again. The English one and her partner were winning a great deal of money over Helen and the Spanish one. It couldn't be that Helen was worried about the money—or could it? It was true that she only played with very rich people. But if it was that, she wouldn't just eviscerate the English one—she'd kill her. She'd find a way to stop the game.

The bidding ended and Mrs. Lawson picked the gossip back up and shook it like a baby bird with a string: "I hear he's difficult to get along with. Snobbish and all."

"He?"

"The Count."

"Oh him. Apparently he hates Americans," the English one said.

"When I catch a remark like that," Mrs. Lawson said, "I just consider the source."

"It was your husband who told me," the English one said. "Last night at dinner. According to your husband, Count Guzmán is in trouble with the Spanish government. It seems the article he wrote was an attack on the American government for supporting the Franco regime. Your husband says both governments are embarrassed over it. Count Guzmán gave some interviews to the foreign press; I gather he talks about nothing else. It all sounds faintly boring. It's your lead."

Mrs. Lawson put a card down sullenly. "Is he really anti-American?" she said to Helen.

". . . Who?"

"Count Guzmán."

"I hardly know him."

"You must *know* him. Your picture's in that Spanish society magazine," Mrs. Lawson said. "I saw it in the lobby. You were sitting at his table at some dinner party in Madrid."

"Yes," Helen said.

Will turned his head enough for Littlejohn to feel the movement in his back. She nudged him with her knee and he glanced over his shoulder. They had both got the message at the same time. Up to then Will had thought Helen's new lover was the German hotel owner, Holtz. So it isn't, Littlejohn thought; there must be another reason for Holtz. So it's a count. It's why she's been holding back. She doesn't want them to know.

Helen folded her cards and sipped her sherry. Then she looked at the sea.

"Are there as many cocktail parties in Spain as there are in America?" the English one said.

Watching Helen, Littlejohn saw her suddenly relax. It was only an infinitesimal movement of her long neck, but it was unmistakable if you knew her. She was out of danger now. The English bird had missed the point of the gossip—missed it cold. Until Helen was ready no one would know she and the Count were more than passing acquaintances. She was safe at the bridge table and she knew it. Look out now, Littlejohn thought. Oh English bird, oh look out now.

"Parties? Not too many," Helen said. She had turned back and was smiling slightly.

"I must say, American cocktail parties are the only things I *couldn't* get used to. . . . It was one after another when I first went over with George. I adored the country. But those awful bashes."

"You adored the country?" Mrs. Lawson said. Her usual bad delivery.

"Oh, indeed," the English one said. "Love at first sight . . . except for Miami."

". . . Miami?"

"Our plane was grounded there for repairs when we were on our way to the Caribbean; I was taken ill. Seriously ill as a matter of fact . . . I couldn't get back on the plane and we couldn't get a room in a hospital or even in any hotel. George had to call a friend of his in New York. Terrible muddle. We ended, of all places, staying as guests with one of those gangster-type Hollywood actors. George's friend had gone to school with him. Wads of dollars in his pockets, he never signed for anything. A real gangster. And if *that* wasn't bad enough you wouldn't have believed the people in that one Miami hotel."

"Ninety-five percent Jews," Mrs. Lawson said.

"So I was told; we don't have the problem in London. . . . No, it was just the hotel and the people. Sequin evening dresses . . . sequin sunglasses half a yard wide, and bathing suits, my dear, *sequin bathing* suits. I said to George, if I had it *in* me to be anti-American, this would do it. . . . Have you ever been to Miami?" she said to Helen.

"No."

"I say, you are lucky. You can't imagine what living there is like."

"No," Helen said. "And I can't imagine living with a gangster."

The English one straightened her cards. "I don't think one could say we lived with him," she said. "I was ill and there was no place else to stay. He was the only person there kind enough to offer us assistance, and we had to accept it."

Helen smiled. "I can't imagine being that ill," she said quietly. "It's still your lead."

"I almost died. It was when I lost my baby . . . they brought an incubator from the hospital to the hotel suite, and they thought my baby would live and I would die. It turned out the other way around. The baby only lived six hours. . . ."

"It must have been a painful experience for you," Helen said.

"It was."

"Yes," Helen said. "All those sequins."

The English one stood up.

"I think I'd like someone to finish my hand," she said angrily. "Does your daughter play?"

"No," Helen said. "Is it the heat?"

"I'm sure you can find someone else to take my place."

"For heaven's sake, it doesn't matter. We'll stop this rubber. You sound so serious. . . . It's only a game."

"Shall I ask the concierge if he can find another partner for . . ."

"You mustn't let it upset you," Helen said

The English one walked off in a jerky way into the lobby of the hotel. She was too angry to walk stiffly.

Helen reached over almost carelessly, and tore up the top page of the score pad.

Mrs. Lawson looked dazed. "What got into her?"

"Not a clue," Helen said.

Mrs. Lawson turned around to Littlejohn. "Do you know, Alice?—What it was upset Mrs. Donahue?"

"No," Littlejohn said. "Unless she left her guts in that purse."

"Her what?"

Helen laughed. "Alice is right," she said. "Mrs. Donahue did forget her purse. Take it to her, William."

"I'll take it," Littlejohn said; she levered herself up against Will's back.

"You?"

"I tend to give succor to war victims when I'm around," Littlejohn said. "It's a simple gesture and it keeps it in the family."

Helen laughed again. Fragile and empty. It's the only real giveaway, her laugh, Littlejohn thought. Like glass tears.

"I wish my daughter enjoyed me as much as I do her." Helen was speaking to the sherry bottle. "We'd have a much better time together."

"No we wouldn't," Littlejohn said. "We'd probably kill each other. We may anyway. . . ."

She and Helen faced each other head-on for a second. Like two warriors with shields: dark glasses to dark glasses. Littlejohn smiled. Helen tried to, and didn't make it.

"I think you'd better leave her purse with the bell captain," Helen said quietly. "You'll have missed her by now." She looked back at the sea.

"Not coming back, the English?" the Spanish one asked.

Littlejohn went inside. The clap of cool in the main building was like entering a cave. Mrs. Donahue was waiting at the elevator. She looked white. "Thank you so much," she said, taking the purse, "so very kind."

"Mother likes to play tennis with razor blades. Please excuse it. She doesn't mean anything."

The English one said, "Here's my elevator now. Till later . . ."

When Littlejohn went back outside there were white birds dipping over the edge of the low tide. Snowy white, converging on fish. A nice clean game, she thought. Just to stay alive.

The heat floated up from the terrace and the sea swayed behind it. Mrs. Lawson and the Spanish one had gone for a swim. Will was on the other end of the terrace watching something.

Helen hadn't moved. "Did you apologize for me?" she said.

Littlejohn went through the heat waves to the edge of the terrace to look at the white dipping birds.

"Is something on your mind?" Helen said.

"Not so you'd notice."

"I wish you'd stop that."

"Stop what?"

"That cheap smart-aleck talk. It sounds as if you got it out of the movies. Be blunt—you usually are. But not snippy. You haven't sounded like yourself since you got here."

"So Will tells me."

"I doubt you're so snippy with him." Helen smiled with her voice. "I always did bring out the worst in you."

"It's not your fault," Littlejohn said, flat. "Maybe we bring it out in each other."

"All right then, let's start over. Is something on your mind?"

Littlejohn raised her shoulders. "I was thinking that you weren't playing bridge for fun. Does the money mean so much?"

There was a slight pause behind her and she could feel her mother thinking about an answer. Before Helen had time to make one, there was a shuffling of footsteps and a man's voice in a heavy German accent said, "How *are* you this morning, Mrs. Locke?"

Littlejohn turned around in time to see a plump middle-aged man with a shiny face bending over her mother's hand.

"Herr Holtz," Helen said absently, "my daughter, Alice Littlejohn."

"So," the man said. He moved forward and touched his lips to Littlejohn's knuckles. "I hope you have a happy stay with us. I have just returned from my hotel in Alicante. Here your mother is our most honored guest. . . ." He saw from Helen's attitude that he had been dismissed. He backed away toward the lobby and disappeared around an air conditioner.

Helen was avoiding her daughter's eyes. Littlejohn went on facing her. "Well?"

"Card games amuse me."

"Do they?"

"And I like the money."

". . . You never told me you were having money troubles."

Helen laughed lightly. "Money is like sickness," she said, "you give it to your children, but you don't let them worry about it. You'll find out when you have children of your own. I hope you're not going to offer to help. You and I have enough problems with each other. I'm capable of taking care of myself."

"The trouble must be serious if you've started playing bridge for it."

"I've played games for money since I was ten years old," Helen said. She kept her mouth open but no more words came out. All at once she raised one hand in an angular movement of impatience. It was a gesture that was totally unlike her, Littlejohn thought.

For an instant Helen gave the impression that she had started to say something more and decided against it. Then while Littlejohn watched, her mother's face relaxed again. "I've been playing bridge for money for years. I enjoy it."

Littlejohn held still a moment more, but nothing further was said. She turned back to the gulls. "Who's Holtz?"

"The owner of the hotel. He has a chain of them."

"And what are you doing in a flashy second-rate hotel on the coast of nowhere? None of your society friends would be seen dead here."

Helen made another slight pause. "I don't mind your asking questions," she said, "if you don't mind answering a few. Holtz is a businessman who overextended himself—he's invested a lot in this hotel. As you say, it isn't chic. It never will be, without something or somebody to stir it up. I plan to give a few parties. I think my society friends, as you call them, may change their minds. You'd be surprised how far society will travel if it thinks it might be left out of something. It isn't knowing who to invite . . . it's knowing who to invite *first*. Even more it's knowing who *not* to invite. It's the sort of thing I'm good at. Like telling Holtz to get rid of these awful umbrella stands, and some of the more offensive parts of the decor."

"And what do you get out of it?"

"A free summer," Helen said. "Superb service. A car and chauffeur. Trips if I want them, for me and for William. I like giving parties. I have good taste, which makes large parties expensive."

"Was it the same last summer? That hotel in Cap Ferrat?"

"A bit simpler. It was just a few dinners there—but then Cap Ferrat has society of its own."

"And what about the hotel in Rome last Christmas? And that ski resort in . . ."

"Yes," Helen said, "all of them. It's not that I don't have money, it's that I don't like to spend it. Now it's my turn to ask questions. I'm sorry if you disapprove of the way I travel . . ."

"I don't," Littlejohn said slowly. "Not if that's the reason for it. It was when you ran after society for fun that I thought . . . that I hated it. . . ."

"Maybe I never went after society *just* for fun . . ." Helen's voice was a shade too elegant; "maybe we never got a chance to know each other, you and I."

"You're being nice," Littlejohn said. "Why?"

"Should I have a reason?"

" 'Don't ask personal questions' was the first order I remember your giving. You're the most evasive woman I know."

Helen smiled. "Is that why you're so blunt? You are, you know. You're a worldly girl, but you're also naïve. That particular combination of extremes could mean one of several things. That you're bored, say. Or confused. It could even mean that you're still a virgin."

Littlejohn kept still. The remark had come out simply. Helen never was given to talking without a reason.

"Why are you interested?"

"As they say in the movies, I'm your mother."

"My question holds."

Helen didn't answer.

"Yes," Littlejohn said. "Worse. A professional virgin. Almost fifty years behind the times. Just an old-fashioned girl."

"Why?"

"No real reason."

"The gentleman you say you're engaged to . . ."

"Oh Jesus. Don't let's go back to tinsel talk. If you want to talk, talk."

"The one you're planning to marry. Is he a real man?"

Two of the birds were swooping.

"I'm not a lesbian, if that's what you mean."

"It isn't," Helen said. "I know what you are. At least I think I do. I think you've been waiting your whole life for something. I think you've been waiting so long, you're . . ."

"Yes. I know what you are too."

"Didn't this man try . . ."

"No," Littlejohn said, "none of them. I'm not all that behind the times. I give a pretty fair blow-job. I think I can figure what you're asking. No, he's not that. Just shy."

Helen was quiet for a while. "You're not in love."

Littlejohn turned her back to the jasmine-white birds to look at her mother. Helen was sitting with her back to the white jasmine.

"We're about to swap lines," Littlejohn said. "I'm worn out."

"We might speak for ourselves."

"You wouldn't like it."

"Try me."

The wind sagged from the sea and the sun was bad on the terrace around them. Littlejohn watched Helen.

For no special reason, she remembered another time, when she was nine and had taken a good look at Helen's perfumes and makeup and clothes and life and said no. That easily. I don't want to live with you. She still remembered her mother's face as she heard the words. Helen had been putting on lipstick in front of her wall-to-wall dressing-room mirror that was rose-tinted on one half and plain on the other—Littlejohn had come in from playing in the street. They were living in New Orleans then—Helen had roots in New Orleans. She had met Littlejohn's father on an ocean liner going to Paris; he was a weak wealthy young man then and Helen had taken him over and they had been married right there on board. It was romantic the way Helen always told it, with candles and the silver glitter of the night on the water and the silence of the mid-Atlantic. But Littlejohn was always sure that Helen had had another reason for marrying him on the ship. The reason was that his family might not have approved of Helen once they got off. So they married and Helen moved to New York and set up an apartment with Littlejohn's father and launched herself into New York society. Everything had been fine until the weak new husband had decided overnight to become a minister. Up to then he had done as he was told and had never contradicted her in anything; but about his decision to join the church he was oddly stubborn. Nothing Helen said made any difference. He listened and nodded and didn't answer her, and just when she thought he was agreeing with her he went right ahead and did it. So Helen had left him for good and taken a chunk of alimony and her eight-year-old daughter and had gone back to New Orleans. It was only to have been a short trip, that return. Only then, Helen had met a young lieutenant who was stationed near New Orleans and almost as soon as the divorce was over she married him. William Charles Locke. Littlejohn remembered him slightly—a tall, trim, sandy-haired man with bulging thighs and clean-clipped shoulders. He and Helen decided to live on in the South after he got out of the service. Helen started making inroads into New Orleans society with her New York connections and her alimony money; finally at the height of the season she was invited to a Mardi Gras ball that fixed her social position in the city. It was while Helen was dressing for the Mardi Gras ball that Littlejohn had come in, scruffy and dirty from playing in the street, and had looked at herself and at her mother in the wall-to-wall mirror and had said it: "I don't want to live with you . . . I don't want to be like you." Helen had taken the lipstick brush away from her mouth and turned, in her crimson and gold ball costume that touched the floor, and looked down at her small daughter with an expression somewhere between mild surprise and amusement and said, "Fine." Then she had turned back to the mirror and put the lipstick brush back on her mouth, and she hadn't even noticed when Littlejohn left the room.

It was after that that Littlejohn was sent to Pennsylvania. Her father's house was in a suburb, and except for the expensive furniture and her governess, Miss Duff, nobody would have known they had money at all. Miss Duff was hired because the minister had made up his mind not to marry again and he wanted a woman's hand in her upbringing. It was a few months after Littlejohn made the move that Helen—who was still in New Orleans—had had the tragedy. The new husband, William Charles Locke, had been sent overseas. Two weeks after he left, on his second bombing mission, his plane had gone down. A month after he died, Will had been born.

Now in the sunlight Littlejohn frowned on the terrace. So Helen had been pregnant that night in New Orleans, the night of the ball, when Littlejohn had told her she didn't want to live with her. She must have known she was going to have another child, when her born child walked up and said it didn't want to be like her. It must have been a strange moment for Helen. She hadn't shown it. She never showed anything on her face and nothing ever disturbed her graceful manners or her cool green eyes that always reminded Littlejohn of glass.

"Well?" Helen said now.

Littlejohn said, "There wouldn't be any point in my marrying for money. You saw to that. I prefer not to marry for love. So I might as well marry for fun."

"I don't believe you."

"Oh, look," Littlejohn said, "what the shit."

Helen sighed. She crossed her legs. "You think I'm affected because my speech is self-consciously refined. It may be. Your speech is self-consciously crude. It comes to the same thing."

"Not to. From."

"I don't want to fight with you, Alice."

"Neither do I," Littlejohn said. "I'd win."

Helen poured another glass of amber sherry in the white

sun under the jasmine and uncrossed her legs in the red canvas chair.

Littlejohn kept her eyes down. She was beginning to regret having asked so many questions about Helen's living at the hotel. She still had the feeling her mother had some sort of silly plan, even if the bridge game was over; Helen was being much too disarmingly direct. Her next move would be to slip under her daughter's guard in some way and point a gun where she could use it to get her own way about something. It was an old game. Though Littlejohn had often seen it, she was never sure when her mother was playing it till her own back went up too far and she said something she didn't mean. When they were together, Littlejohn knew, she was apt to be more than blunt; her angers were too sudden. In reacting to her mother's deviousness, she herself hit too hard. Helen was looking out to sea again, with an expression that lay somewhere between innocence and the blank self-control of a stalking cat.

Littlejohn said, "I think I'll go sleep on the beach."

". . . Didn't you sleep last night?"

"Not much."

"Sometimes I can't sleep either. It doesn't happen often. I can usually find the reason—I just go down the list. What keeps you awake? Conscience?"

"No."

"Happiness?"

"No."

"Fear?"

Littlejohn didn't answer.

Helen smiled. So the gun was pointed.

"The heat?" she said softly.

"I'm not in heat," Littlejohn said. "You are."

She saw her mother's face go pale in the sun. Helen didn't move. She didn't even blink. She was a trooper, you had to give her that.

"I'm tired," Littlejohn said. "Plain tired. I don't want to hurt you and I don't want to talk like you. I don't want to talk . . . I just want to go lie down on the beach until lunch. I'm sorry if I knifed you just now. I am sorry."

She turned fast and went to the terrace edge.

"I'll be right here when you wake up," Helen said behind her gently.

Littlejohn smiled, going down the steps. She did almost like her mother sometimes.

She avoided the stares of the lifeguard and the big Texan and she took her sandals off at the bottom and put them in her straw bag. She shouldn't have. The sand in the sun was like hard glitter. It was deep and coarse and it was like walking through crushed diamonds in a furnace. Littlejohn ran to the cool sand under the blue beach umbrella. She got her feet out of the fire and spread out her blue towel and knelt on it. Will came up behind her, holding the dog. He was barefoot too but he was walking slowly. He didn't seem to notice the hot sand.

He put the dog down and crossed his fists behind his head and carefully cracked his neck. "Did she say something to you?"

"Mother? Sure."

". . . Bad?"

"I wasn't running away from Mother," Littlejohn said, "I was running out of the sun. Will, I need some sleep." She lay down on the towel in the shade.

"Didn't sleep last night?"

"Look. Don't you start," Littlejohn said. "Just a half hour's rest and I'll be fine."

"Sure." Will shuffled in the sand with one foot and turned away. He coughed. "Can I ask you something?"

". . . If you make it quick."

Will yawned nervously. He cracked his knuckles and yawned again. Then he fastened his eyes on the bottom of the umbrella.

"Are you a virgin?" he said.

Littlejohn shut her eyes.

"For Jesus Christ's sake," she said evenly, "and for Alexander the Great's and Madame Curie's and Alexander Hamilton's and Joan of Arc's sake, and for my sake, just shut up and go away."

"Sorry," Will said.

"What did I do; what did I ever do? I wish I were dead. No I don't, I wish I were alive. . . . I don't wish anything. I wish you would just please for God's sake take a walk, Will, I'm tired."

"You don't believe in God. You told me."

"I don't believe in a Supernatural Being, that's all I ever told you. . . . I didn't say I don't believe in God, that's a word with many definitions. . . . I wish I were a bird. I wish I were floating in the middle of a very cool ocean on a whale. I wish I were the whale."

". . . Why a whale?"

"They can dive two thousand fathoms in a second without adjusting to the pressure," she said. "That's why a whale."

"How do they do it?"

"I don't know how they do it," Littlejohn said, "if I knew, I wouldn't be here. Yes I would, but I could sleep. . . . It wouldn't matter about Mother or the sun or you or all the questions because I'd just dive two thousand fathoms deep into my mind where it's cool and lie down and sleep. Please, Will . . ."

He waited a second.

"Okay," he said. He lifted the dog and started to walk.

"Don't be angry. I only need a half hour alone."

"I said okay," Will said.

She got the other towel out of the bag and folded it into several thicknesses and lay down and put it over her eyes. It wasn't cool but it was better than nothing. It blocked out the big bloated sun. The silence was complete now. She felt woozy and there was a circling in her head. She could still see flights of white birds like snow birds. Just cool white floating birds. She had always wanted to be as weightless as a whale in water or a bird in the air.

She tried to follow the white birds with her mind. They were like circles of cool. In her head they were over the beach above the hotel and over the different-colored bungalows. So if you have the blue bungalow, then your beach umbrella is blue and your cabin on the beach and your tablecloth in the dining room. Your napkins and your thinking.

So there's the circling of white in the blue, and you inside it. Blue-safe, blue-cool, blue-quiet. Blue-lifting, blue-sailing, blue-blue. Blue blue blue until you don't know what it means till blue blue blue blue BLUE is just a line of letters way below you, and way above you, in the blue. Of course I'll marry you, why wouldn't I, we'll live in a house in the blue country. I won't even use the words. I won't say I learned to give head at Harvard. On weekends in cars to keep from letting them do it. We'll call it love: 'I'm a minister's daughter, you can say God is love, it just goes in one blue and out the other. Yes, let's marry, let's promise not to use the words. I want to live in a blue euphemism. . . .

And turn over on my side like this and you'll think I'm listening. Just so it's blue. Not orange. . . . Pause . . .

Not the sun. Don't let it happen. It's turned bright red. Staring. You promised. E. J., you promised. The ghost-shape. I asked you, I begged you not to let me out of the blue; blinding awful red. The shape of emptiness cutting out its way. Somebody help me. Anybody . . . There. Blackness . . .

Not blue, but sharp cutting shadow black: open your eyes.

You know you're dreaming but you can't stop. Yes you can if you open your eyes. Peel yourself out of it. Lift yourself out of it. Open your eyes.

Ugliness and the sun. The sun through it.

Between me and the sun. Look up.

Very old man. Ugliest face I've ever seen. Uriel.

"Christ," Littlejohn said, loud.

She waited a while and caught her breath. A wave of nausea swept through her like a low roll of surf. The skull-face in front of her was almost inhumanly ugly.

"They told me my wife was this blue umbrella," he said.

". . . What?"

"I must have misunderstood."

"What?"

"They must have said to me some other color of umbrella. You have not seen her, I suppose?"

The bone-ugly old man walked around the umbrella letting the sun go like a slap in Littlejohn's face. He walked a full circle and came back to where he had been standing before between her and the sun. Like a walking shadow. Ugliness of ugly.

"I see my wife is not here?"

"You don't miss a thing," Littlejohn said. "Go away."

". . . Excuse me?"

"Good morning."

"Good morning." Smiling.

"Not exactly. *Adiós, buenos días y adiós.*"

He shook his head. *"Buenos días y adiós* is not correct; it's the other way . . . *Adiós, buenos días."*

Littlejohn sat up hard. "Look, I lie down on a beach in a private hotel and . . ."

Will came up around the umbrella. "Something wrong?"

"No," Littlejohn said.

"I believe we have not met," the hard ugly skeleton said to her.

"We have not. I don't know you, I don't want to know you, and I don't like being molested on the beach."

That did it. She saw the change.

"I beg your pardon," the old man said. He stood frowning and his body went thinner. His face got really ugly. It was a death's head; he stared at her for one more second with the sun coming out of his eyes. Then he turned and walked off. Fire of bones in the sun.

"Fine," Littlejohn said. "I hope he stays mad twenty years."

"Why?"

"No particular reason. I shut my eyes for two seconds because I'm so tired I feel like dying, and some old bastard comes up and trips over me. The sun got under the umbrella and I must have turned over and knocked the towel off my face, and then he walks up and . . ."

"You were asleep over two hours," Will said.

She looked at him. He wasn't lying. He was watching the bone-ugly old man walk up the steps. There was something about the way Will watched him.

"He didn't trip over you either," Will said, "he never went anywhere near you. You must have been dreaming."

". . . Do you know that man?"

"Yes," Will said. ". . . No. That is . . . I've seen him."

"Seen him?"

"Yes," Will said, "once before. You better wash up for lunch . . . Mother called down ten minutes ago."

"Oh boy," Littlejohn said. She stood up and stretched. "It doesn't stop, does it?" she brushed the sand from her right shoulder.

"I'd like to know now."

". . . Know what?"

"Who it is you're going to marry."

"Ernest Jeremy Williams," Littlejohn said. "Law school, athlete. Phi Beta Kappa. You'll like him. He'll like you. We'll all live happily ever afterwards, if we can just get through lunch."

They walked back up across the beach. Littlejohn waited for the sand to get so hot she would have to run but it didn't. It must have got cooler, she thought. Or else she was getting used to it.

She washed and changed in fifteen minutes. Will was waiting in the living room of the blue villa when she came out. He had left the bandaged dog in a makeshift crib he'd put together in his bedroom.

"They won't let you wear those bluejeans in the dining room," he said.

"Good . . . you and I might have to go out and sit on the terrace or someplace and eat alone. Won't that be awful?"

Will grinned.

It didn't work. The headwaiter in the dining room looked at her critically but he decided not to do anything. "Today you are at the gold table."

"What about the red one?"

"*Señorita?*"

"Our mother is in the red villa. We all eat at . . ."

"Not today. Gold table, please."

They walked through the bright pastel colors and the smiling people. The English bird kept her face in her menu. Her big Texas husband blinked discreetly.

Will stopped so short he almost made Littlejohn fall. When she caught her balance she followed his gaze. It's true, she thought. Will does have vision.

"Sit, children," Helen said, "you're late. My son, William. My daughter, Alice Littlejohn . . . Count Guzmán and his sons, Juan Alberto and José Ramón. Count Guzmán has kindly asked us to join . . . What seems to be wrong *now*, Alice?"

"Nothing."

"Do you often laugh at nothing?"

The two sons were standing. About nineteen and twenty-two. Nice-looking. Frightened eyes. Hand-kissers.

"You and I need not say how do you do," the Count said. "We have already spoken on the beach. We are acquaintances since twenty minutes. We did not begin very well; now we shall see how it goes."

LITTLEJOHN sat and didn't look at Will and picked up her napkin. Will was bursting with it. She had outdone herself this time, insulting Helen's new beau before she met him. They were both at the point where one snicker would land them under the table. "Don't," Littlejohn said.

"Can't help it," Will said.

"Children, if you have anything to say," Helen murmured, eyes on the menu, "speak up."

Littlejohn tried to hold her breath and keep a straight face but it wasn't going to be easy; the sons were staring at her. The older one, Juan Alberto, was handsome in an even-featured way. The Count wasn't as ugly as he had been on the beach. Not as old either, but older than Helen. You wouldn't figure Helen for that—as a rule she liked them her age or younger. This one was silvering gray. Maybe fifty, maybe a lot more. It was hard to tell; it was the eyes that made him seem so strange. When he squinted at the menu he was ugly again. Some men should be careful of their eyes, Littlejohn thought: his were too pale blue and they slitted when he watched something. Eyes of devil. Bones out of face. Either as repellent as death or as simple. Skull.

"Where's your wife?" Will said.

Helen fumbled her menu.

"She has already left," the Count said, "I was misinformed twice. Once for my wife and once for the blue umbrella. Evidently she left last night. I would suggest the sole. Mrs. Locke?"

"Helen," Helen said.

"A pretty name, a pretty woman."

Helen blushed. She had it ready and she was good at it. It came up fine—high pink on the cheekbones and under the hairline. Littlejohn swallowed a smile. She had always been tickled by her mother's technical proficiency; Helen could produce a blush on no notice, the way some people can belch. "Yes, the sole."

"... William?"

48

"Sure."

"Yes, sir, please," Helen said.

". . . sir, please."

"The sir is not necessary for me," the Count said, smiling, "would you care for a green salad?"

"I think we'll leave it all to you," Helen said. Littlejohn watched her. She knew Helen's technique by heart. Menu down. Cigarette slowly up. Eyelids down. Foot accidentally next to the Count's under the table. Snatched away too quickly. Cigarette out. Caught Littlejohn watching her. "Bluejeans, Alice. . . . Did you think we were going on a picnic?"

"I still think so," Littlejohn said.

"I like very much bluejeans," Juan Alberto said to her. Serious smile. Photograph. Eight by ten glossy.

"I also," his brother said.

"Charming. Very American."

"They're Spanish," she said. "I bought them in Madrid."

"Alice has dozens of pairs of bluejeans," Helen said fast, "from all over. . . . It's all she wears in the summer."

"Charming."

"You speak English very well," Helen said to the sons while the Count was ordering.

"We were at university in England. My brother and I."

"I see."

"Have *you* been to England?" From Eight by Ten Glossy to Littlejohn.

"Yes," she said.

"Did you like it?"

"Yes."

"Did you like London?"

"Yes."

"And the Tate Museum?"

"Yes," she said.

Will snickered. He faked a sneeze to cover it.

"Alice has traveled a great deal," Helen said, looking at her.

We all have, Littlejohn thought, but she didn't say it. Helen was still up to something. Littlejohn knew the signs; she could feel herself bristle.

"Do you agree," Juan Alberto said, "that it is most diverting to travel from culture to culture?"

Littlejohn glanced at him. "You have to be kidding," she said.

"Excuse me?"

"Yes," she said. "Most diverting."

"I hope this wine will suit," the Count said, "it's not of the sherry variety, but volatile."

Helen sniffed it and shut her eyes. She let a little touch her tongue. "Lovely."

"I don't believe this whole day," Littlejohn said.

". . . Excuse me?"

"Alice, do be careful of your water glass." Sharp.

"I'll be careful."

"I sometimes find the American language difficult to follow," the Count said.

"Here we go again," Littlejohn said: " 'the American language.' "

"I find it charming," Juan Alberto smiled. "Since I learn it."

"It grows on you."

". . . Excuse me?"

"Juan Alberto plays championship tennis," Helen said, staring at Littlejohn.

"Charming," Littlejohn said.

"Not championship; only to enjoy."

"Your father said you'd won several prizes."

"Amateur competitions. One would hardly call them prizes."

"You are modest," Helen said. Flash smile to the son. Foot to the Count. "Alice plays tennis."

"Not any more."

"You played last summer . . . you must have forgotten quickly."

"Faster every minute."

Eyes of the Count wider. He had been watching Littlejohn and frowning.

"English university, tennis, travel . . . I'm surprised you have time for so much," Helen said to Juan Alberto.

"How is that, please?"

"You'll be a count too one day; you have to prepare, I suppose."

"Oh no," Juan Alberto said. "To prepare for what? A count is not so much . . . I'm already a count. I have a title from my mother's side of the family."

"I see," Helen said.

"Would you prefer a different dish to begin besides the shrimp?" From the Count.

"Indeed no," Helen said. "I never eat much lunch. . . ."

"In Spain lunch is the big meal. Supper is only light. I believe in your country it is the opposite?"

"Yes," Helen said, "isn't it interesting?"

"They are surprised to see us together this way," Juan Alberto said, "the waiters."

"Are they?"

"Oh yes. Everyone knows my father doesn't like American politics. He's famous for it. Particularly in this province. The Guzmán palace is in Sanlúcar—just a few kilometers on the other side of Puerto de Santa María. The people here know my father by sight. The hotel employees are shocked to see him sitting with Americans. It is amusing and very nice."

"You exaggerate a little," the Count said.

"No," Juan Alberto said, "it's important that they see you this way. I hope it becomes known in Madrid. No one there would believe you would sit at the same table with Amer—" He saw something in his father's eyes and stopped. He smiled. "Of course," he said to Helen, "you are not typical Americans. *Es decir,* you're not at all the usual type. One wouldn't guess unless one were told. You seem so much more European. . . ."

"Did you know," he said, turning to Littlejohn, "your mother and I have discovered some mutual friends in Paris? The Vicomtesse de Lerague and her family—she is a friend of *my* mother's, not of mine. It's nice that our mothers have a friend in common, yes?"

The itch in Littlejohn's scalp was the same as it always was when Helen was up to something; she looked at the Count and at Helen and then at Juan Alberto, carefully, one by one. Then all at once she got it. The bridge game and the are-you-a-virgin bit, and Helen's being so nice, and the two counts, the ugly one and the eight-by-ten glossy one, and lunch. Even Helen's putting up with Juan Alberto's brand of patronage. The whole picture. She whacked a look at her mother. Helen turned away and wouldn't look back. Then she was sure.

"Perhaps," Juan Alberto said to her, "you'd remember your tennis again if you allowed me to teach you?"

"I doubt it."

Eyes of the Count. Slits in the skull. Tore open.

"Do you find us hostile?" he asked, "the Spanish?" Straight at Littlejohn.

"No," she said.

"I sense a hostility in you."

"If you mean on the beach, yes—I was angry. I was asleep and you startled me."

"No," the Count said. "I meant now."

"Alice hasn't been sleeping very well," Helen said.

"I woke her," the Count said, "I am the guilty one . . . the chambermaids misguided me. I had not yet learned the custom, that the color of one's bungalow . . ." He stopped and looked behind him. The concierge was standing at the back of his chair with an envelope on a platter. Count Guzmán took it.

He opened it and read it. Helen didn't talk. The Count didn't move. After a moment the skull stood out sharper.

"Otra vez?" Juan Alberto said.

"No. Nada," the Count said. *"No tiene importancia.* Excuse me," he said to Helen, "it isn't important. *Gracias,"* he said to the concierge.

"Algo es," Juan Alberto said. *"Algo debe de ser."* His voice had gone strange.

"We must not speak Spanish," the Count said. "It's rude."

"Not at all," Helen said.

Juan Alberto was white under the tan.

"What's wrong?" Will asked.

"Only that my father has many *denuncios* lately. I don't know how you say *denuncios.* They come one after the other."

"I have troubles with my government," the Count said. "With the military and the civil . . . I am frequently denounced . . . no, it isn't denounced. I don't know how you say it either."

"Charged with something?" Will put in.

"Thank you, that is close, yes. Charged with something . . . the police would like to get rid of me. I'm a nuisance, you see. No one agrees with my political beliefs, certainly not my wife. Up to now I fool them with the cape, as the bullfighters say. Sooner or later my government will find a way to catch me."

". . . Why not leave Spain for a while?" Helen said.

"No," the Count said, holding the letter up, "now they have made another demand. I must surrender my passport. Both of them. My diplomatic and my regular passport."

"No pueden . . ." Juan Alberto half rose from his chair.

"Sit down," the Count said. "They can; yes. They just have. . . . But I would not leave the country if I could. . . . It is after all my country."

"Yes," Helen said.

"What did you do to make them angry?" Will asked.

"I speak out against the government of my country and the government of yours. Against yours for supporting mine."

"You're a monarchist?"

"I am what we perhaps do not have in either one of our countries. I am a democrat."

"They *call* him a Communist," Juan Alberto said. "But it is not. The Red Count. The press labels him that. It's a lie."

"Not a very unusual lie," the Count said, "they do it everywhere now. Also in America, no?"

"Do what?"

"They take those of us who do not like Fascists and they call us Communists," the Count said: "it's always a convenient way to frighten the people. Your Mr. McCarthy knew. Many will believe it. You have no way of knowing what goes on here," he said to Helen. "You don't see the people or how they live. You see the hotel, the pretty villas, the things they wish you to see. The Ministry of Information and Tourism is clever at diverting your attention from what exists. But it is bad. Without the American government's support, our military government would have fallen long ago. If you saw what goes on in Spain, you would not like your Presidents for supporting it."

"I don't want to see it," Helen said. "I'll take your word for it."

"I won't take your word for it," Littlejohn said. "I'd rather see it."

The Count blinked blue and smiled. "No. That perhaps is not a good idea . . . it's good, though, your willingness to learn. I had the feeling on the beach that I might have seen you before. I had it again just now when you spoke. . . ."

"Will's seen you," Littlejohn said. "No, Will?"

"Passed us in the car last week," Will said, low. "Going in the other direction. The day you got here."

"The car?"

". . . Yes," the Count said beaming, "quite right. I remember; I did pass you . . . just the two of you. It was a convertible and you were driving," he said to Littlejohn. "It was on the road that leads to the American naval base."

". . . I didn't notice."

"Did you go to the base?"

"Past it. To Puerto de Santa María."

"The day of the automobile accident? Did you notice what happens to the coast as a result of accidents like that? The child was killed, you know. They took him to the hospital with the others . . . he died the next day. He had done nothing—he was only following a stray dog on the sidewalk when the car ran him down. The family—his family—took it very hard. I did not hear about it in time; I went too late to help. The people were fishermen. They had no money for a proper funeral. They drove with the coffin back to the part of the coast where the child had died. The coast has many American homes occupied by families from the naval base. The mourners carried the coffin from home to home. They did nothing . . . there was no violence. When a child dies here, people use a small white coffin. The family carried it for a day and a half. They carried it through two towns. Whenever they came to a house where American military personnel live, they stopped and held the coffin up and stared at the people in the house. If they could not see anyone, they stared at the house itself. Then they went onto the next American house and did the same thing. Many Spanish people joined the procession. They were dressed in black and they maintained the silence and kept on holding the white coffin up until the police intervened and forced them to bury it. Do you know the punishment that your navy gave to the American sailors? The Puerto de Santa María and the area around it are off-base for a month. One month. And even that is to protect the sailors, not the town. Your navy is afraid of what the fishermen might do if American sailors were allowed to roam the streets too soon again. They needn't be, but they don't know that. The fishermen wouldn't do anything. They are not a violent sort of people . . . if they were, it would have shown before this. They would have objected months ago to the spoiling of the waters they fish in—or to the use of their land for a foreign military base when they need it themselves now to raise cattle and crops. It's their land, of course—it has been for centuries. Then Franco came in, 'con sangre y muerte'—with blood and death—and then the Americans came in behind him. No, the fishermen are not a violent people. They've been betrayed twice in the last twenty years . . . once by their own country, and once by yours." The Count paused and took a sip of water.

"I'm sorry about what happened to the child. I suppose any poor town next to a navy base is apt to be corrupted," Littlejohn said. "In any country."

"But then the navy must also do some good for that country."

"Our navy wouldn't be here if you didn't want us."

There was a second's silence. Littlejohn had raised her voice to cover herself; she was at her most perverse. Will looked at her. She was trying to drown out her thinking, he knew. Her left eye was starting to list almost invisibly toward the center and both of her eyes were flashing. She was about to lose her temper.

"No. Not me," the Count said. *"I* don't want you . . . my government wants you . . . it wants your dollars. You pay for military bases, and the dollars go straight to the big ministries in Madrid. A few ministers grow rich. The people remain poor."

"If your ministries are corrupt," Littlejohn said, loud, "it's hardly the American government's fault, and if you're going to misuse our dollars you damn well shouldn't take them."

"That's enough, Alice," Helen said.

"No, please," the Count said. "I like to talk."

"You are talking too loud," Juan Alberto said in a strained voice.

"I shall be careful, don't worry. . . . My sons protect me," the Count said, laughing.

"He is *not* careful," Juan Alberto said, "he will not ever be careful. . . ."

"Yes. I talk and I think out loud too much. It's your government that's to blame. Not you. You aren't typical Americans. My son was right."

"Your son was wrong," Littlejohn said. "We're typical, and I'm sick of your compliments. I've heard all the anti-American chitchat I can take in one day. It's noble of you to have such high-minded thoughts about the Spanish people. It's especially noble considering you're a rich aristocrat having lunch in an expensive seaside tourist resort restaurant with the foreigners who support the resort. If your conscience is so fine and you object to us so much, why the hell don't you go out and do something about it? Instead of ordering vintage wine and giving us expensive lectures? I'm not ashamed of being American, I never have been and you can't make me. . . ."

The Count kept staring at her and the more she talked the more his eyes kept burning out. They were awful eyes, too pale ice-blue in the bone face. "It's strange," he said slowly. "I do not believe you speak the truth now. I think you were probably very much ashamed that day in Puerto de Santa María."

Littlejohn could feel the blush start from the small of her back. She tried to stop it but it flooded up anyway. It bloomed in her face and her eyeballs felt hot as fever. "I don't much care what you believe."

"Alice . . ."

"It's nice of your son to want to prove to everybody that you can be seen with Americans . . ."

"Ali—"

"But you could at least go through with the game and

keep on talking about tennis and wine and how goddamn charming it all is."

The Count said softly, "Nothing I say does anything but make you angry."

"Don't sneer at my country," Littlejohn said, "I reserve that right. It's not for you. Not when you're using us as decoys. And don't patronize me."

"Alice . . ."

"But most of all, don't lead my mother into thinking she can hold you up as bait for her fancy friends from Paris. She will invite them down here and show you off. Only she doesn't know you'd back out of it. . . . Your son wouldn't; but you would. You'd let him lead her on, and then you'd claim you didn't know anything about it at the last minute. You're willing to go that far, though. And you're willing to let her think she can pair me off with your son and have a title in the family. That's what Americans call, in our language, which incidentally is English, very bad taste. . . ."

She stopped because she was out of breath and sat still.

Helen had turned dark angry red and everybody at the table was staring at Littlejohn. So were three or four other tables, including the English bird and her Texas husband, and so were several waiters.

The Count's eyes had gone out. They were only cold ice-blue.

Helen whispered, "Leave the table, Alice."

Littlejohn stood up. The Count and the two sons stood. The Count watched her.

Juan Alberto kept his head bowed down and his eyes on the floor.

Littlejohn said, "Come on, Will."

"William is staying," Helen said.

"No, William isn't," Littlejohn said.

She watched her mother.

Helen bit the inside of her mouth. "Take William to the terrace," she said, low. "Leave quietly and leave now."

"Done," Littlejohn said. "You got yourself a bargain. I've enjoyed doing business with all of you."

Will followed her out. The hotel guests on the way tried to pretend they hadn't been listening but you could have heard a pin drop in most of the restaurant. Bird beak from England was smiling. The headwaiter stood back against the wall as if Littlejohn were carrying an open electric wire. She walked through the lobby and out of the hotel.

Will pulled two chairs under the awning on the terrace. They sat against the light. The sun was high and blinding over the tiles. "The son of a bitch," she said over and over, "the dirty son of a bitch."

"I don't get it. You feel the way he does about the American bases in Spain. I didn't like what you were doing. . . . Why were you talking against yourself?"

"Because I felt like it." For half a second Littlejohn's left eye swam over until it was just a fraction short of being crossed. It looked as if she couldn't see at all. Then it swam back.

"You really let them have it," Will said.

"Not enough," Littlejohn said. "I should have given them a free line just to see. I bet they'd have brought up the integration problem, and how they don't have *that* in Spain. . . . I hate snobs, and I hate finaglers . . . I hate radicals and Communists and middle-of-the-roaders and conservatives and Fascists and liberals," she said. "Especially liberals. I hate them all."

"Aren't you a liberal?"

"Yes. I didn't say I wasn't one," Littlejohn said, "I said I hate them. Myself included. Guilt incorporated. The people who think they can identify with all pain and all hunger. Who get rid of our own pain by curtsying to worse pain. Who sleep in our neat beds with our neat minds and our neat consciences; who sleep," she said. "Who just sleep."

"I bet you sleep tonight," Will said.

"Yes, I'll sleep tonight," Littlejohn said.

Will looked at her. She was lying.

THE THING that worried him worst was about his father.

In the end there hadn't been a lot of his father to bury, they said; but then how did they know that the body they had was the right one? If it was burned so bad there wasn't much of it left? They never had needed to identify his father's body—none of the people in the plane survived. Will had heard Helen say once a long time ago they didn't even know exactly where his father's grave was located. So how could you be sure?

It was ten days since Littlejohn had made the scene in the dining room and lying in bed in the morning Will found his mind on his father all over again. It was a bad way to wake up—he could tell right away it wasn't going to be his day.

He slid his hand down under the bed sheet and felt it there. What he generally did when his mind took to thinking about death—he touched his piece.

The bed was warm from his night's sleep and the single sheet felt heavy and wrinkled over him. It was crazy how a life feeling could come from thinking about death. He worried in private ways. When Helen first took him to the Tomb of the Unknown Soldier in Paris he wondered why that soldier who didn't have a name was buried there and his father who had a name had no tomb; but when he considered about it, it made sense. The unknown soldier might be his father except for its being the wrong war. The thing that worried him couldn't be put into words. It was like Will himself was born out of a war. He was born out of death, into the in-between of wars.

It was like death was really his father. So he was an in-between person. That was what worried him. Right there.

It worried him that he would always be in-between.

He could hear the maids now, loudly cleaning up the living room and chattering. He lifted his arms straight up and pulled his neck out until his backbone cracked. Then there was a thumping in the room with him. For a second

58

he couldn't think what it was; then he remembered and sat up. The dog named Sneakers was lying in the crib he had made for it, watching him. Will got out of bed and looked down at himself. His piece was too stiff to go out through the living room where the maids were; he put his bathing suit on over it, and lifted the dog and carried him through the back door in his bedroom that led outside. He put him down on the deserted back lawn. The dog still couldn't walk for the plaster on his two front legs but he could hobble a little. He made it to a flower bed and managed to lift one hind leg enough to wet on a small bush. After that he went a few steps farther and squatted. Will stood behind him and waited. The sky was solid gray and the gray had come down like a blanket over the pastel villas. You couldn't tell whether it was fog or dew, or just that kind of day. The air smelled faintly of lemons. The villa next to theirs was pink; it was lived in by another American, a man in his twenties named Jim who shared it with an older man that came down on weekends from Madrid. Out of the corner of his eyes now Will could see the one called Jim in the living room of the villa looking through the window. Jim was thin but well shaped and he wore a leopard-skin bikini all day long. It sometimes made Will feel creepy the way Jim looked at him, and he turned away now and pretended he hadn't noticed him. The lemon smell was coming from a tree between the two villas that was draped with pale yellow fruit and Will liked the look of it. It wasn't strange for him any more, waking up in Spain. Helen had taken him out of the States the first time when he was only six; right at first it had been peculiar waking up in foreign places. It was mostly the smells he minded then, the black tobacco and the wine and the tinge of olives. He would dream about being back in the States and in his dream there would always be a familiar American smell that was kind of a combination of peanuts and erasers. Then he would wake up in a different country and the waking was always worse than the dream. But now, bit by bit, he had got used to it: the waking smells of strong coffee and tobacco and the sea, the naked broken purple look of the bougainvillea on the roof of the villa—the first quick breeze and then the sense of sex like a quivering odd stillness in the air—were colors in a bright mosaic that lay around him like pieces of sleep. It reminded him of the mosaics of forty-colored tiles in the main building. He carried the dog back inside and went into the bathroom. His piece was still hard. He stood at an uncomfortable angle bent almost double but he had to wait what seemed like forever before he could make water. It was one of the ways his body wouldn't help him out.

"*Buenos días*," one of the maids said to him when he went into the living room. It was Eugenia and they were friends. All the maids in the hotel were young except for her; Eugenia was going on sixty—gray hair pulled back into a tight bun and tiny gold earrings and a crooked grin. She had had an attack once and it had left half her face at a squinched angle. The first two letters were two separate vowel sounds in Eugenia's name and she couldn't say his name either. She called him "Weel" and they practiced on one another's names all the time. Will had learned hers after a couple of days but she still called him Señorito Weel. There was something simple and open, almost gay, about Eugenia, that he liked—she was a pure Andalusian. "Did you have a good night?" she asked now in Spanish. He nodded and asked politely about her family and they chatted a while. He was discovering that a sort of ritual of manners is necessary in Spain where manners long ago became a means of survival. He asked formal questions every morning about the health of Eugenia's husband, who was not well, and about her son, who was a fisherman in Sanlúcar. He used the respectful *usted* and Eugenia called him by the familiar *tú* because of the difference in their ages. She was worried about her son, he knew, though he wasn't sure why. When he looked over, Littlejohn was standing in the open doorway of her bedroom. She was smoking, watching him. Her arms were folded and she was very still. The blue villa had two bedrooms and a living room and a porch. Littlejohn had been awake again most of the night, he could tell. Her face was pale. Her left eye was just a tiny fraction off center again. It flicked back while he watched it. It hadn't stayed completely centered for longer than six hours since the day when she had talked against her mind in the hotel restaurant. Only instead of looking like a defect, it gave her face a strangely sensual look these days. She had been quieter than usual, too, as if she were thinking about something all the time.

The maids went into his bedroom to clean it up and Will took the dog to the terrace and opened the packet of daily scraps Eugenia had brought for him from the hotel kitchen. Littlejohn came and stroked the dog's back quietly while he ate. Then she straightened.

"If we're going fishing," she said, moving inside to the sofa, "we'd better get started. The man who runs the boat says by afternoon you can't stay out very long in the heat. . . ."

For ten days now they had been going wherever they liked together. Sort of roaming the countryside and picnicking where they wanted to, or eating in little country restaurants. Littlejohn hadn't gone into the hotel dining room since the scene she had made; Will had been back once at Helen's insistence, but other than that he spent all his time with Littlejohn. They stayed off the beach and thought of things to do away from the hotel. Their mother stayed in the red villa or went out with the Count and left Littlejohn alone. Helen was angry.

"Still want to fish?"

"Sure," Will said. ". . . Wonder what we'll catch."

"Don't know," Littlejohn said. "I'll settle for anything but people." She put her fingers up through her hair. "How do I look, tired?"

"You look good."

She lit another cigarette and smiled at him. "I'm proud of you," she said. "You're a lousy liar. Do you have rubber-soled shoes?"

"Yup."

"Why don't you get out of your bathing suit into some jeans. . . . I just talked to the kitchen about making sandwiches for us. The electricity was out for a while this morning; now everybody's awake, but nobody can get coffee. Not enough waiters and bellboys to go around. Maybe I'd better dig us up some breakfast. . . ."

She went out the front door and it slammed behind her. Will sat and waited for Eugenia to finish in his bedroom and in about a minute Littlejohn came back.

"I caught a bellboy on the lawn. The electricity's out again. No room service for a half hour and nobody's calm. And it's drizzling. Come to sunny Spain."

"It only drizzles in the morning."

"The bellboy claims it'll stop in a few minutes. They're expecting something called the *foreño* later on. What's that?"

"African wind."

"Very hot and muggy and very hard on the eyes?"

He nodded.

"I read about it somewhere . . . throws sand in your face? Can't walk in it? Too hot to sleep in it? Can't live in it?"

"That's the one."

Littlejohn said, "I'm going over to the kitchen and make sure they put the sandwiches together right. My Spanish still gets me noodles and raw fish. I'll be back in time to make a noise and wake you again."

"You didn't wake me," Will said. "Eugenia did."

She went out behind him and he heard the front door slam again. Eugenia came out of his bedroom with the other maid and went on to clean up another villa. She slammed the front door too. Everybody slammed the front door.

Will left Sneakers on the terrace and took his bathing suit off. He passed himself in the mirror over his dresser and tried not to look. His body always made him nervous. He went over and lay down on the bed. Eugenia had made it up and the blue cover scratched his back. Then he felt along his ribs with both hands and tried to locate his liver. Once he had touched it and it was a relief to him that his liver was where it was supposed to be. He thought of his organs as stuck together, all miserably pushed up against each other inside a cage that wasn't big enough to carry them, like people in an overcrowded bus. It was like his glands were jostling for position all the time and the wrong gland always got to sit down. Not having enough room inside himself was only part of being an in-between person. He thought about that again and felt his piece. It came up to meet his own hand. He could see he would have to fight with it if he was going to get anything done today, and he pushed it back down for a while and then decided to get it over with and jerk off. He kept his mind on naked women with naked men on top of them and tried not to think of her. He always tried, but at the very end he couldn't help it. Just before the click, when it was too late to stop and the stillness happened, his mind broke open and got onto the subject of Littlejohn. Like without her his body wouldn't know how to finish. He didn't have a well-run body any way you cut it.

Then he was catching his breath with the pool of white on his belly when he heard the front door slam again. He jumped into the bathroom in one move. He took a shower and got dressed. But when he came out there was no one in the living room. He figured the door must have slammed in the wind. . . .

The living room was all blue—sofa, chairs, lampshades, tiles. It was so blue you couldn't see the blue in it. A plain white scarf of Littlejohn's caught his eye and he went and sat down next to it. He felt a little raw-stomached and he turned on the blue radio to wait for breakfast. The dog hobbled in and collapsed with a grunt at his feet. There was a pause and then some bad castanet music blared out. A lot of what the radio played was "Granada" and "Lady of

Spain" and other tunes written by non-Spaniards. This time it was a bad flamenco singer cheapening a song for the general public. The general public didn't know good flamenco even in Spain and the radio was a dead loss. He could see again it wasn't going to be his day and then she came back with a tray.

"Fishing is out," she said. She kicked the door closed with her tennis shoe. It didn't catch, and it blew open right away. "The wind has started. It isn't muggy yet."

"It will be."

Littlejohn laughed. "Now you sound like me," she said. He could have told her why.

She put the tray down and Will had some of the scrambled eggs and a splash of black coffee in warm milk. The milk was thin and bluish. Littlejohn wasn't hungry. She was smoking another cigarette.

Through the open door there were smells of damp grass and early morning earth and the fresh rotting smell of the sea. The air felt like it was going to go on raining for the rest of your life.

"We could always drive to one of the other towns," Littlejohn said. ". . . Like Arcos de la Frontera."

"Sure."

"Or Sanlúcar."

Littlejohn's voice had gone almost inaudible. Will turned to her.

She was staring out the window. There was a softness in her face. Will followed her gaze. There was nothing on the lawn at all that he could make out. The drizzle had almost stopped, but the side terrace of the main building and the beach were still empty. In the distance, on the other side of the main building, Count Guzmán was crossing a gravel path to the pier where the pleasure boats were docked. He went into the shed that was used by the dockkeeper to store fishing tackle and life preservers for the hotel guests. Littlejohn turned back into the room. When she saw Will looking at her she dropped her eyes. She started to light another cigarette and then she blew the match out instead. "I didn't ask the one who runs the boat," she said.

"About what?"

"Fishing," Littlejohn said, "he may want to wait and see if it clears. . . . I did reserve the boat, after all. . . ."

Will watched her but she had turned and was putting on her yellow slicker. "I'll be right back."

"I'll go with you," Will said.

"You needn't."

"I'm going to," he said. He said it with a stubbornness he hadn't known was going to come out. It was almost like he wanted to pick a fight with her, though he couldn't have said why.

Littlejohn didn't seem to hear his tone, but she didn't look at him either. "Fine," she said. "Come along."

Outside, they ran through the drizzle to the shed and Will opened the door for her. It was shadowy inside, and the electric light wasn't on. The room smelled of seaweed. The dockworker and five fishermen in high rubber boots were standing in a corner around a big barrel that they were using for a table. There were some small brandy glasses on it and a bottle. Count Guzmán stood near the six men. He was holding another brandy bottle and a corkscrew.

One of the men stepped forward. It was a dockworker. *"Sí, Señorita? . . . Buenos días,"* he said.

"Buenos días," Littlejohn said.

"Good morning," the Count said.

Littlejohn nodded.

"Ask him," she said to Will, "if any fishing boats are going out."

"Ask who?" Will said.

"The dockworker."

"No," the Count said, "I can answer for him. The pleasure boats don't go out unless the weather is clear. You can always tell from the flag on top of the main building. It's the flag for all craft warnings."

"I see," Littlejohn said.

"Is there anything else?" The Count took a step forward. "I wanted to . . ."

"No," Littlejohn said. "Thank you."

She cut him off, but instead of turning away she stood her ground. She grazed his face hard with her eyes. It was as if she were looking for something. Will studied her. It was too dark in the shed to see the Count's face very well. The way Littlejohn looked at him, she could have been trying to be certain who he was. Will couldn't make any sense out of it.

Then she turned abruptly and left.

Will followed her across the lawn without talking. Back in the blue villa he took off his own slicker and threw himself into an easy chair. "What was that about?" he said.

"Hmmm? I just wanted to make sure of something."

"You already knew about the warning flag."

"Did I . . . I must have forgotten."

Will didn't bother to go on with the conversation. Littlejohn was a worse liar than he was. It took Helen to know how to tell a lie. Littlejohn didn't usually try and if she did, it was a sure sign she wasn't going to haul off and give you her reason. She'd only get angry if he pressed it. Will shrugged to let her know that he knew, and then forgot about it. "So where'll we go?"

"Wherever you like. Arcos?"

"It's a long drive. It's way inland. It's too hot."

"That it is."

"It's still drizzling."

"Cheer up," Littlejohn said. "It'll get worse."

Then it did.

"Let's try Arcos. It . . ." Littlejohn stopped short. She was looking over his head. Will was sitting with his back to the front door and he saw her face change. He stood up so fast he slopped a little of the coffee over the saucer in front of him.

The figure was standing behind him in the open doorway. For a second it didn't speak.

"No. You want the red villa," Littlejohn said. Her voice was flat and hard.

"Forgive me . . . the door was open. I tried to tell you just now . . . I knocked on this door a few moments ago, but no one answered. I came in to look, but no one was here. . . . They should put doorbells on all the villas."

"That they should," Littlejohn said. "She's in the red one. I'm sure you know the way by now."

"Oh no. I am not mistaken this time. I know where I am," the Count said. "I came for you."

Listening, Will thought he heard Littlejohn sigh, sharp and deep. Not so you could see her do it; you had to know her. It was a hard whispering sigh, like something dying. She didn't answer.

The Count came in and stood by the other easy chair. Will could see him clearly now in the light. He looked kind of scruffy. He hadn't shaved—he had a stubble beard and his eyes were red and pink-rimmed. He had on a pair of old pants and a long hunter's jacket. "May I sit down . . . or should I speak first? I came to tell you something. I'll be brief . . . I am thinking since ten days. At first I was angry . . . I thought you had been rude to your mother and rude to all of us. But now I think that I am wrong and you are right. Not about my political belief—I don't apologize for that. I meant what I said. But you were right about my patronizing you. . . . It was rude. It was much ruder than you were. . . . I think it was not true what you said about my leading your mother on . . . but I cannot blame you for thinking it after the way I had talked. I would be happy to meet any friends of your mother—I would not 'back out,' as you said, unless of course, your mother's friends had some political significance, and I don't think they do, any more than she does. It's true what you noticed, that my son wants me to be seen with Americans. He has been insisting on it for a year. It was because of his insistence that we all have lunch now every day. But it was the game of patronage, as you said. Yes, I think it was a very ugly game we were playing. That I did not see it at the time was only stupid. That is all I came to say and that I am sorry." He sat down as if he couldn't keep standing.

Will watched him. You could see what it had cost him. His eyes were like the first time in the car. He was a funny color too. His face had gone sheet-white and there was a yellowish tinge around his mouth. His lips were blue and trembling. He had been speaking almost feverishly.

"It's a shame," Littlejohn said.

"Excuse me?"

"Your apology is accepted," she said, "thank you for taking the trouble. You shouldn't have. I was perfectly content not speaking to you. I really don't like you at all."

Will frowned, listening to her. Littlejohn seemed to be saying one thing, and yet he had a feeling she was saying another. Her face had taken on a sudden hardness.

The Count folded his big hands on his knees and faced her. He had long heavy fingers and dark skin and no wedding ring. "I understand," he said.

He didn't move. Littlejohn's left eye jerked a minuscule fraction. She looked away.

"Would you like some coffee?" she said suddenly, "you look as if you need some."

"Yes."

She poured him a cup and then mopped up the coffee Will had spilled on the table. There was a silence.

Will tried to keep his eyes on them both. He thought that something had passed between them that both of them knew about; he couldn't tell what. He waited to find out, but whatever the thing was, it was gone.

"The east wind is coming now," the Count said dully. "It is exceedingly debilitating. The *foreño*."

"It's in the guidebooks."

"In . . . ?"

"There've been articles written about the *foreño*. . . . I've read about it." The sound of Littlejohn's voice was tight now and there was a peculiar edge in it. She was staring at the Count.

Count Guzmán had got out of his chair to take a pack of cigarettes from his pants pocket. He had stood up too fast and when he sat back down his face was the color of bone. The blue in his lips had gone darker. "What?"

"The *foreño*."

"Oh yes ... the *foreño*."

"Aren't you feeling well?"

"Yes," the Count said. "Of course, yes. It's an extremely bad wind. The *foreño*."

Then he passed out.

It happened in a plain way, and there was no warning. Will wasn't even bothering with him. There was a soft double crunch and right while Will watched, the Count wasn't on his chair any more. He was lying stretched out on the floor with the coffee splashed out in front of him and his head partly in it.

Littlejohn stooped fast and pulled his face out of it and Will helped her. They yanked him to a sitting-up position, but he kept falling over. His face was an awful color. "Is he dead?" Will asked.

"Undo his collar."

"What's his name?" Will said. "Call him by his name."

"Just keep calm and prop him up there if you can," Littlejohn told him.

She went to the phone and asked for the gold bungalow and got one of the two sons. "The blue villa," she said. "The Count's not well." She came back and sat by him until he woke up.

"Just one moment," he said. He spoke in slow motion. His eyes were open straight at her but he didn't look like he was seeing her. He looked drunk.

"It's all right," Littlejohn said. "You fainted."

"One moment, please. No ..."

"Is there a special medicine you should take?"

"In one ... in one moment ..."

"There's some brandy somewhere." Littlejohn turned to Will. "The cabinet, I think."

"No. Thank you," the Count said. "Thank you so much, I will now get up. No brandy." He pushed himself up into a sitting position in the chair and looked down at his jacket.

"It's just coffee," Littlejohn said. "Here." She held out a clean napkin but the Count didn't take it. He didn't seem to see it. Littlejohn wiped the side of his face with it and then stuck the napkin in his jacket.

Juan Alberto came in fast, latching the door behind him. *"Cuando volviste? Qué pasa aquí?"*

". . . No pasa nada."

"Se desmayó," Will said.

"Claro," Juan Alberto said. *"Cómo no se va a desmayar? Si no se cuida,"* He sounded angry.

"Is he sick?" Littlejohn said.

"Que va! He isn't, but he will be if he does not stop," Juan Alberto took the Count's face in his hand. *"Has comida o no?"*

"No sé; no me acuerdo. Creo que sí." The Count still looked kind of drunk and blank.

"What is it?" Littlejohn said to Will. "What are they saying?"

"He doesn't remember whether he's eaten," Will said.

Littlejohn took the metal cover off her untouched breakfast. "Will this do?" She stuck the plate in his lap.

"Oh yes," the Count said, laughing childishly. "Very nice. I am fond of scrambled eggs. . . ." He swayed out again.

Juan Alberto caught him.

"The sofa," Littlejohn said. She grabbed the plate back.

Juan Alberto picked his father up and carried him over to the blue sofa.

"Undo his belt," she said.

"I am very fine now," the Count said. "I do hear every word. I only sat up too fast."

He said formally, "I very much apologize for this performance." He smiled at them all.

Then he passed out again.

"Get a doctor," Littlejohn said.

"No," Juan Alberto said, "there's nothing wrong with him. It has happened twice before. He forgets to eat sometimes for two days. How can a man forget to eat? He'll be fine in a minute. . . . He's been out all night; he has much wine and brandy with the fishermen and puts nothing else in his stomach. I ask myself, how is it possible that a man his age forgets to eat? It isn't the first time. . . . His doctor is in Madrid."

"Won't any doctor do?"

"No."

"Why not?"

"He must have just come back to the hotel. He's been to the bars, to drink with the fishermen. There was another incident yesterday—some American marines fighting in the town of Rota. They say a Spaniard was hurt. He talks too much when he's like this. He always . . ."

". . . What kind of fishermen?"

Juan Alberto looked at her and then sat back with the Count's head in his lap. "Just ordinary fishermen. I also talk too much," he said. "If you will allow us to wait until he can walk, we will leave quite soon. What you can do for him is not to say anything. That's all you can do. Now we will not speak about it."

It took about fifteen minutes and the Count sat up.

He laughed.

"I am something of a woman," he said.

"You're better now," Littlejohn said, "your color's back. You were white as a ghost when you stood up to get your cigarettes."

"I am a woman," the Count said. "Like a woman. Not like you," he said to Littlejohn. He laughed again. "You are something of a man," he said.

He had a funny laugh, Will thought; it didn't go with his face. It was a little boy's laugh.

The Count asked for the scrambled eggs and Littlejohn gave them to him and he ate some and drank some coffee with four spoons of sugar in it and then had some toast with marmalade. "Excellent cold breakfast," he said.

"I'll order fresh coffee and . . ."

"No," Juan Alberto said, "no waiters until he takes a shower and shaves. He is fine now. In a moment we shall leave. I don't know why he came here."

"Neither do I," Littlejohn said.

"It was because I decided since three days to speak. Seeing you in the shed made me sure. Did I speak adequately?" the Count said.

"Yes."

He stood up. Juan Alberto stood beside him. "No," the Count said. "It is over."

"This one is over," Juan Alberto said; "*this* one." He still sounded mad.

"I came also with an invitation for you and your brother to have drinks in the bar of the hotel. With your mother and my two sons this evening," the Count said. "All of us."

Littlejohn studied his face before she answered. "I don't think so. I don't think Mother would dance at the idea either."

"I understand you and she are not speaking? Or that she is not speaking to you?"

"I like the second one better, but I'll buy either one."

"It's what first troubled me. That I had caused trouble between you. I had no wish to cause trouble between you and your mother. I have already talked with her. She has agreed."

Littlejohn sat down and lit a cigarette and watched him through the smoke. "What are you and Mother cooking up now?" she said. "An international bomb syndicate, or just another war?"

"Will you accept my invitation?"

"No."

"I'm sorry."

"Don't apologize again," Littlejohn said. "You know what happened the last time."

"You must not speak to him that way," Juan Alberto said.

Littlejohn sat back and took another drag of her cigarette. She was looking at a carnation growing outside the window. "I should explain. . . . I can't join you for a drink. I'm going to do some shopping and have my hair washed today. But my brother can."

"No," Will said.

"Yes," Littlejohn said. She was still looking at the flower. "You can't come traipsing with me into the she-barber's, and there's no sense your waiting in the car. I believe the Count means his offer well. You should accept it for me."

Count Guzmán tipped his head forward. His eyes did it again, Will saw, like they had in the car—only this time they stayed that way. "Perhaps another day you also?"

"I think not," Littlejohn said. "I won't have time. I'm not staying in Suelo long."

He took his eyes off her and went out, and Juan Alberto bowed his head formally without looking at her and went out after his father.

Littlejohn turned her back to Will; she tackled the second coffee mess on the floor. Will watched her. She was framed by the open window. On the other side of her, through the window, the drizzle had stopped, but it looked now as if the sky were sweating. Will got up and went into his own room and sat in a chair.

"Okay. Knock it off," Littlejohn called.

She came to the door.

"I'm not throwing you to the wolves," she said. "Let's not pout. I do have a hair appointment; I made it from the hotel when I was seeing about breakfast."

Will didn't answer.

"And I do believe he means well," Littlejohn said, "I just think I'm better out of it. You won't get tangled in it. I might. Okay? You're plenty old enough to handle it."

Will shrugged.

"Come on," Littlejohn said. "Let's not everybody get angry. . . . There isn't time. Let's go for a drive."

"Okay," Will said.

It was generally like that. He couldn't stay mad at her.

They went out and got in the car. The top was up. Will carried Sneakers. The clouds were lifting but the hot wind was heavy now off the sea. The dry desert heat was blowing from Africa over the sea-wet. It clogged your brain. The sky was dirty.

Will watched the shell road that wound between the bungalows under the soggy clouds. There was a bitter smell in the air like raw fish. He settled back in the car and relaxed. He wasn't worried. He figured that everything that was going to happen that day had already happened. Much later, it seemed to him he should have known by now what was to come after. He could have known. He already had all the clues.

"Where shall we go?" Littlejohn said. "It's too hot for the towns."

"There are some salt field marshes on the other side of Sanlúcar. There's a farmhouse out there and piles of salt. There's a game preserve. It isn't so hot in the shade."

"Show me," Littlejohn said.

They drove out of the hotel for a long time in silence. All at once for no reason at all Will began to be uneasy again. There was something unsaid between them. Littlejohn avoided Puerto de Santa María and took the other road that cut across the train tracks toward the town called Sanlúcar de Barrameda. There was dust floating from the African wind. There were men walking along the side of the road through the thick air as if they were going someplace to breathe, and the light was hard. There was a donkey with two baskets heaped with oranges like bubbles of heat.

"It isn't any better with the top up," Littlejohn said. "It's not the sun. Today it's the wind. There isn't any way to get out of it. . . . Did you believe him?"

"Who?"

"You know who."

"*Him?* No."

"You're wrong," Littlejohn said. "He was speaking the truth the whole time. I think he's a very good man. I thought so the minute he walked in the door. Even before that. I knew it when I saw him in the shed."

"Then how come you kept knifing him?"

"I don't like him," Littlejohn said.

Will shrugged. He didn't get it, but he didn't care.

They drove through the gray-green fields and Littlejohn had to keep swerving to avoid the ruts. The road was very bad. They drove for fifteen minutes.

"What don't you get?"

It made him jump. It was a trick she had done a lot of times when they were little. In those days Will used to believe she could hear people think. Only, she had explained that a woman who loves a man, even if he's her brother, can think right along with him no matter how young he is.

"You. I don't get you," he said.

"What don't you get about me?"

". . . The way you're talking."

"I'm not difficult," Littlejohn said. "I don't like people who take advantage. . . . I just don't like people," she said, ". . . I'm a minister's daughter, don't forget that. In a way I'm the purest minister's daughter you'll ever see. That's the whole point of me."

She drove a while with the hot wind behind them.

"*He* got it," she said.

Will ducked that one.

"I wish you'd tell me what's so difficult to understand about me."

He let that go too. He was getting tired of the whole conversation. Besides it was making him nervous—there was a sound in Littlejohn's voice he didn't like.

". . . Look at the wheat fields," he said.

"Isn't that something? Look at that green," Littlejohn said. "He takes advantage."

"Who does?"

". . . Him. The man. It's not a nice quality. The other time he just let his son flirt with me. . . . Now *he's* doing it. . . . I was wrong about Mother, I doubt she's got him yet . . . she's still setting it up probably—but it wouldn't much matter if she had. The Count would change horses in midstream so fast none of us would know what hit us. There's something big and quite cruel in him. Did you notice the way he looks at people? He's got the worst eyes I've ever seen."

"I've seen his eyes," Will said. "You just got through saying he's a good man."

"So what?"

"So now he's cruel."

"Good men are," Littlejohn said. "Only the best. He's about two and a half years old. He'd take me the way a baby would pick up a lollipop. He wouldn't even know he was going to do it. He didn't have a clue what was going on at the table the other day. . . . His son did, yes, but not *him,* not the man. And still, he's the one who comes to apologize. Did you hear him flirt? Did you hear *him* apologize. . . ."

She took a long breath, and Will turned to look out the window. Littlejohn sounded as if she were giving one of her father's sermons from the pulpit, only she wasn't making much sense. After the years of her silences it was like a big bunch of words had poured together in her, and she couldn't stop talking. Will watched the green passing fields and let her go on. The dull green glittered in the dust and her voice hummed over him, preaching.

". . . it's the look around the eyes. That's why I went to the shed—I knew it the other day when I blew up at him. He's the most sick-makingly innocent thing I ever saw." She turned another curve on the rain-rutted road. "He's got the look of a baby. There's nothing crueler in the world than a baby's eyes. That's what the ministers don't understand. The ones like my father, they miss it cold. They think the world is still heading toward innocence. See?"

"No," Will said boredly.

"It's simple. We're outside Eden now. Innocence isn't ignorance any more . . . now it's just evil . . . do you know where we're headed now?"

"The salt field marshes," Will said.

"Don't be funny," Littlejohn said. She took a deep breath and said, "We're going away from innocence as fast as we can. Because you have to. Once you're out of Eden, you're out. The only road back is the fastest road away from it . . . the way light travels—because if light once rises it has to go straight up, way out into space and never waver and never, never, turn back until it goes through the universe—all the way of time through the whole entire curve of the universe without stopping, until it comes back to earth from the other side; because if it ever stops once, just once, it's dead. It would just sputter and go out. Burn up and go out. That's why I'm never going to see him again."

". . . Why not?"

"Don't be stupid," Littlejohn said. "I'm in love with him."

Will jumped hard and turned. Up to then he hadn't really been listening. He knew she was talking in a funny way but the thick blowing heat could make anybody talk too fast. He watched her now. She looked the same. She was wearing her dark glasses against the swollen gray of the sky and she was just watching the road. Nothing in her face had changed. Will asked:

"Were you ever in love before?"

"No."

"Then how do you know?"

"That's how."

"You're not."

"I would be if I saw him again. . . . I'm falling in love right now, can't you hear it? He doesn't even have the sense to eat. There, did you hear *that*? I *am* in love with him."

"He's . . ."

"What?"

". . . an old man."

"Not as old as he looks; he's mostly bones with a lot of muscles over them."

"He looks like a skeleton."

"Yes," Littlejohn said. "I think he's very ugly. How old would you say he was?"

"Ninety-nine."

"Seriously."

"Forty."

"No, seriously."

"I don't know."

"That's the point," she said. "See?"

"I don't see anything," Will said. "I think you're crazy. I don't know what you're talking about. What in hell's got into you?"

"That has," Littlejohn said. "A little bit of hell has. Only it's all right, I caught it in time. . . . I practically caught it in the act. Maybe I haven't been sleeping for a reason. I must be ripe for it. . . . It's only just got a foot in, I know how to get the door shut. Will you help me?"

". . . Sure."

"I'll make it. I'm going to leave this afternoon and go back."

"Where?"

Littlejohn's voice was dry. "I'm going home and marry E. J. Williams," she said, "like any normal schizophrenic American girl. I've already made my commitment. You just keep them in the bar for an hour or so. Throw a fit if you have to. I'll pay my bill upstairs and leave. . . . I don't want to see him again, understand?"

He stared at her good and flat. Then he knew she was serious.

She drove for a minute.

"Why should I keep them in the bar?" Will said. "Why don't you just drive off if you want to?"

". . . I don't trust myself driving alone any more—I get angry."

"Why?"

"I don't know. . . . But I can't seem to drive alone," Littlejohn said. "I'm going to take a taxi to Cádiz and catch the night train up to Madrid. There must be one. I'll fly from there."

"What about the car?"

"The hell with the car," she said.

"You can't just leave it."

"Mother can have it. I'll buy it for her from the rental company in Madrid." Littlejohn smiled. Will didn't much like the look of the smile.

"When will you come again?" There was a tightening in his throat the way it always happened whenever she had to leave. He could hear it.

She reached over and slid her hand hard over his hand on the seat. "I'll come back when I'm married. Or maybe send for you. . . . I'd just like your help now, that's all."

Will nodded. He still couldn't put any of it together but it was better to go along with it, he thought.

Her hand pressed harder down and then she took it off and put it back on the wheel. He didn't notice when she touched him. But as soon as she took her fingers off he knew she was cold.

"What'll Mother say?"

"That I left because she's mad at me," Littlejohn said. "She'll cool off and write me—she always does. She's been mad before, it doesn't last. . . . The second she needs me for something she'll repair it. Only she can't ever know the real reason. . . ."

"Okay."

"Don't tell her. Promise."

"Okay," Will said.

"And don't tell *him*. Let *her* tell him. . . . He'll believe whatever she says."

"Will he?"

"Oh yes," Littlejohn said softly. "He'll believe anybody."

". . . He doesn't believe the Spanish government or the American government or the Russian government."

"That's different. You have to be so innocent it hurts to know how full of shit they are. He even thinks he can change it all by himself. . . . Where are your goddamn salt field marshes?"

They both heard it in her throat at the same time and Littlejohn had barely time to pull the car over on the side of the road. Will didn't know what to do. She put her hands on the wheel and her head down on the backs of her arms. He wanted to touch her. You didn't hear anything in her crying. There was no sound at all and she didn't shake. She kind of rocked. There were spasms of it, one after another ripping out of her without any sound till you thought she would die there on the wheel. Then he did reach over; he put his arm on one of her shoulders but it didn't seem to make any difference. But the hard spasms stopped after a while on their own.

Littlejohn picked her head up and opened her purse. She took out some tissues and wiped her face. Then she laughed, short. "It's mighty peculiar. I used to daydream about falling in love like this. Only now . . ." She let the sentence hang in the air like a torn piece of paper. "Who else do you know would have hysterics with dark glasses on?" she said. "Almost anybody knows better than that." She wiped the glasses and blew her nose. Her left eye was normal now, Will saw, as if it had never been crossed at all. The tears had washed it straight.

"You have gold hair," he said.

"If you say so," Littlejohn said. "Do you seriously want to go to the salt field marshes or where the hell do you want to go?"

"I don't care."

"What's out there?"

". . . Birds mostly."

"Let's go," Littlejohn said.

They drove through the earth-rolls of white houses that led through Sanlúcar de Barrameda. The dust was hot and the little Andalusian town was on the edge of the Guadalquivir River at the mouth, just where the river opened into the sea. High in the town the roads were of dirt and cobblestones and you could see the green water below. The town smelled of sea and of wine. There were men on bicycles and in bars and dusty courtyards. It was rocky and bumpy with the dust rising in the wind. They had to creep along the narrow streets and once they had to wait for a truck that was emptying sand.

"What are you going to do about it?"

"What?"

"Being in love."

"It'll go away," Littlejohn said. "I'll think I dreamed it one day. . . . You can't fall in love because somebody's eyes are pale. It would be ludicrous. It would be like falling in love because somebody faints on your breakfast."

"There are the marshes."

"Yes, look at them," Littlejohn said. "Yes."

They were out of the fishing town now. They were passing flat long rectangles of water where salt farmers had let the sea water in from the delta and then trapped it and let it evaporate in the sun to pure salt. There were long roof-shaped piles of coarse salt by the sides of the road maybe twelve feet high and fifty feet long. Then you could see the birds.

They were sitting or standing in the long shallow salt water lakes. There were all kinds. There were ducks and there were little birds with long skinny legs and thin long beaks and fat birds and big birds. There were birds that swooped for fish and other birds that darted their heads under the water. There was everything but eagles.

They got out and walked. Will left the dog in the car.

Littlejohn's hair was matted. Against the big grass and the shivering heat of the marshes she looked like a boy in a school play.

"It's a nice place," she said. "How did you find it?"

"Spanish kids at the hotel," Will said. "Their parents brought us here on a picnic. There's a game preserve across the river . . . sometimes there are herons. I've never seen the herons."

"I didn't know you liked birds."

"You taught me."

"I love herons."

"Me too."

"I don't love a lot of things," Littlejohn said. "I love you."

". . . What about your father?"

"Sometimes it's hard for me to think about him."

"He still just a minister in that Pennsylvania town?"

"He never wanted to be anything else," Littlejohn said. "That's all he ever needed. The money my grandfather left him didn't do anything but make him unhappy, he doesn't even want to be higher in the church. He wants to be a simple minister. Know why?"

". . . Why?"

"Because it *sounds* good. He's looking for it," Littlejohn said, "can you imagine? *Looking* for innocence. . . . He's even looking in himself. You don't find it that way. He's a nice man, he's just small . . . he's not like the Count," Littlejohn said, "you have to be bigger than life if you want to live. . . . He never was, my father; he's only a nice little man. Yes, I think I love him. Will, promise me something."

"What?"

"If she isn't ready to go back to Madrid in the fall—if she

says the way she sometimes does that it won't matter if you wait till December for school . . . get the hell on a train. Just leave her with whatever man she's with . . . walk out and take the first train and go back to Madrid."

"Sure."

"Say it."

"I promise."

Littlejohn said, "Let's go now."

They went to the car and drove through the wet marshes and then through Sanlúcar again and out on the long road to the hotel. It took well over an hour. She didn't talk all the way. Then she parked the car.

They went toward the villa in the muggy blowing air and she kept glancing over her shoulder like somebody walking through a haunted field. It was like she was afraid the Count would walk out of a bush or somewhere. He didn't.

She phoned from the living room and spoke to the beauty parlor in French but they couldn't make the appointment any earlier.

"It's dumb," she said after she put the phone down. Her fingers were shaking and she was looking at them. "I'm sick of my hands . . . I'm sick of the problems of the lucky. I'm going to be a *real* coward now. . . . I don't want to sit and wait here if he's around the hotel. . . ."

Will didn't answer, and Littlejohn said without looking at him, "Go ask where he is, Will. Don't let them know it's for me. Don't look at me. Go ask, Will." She ran in her bedroom and shut the door.

Will went to the main building and asked in the lobby where Count Guzmán was. The desk of the concierge was a mosaic of tiles on top with the standard forty color combinations of the hotel. The concierge said that the Count had gone away for the day on business and wasn't expected back till late afternoon.

When he went back to the blue villa Will had to shout for Littlejohn before she knew it was him and came out of her room. He told her.

"Good," she said, looking away. "Let's play chess and just stay in here. The two of us."

They sat down and played till it was time for her to leave. There was an anger in Will that kept moving up inside his chest like a claw. It was too hot and wet to breathe and the clock got louder and the games went slowly. Every time somebody walked past on the gravel path outside he saw Littlejohn's face go whiter.

"I don't see why you're afraid of him," he said.

"Him?" She frowned.

". . . The Count."

"Oh no. Not him . . . I'm not afraid of him," Littlejohn said.

"I don't get you. Of what, then? . . . Of what the hell then?"

"Everything except him," Littlejohn said. "*He* wouldn't ever hurt me. . . . It's all the rest. Don't you see?"

"No."

"He can't last," Littlejohn said in a flat way, as if Will had asked her the time. "They'll put him in jail and then they'll just kill him. His son knows it. . . . People like him don't live as long as other people, they just live harder, and it won't take him long to die. Just take a look at his face. . . . It's me. I don't want to be anywhere near him when it happens. I don't want to know him. That's all."

Will sat still and listened and tried to hold the claw that kept rising in him. He couldn't make sense of anything she was saying and he figured it was better to stop trying. They started another game of chess and Littlejohn remembered they hadn't eaten anything all day. She ordered some food by phone and then she forgot she'd ordered it. When the waiter knocked on the door she stopped breathing.

"Go see who it is."

"I can see him from here."

"*Him?*"

"The waiter."

"Yes," Littlejohn said, "him. Let him in."

"That's what I was going to do," Will said. "You're acting crazy."

The waiter came with a tray and set a blue cloth on the table. There was cold gazpacho and tiny lamb chops with string beans. There were two glasses of iced tea. The waiter left. Littlejohn had a spoonful of the gazpacho but she didn't eat anything more. Her eyes had a glitter-glaze to them like burning. "You know what I'd like now?" she said, "I think I'd like a little of that brandy."

Will got it for her from the cabinet. She poured some and swallowed so fast she almost gagged.

Then she laughed but without any sound. "Thanks, Will," she said; "if I can get through today I won't ever have another problem like this one. After they finish with my hair, I'll go to Cádiz and look at museums till the train leaves. Do you need money?"

"No."

"Let me know," she said. "If you need money."

It was such a dumb remark he knew her mind was completely away now. It was Littlejohn who paid his allowance, not Helen. The arrangement had been set long ago when Littlejohn herself asked to do it; she had made Will promise if he ever needed more he would phone her collect. He never had. He didn't get a kick out of it any more than Littlejohn did and she knew it. It was Helen who liked money.

She quit talking and they went on playing chess and she lost three games. The brandy made her begin to sweat under the armpits in half moons. There was an odor about her like vanilla beans.

At six o'clock she stood up to get ready. Her face was white and she pushed her damp hair back. "I'll have them send my hotel bill over," she said. "As long as the car's outside Mother will think I'm still here; I'll send her the car papers from Madrid with a note. . . . Unless she asks the concierge or you, which she won't. But if she does, tell her I didn't like the hotel. But listen, Will . . . it's important to me . . . don't tell him anything about me. Not what time I get up in the morning or what food I like. If he asks about me, don't answer."

"If he wanted to ask about you," Will said in a bored voice, "he'd ask Mother."

"Let him," Littlejohn said. "She doesn't know me. Let him believe whatever *she* says. It's what he deserves."

". . . Why are you getting angry at him? . . . Are you crazy?"

"Right now I am," she said. "Right now maybe I'm a little crazy. Come help me pack."

She put her cigarette out and took a jerky breath and went in her bedroom. The way she walked you'd think she was marching onto a battlefield; you wouldn't think a girl you had known all your life would meet some man three times her age and turn into somebody you never met.

Will sat still while she packed. He wanted to think about her—about all the things that had been happening—but it was all going too fast. He almost wished she was on her way already. If you love somebody who's going to leave you, sometimes you wish they would be gone.

Besides he wanted to be alone and consider. He knew there was a pattern to everything that had happened since she came to see him this time, but he couldn't follow it. He kept catching glints of it. It was like moving through a strange landscape in a dream and the landscape was this strange mosaic of facts. He couldn't make it out where he was or where he was going. Sometimes there was light around him and he could see a little distance, but not enough to help. Thinking about that made him angrier and by the time Littlejohn got ready to go he was as anxious for her to leave as she was. She didn't look fevered any more. The glitter was gone. She just looked burned out and kind of bored. She had put on a pair of brown slacks and a clean shirt and she had a scarf over her hair. She phoned and had the concierge send the bill over and she paid it and then had them phone for a taxi.

Waiting for it to come was the worst part of all. They had waited together for Littlejohn to leave in lots of places—in airports and train stations and boat docks, but nothing like this. For the first time in his life Will felt strange with her, and he couldn't think of anything to say. First off, he took to itching all over his body in every different place. He scratched one section after another. In the silence it was embarrassing how many spots tingled. Then they heard the taxi.

Will carried Littlejohn's two bags out one by one and gave them to the driver. When he came in for the second one, she was standing inside with her back to the front door. She was watching as if she wanted to forget the room for always —or maybe remember it—he couldn't tell which. Her face was hard, like a gypsy boy's. Then she walked past Will and out the door. She got in the taxi without kissing him good-bye. She looked at him from the taxi window but she hardly seemed to see him. "Thanks Will," she said. "I won't ever be like this again."

The taxi took off along the gravel. She turned and waved suddenly, as if she hadn't known it was going to start moving yet. She went on waving till it was out of sight.

Will waited a while watching the dust cloud the taxi left behind when it got to the main road. Then he went and got the dog and sat on the stone steps twenty feet above the sea. There was nobody down on the beach today. There was too much wind. There were whirlpools of sand and there were streaks and flat shapes of it in the air about a foot over the beach. He didn't understand her looking like a scraggly beggar boy running away, and all he could see was the flat whirlpools of sand underneath him. Nothing made any more sense than the curls and wheels of it—the flat designs in the rising wind on the shore. He sat there watching the sand shapes in the wind for nearly two hours.

When he got up, his shirt was sticking to him in the thickness of the heat and Sneakers was whining. He carried him back and took a cold shower. When he was drying himself he looked at the clock and saw that it was eight forty-five. In Spain that is cocktail time and when the phone rang he knew who it was.

"I'm waiting for you," Helen said. "You're late."

He got dressed and walked to the red villa. Helen was standing pulling her dress straight in front of a full-length mirror. She turned her waist back and forth until the dress looked right. It was pink and gold and she had gold sandals on and two yellow bows in her hair. She looked beautiful. Will couldn't think of anything to say, so he told her so.

"William," she said absently, "you haven't said that in years."

She was right—he used to say it sometimes.

"Come along. This heat," she said. "This *foreño* . . ." She wasn't going to mention Littlejohn; you could see she was still angry.

Will followed her to the main building. The wind was the highest it had been all day and Helen had to keep a hand on her hair and another on her skirt. It was like walking against the turn of the earth through the wind. They passed the blue villa with Littlejohn's car still parked outside. Will had left a light on in the villa for Sneakers. Helen kept going and when they got to the main building she had to stop in the ladies room and fix her hair again in front of another mirror. Then they went downstairs.

The bar was by far the hollowest part of the hotel. The whole room was one huge mosaic. All the colors of the different villas were laid out in bits of tile on the wall from floor to ceiling, and the room was lit by torches on the wall and candles on the tables. Nearly every torch was a different color and every bar stool. Will followed Helen and wherever he looked he kept seeing Littlejohn's white face. The air was cool and the orange light from the flames wasn't bad if you didn't look at the waving colors. There was a man at one end of the room with a machine, playing records. His whole job was to play records. The bar was over half full of people. There was American pop-music playing. The Count was talking to the bartender; his two sons were sitting at a table. Helen paused halfway down the stairs, pretending she was looking for them. She wasn't, Will knew, she was posing.

The sons stood up before Helen got to the bottom, but she went on pretending she hadn't seen them. Then she looked at them and flashed a quick smile. From the way she started to walk to the table Will could tell she was annoyed. The Count was still at the bar with his back turned and Helen's entrance was wasted. Helen liked to make entrances. Will

watched the Count from behind. He did look like what Littlejohn had said he was—a skeleton with muscles. He was in a
solid black suit. The sons wore sports jackets and pants. The
table the sons were at had an awning with the hotel colors
in it and there was a parrot somewhere cawing loudly and
there was a fountain of water in the middle of the room lit
by two torches. The fountain had stones around it. Looking
at the fountain and the bird and the colored stones, all at
once Will wanted to cry.

Helen spoke to the sons and they kissed her hand and they
all sat down.

"I shall call my father," Juan Alberto said.

"Please don't disturb him."

It was like people talking in a play.

A waiter came up and Helen ordered a dry daiquiri and
ordered Will a Coke. The Count saw her and came over fast.
You could tell he was going to say he was sorry for not noticing her sooner.

"Black," Helen said before he could talk, "you *are* brave
in this weather. Is it an occasion?"

"That we are all here together," the Count said. He smiled.
He looked better than he had that morning—you could see
he had rested. He did have baby eyes, Will saw. Long and
pale now, like stones. "I am so much in the ocean. Perhaps
you do not recognize me with my clothes on," he said. He
didn't mean it sexy. Littlejohn was right. The way a child
would say it—like a character in a school play. The last act.
You don't recognize me with my clothes on. Death's entrance
line.

Helen showed an edge of her upper teeth and the Count sat
down beside her and they began to talk. Will stopped listening. The conversation was like the swirls of sand. He missed
Littlejohn so much it was like a band around his chest. He
tried not to think about her leaving the way she had, and he
listened to the music and finished the Coke and chewed some
of the ice too loud.

"William," Helen said. "You sound like a factory."

"Would he care for another Coca-Cola?" Juan Alberto
asked. Would *he* care.

They went on talking and now and then some people came
up to say hello to the Count. You could see wherever the
Count was sitting turned into the center of the room. He
didn't seem to know it. Or maybe he just took the attention
for granted. Like a baby.

"We were sorry your daughter couldn't come today," Juan
Alberto said in a stiff way to Helen.

"Yes," Helen said. ". . . Isn't that music a bit too loud?"

"Of course," the Count said. He turned around to the man who was running the big record machine; he raised one hand and lowered it, flat. The man turned the music down so fast you would have thought the machine had heard the Count.

"It's delightfully cool in here," Helen said.

Click, click, click, like a play.

"I do hope Alice will change her mind and come," the Count said.

"She said definitely not," Juan Alberto said.

"I am *sure* she will come," the Count said happily. "I am certain of it."

"She won't," Will said.

It was out before he could squelch it. The Count had sounded like a brat who knows everything and it irked him.

They all looked at him.

"If she said she wouldn't, she won't."

"Does she not ever change her mind?"

"I don't know," Will said.

"If you don't," Helen said, "you needn't offer an opinion."

"I'm interested in what you think," the Count said. Still like a little boy.

"I don't think anything," Will said.

The Count smiled wide. "I think she wanted to come and was only being stubborn. . . . She *will* change her mind and come," he said. "She is a fine person."

"She already left," Will said.

In the silence he could hear the ice in his mother's glass.

The Count shook his head. "No . . . I'm sure she hasn't left yet. . . ."

"She's on her way to New York," Will said. "Right now." He felt like he was arguing with a five-year-old.

"Please don't tell fibs, William," Helen said in a thin tone. "Her car was in the driveway when we crossed the lawn. . . ."

"She's going by train," Will said.

Helen looked at him.

"In that case, she has not gone yet," the Count said grinning like a baby, "the train doesn't leave till eleven at night." He still sounded like a happy infant.

"*Yes*, she's gone," Will said.

"William, drop the subject," Helen said. "We had one demonstration of bad manners last week. I don't intend to sit through another. If you can't behave yourself . . ." She watched him.

"I'll leave the table."

"No, please," the Count said. "I always seem to make everyone angry. . . . Please."

"He'll stay," Helen said, "if you'd like. . . . Only we won't have any more discussions." She said it to Will.

"I could telephone," the Count said. "I could reach her by calling the railroad station. Do you think another invitation . . . ?"

Will mashed his left cheek hard into his teeth with one finger and looked down. He had talked too much and he knew it. He had sold Littlejohn down the river whether or not anything came of it, just because the Count had made him mad. He could feel both pairs of eyes on him now—Helen's and the Count's.

"Or perhaps it's better not," the Count said slowly. "I mix in what is not my business. . . . I am something of an old woman. Perhaps I shouldn't call."

"Hey, Count," a drunken-sounding American woman from the bar said. He turned.

It was over, Will knew. But the Count had won. He had made up his own mind not to call. If he had decided to phone Littlejohn at the Cádiz station it would have been Will's fault. Will sat there feeling like a Judas.

"Hi, Count," another woman from the bar said. "You're a Spanish count." There were two women, blowzy-eyed and liquored up. Will thought he remembered the second voice from somewhere. He didn't know the face.

Count Guzmán turned around looking puzzled. "Excuse me," he said. ". . . I am with friends."

"Friends?" the second one said. She got off the barstool, a little wobbly, and came over to the table. She had a swollen face and fuzzed stringy hair like fur piled on top of her head. She wasn't very old.

Helen turned away and crossed her legs and looked at the other side of the room. "There must be something in the air," she said.

Juan Alberto signaled the bartender.

"You're a count," the woman said, "that's what I heard. You're the one they call the Red Count. . . ."

Then Will remembered her voice, it was the soft-throated one from inside the bar in Puerto de Santa María. The voice that had stayed in the dark. The way things were going today he could tell that she was going to recognize him, but the way things were going today he didn't care.

The Count stood up.

"How do you like being a count, Count? I'm Nell," the woman said thickly. "Little Nell Napkin with knickers."

"*Señora,*" the bartender said behind her.

"Bugger off," the woman named Little Nell said.

"*Por favor . . .*"

"Not going to make a big scene . . . I just came over to introduce myself to this count . . . how'd you do, Count?"

"How do you do, Nell?" the Count said.

The woman started away and then stopped. "Hey, kid . . . how's the dog?"

"Fine," Will said.

"Swell," the woman named Little Nell said. "You don't see him around that bar any more. I figured you had him."

"Yup."

"Great," she said. "Dog's not so dumb." She walked away.

"You are friends?" the Count asked, sitting down.

"I saw her once."

"William," Helen said, "William . . . what a summer."

"The *foreño* will go down soon," Juan Alberto said.

The woman who was with Little Nell was shouting now at the bartender.

"The summer will be very hot till next month."

They went on talking. . . .

Then he could feel it happening. It was like in Puerto de Santa María that second before the car hit the dog—only this time he knew.

He was looking at the tablecloth and there, clear as crystal in his mind, was the last picture in the mosaic of facts. He just plain knew.

"Would you like another daiquiri?" Juan Alberto asked.

Helen smiled.

"My father forgets to order," Juan Alberto said.

"Look . . . you *see?*" the Count said suddenly. He got up fast.

And Will knew.

The Count lifted his hand quick and high; the man on the record player thought it was meant for him. The needle screeched off the record.

You could see the Count was only waving at somebody, and if Will hadn't sensed it before, he would have known it now from the man's face. The Count looked like a baby watching a lollipop. His eyes weren't glowing anymore—they were just lit up like anybody's sky. They made Will sick and he turned his back to the Count and saw her.

She was standing at the top of the staircase and the whole bar was quiet. The woman called Nell stopped shouting at the bartender. A lot of people were looking at the staircase.

If they weren't, they were blind. Even Helen sucked her breath in once, short, to clear her throat.

But if Will hadn't known who it was, he might not have recognized her. She had a plain white dress on and white high-heeled shoes and when she started downstairs it was like a bird that had waited forever high on the wind, settling down slowly in the first long downdraft it could trust. The white dress had a long skirt. Her hair was soft back from her face and she was the most shining thing he ever saw in his life; she came down like that, like a cool white winter bird shining, and she didn't stop at the bottom of the stairs or speed up or slow down until she was standing face to face in front of the Count. Then Will saw her eyes and she didn't even look unhappy. She looked so happy you could have yelled. She had lipstick on and she looked like what Helen had tried to look like all her life. She wasn't a gypsy boy; she wasn't a boy. Go figure a woman.

"Hello," she said.

"Good evening," the Count said.

They stared at each other for a minute.

"Hello, Will," Littlejohn said, "I didn't make it."

TWO

Spaniards

THE TOWNS along the coast were dry and breathless by July and at night the hot wind still blew. Life in the summer appeared to have come to a standstill. The wind was more than three weeks old and it did not show any sign of stopping. Nights were dusty with heat, hard and stale as used air. The sky was thin and starless, curled at the edges as if some part of it had cracked and peeled. Following the coast in a jerky wavering line west from Suelo were Cádiz, Puerto de Santa María, Rota, where the American naval base was, and Sanlúcar de Barrameda which was topped by the broken-plaster palace of the Guzmáns. Farther west there was the province of Huelva, then Portugal and the Atlantic Ocean. At night to the towns the sea came in little folding waves, creasing and slapping and hissing, tilting at the land; but from the continent above there was no noise but the occasional screech of a night bird that floated on the wind, its black body rigid, just a bird sliding across the sky like a loose piece of darkness.

The fat man came to kill Pepe Luis Sanchez in the town of Sanlúcar de Barrameda at three o'clock in the morning when he was finishing a dry *anís* inside one of the open bars that lined the beach where the smaller fishing boats docked. Pepe Luis had been drinking in silence, listening to one of the screeching night birds that soared overhead. Dry *anís* is stronger than sweet *anís* and the thinking of Pepe Luis had become bright and luminous as though his brain were lit up by a thick white glow. There were four other fishermen talking at the table with him but he paid no attention. Outside of the sound of the bird his mind was busy caressing the shape of the bar he was in. It was not quite rectangular. The bar was one room and the walls were white plaster. They were lined with pictures of flamenco singers. Most of the singers were old or no longer living, and no new ones were being born—none who could sing *por siguiriyas* or *por tientos* or even produce a fairly decent *soleares*. Here and there you sometimes found a gypsy who could start something, but most of them today could not get beyond *bulerías*, the clownish song that shows a certain humor. The true *cante jondo*, the deep song, was dying out slowly along the coast as it was every place else; like the deep song of the black man in the southern states of North America, it was being replaced by watered-down yelling and verbalized outrage. Though Pepe Luis did not know of the great formal echo of the black man's voice from across an ocean he did know that *cante jondo* was ending; he loved it better than anything. He came every night to one of the cheap bars on the beach near the dock to hear it, but if you found a man who could give you even a few minutes of it once a month you were lucky. Tonight there had been none and Pepe Luis's mind was glowing around loosely in space. He had become aware of one corner where a couple of walls jutted in and met near the door with no visible purpose except to make the room smaller. There are two separate words for "corner" in Spanish where in other languages there is only one: *rincón* is an inside corner, like the corner of a room; *esquina* is outside like a street corner. This one that Pepe was looking at was an *esquina*, an outside corner. It was like having a street corner in the room. It was in his mind now to ask one of the other fishermen or maybe the bartender about it but the sharp glow of his thinking was too bright for speech. The *anís* had made a blinding halo and he could not get the words out. In the five years since he had come to Sanlúcar he had not often drunk this much. His own home was not here, but in Suelo. Pepe Luis had moved here to find work and he had got drunk tonight because it was his saint's day, the night of Santo Tomás, July the fourteenth—for although he never used his first name, Tomás, he still celebrated the day. He had bought drinks for everyone. Now it was time to go, and his mind ran in circles around the strange corner of the familiar bar that he had known since his first coming to the town five years before.

He had come to Sanlúcar for a reason: there were no more jobs in Suelo for a man of his profession, fishing. There were only jobs for people who would work in hotels. His mother, Eugenia, worked there in a hotel. Pepe Luis had tried it himself but he had not been fit for such work. Men are born in the breaking of water, they use the ocean salt in their veins, but only some men need to get something else from the sea; a fisherman is often such a man. So his father had told him. So Pepe Luis had looked along the coast until he found work in the town of Sanlúcar, which had not been invaded yet by foreign tourists as Suelo had, or occupied by a foreign navy like Rota.

He had taken a job on a shrimp boat that went out for two days at a time, trawling and dragging in the nets and then separating the shrimp from the other life: the fish that flipped sharp silver around the eels and the squid and the agonized octopus eyes, and little crabs with eyes on stilts and other things. It wasn't much of a job but it was on the water. You didn't have to clean up after tourists, or run to get out of the way of foreign sailors who made a graveyard of the land, who had never sailed on anything worth sailing on. He liked working in the salt air and the touch of the sea and it paid him enough to live most of the time. He was not much of a talking man, and he was never lonely. It was an all-right life except for the lack of a woman.

He had noticed quickly though he had not complained about it that he could not save any money. His salary and percentage of the catch were so small that even when the shrimp were running, he spent what he earned as he earned it. To support a wife you must have money; he had been engaged to a girl for three years. Her name was Lupe. Her hands were all separate. The fingers were long and white, they swooped and chattered in the air, and there was almost nothing that she could not say with her hands. On Sundays after morning Mass he and Lupe would walk in the country and sometimes toward evening she would put her hands on the sides of his neck. Then she would sit with him and if he pressed her she would let one of her hands lie in his lap. She would feel him there through his pants. Now and then she allowed him to put his hand inside, and the touch of her white hand brought him to a sudden violent climax when he kissed her. Lupe could do no more. In Spain a girl is either Good or she is Bad, and in the smaller towns of the South a girl is not even seen alone with a man unless they are engaged. It may last several years while the man saves money for a place to live and furniture, until he can afford a wife and children, but after three years when Lupe's parents saw that there had been no increase in his salary and that Pepe Luis had been able to save nothing, they forced her to break the engagement. For a month after that he did not see Lupe at all. He dreamed of her walking next to him. When he thought of her hands he nearly went crazy with it. After another week, a friend who worked on another boat told him about the blessings of the Communist Party and he listened. The friend's name was Jaime. Pepe Luis himself knew nothing about the Communist Party or about politics in any form and cared less, but Jaime explained that the Communist Party would take into account that Pepe Luis needed enough money to be married on and needed it fast. Four times he went to meetings with Jaime in small dark rooms at night where wine was drunk and six or eight men discussed the importance of Carlos Marx and other people with strange names and many plans were made though nothing was ever done about them. The meetings were illegal and even though they accomplished nothing they made everyone feel a little better. There was talk about organizing the grape pickers in the sherry wineries in Jerez, but strikes were illegal too and talk was just talk. Organizing anything was difficult. It had been difficult for centuries and it would always be difficult. Spain is not a country of members. It is a country of loners and each man prides himself on his individuality so that their only real bond is that pride. The different provinces don't agree with one another any more than the different villages within a province do, and within a single house the people don't agree. Andalucía is a place of loners who talk. They make bad revolutionaries and the Communist Party was a washout. Even Jaime who believed in it deeply could not organize the Party in Sanlúcar. He tried everything. He tried promises. He tried important people. Once he took Pepe Luis and three other prospective Party members to the poor-looking plaster palace at the top of the town to ask help from Count Guzmán who was known to have spoken out against the Franco regime, but that came to nothing too. Everything came to nothing. Guzmán listened and served them each a glass of brandy and then politely showed them the door. It was the worst disappointment of all, for Pepe Luis had liked the look of the man, muscular and gaunt, hard, with eyes that paled near the edges to a distant unbelieving blue. The Count's eyes made you trust him and it was the day that the Count sat in respectful silence and rejected the theories of the Communist Party that Pepe Luis had stopped believing in it himself. Still he had lingered, going to a few more meetings, hoping that Jaime was right and the Party would recognize the urgency of his need, the things he could not talk about, the white hands. He hoped it was true about the heads of the Party in Moscow knowing how to provide enough money for everyone and that they would send advisers to Sanlúcar soon. Two months more he waited. He looked for Lupe in church every Sunday but she never appeared. Once he heard that she was engaged to marry a man twice her age but he didn't believe it. The man was a police captain. Pepe Luis tried, but he could not stand to think of her hands and another man. It made him sick to think about it. The police captain was known for his cruelty, it was said that he liked to beat prisoners. He kept order in the town. He was rich, he owned his own house and drove his own car. Nearly everyone knew him by sight. While Pepe Luis was busy not thinking about it, the police captain married Lupe after knowing her only six weeks. The engagement was so short that there was some talk in the town, but the captain was a man to stay away from and the jokes soon died down.

Still Pepe Luis could not think about it; he allowed no picture of the marriage in his mind. He had never seen the two of them together. He had never seen the police captain and he hadn't seen Lupe since she left him. He went on working, hauling in the nets, and it was as if his head had filled with an early mist. He kept to himself when he wasn't working. He would go and sit on the gunwale of the boat and stare at the running sea. The other fishermen saw him. He would sit there and shake his neck hard from time to time, as if he had got a headful of spray. But his head was dry. He was waiting for his thinking to clear in the sun. The only other time his mind had felt this way was when he was much younger. It was when his brother and he, both, had become ill with a disease, and his brother had died from it. It had seemed impossible to Pepe Luis at the time that his brother had died and was not coming back ever, died, just died, was gone, and it was like a mist. For several years when he was young he kept expecting the sun to burn off the fact of his brother's death. Now he expected that it would burn away the marriage between Lupe and the rich police captain. He went on working and three times a week in the mornings he came back from his two-day trip with the other fishermen; they docked the boat and arranged the catch in wooden boxes on the long pier that was the town's fish market. The shrimp and the fish and shellfish were separated into big open boxes according to type and size, and each box was auctioned off to people who came from all over the province, from hotels and inland markets and restaurants. The work was done early to avoid the worst of the heat and the boxes were auctioned in the morning to keep the sun from spoiling the fish. Pepe Luis had always worked quickly; his hands were dark and rind-yellow, partly from tar and from having been jabbed by so many things. He thought that his hands were the ugliest he had ever seen and quite early one morning he was pouring shrimp from one box into another on the pier when he looked up from his two huge hands and saw the other ones. They were holding onto a shopping net of woven string and he could not stand to see them. He was squatting on his haunches; he tightened his flat belly. He held on hard to the box of shrimp and something flushed inside him so that it felt as if his heart had swelled up to the size of his chest. He could feel the blood surge and eddy in his neck. He did not look up beyond Lupe's hands. The mist was worse than ever; he went on pouring the shrimp and when the box was empty, he straightened. There was a crowd of women waiting for the auction to begin. She was among them. One of her hands had a bruise on it. He knew that she was looking at him but he could not look back. He didn't know what to do and he shoved his own hands in the pockets of his pants. When he raised his eyes and looked at her it was with such force that Lupe winced for a second and turned away. She pretended to lift a wisp of hair from her forehead. They were silent like that, standing and not speaking.

Women milled around them, some with children who were trained to pick up a clam or a shrimp that had fallen from one of the boxes; sometimes a child would pick up enough so that its mother could leave without buying anything. Then there were the rich women with maids. The maids didn't earn much more than room and board, and almost any girl would add a few pesetas to her pay now and then by padding the market bills, so the mistress of each house went shopping with her housemaid every day. Pepe Luis noticed with a sort of numbness now that there was a maid standing next to Lupe. Lupe was married to a man rich enough to afford a uniformed maid. You could see that she was not used to it yet or she would have given the maid the shopping net to carry. They were waiting for a giant box of fresh sardines to be auctioned off, so that they could bargain for a small portion of its contents from the buyer. You couldn't buy direct from the fishermen because it was not the custom. You didn't even take more than one or two fish free from a fisherman, unless you were his mother or his sister or his wife, or in some much less proper way belonged to him. Such rules had been set down over centuries, so that what Pepe Luis did now was unheard of and insulting, though he didn't mean it to be; it was just the only thing he could think of to do with his hands. He could not stand there any more with them hidden. It was if they were growing in his pockets. He took them out and squatted again slowly and made a cone out of a gray thick piece of paper and filled it with shrimp from the box. Then the feeling in his chest lifted and, as he walked past her, he tossed the cone full of shrimp into the half-empty bag of woven string dangling from Lupe's long white fingers.

It would have been up to her then to send the maid running after him either with a few pesetas or to return the shrimp; it would have been the only gesture she could have made to counter the open gesture of ownership. Lupe did not make it. Pepe Luis had met her eyes again in the instant after dropping the packet into the net under her hands; this time she didn't flinch away from his look. She stared back at him in a bold way and her eyes had an odd black glow to them almost as if they were sending him a message. He had never seen her eyes look that way before. Lupe was not a pretty girl, her skin had a sallow yellowish cast. Except for her legs and her long hands and a certain sexual hint in her eyes, no one would have looked at her twice. Pepe Luis took the secret message from her now without knowing what it meant, but Lupe knew that he had received it. The corners of her mouth twitched up quickly, and, for just the time it took him to catch his breath, Pepe Luis saw her face contort into a nasty smile. It was an ugly look and there was something in it that he didn't comprehend. Then it was gone and Lupe's face was serene and expressionless as it had always been. The whole thing had taken place in perhaps ten seconds, but Pepe Luis went past her and walked along to the boat, still with the mist in his head and half certain that a sort of signal had passed from Lupe to him, something that he could not name. When he came back to empty another box of shrimp, Lupe and her maid were gone from the pier.

He waited for her every day after that on the mornings when his boat docked but Lupe knew what days he would be there and she only came to the fish market on the other days, when he was at sea. She didn't come again while he was on land. The gesture of ownership that was insulting to a married woman had not been seen by anyone but Lupe, so there was no trouble. But the haze in his mind still had not cleared, and after a month Pepe Luis found himself late one night walking up a dirt and cobblestone hill in the town through the blunt smells of coffee and black tobacco and the soft endless tang of the sea. He stopped and asked for the house and was told where it was. He found it on the river side of the town, halfway up—a clean white house with a garden behind it of fruit trees. It was a two-story house and a light was on in one of the upstairs windows. He could not see Lupe anywhere. Pepe Luis stood opposite the window across the street in a doorway. He waited there

for an hour and a half. Then the light went off and he was
standing on a dark street with only the glow of the sky.
Some moonlight came through the trees next to the house
and lay in crazy pale green patches on the sidewalk. Pepe
Luis stood there all night until just before dawn when it was
time for him to go out on the boat. Then he walked back
down through the town to the beach in the heavy morning
mist.

After that he came nearly every night when he was on
land and stood in the doorway across the street, waiting.
He never saw anything and he didn't know what he was
waiting for. One night it rained and he stood back in the
doorway only partly protected by the low eaves and by the
time he had to leave for the docks his clothes were dripping
into his shoes; going down into the town he sounded as if he
were walking on wet sponges. He caught cold, but the cold
was slight and it didn't last long. He was back in his place
in the doorway two nights later when his boat docked again.
He never saw Lupe at the window or in any other part of
the house. He had no idea whether she knew he was waiting there or not. It was over a month of standing in the
dark doorway in front of the darkened house before he saw
the fat man for the first time.

It was after the *foreño* had started that he first saw him,
on a night in June. Pepe Luis had been in the doorway
for about an hour. By now the new habit had become a
ritual: he went first to a cheap port bar near the docks
and had some wine and then a wedge of potato omelet
and some slices of cold marinated fish roe that were the
specialty of that bar. He spoke a few words to his friends
among the other customers. He ate a roll with the roe and
mopped at the leftover marinade with the last of the crust.
Then he had some black coffee and a couple of cheap
brandies at a café on his way up through the town. By
the time he got to the house it was usually around two
in the morning and the street was dark. On this particular
night it was both dark and soundless; everything in the
whole town seemed to have gone to bed and was sleeping.
The light was out in the upstairs window of the house and
Pepe Luis looked to see if the usual stars were there but
there was nothing. It was cloudy. He was left alone. He
could feel the wind. The thin peeling at the edges of the
horizon had finally reached the top of the sky and there
was only a black hole left directly over his head, as if the
world had yawned at him. There was no noise at all and
when the footsteps started, they were so separate and exact

in the blackness that standing in the vacuum of silence for a moment he thought they were hooves. They began very small and they echoed in the street and clopped on in his head; they were like the hooves of an animal with only two feet. Then he heard the tiny ringing of the chain. He stood still in the doorway and tried to pierce the darkness with his eyes but for what seemed too long to live he could see nothing. The beating of his heart increased in tempo, growing louder in a queer way as if it were adjusting to the bodiless footsteps. Then the wind stopped and standing stock-still, all at once the mist in his mind cleared and Pepe Luis felt out of breath—without air—in the night. He had never before felt panic and for a few seconds he did not know what the feeling was. When he did, he still didn't know why he felt it. There's a moment in every man's life when it seems as if all the past of the human race congeals and squeezes together into one sense, a single smell or a single sight or sound, even a taste or touch, and this was the moment for Pepe Luis. He didn't recognize it for what it was; he only stood quietly, waiting, knowing that whatever it was that was coming to join him at this place, at this time, was the thing that he had been standing here waiting for. Along with the panic there was a sense of relief, because he had been waiting a long time. When the footsteps stopped, he held his breath.

Just then his heart hit the insides of his ribs so hard he thought the earth had cracked and moved under his feet, and he saw the fat man. The man had stopped to light a cigarette; in the flare of the match Pepe Luis made out his face. The short flame rose around it from below. It was a face he was to see again, and though he had never seen it in his life up to now, it was instantly familiar, like some things seen in dreams. It was happy looking, round and shiny, with a loop of flesh hung under it as if the face had melted from the effort of climbing the hill. The eyes were little and partly hidden over the thick red cheeks and the face did not look like it had a bone in it. Then the match went out and the footsteps started again and the tinkling of the chain. In the dark the fat man was breathing heavily from his climb; you could tell that he had had too much to eat and was uncomfortable. Pepe Luis could make out the shape of him now. He was swaying slightly but he stepped with incredible delicacy for a heavy man, a decorous grace, as though he did not want to damage the sidewalk. It was the step of a fat man who is wearing new shoes. He halted again at the house across the street. Then he fumbled with the keys at the end of the tinkling chain. The dark olive green cloth of the uniform with the black belt was stretched taut around the man's big belly. He let himself into the house and was going to close the door behind him when Pepe Luis crossed the street and spoke his name:

"Capitán Herrera."

The fat man frowned and squinted at Pepe Luis through the darkness. "Yes? Do I know you?"

"No," Pepe Luis said, "I have to speak to you."

". . . At these hours?"

"Yes," Pepe Luis said. "It's important. She sent me."

"She?" The fat man moved a hand in front of his face as if he wanted to wipe the night out of the air between them.

"She sent me," Pepe Luis said again. He spoke simply and with a sort of quiet accuracy; he wasn't used to talking much and he wanted the other man to understand him.

"She who? Who is she? . . . Do you know who I am?"

"Yes," Pepe Luis said.

The fat man moved the cigarette butt over to the corner of his mouth with his tongue. His hard little eyes stared straight ahead. He didn't speak for a minute. Then he said, "Are you drunk?"

"No."

"She sent you? Who?"

"Her. Lupe."

". . . You must be drunk," the fat man said. "You know what time it is?"

"I had two brandies. I have two brandies every night. I'm not even feeling good," Pepe Luis said. "I'm not drunk."

"Who are you waiting for here?"

"Not here. I was waiting across the street. Only I didn't know it—I was waiting for you."

"For . . ."

"You," Pepe Luis said. "I was waiting for you."

The fat man turned slowly and glanced at the staircase in the house behind him. Then he looked back at Pepe Luis. "My wife is upstairs," he said carefully.

"I think so. It's over two months that I haven't seen her."

"Two months? She sent you two . . ."

"Yes," Pepe Luis said. "Only I didn't understand it. Not till just now."

"Understand what?"

"That she was asking me to speak to you. That she was sending . . ."

"But when?"

"When I gave her the shrimp," Pepe Luis said.

"The *what?*"

"First I gave them to her. The packet of shrimp. Then she sent me. I don't say it well, but you'll understand me. You're a man of much knowing. I'm not very good at talking," Pepe Luis said.

The fat man took the cigarette butt out of his lips and flicked it away delicately with two fingers. It made a short arc of fire in the air and there was a puff of sparks as it hit the cobblestones. He started to close the door. "I don't understand anything. Come see me at the office tomorrow. *La Jefatura de . . .*"

"No," Pepe Luis said. "Now."

"Oiga," the fat man said: "Listen." He threw the door back hard and stepped out. Then he thought better of it and held the door again. "I've put people in jail for molesting and drunkenness . . ."

"Ya lo sé," Pepe Luis said. "You beat some of them with a piece of pipe. Everybody knows."

The fat man stared at him again and in the night Pepe Luis could make out the rims of the tiny eyes. They were red and the eyes were like pebbles set in the flesh. "Let me understand," he said slowly. "My wife spoke to you and . . ."

"No," Pepe Luis said.

"You just said . . ."

"She didn't speak to me. She sent me."

"How could she send you without speaking?"

Pepe Luis tried to answer. His lips moved but nothing came out.

"The maid? It was the maid who spoke to you?"

"No," Pepe Luis said. "Nobody spoke to me."

"Then how? . . . How did my wife send you to me?"

Pepe Luis wrinkled his forehead in an agonized way and looked at the darkness next to the police captain. "I don't know," he said.

"You're crazy," the fat man said. "It's three o'clock in the morning. My wife's asleep in her bed. Two months ago you say she gave you a message for me. You don't know how she gave it. You wait two months and then you come to me at three in the morning. Do you even know what the message was?"

"No," Pepe Luis said. "I think . . ."

"You *think?*"

"There was something about her hand. A bruise. I saw a bruise on her hand. Or something about . . ."

"*Hombre,* what's on my wife's hand is my business. No?"
Pepe Luis waited a moment more. "No," he said.

"*Cómo?*"

"No. You see . . . No."

Captain Herrera watched him through the darkness.

"She belonged to me before. It was other things that stopped. She doesn't know it herself. It was the money . . . I have no money. The wedding was for money," Pepe Luis said hurriedly. "You see, Captain, it isn't about talking. You have all the right on your side. But it isn't about right. It isn't about anything. You have the church, you even have the law. But it's strange. She belongs to me."

The fat man chuckled once. He sniffed and spat precisely into the darkness by Pepe Luis's left foot. "You're a half-wit," he said. "You think Lupe would send you to say that?"

"No. She doesn't even know it. She sent me to say . . ."

The captain waited.

"Wait. She thinks . . . wait . . she isn't for sale," Pepe Luis said. "Or wait. No. That she may be for sale . . . that she may be. That your price was too low. *Allí está.* A house, a car. A maid. It wasn't enough. A kilo of shrimp was worth more. . . . She sent me to say it. That's it. That's all. . . . That your price was too low." He finished and stood quiet, panting a little and sweating from the strain of forming the words.

The fat police captain was silent a minute or two. Then he reached in his pocket and took out another match. He lit it and held it up between them. The two faces looked at each other across the match. Pepe Luis saw it burst into two flares reflected in the fat man's minuscule eyes. The captain looked down at his clothes.

"A fisherman?"

"Yes," Pepe Luis said.

The fat man studied him. "I understand why you preferred to come at night. It won't help you. I'll remember your face."

"Just in case you don't," Pepe Luis said, "I'm at the docks Tuesdays and Thursdays and Sundays. Pepe Luis Sanchez, to serve you."

"*Ya lo veo. Ya* . . . A complete idiot," the captain said to himself on the other side of the match.

"Just since I was sick. I was sick when I was small. . . . My brother died from it. . . . I don't like to talk much since then," Pepe Luis said. "The disease affected me in some ways. It's why I limp a little."

The fat man said nothing. In the shrunken flame he swore

and dropped the match. It had burned his hand. The darkness took over and the captain swore again and rubbed his thumb and forefinger against the leg of his uniform. "I'll be seeing you again," he said. "And as far as my wife . . . but there's no problem. She'll be kept in for a few weeks and . . ."

"No," Pepe Luis said. "I forgot. I wouldn't allow that."

In the airless night there was a silence and then the captain said the word, "Allow." He began to laugh in the darkness as though he had just said something very humorous. Then the laugh stopped. The black shape in front of Pepe Luis faded away from him and after a moment he heard the door snap shut in his face. The street was empty again except for him.

A few seconds later Pepe Luis stepped forward out of the deep shadows; he turned and stood watching the locked door. Somewhere inside the house a switch had gone on—there was a glow like an echo of light in the upstairs bedroom. On the street it was as if he could see the fat police captain mounting the stairs to Lupe's bed. Then the wind began again. In the silence Pepe Luis felt it, gusty at first, then steady and thick against his shoulders. He waited until the light had gone out before walking away from the house. It took a long time and he kept his eyes on the window. Standing on the cobblestones he shivered suddenly in the hot wind.

Exactly when it was that the fat man began to have him followed he was never sure, but it was not more than a few days after that: the crazy African heat wave was still blowing in the town. Instead of sending for him the next morning from the police station as Pepe Luis more or less expected him to do, the captain did nothing. The morning was fevered and slow. Apparently the captain didn't want to continue their conversation. It was a fishing day and Pepe Luis went out on the boat. He came back two mornings later, but there were no police waiting for him on the pier. He separated and boxed the fish as usual and then went to the single room he rented in a house in town; he washed, then slept for a time. When he woke he threw cold water on his face and went down to the cheap bar he liked best for a glass of beer. Two of his friends were there and he sat and listened to them. In Andalucía a man who does not talk is a listening man, and there had been no one that Pepe Luis could share things with since his friend Jaime had left. Jaime had given up trying to organize the Communist Party in Sanlúcar and had gone to Madrid where things get done a bit late but at least they sometimes get done. There was no one else Pepe Luis had ever talked to in the town, not about anything private; though he had several friends who came to the bar every afternoon, his position was established as a listener among them. He sat while they played dominoes and spoke about many subjects—who had died recently or the world situation. They couldn't discuss Spanish politics because it was against the law; but they could talk about other countries and they did so with great sweeping gestures and grandiose statements, though few of them had been outside of Andalucía and none had been outside of Spain. The bartender would occasionally throw in a phrase, agreeing or disagreeing, just stoking the conversation until it became heated and they ordered more wine. Only if a policeman came into the bar for a drink did the conversation cease or diminish; otherwise it went on all afternoon and late into the night. You could leave and come back two hours later and there would be the conversation. After a while Pepe Luis tired of it and went for a walk along the docks. He would have liked to walk along the beach but the sand was blowing. He kept to the wooden piers and the streets near the sea. He was walking the wine off. The shacks and warehouses closest to the docks were empty and gray in the evening. He found a dirt road that led down to the water. The sand came at him like needles and he turned and started back. The wind was thick on the street. A wiry small man in blue overalls with a face like a rat or a weasel was standing halfway up, paring his nails with a fishing knife; he asked for a match and Pepe Luis gave him one. The stranger offered a cigarette in return and Pepe Luis took it; he didn't feel like smoking but it would have been rude not to accept, and he put it behind one ear. Then he went back to the bar in a roundabout way and sat at the same table; he listened to the conversation some more. In the back of his mind he still half-expected that the police captain would send a message to him, but none came. At the bar after a while he saw the man in blue overalls who had asked him for a match. He was not one of the group of regular customers and he stood drinking a glass of wine alone. When Pepe Luis felt sorry for him and asked him to sit with them, the man came, but he seemed to have nothing to say and he didn't join in the conversation. He sat silently, exactly the way Pepe Luis did. The man was a listener too.

After that, Pepe Luis saw the rat-faced man in blue overalls almost wherever he went; he didn't give it any particular attention. The town was full of loners. Once when he came back from a fishing trip the man was sitting on one of the pilings of the pier. Pepe Luis waved and joined him. It wasn't until the night of Santo Tomás, his official saint's day, that Pepe Luis began to notice anything odd about the man, and even then he wasn't sure just what it was. Pepe Luis had bought one drink apiece for everybody because it was his name day, and everybody had congratulated him. Then he switched to drinking dry *anís* and the hard white glow began in his mind, and he knew what it was that had been bothering him. The man in blue overalls was not drinking. The first glass, the one that Pepe Luis had stood him, was still on the table; only a sip of the brandy was gone from the top. There was another full glass next to it from a round of drinks someone else had paid for. From time to time the man in blue overalls raised the first glass and wet his lips with it, but he only pretended to drink. He sat, sober, with a sneaky stiff look that gave him an air of a school-teacher, gazing at the rim of his glass as motionless as though something inside him were gathering to spring.

Pepe Luis reached over and pushed the glass two or three millimeters closer. The man nodded and raised the glass again and took a small sip. Pepe Luis shook his head. *"Así, no."* He took the man's glass and lifting it flung what was left down his own throat in one swallow. *"Así,"* he said. He pushed the man's second glass closer.

The man in blue overalls smiled at him and Pepe Luis smiled back and then turned away to scratch his ear. He did not see the smile drop from the man's face like something that had been pasted on and come loose. While Pepe Luis was busy scratching his ear, the white glow from the *anís* in his stomach lit up even brighter, and he saw the corner of the bar that was sticking awkwardly into the room and focused on it. He was at that stage when you can't concentrate on more than one thing at a time and each thing is fascinating. The awkward corner challenged him and he accepted the challenge; he could feel all his mind pull back slowly like a giant wave that would cover it with his thinking. The big corner didn't have a chance with him, he decided. Give him time and he would think it right out of the bar. There was nothing that his mind could not do, he thought. It was then that he heard the singing of the *siguiriyas.*

It began after the guitar so that at first he had paid no attention. It was in the bar next door and it was just a guitar. But the singing was something else—it was the real thing, and you could tell it on the first note. As in the hands of a great poet you know from the first line where you are, or the first step of a great dancer or of a great anything, there's no mistaking the opening cry of a great singer of *cante jondo,* and Pepe Luis felt the hair crawl on the back of his neck before he even knew what he was listening to. The white glow inside his mind went cold; then it went white hot like molten steel. The circle of this thinking grew smaller until it was only like the tip of an icicle, a pinpoint of fire. He hardly breathed. You didn't want to breathe. The man singing *por siguiriyas* in the bar next door *knew*. There are not many left, but he was one of them and that was what you heard in the birth-cry of the song. It was an old man, Pepe Luis could tell from the voice. Then he stopped noticing anything but the voice itself. The grace of it. Just that. The *siguiriyas* and the varied incredible grace of it. The raw guttural sound and the outrage in grace: the scream. The rasping harshness, but the grace of it. The true deep song—the sound of agony, of the death of a country. The voice of a people singing under the whip but the grace of it. The always grace of it. The voice rose, twisted, rose again, slid high, caught in space; held, then opened, and broke; and then broke open.

The *siguiriyas* flowed through the little bar by the sea and shattered the air. It was a love song. The words to the Virgin, obscene and marvelous. The voice caught in ritual rhythm, straining. The straining as in sex—you listened and it was like sex. Then it was like dying. Pepe Luis heard it all. The deep thing in it, the insultingly physical compliments to the Virgin. The not-quite release. The song holding back. The denial that is always in possession. Then something lost and loved and killed and forgotten and wild until there's not much left but yearning. And the denial of that, of even the yearning—the final self-denial—until that too is gone and there's another kind of emptiness that is only hunger; and another, the least important of all because it's only death. And then the death of death: the pulse of song. But all of it in the end of it, in the one last throb of it, transcending all the final sex-cry cut short in triumph: transfiguration. Pepe Luis rose from his chair.

He stood rocking back and forth on his feet for a moment. There was nothing to say to show what had happened in his heart because of the song. He didn't know the words to say it and anyway even if he did the words wouldn't matter. He managed to get out one *"Olé."* It came out in a whisper as sharp as the white pinpoint of fire from

the *anís* in his brain. Then he sat back hard into the chair
as the singing began again. It was light song this time, accompanied by clapping and shouts—*bulerías*, the comedy of
ritual, a kind of pain in it too, but just the pain of humor.
The *bulerías* rang out over the water and echoed in the
dock like a bawdy laugh. In the cheap bar with the smell
of *manzanilla* wine and the sea, Pepe Luis began to clap
along with the song. He sat staring at the floor and the
laughter stabbed at his heart. The *bulerías* finished and
started again and he went on clapping. He had clapped for
a long time staring at the floor before the song ended and
he heard the two footsteps, and moved his eyes a fraction
and saw the new shoes, and knew that the fat man was
standing in front of him.

For a few seconds he didn't believe it. He couldn't understand why he had not heard the captain's footsteps coming down the street to the bar. Then he knew that he hadn't
heard them because of the *bulerías*. The double clop of the
shoes that sounded like hooves had been drowned out in
the song. It was as if the captain had walked right out of
the singing. It had stopped and there was silence along the
dock now; Pepe Luis kept his eyes on the fat man's shoes.
They were still new, only a few weeks old at most, the heels
were still squared. They had been shined recently and there
was a new layer of dust over the gleaming black polish.
Then Pepe Luis thought of something. When he raised his
eyes, it was to look not at the captain but at the rat-faced
man in blue overalls who was still sitting at the table. The
man was no longer staring at his glass; he was staring up at
the captain, and he nodded, once; it was a curt nod that
was not seen by anybody else in the bar, but the little man
had a funny look, as though the thing that had been gathering inside him to spring had shot suddenly out of his eyes.
"Get up," the fat man said.

Pepe Luis moved his weight forward and tried to settle
it onto his feet. He made a motion to stand, but the *anís* was
sliding down into his legs. His ankles felt like liquid and they
wouldn't support him. He swayed back into the chair and
looked apologetically at the captain. There were two other
policemen in dark olive green uniforms standing behind the
captain. Pepe Luis watched them. The three faces stared
back at him like fish heads lined up for sale. *"Lo siento,
Capitán,"* Pepe Luis said, excusing the behavior of his body.
His own voice sounded foolish in his ears.

The captain stepped back. *"Mejor que le despiertes,"* he
said to one of the men: "Better wake him up." The younger

of the two policemen put his hand out and lifted Pepe Luis off the ground. The policeman held him by the shirt and slapped him with the back of his other hand across the face. Pepe Luis didn't feel the slap; then he couldn't get his feet on the floor. When he put his arm for balance against the policeman's chest, the second policeman took a green bottle of *manzanilla* and broke it in half on the bar and swung out with half the bottle. The jagged glass looked big and then it was gone. Pepe Luis heard something crack in his mouth. Then he felt silly. He was looking at one of the captain's new shoes from very close. The shoe was only about a millimeter from his face. He couldn't think how it had got there and he pushed away from it. There was a mountain in his mouth and his tongue wasn't working; he couldn't feel anything and he rolled over on his side and tried to spit out the thing that was in his mouth. It was choking him and he coughed; a red piece of something fell on the floor under his face. It looked like a starfish. He didn't like the look of it. He coughed again and another starfish fell out of his mouth and one of the policemen lifted him up again by the back of his shirt. "He's trying to get away," the policeman said. The fat man said: "Not in the face . . . he'll need his face to testify." "He'll testify," the young policeman said; "I want to show you how he'll testify." "Not in the face," the fat man said. "It takes too long." "If you don't want it to take long," the young policeman said, "it won't take long." "That's when he's in jail," the fat man said. "What's he doing now?" "He's trying to get away again," the policeman said. "All right," the fat man said. "Jesus. He won't be able to talk. Can't you understand? Not in the face. Look at it." "I don't like to look at it, Captain," the policeman said.

They were outside somewhere and Pepe Luis could hear the lap of the sea. There was a policeman on either side of him and his feet were dragging on the ground. The fat captain moved ahead of them. They came to a stop.

"He'll have to get in," the fat man said. "Show him." "He doesn't want to, Captain," the young policeman said. "Listen," the fat man said, "I don't like what you did to his face . . . I'm going to be very angry in a minute." "You know how it is," the policeman said, "he's still resisting." "I don't care what he's doing," the fat man said; "oh God. Can't you handle him?" "I didn't know he was going to do that," the policeman said. "You don't know anything," the fat man said, "you don't think of anything. He got it all over me." "We got a rag in the car," the policeman said,

"I'll get it, Captain." "Never mind no rag," the fat man said, "watch him. He's choking." "I don't think he can swallow," the young policeman said, "I think that's why he's choking." "That's for later," the fat man said, "can't you do anything right? I need the testimony. Can't you understand that I need it for the record? What's he doing now?" "He's cutting up something awful," the policeman said. "What's that sound?" the fat man said. "I not sure," the policeman said. "I don't like it," the fat man said. "I don't like it either, Captain. It sounds like he swallowed his tongue," the young policeman said, "I bet you that's what he did. I bet you anything that's what he did, Captain."

They were driving in the car and the sea was in his stomach. Then it happened again. It came out of his stomach and then suddenly there wasn't any place for it to go. He put a hand up but he couldn't hold it in his mouth.

"He's all right," the policeman said, "he's at it again."

"Did he do it?"

"He tried to," the policeman said. "He couldn't get it out."

"What's he doing now?" the fat man said.

"I think he's trying to find his mouth," the policeman said.

The fat man giggled.

"He must be drunk," he said.

After a while he woke up. He didn't believe the way it felt and he tried to think he was still asleep. Then he tried to scream at the man who was standing over him. The man leapt back and Pepe Luis could see the ceiling. There were two other men. The one who had been standing over him came back; he was holding a wire in his hands. "I knew it," he said.

"How did he get that way?" one of the others said.

"He started a fight in a bar."

"I never saw a thing like that."

"It was a bottle."

"I never saw no fight made a man look like that."

"You better hope you never do," the first man said. "You'd be surprised what a bottle can cut. I knew he'd wake up. You better keep holding him."

"We got him," the second man said. "He's not going nowhere. Look at that, will you? Look at that."

"I'm trying to finish," the man over him said. "It's just this one place that's left. *Me cago en la leche.* I knew he'd wake up. *Me cago en la puta leche.*"

"I sure don't see how it got on his chest, Doctor," the other said. "He ain't moving now."

"He's waiting to see. He's still awake," the doctor said. "He ripped the wire clear out of his jaw just now. I had to thread it again, it's all right now."

"Look at that," the other said. "What about that? Is that his tongue?"

"Never mind looking," the doctor said. "Just hold him. Here we go."

"We got him," the other man said.

"You better make sure," the doctor said. "I nearly got his handcuffs right in my chest before."

"Don't you worry, Doctor," the other one said.

"I'm not worried," the doctor said.

"Please don't you worry," the third one said.

"I'm not worried," the doctor said. "Just hold him. He's going to yell."

When he woke again the ceiling was gray and wet. They were getting ready to feed him. When he took food in his mouth, his stomach rebelled. It went that way for a few days. All he could swallow was water. Then they withheld the water until he swallowed some of the food. He still didn't want it, but the vomiting was worse than the swallowing, and he practiced keeping it down. It seemed to him a lot of time had passed and other times each second was as big as his tongue. He knew that he had soiled himself several times but there wasn't enough water to wash with even when he could stand up alone.

The day they took him out of the cell he could almost walk by himself; they gave him a pan of water first so that he could wash some of it off. Then they took him down the corridor. There was a door at the other end and he went through it and sat in a chair. The light was gray; he was facing a desk and a window. The doctor was on one side of the room smoking. The two men who had brought Pepe Luis in stood on either side of him. The doctor was silent and the fat man was sitting behind the big desk doing something with a piece of paper. He was writing on it. His face looked jolly in the light. Pepe Luis coughed. Another man came into the room and sat down with a pad of paper and a pen. "When you're ready, Captain," he said.

"How long have you been a member of the Communist Party?" the fat man said.

"He doesn't understand."

"He smells," the fat man said without looking up. "Jesus but he stinks. Couldn't you wash him?"

"We gave him some water, Captain," one of the men said.

"He probably never washed in his life," the fat man said. "Can he talk?"

"He can talk," the doctor said, "it wasn't as bad as it looked. It was just that the jaw was hanging loose from one side. Painful, though. It always takes them a while to get used to their tongue again."

"I asked you if he can talk," the fat man said. "I didn't ask for a diagnosis."

"He can talk," the doctor said.

The fat man folded the paper he had been writing on and put it in a drawer in his desk. His round face tilted slightly like the head of a bird at Pepe Luis and he looked away. "I see what you mean," he said to the doctor. He put one foot up on his desk and crossed it delicately with the other one. The shoes no longer looked new. The heels were slightly worn down, rounded from the weight of his walking. "How long you been a member of the Communist Party?" he said.

"He still doesn't catch you, Captain."

"Get Rafael in here," the fat man said. "Do I have to think of everything?"

The doctor snapped his fingers, and one of the men standing next to Pepe Luis went outside. He came back with the rat-faced man who had worn blue overalls in the bar with Pepe Luis. The man, whose name was Rafael, was dressed in a suit and tie now. He sat down. He looked at the table leg and avoided Pepe Luis with his eyes.

The fat man sighed. "I wouldn't bother if Guzmán wasn't in it," he said. "I'd have let this one die."

"The Count?" the doctor said. "He's in it?"

"He's in it up to here," the fat man said.

"How'd you find out?"

"Rafael," the fat man said, "he dug it up talking to people. They had a meeting up at Guzmán's place. This one was there. That's what we need on the record."

"How did you know this one was a member in the first place?"

"I smelled it," the fat man said. "I got a nose for it. I needed something on him and it turned up."

"Why did you need something on a fisherman, Captain?"

"He insulted me," the fat man said.

"How come you want Guzmán?"

"I don't. They been after me for a year from Madrid

for something on Guzmán," the fat man said. "That's why. We started looking into it, turned out Pepe Luis was one of them, then it turned out they met once up at Guzmán's place. So Guzmán's in it too. Guzmán probably gave this one his orders. He . . ."

Pepe Luis opened his mouth and made a bad sound with it.

The fat man looked at him.

"No," Pepe Luis said.

"Cómo? . . . What did he say?"

"I think he said no," the doctor said.

"He sure doesn't talk so good. Couldn't you have fixed him up to talk any better than that?"

"He can," the doctor said. "He just hasn't tried."

"How come?"

"I don't really know," the doctor said, "but he can."

The fat man uncrossed his legs and lifted them one by one with precision down onto the floor. He looked like a boneless toy bear and there was a flat twinkle in his eyes. "I think you better explain to him," he said, "that he has to talk clearly now . . . maybe you better explain that to him."

"He understands that," the doctor said.

There was a silence.

"See? I don't like the way he's acting," the fat man said.

Pepe Luis looked at the fat man. The fat man stared back at him evenly. *"Mejor que le despiertes:* Better wake him up," the fat man said.

Pepe Luis made another sound in his mouth.

"I tell you," the doctor said, "he understands just about every word you say. He just isn't very bright."

The fat man sighed. He said to Pepe Luis, "How long have you been a member . . ."

"Excuse me, Captain." The man with the pen sat up straight. "Pardon me, but you ought to begin with the form. If you want it for the record."

"The form?" the fat man said.

"The family."

"The what?"

"The antecedents."

"Do I have to?"

"It's the form." The man with the pen smiled.

"Oh Jesus," the fat man said. "The form."

"First you ask . . ."

"I know how to do it," the fat man said. "Don't I? Who hired you?"

"Yes, Captain," the man with the pen said.

The fat man lifted his legs back up on the desk and re-crossed them and then crossed his hands in his lap. "Father's name. What's your father's name?" he said to Pepe Luis.

"Ah . . . Captain," the man with the pen said. "You'll have to say *usted* to him. You have to use the formal you. You can't say *tú* to him like that. It won't look right on the record."

The fat man stared at the man with the pen.

"I'm sorry, Captain," the man with the pen said.

"Listen," the fat man said softly, "I am going to ask thee a question. Thou must answer truthfully. Dost thou wish to be fucked up the ass in the town square?"

"No, Captain," the man with the pen said.

"I am going to ask thee another question. The army has no women. The sex life in the army is very poor. They will give it to anything. They would give it to a sheep. Dost thou wish to be fucked up the ass by the entire army?"

"No, Captain."

"Then," the fat man said carefully, "let's make a bargain. When I say the word thou, thou must do me a favor. Every time I say the word thou, thou must write down the word you. Understand?"

"Yes, Captain."

"Let's practice. I say Jorge, thou wilt be fucked up the ass. Now what dost thou write?"

"You," the man with the pen said. "I write you."

"The whole sentence."

"Jorge, you will be fucked up the ass," the man with the pen said.

The doctor laughed.

"I think thou hast got it now," the fat man said. "Hastn't thou?"

"Yes, Captain."

"May we proceed?"

"Yes, Captain."

"I thank thee," the Captain said. He settled back in his chair. The light from the window behind him was getting brighter. "Father's name," he said.

Pepe Luis blinked at him.

The Captain sighed. "Everybody in this room," he said, "is trying to annoy me. Maybe you better wake him up," he said to the doctor. The doctor stood up.

Pepe Luis made another sound.

"I'm tired of those noises," the fat man said. "I don't

think he's trying to be cooperative. Maybe you better show him."

"Should I show him like a doctor," the doctor said, "or shall I show him like a policeman?"

"Which is which?" the fat man said.

"Well," the doctor said, "a doctor would hit him in the kidneys. An ordinary policeman wouldn't know where the kidneys were."

"I see what you mean," the fat man said. "Where would an ordinary policeman hit him?"

"Anywhere," the doctor said. "In the face."

Pepe Luis opened his mouth and made a loud noise and then shaped it into a word.

"Wait," the fat man said, "you can sit down for a minute. I think he understands better now. That sounded like 'Enrique.' Was that what you said?"

Pepe Luis nodded.

"Cómo?"

"Yes," Pepe Luis said.

"Your father's name is Enrique?"

"Yes," Pepe Luis said.

"Enrique what?"

"Ver-gara."

"Enrique Vergara what?"

"Sanchez," Pepe Luis said.

"His father's name," the fat man said to the one with the pen, "is Enrique Vergara Sanchez. Dost thou have that?"

"Yes, Captain."

"Fine," the fat man said. "Fine. Father's profession?"

Pepe Luis moaned.

"He's crying for God's sake," the doctor said disgustedly. "They're all sissies. All fishermen."

"I thought you said . . ."

"I didn't say it doesn't hurt him a little to talk," the doctor said. "Did I?"

"I don't understand why he isn't trying harder. It's going to hurt him worse if he doesn't."

"Maybe he likes pain," the doctor said. "They got them like that."

"They got all kinds," the fat man said. "I'm going to give him one more chance. Father's profession?"

"Fish-erman," Pepe Luis said.

"See?" the doctor said. "His father's a fisherman too. They're all sissies and queers. I bet you his father's a queer, Captain."

"How could his father be a queer?" the fat man said. "I

understand how *he* could be. But how could his father be
a queer, if his father gave it to his mother?"

"Maybe he just *thinks* it's his father," the doctor said.

The fat man giggled.

The doctor looked pleased. "Do you mind if I smoke?"

"Go right ahead."

"Usted?"

"No thank you," the fat man said.

The doctor lit a match and put it to his pipe.

"Father alive or dead?" the fat man said.

"Alive," Pepe Luis said.

"Father's place of residence?"

"Suelo."

"Place of work?"

"No."

"What?"

"There is none," Pepe Luis said. "For him . . ."

"I told you," the doctor said.

"Quiet," the fat man said to the doctor; "don't make me
laugh. If I laugh it could take all day."

"Sorry, Captain," the doctor said.

"Mother's name?" the fat man said.

Pepe Luis tried it. There was a *g* in it and everything
in his stomach almost came up.

"What's he doing now?"

"Gagging," the doctor said.

"Doesn't it hurt him to gag?"

"Yes," the doctor said. "I told you. He isn't very bright."

"I bet you I was right," the fat man said. "I bet you he's
the one that's a fairy."

"If he is," the doctor said, "he isn't going to be able to
take it in the mouth any more. He's going to have to take
it up the ass like your new secretary."

"Por favor," the man with the pen said stiffly to the
doctor, *"oiga, por favor* . . . I haven't offended you, no?
You have no reason to offend me. . . ."

"Sorry," the doctor said.

The fat man took a handkerchief out of his pocket and
wiped his eyes. What the doctor had said had tickled him,
and when he laughed too hard he cried. "What did I tell
you?" he said to the doctor. "About not making me laugh?"

"Sorry, Captain," the doctor said. He winked.

"You just stop that," the fat man said, laughing.

"Ye*sss*, Captain. Sorry, Captain."

"Stop that right now."

"Yes, *sss*ir, Captain. Yes, *sss*ir," the doctor said.

The fat man was crying. The doctor saluted the fat man.

"You're awful," the fat man said. "You're just awful."

The doctor put his saluting arm down and the fat man dried his eyes and blew his nose. The man with the pen looked very angry. The other man, the one called Rafael, hadn't taken his eyes off the table leg.

"Where were we?" the fat man said.

"Mother's name," the man with the pen said through his teeth.

"Mother's name," the fat man said.

Pepe Luis bit the inside of his good cheek hard and got the word out. "Eugenia."

"Good," the fat man said. "And where does your mother Eugenia work?"

"Hotel."

"Which?"

"The Malage."

"In Suelo?"

"Yes."

"Profession?"

"Chief maid."

"We'll have to be careful. His distinguished mother," the fat man said, "Eugenia, is *chief* maid. Don't answer me, you," he said to the doctor, who was going to make a joke. "Can you read and write?" he said to Pepe Luis. "Is that the next question?"

"Yes, Captain," the man with the pen said.

"Well?"

"No," Pepe Luis said.

"Nothing?"

"My name."

"Have you ever been in love?" the fat man said.

"Yes."

"Without writing? What do you do when you want to write a love letter?"

"He jerks off," the doctor said.

"Look," the fat man said. "You . . ."

"Sorry, Captain," the doctor said.

"Captain," the man with the pen said. "Do you want me to include that? About the prisoner's being in love?"

The doctor shrugged at the fat man and pointed his head at the man with the pen. "I told you," he said.

The fat man put his face back in the handkerchief. "I swear," he said when he had stopped laughing and could breathe, "you're just terrible."

"*Mi Capitán?*" the man with the pen said.

"Not you," the fat man said. He took his legs down again and rolled forward and they could hear him wheezing with it. Then he blew his nose hard. *"Una mierda,"* he said.

The man with the pen said, *"Solo quería saber . . ."*

"No," the fat man said. "Of course not, idiot, read the form. Does it say anything about love on the form?"

The man with the pen clamped his mouth shut and looked down at his hands. He was furious, and his face had turned dark red.

"The question about love was my own," the fat man said. "It's a private joke. This prisoner isn't just an ordinary man. He thinks he's a Don Juan Tenorio. He comes calling at night on ladies. He needs a guitar, nothing more."

"Nothing more?" the doctor said.

"I'm going to send you out of the room in a minute," the fat man said.

"Sorry," the doctor said.

"By the way. I can't remember if I asked him his name," the fat man said to the man with the pen.

"Whose?" the man with the pen said.

"The accused's," the fat man said. "Yours I know. It's Jorge."

"The accused's name is Tomás José Luis Sanchez. He calls himself Pepe Luis. You didn't ask him, but I filled it in. I put it at the top of the form," the man with the pen said.

"Good for you. Everybody's learning. The heat," the fat man said. He had opened his collar and was mopping his neck with a handkerchief. *"Este puñetero foreño.* Is the window open?"

"It's worse with the window open, Captain," one of the men next to Pepe Luis said, "the wind comes right in."

"Never mind what comes in," the fat man said. "Maybe his smell will go out. I can't stand a whole lot more of this. His stink and the heat. It's like hell in here."

The man next to Pepe Luis who had spoken walked over and opened the window behind the fat man and came back.

"That's a little better," the fat man said. "Jesus. He must like it."

"You'd be surprised. They got them like that too," the doctor said. "They got them that they like their own smell."

The fat man took a sip of water from a glass on his desk and put the glass back down. "Don Juan Tenorio," he said. "Romeo. Jesus."

"I don't think he's going to want to play Don Juan any more," the doctor said, "I don't think he's got the equipment."

"You cut that off too?"

"I couldn't see that tiny."

The fat man giggled. "You wouldn't have believed it," he said. "Right out in the middle of the street at night. Standing under a lady's balcony. Just like Don Juan Tenorio in the play."

"How'd he insult you?" the doctor said.

"I'm telling you. The only difference was at least Don Juan had the sense to climb up to the balcony and sneak in. This one stood and talked to me about it. He *talked* to me about it."

"They got them that they like to talk about it."

"What do they call them?"

"Talkers," the doctor said. "Talking men."

The fat man looked at Pepe Luis. "Anyway," he said, "he don't like it now. I guess it must hurt him to talk now."

"It hurts him," the doctor said.

The fat man took a sip from a glass of water, and put the glass down.

"Captain, if he insulted you, why couldn't you have punished him just for that?"

"I had in mind more than punishing him," the fat man said. "I had it in mind to get rid of him. Until Rafael dug up this other business."

"About his being a member?"

"*Que va*," the fat man said, "no, I wouldn't have given a damn about that. It was when I found out Guzmán was in it. It was when I finally figured out that Guzmán gave this one his orders."

Pepe Luis opened his mouth again and made the sound that was like a foghorn. He had meant to speak but the saliva had collected in his mouth and he couldn't swallow.

"There he goes again," the fat man said. "Like a ship in a mist. Let's get through the rest of it. Can you give the evidence fast, please? The wind is killing me."

The man named Rafael took his eyes off the table leg for the first time since he had come into the room and removed several sheets of paper that were folded together in the inside pocket of his coat. He unfolded and pressed them out on his knee with his hand. He began to read out loud. " 'On May the . . .' "

"Wait," the fat man said, "not the whole damn thing. You can put it in the record as it is. Just tell what you heard him say—then tell what the other people you talked to said about him—and then explain that you got a whole lot more evidence written down to submit—and then submit it."

Rafael slipped three papers off the top and looked at the fourth one. He cleared his throat. He said in a monotone, " 'I heard the accused make references to a man called Jaime. This man called Jaime did not appear. I began to suspect that he did not exist. It was then I began to suspect that the name Jaime might be a pseudonym for another name too well known to be used. Accordingly, and on further investigation into the matter, I discovered that the members of the Communist Party, of which the accused was one, had had a meeting in the residence of Señor Don Juan Alonso de Muñoz, the Count of Suelo Guzmán, on February the . . .' "

"Coño," the fat man said. "It's going to take forever. Just take the whole thing and insert it into the record," he said to the man with the pen, "I'm not going to sit here with the heat down the back of my neck just because Madrid wants something on Guzmán, am I?"

Rafael handed the sheets of paper to the man with the pen. Then he looked back down at the table leg.

"So this Pepe Luis is really one of them?" the doctor said. "I never saw one before. Are they all this dumb?"

"Are what all?" the fat man said.

"The members of the Communist Party," the doctor said.

"What Communist Party?" the fat man said. "In Sanlúcar? Are you kidding?"

"I thought you said . . ."

"Of course I *said,*" the fat man said. *"Claro.* What am I going to say?"

"Oh," the doctor said. "I see."

"I don't think so," the fat man said. "I don't think anybody in this room sees. It's just me and the wind. And the smell. What the hell would a Communist Party do in Sanlúcar?"

"They could organize . . ."

"Organize what?" the fat man said. *"Organize?* Here?"

"I don't come from here," the doctor said. "I come from Barcelona. I'm a Catalonian. It's difficult for me to understand. In my *tierra* it's different. People read; they organize all the time. They . . ."

"Oh, shut up. I'm too tired. It's hot for speeches. Besides, don't give me any of that Catalonian crap," the fat man said.

"Sorry, Captain," the doctor said.

"Go back to making me laugh," the fat man said. "You're better at it. Maybe they got Communists up in Catalonia. Around here the people know better. If we get an idiot, he's a Don Juan Tenorio . . . he isn't any Communist. This one doesn't even know what the word means. He probably needed some money and somebody told him the Communists had money, that's all. Don't talk to me about what goes on in Andalucía; this is where *I* come from. This is my *tierra*. People don't hate their own government here like they do up in Barcelona. Understand?"

"Yes, Captain."

"Then don't give me any of that Catalonian crap," the fat man said.

"I only meant . . ."

"I don't care what you meant," the fat man said. "I was in Barcelona once. I saw what they got up there. Give me an idiot like this one any time. I'd rather have a Pepe Luis any time. At least I can understand him . . . he's an Andalusian. He's a good man. He's just an idiot, that's all. He isn't any Catalonian. He isn't even any Communist."

"Yes, Captain," the doctor said.

"What are you writing down?" the fat man said suddenly to the man with the pen.

The man with the pen lifted the pad he had been writing on and read formally from it. " '. . . an idiot, that's all. He isn't any Catalonian. He isn't even any Communist,' " he said.

The fat man stared at him for a moment. Then he shuddered and put his forehead in one of his hands. "*Coño*," he said finally. "I give up. The world is a big cunt: you put something in, you wait a little, you don't know what the hell's coming out. I don't know why I even bother. . . . I should just have killed this one and scrapped the whole business about Guzmán. They can go screw themselves in Madrid. I hate Castilians worse than Catalonians. But no. I try to do my duty, and look what happens. I try to keep law and order. I try to be a decent police captain and look what happens. Tear up that pad," he said to the man with the pen.

"*Mi Capitán?*"

"Tear it all up. The whole *puñetero* pad," the fat man said. "Tear it up and start over. Doesn't anybody understand what this hearing is about? Why do I try? I shit on this hearing. I shit on myself. I shit on the sea. Did you tear up the pad?"

"Yes, Captain," the man with the pen said.

The fat man took his head out of his hand and sat back. There was a silence in the room and you could hear his heavy breathing. "I'm going to tell you all something," he said. "Spain is a mess. Don't start writing yet. Spain is a big pile of shit," he said. "I wish there *were* a Communist Party. Maybe we could get something done around here. Maybe I wouldn't be surrounded by idiots, who knows? I wonder if it's this bad in Russia. Maybe the Communists have something."

There was another silence and the doctor coughed and politely covered his mouth. No one else moved.

The fat man said, "I'm going to tell you something. Guzmán isn't a Communist either . . . he isn't any more of a Communist than I am. . . . He's just another kind of idiot. And if any of you in this room ever repeats *that*, I'll put you in jail, and by the time I get through with you, you'll look worse than this one does. Is that clear?"

No one said anything and the doctor coughed again.

"Guzmán isn't even a Fascist," the fat man said. "He's a nothing. A dramatic actor. He's a loudmouth, that's all. He thinks he's very important. Did you ever meet him?" he said to the doctor.

"No, Captain."

"What a speechmaker . . . I'd like to know what he thinks he's done."

"What's he done, Captain?" the doctor said.

"Nothing," the fat man said. "He wrote a couple of articles, that's all. It's whaleshit. Madrid gets annoyed at anything. Now he's screwing some American tourist."

"Which one?"

"Some little blonde. . . . We keep a man up there watches the house at night."

"Can't you get Guzmán on that?"

"On what? Screwing an American tourist? . . . Fortunately it's not a felony," the fat man said. "Half the coast would be in jail. Don't they screw tourists in Barcelona?"

"I don't know, Captain."

"What were you doing there?" the fat man said. "Reading? It might be used against his character once we got him. I mean, if his wife chooses to bring charges. Once we got him it might help, but first we got to get him. Doesn't anybody understand that we have to get him?"

"Yes, Captain," the doctor said.

"Could we commence?" the fat man said. "Could we?"

There was another silence and Pepe Luis tipped forward slowly and fell out of the chair.

"Oh shit," the fat man said wearily. "He fainted. Put him back. Just put him back."

The two men lifted Pepe Luis up and put him back in the chair. After a while he moaned and blinked.

"There he is," the fat man said. "Let's go. I'm trusting you," he said to the doctor, "to make it clear to him ex-actly what's going to happen to him if he doesn't incrimi-nate Guzmán. Do you think you can manage that?"

"Yes, Captain."

"Can you fill the rest in?" the fat man said to the man with the pen. "The part about the form? His mother and his father and all?"

"Si, mi Capitán."

"All right," the fat man said. "I'm tired today. Let's get it over." He yawned and leaned forward and looked at Pepe Luis.

"How long," he said, "have you been a member of the Communist Party?"

THREE

Morning

ONLY a few days later the earth along the coast looked white and cracked. Now and then the roots of things showed. Most of the towns were hard to see from the water; there was a permanent sheen in the air from the blowing dust. In the early dawn the coast itself looked brittle. In the town of Sanlúcar where the dirt rose in the streets, women walked with scarves around their faces and forgot to gossip. While it was known that a blond American girl came almost every night to stay with Count Guzmán, people no longer stopped to talk about it. No one knew about the plainclothesman who squatted on the flat roof of Guzmán's home at night and no one would have cared if they had known. No one saw him. No one was aware when he began to carry a gun.

In Suelo things were not much changed and the tourists felt brave about the weather.

EUGENIA moved with a slow steady rhythm that looked both solid and boneless. She walked to the door and put her head out, blinking at the dawn. The street in Suelo looked dusty. It wasn't fully light yet but she could tell from the feel of the air on her eyes that the day would be another bad one. The African wind hadn't stopped. It was a freak of nature. It was the bastard of the world, and for two months now it had seared the coast to powder and dried people's souls up like grass. *El foreño* had never lasted this long as far back as she could remember; she shook her head and grunted at it.

"*Madre mía,*" she said and let the door slam and went back into her small house. She wore a black dress with rope-soled black canvas shoes. When she moved, her body swung forward with a kind of effortless grace. She didn't waddle; she rocked. She opened the door of the bedroom—the only room besides the kitchen—and looked at her husband lying sprawled asleep on his back. Enrique was as heavy as she was; the mound of his stomach rose like a naked mountain in the air. He looked like a beached whale. He snored like a monster and she loved him very much. He was dying slowly of not finding work and of something that had gone wrong with his liver.

Eugenia closed the door and went to the stove. She had already started the morning fire. The kindling had caught and she stoked the hard coals now with a black iron poker, fanning them mercilessly with a leaf-shaped straw fan. She had no gas in her house and she cooked with coals as she had always done, with the same quiet attack and deadliness of purpose she showed in walking or in just breathing. She was accustomed to waking up this way, and her face had a certain inertia of living, a kind of startled repose—that always sudden, expressionless look of survival that is sometimes seen in the faces of the very old or the very used. She jerked the poker into the coals and fanned them until showers of sparks flared out in vicious arcs over her hand;

126

then she put the poker and the fan down and placed a pan of milk on the stove to warm. Every morning she had the same breakfast: slices of toast cut from yesterday's loaf spread with sweet butter or *manteca*, the rust-colored lard made from pork, and coffee made with milk. She lit the stove in the morning and left it lit for Enrique's breakfast and for his lunch later in the day. Though she knew he wouldn't use it, except possibly, with much grumbling, for coffee. The rest of the day he would spend drinking at a café with his friends and discussing business matters while she worked. Enrique had not found work in years except for the occasional small contraband articles brought into Suelo by the boats from Tangiers. When he had none of those to sell he discussed things with his friends over coffee and brandy, because a man who does not discuss business matters has no more reason for living. When there were no business matters to discuss he made them up, and everyone knew this, but everyone still listened, because to disrespect a man's reason for living is to insult him and because it might happen to them too. It had already happened to some of them: they had been pushed into the back of Suelo and they sat in the cafés all day and had serious conversation. There was nothing else to do. Enrique had been a fisherman.

Eugenia took several of his shirts now and dropped them in the corner basin to soak before washing them; she had got up early to clean Enrique's clothes before going to work. A fisherman doesn't wash his own clothes, and all the men in Eugenia's family as far back as she knew had been fishermen. Her father and her grandfather and her great-grand-father. Her great-great-great-grandfather had been one of the sole survivors of the seismic sea wave that had destroyed Suelo the night after the African earthquake; he had been a fisherman too but on that day he had been in one of the inland towns visiting a friend. It gave Eugenia a particular distinction, as if she was related to the wave. Everyone from Suelo knew that her ancestor had beaten it. So she had married a fisherman and her two sons were raised to be fishermen—only there was no more work. One of her sons had got sick and died and the other one, Pepe Luis, had gone to Sanlúcar where there were still boats and shrimp and oyster luggers and a way for a man who knew the sea to make a decent living. Eugenia had stayed behind, moving into the back of town and walking daily to work since she found the job as chief maid in the Hotel Malage. She had done her best with her children and now she was worried about her husband. It wasn't right for a man to die for this reason. Of other things yes—but no man should swell up and die of decaying pride.

She cut some more slices from the loaf and lay them flat on the black iron stove to singe brown. Then she sat next to the stove and used the straw fan on her face and neck. She unbuttoned her dress to the nipples of her breasts and fanned a few gusts down over her body. At least this early, the *foreño,* the shit of a wind, wasn't as bad as it would be at noon; the whoreson wind was cooler in the morning. Though you didn't feel it so much anyway working in the Hotel Malage where the rooms were air-conditioned. She smiled now, thinking of the name of the hotel. It had been the running joke along the coast for some time. When the local people first heard the name of the hotel they couldn't believe it. Malage is a corruption of the word *malangel.* It is used in Andalucía to denote a special kind of evilness, and the meaning may be anywhere from fate to a vicious wit to plain bad luck: an evil grace. The word *malangel* divided into two is bad angel. Only the Andalusians speak with a southern accent and you do not hear either the *n* or the final *l,* so the word sounds like "maláge." When the German hotel owner came to Suelo and was told he had a great deal of that, he mistook the insult for a compliment and named his hotel after it. By the time he found out his error he had done too much publicity on the hotel to change the name. Now it would be the Hotel Malage for as long as it lasted and no explanation of its meaning was safe to give the guests. The name of the hotel was only one of the many things about the foreigners that amused and mystified the people along the coast.

Eugenia turned the slices of toast over and pushed herself out of the chair and took the lard from the icebox to spread on them. She kept it there in a can. The icebox wasn't electric and there had been no ice in it for three months—there wasn't any point in summer, especially with no one in the house most of the day—but she still kept perishables there out of habit. A lot of her life was habit. She sat down again and scooped some of the red lard out with a knife and laid it on the hot toast to melt. The coffee was made with hot thin milk and now she began her breakfast slowly, chewing and swallowing in a ponderous manner, the way she did anything that was a part of staying alive. A country with a history of civil wars if it has managed to survive at all has done so mostly through ritual and manners, and by now in Andalucía there was a way to do everything and only one way. There was a determination in the way people ate or made love or sang, though there was humor in those things too, great gut-laughs of it, when the gut was full and sometimes even when it wasn't. You could laugh the way you could live; nobody had ever lived easy. Eugenia had been expecting to die for over five years, but the more she expected it the harder she seemed to live and the longer. She worked all day and at night she came home and made supper for herself and Enrique. Very often they argued, and if he was drunk enough he hit her. Then she would cry and sometimes at night they made love, heaving and slapping and laughing, moaning heavily in the soft dark. The arguments were fine when they ended in bed. They made love like two great fishes surging at each other. Then in the morning she got up in time to do whatever needed to be done before she left again for work.

Breakfast took twenty minutes and when she had swallowed the last piece of toast she cleaned the top of the stove and then took some of the water from a metal cauldron that had been heating and went to the white sink that had a washboard built in it and began to wash her husband's shirts. After the shirts there were underclothes; she was a half hour washing and she hung the clothes up on a line over the small patio in back that she shared with four other families. Then she put some cold water from the tap into a basin and opened her dress further and began to wash herself. There was no hot water from the taps, but you didn't need much in summer; you heated it yourself, and you poured a bucket of water into the toilet when you wanted it to flush. After she had bathed herself she buttoned her dress and looked in again at Enrique. He had stopped snoring. He was swearing now gently in his sleep. She could only hear a few words, but she knew what he was angry about. "*Que malage tengo:* What an evil grace I have," he went on mumbling, growling at the ill-natured fate, the bad angel that had brought him to this state of uselessness. There was a fly crawling on his stomach like a mouse on a mountain and she whooshed it off with her hand. "Let him sleep, daughter of a whore," she said to the fly. "He hasn't got enough to put up with without you?" Then she left him and went out of the house and down the street to work.

Even in back of town this early in the morning not everybody was awake. It was just after five—she had to be at the hotel at six—and only those who went to work as early as she did were on the streets. Pedro Suso the milkman was in the act of receiving his milk for the day from a donkey cart; he wouldn't open his *lechería* for another hour and a half; *"Buenas, Doña Eugenia,"* he said as she passed, and she answered him in kind. She stopped beside the cart long enough to let him complete the ritual. "How is Don Enrique?" he inquired, and she said her husband was well enough considering and that he would be better soon, God willing. *"Si Dios quiere,"* Pedro repeated after her, handing the whole business back to God. Eugenia stayed long enough to ask about the health of Pedro's family and went on down the street. "This *foreño* is the son of its mother," he yelled lightly after her in a friendly way. *"Ya lo creo,"* she said, agreeing with him over her shoulder without stopping again.

It was because of the ritual good mornings that she had to leave her house so early—sometimes it took her forty-five minutes to walk what would otherwise have been twenty minutes to the beach hotel. She stopped when people spoke to her, it was the way things were done. Many spoke because of her fame. She was well known and respected in the town both because of her ancestor beating the wave and because of her vision. She had had a vision, and God had performed a kind of miracle on her behalf. It was a great many years ago, when her younger son, the one called Pepe Luis who lived now in Sanlúcar, had become sick with a nameless disease that had paralyzed him temporarily. He was a boy at the time and the disease had already killed his brother; the doctor had said Pepe Luis could not live either. Eugenia was a woman of great will and she would have done anything to save his life—she would have taken him to Madrid, if taking him to Madrid would have helped. Instead, she made a promise to the Virgin of Pilar who was in a town fifty kilometers distant that she would walk there and back if her son became well. The next day Pepe Luis had started to improve, and within two weeks the paralysis had left him. The month after that, Eugenia had walked the fifty kilometers to the shrine of the Virgin of Pilar which was on a hilltop church over a town called Chorro del Agua. It had taken two days and at night she had slept by the side of the road in the fields. When she got there, she started up the cobblestone road of the hill on her knees, climbing up to the shrine, which was a part of her promise. That had taken six days because a fifth of the way up on the second day her knees began to swell with blood and crawling even a little way on them made her feel like vomiting. When that happened she kept still and moved forward only when the nausea went away. When some of the townspeople of Chorro del Agua saw what had happened to her knees, they brought her a rubber pad to use. But the pad had not been part of the promise and Eugenia refused to use it except to sit on during the day while she was summoning the strength to climb farther. The woman who had brought it said that it was customary to use such a pad when making a pilgrimage on this hill to the Virgin of Pilar, but Eugenia could tell that the woman was lying. People will say anything to stop blood on the street, and she paid no attention to the woman and went on crawling up the hill without the rubber pad when she could. The sixth day she thought she would die on the hill. That was the day it had happened. She had been moving a bit every hour all afternoon, and though she was only two thirds of the way up, her knees had gone soft and were hurting so badly that she had to stop breathing when she used them. She held her breath and pushed all her strength down, and after a moment the pain was so bad she could not even feel it. There was only a light-headed dizziness and a sinking inside her as if her whole stomach were being pulled out through her knees. Then it had come to her. It was when she thought she had better sit down again and wait for new strength, and just then the last of the pain had disappeared and the dizziness and the sinking feeling too. All at once they had all gone away. She felt as if she were falling a great distance into a wondrous cushion of soft air, and then she had seen it. It began as a pinpoint of light way in front of her eyes, and it grew until the light exploded in the air around her. She could see nothing but the white bursting light and then she heard clearly the voice of the Virgin in the light telling her to go back. The Virgin had come down one third of the hill when She saw that Eugenia could not make it the rest of the way up. With her blood behind her, still kneeling on the stones leading up the hill to the shrine Eugenia had spoken to the Virgin. They had had a talk and people had gathered around Eugenia to hear her part of the conversation. When it was over she was unconscious, and they had carried her into a shop on the hillside and called a doctor. When she became conscious again, half her face was paralyzed. Eugenia had had nothing else to offer and she had given up half of her face when the Virgin had told her to go back. So she never saw the shrine. When she was well enough, she walked back down the hill, and despite the protests of the doctor and the shopowner and his wife who had taken care of her, she walked all the way back to Suelo. This time it took her four days and three nights and when she got to Suelo word had already reached them of the vision she had seen. Enrique came out of the house with his arms open and when he saw what her knees looked like he beat his own head with his fist. That time too he had said it, *"Que malage tengo,"* and he had taken her back into the house and Eugenia had slept for forty-eight hours, waking only to go to the toilet; a neighbor woman looked in once or twice and forced her to drink some broth. The thing was well known among the people of Suelo. Her son Pepe Luis had never again suffered from the childhood paralysis, and he limped only very slightly. Though he seldom spoke much after that, it was because of the suddenness of his brother's death, not because of his own illness. After he left, Eugenia had gone on living in Suelo with this new mark of respect, the half of her face she had given out of love for the Virgin.

She walked around a pile of straw-filled dung in the street and crossed over to the other side and continued toward the hotel. Eight more people said good morning to her; five times she was forced to stop and hold a brief conversation. One woman leaning on a balcony above the street discussed Eugenia's job with her and all of them discussed the weather. By the time Eugenia got to the hotel, the *foreño* had a serviceable array of titles that questioned everything from the wind's birthright to the excretory matter that had been used instead of earth on the graves of its ancestors. It had been called a homosexual wind, and a wind without testicles, and a wind that had had its beginnings in a Moorish latrine. The father and mother of the wind had been widely sullied, and the wind itself had been called the great African fart of the century. Even the African continent where the wind originated had come in for its turn, and the smell of the African desert had been compared to the dry asshole of an elephant that had died of boredom. When Eugenia walked down the steps toward the back entrance of the hotel, she was smiling contentedly with half her face. There was not much left of the wind but the wind itself.

Ahead of her now were the villas dimly seen in a thin shroud of fog. Walking down the pebble path that wound through the pastel colors, she thought about the summer inhabitants of the hotel; they were as foreign to her, most of them, as creatures from the moon, but in a way they were more acceptable than the people from Madrid or Barcelona who thought of themselves as Spanish like herself but who were peculiar. Eugenia could take out-and-out foreigners much more easily than she could Spaniards who came from a different province. The foreigners at least *announced* themselves as foreigners and you knew what to expect—

people who couldn't speak God's language and who communicated with her by flailing their arms and making awkward sounds in their mouths and throats. She didn't feel threatened by them any more than she would have by a vast crowd of diapered infants who yelled when they wanted something. But the Spaniards from Castile or Catalonia or Asturias or Galicia or the Basque provinces were another matter. All of them spoke Castilian with different accents, and they all thought of themselves as just as Spanish as she was. She did feel threatened by them. They crowded her mind. If each had his way, Eugenia knew, each would make his province the capital of Spain. She didn't understand or enjoy those people. There was no point to them. Better deal with an alien than with someone from your own country who is hostile and "superior."

She used her eyes now in a kind of triangle shape on the lawn ahead. The villas were spread out before her like multicolored cakes. Under the fuzzed gray sky the lawn was green and soft-looking, and the villas were separated by fruit trees and crêpe myrtle and green bushes that smelled like new milk in the morning. She could see the blue villa, the color of smoke through the fog. Take for instance the boy in the blue villa. He was a moody child who preferred being by himself, but she liked him. The boy had learned to speak Spanish with an Andalusian accent. He seemed to support a small invisible cloud that hovered over him wherever he was; now that he was left alone most of the time he went for walks with his pet dog and stayed away from people almost all day. He behaved as if something was eating on his mind. She had asked him what was wrong but he had answered only that he had many things to think about. She wondered now, passing the villa, whether one of the things he had to think about had to do with Count Guzmán. The boy's sister wasn't like some of the other young foreign women who came to spend the summer; she wasn't Bad, Eugenia could tell. It was common knowledge at the hotel that the girl had taken an immediate dislike to Count Guzmán and then changed her mind; the dislike had become anger and the anger had turned to something else, as anger will. Eugenia knew more about the facts of the case than anybody else in the hotel. She just didn't talk. She made it a rule. What people did with their lives was their own business. But the sister of the boy named Will hadn't spent a night in her own bed in more than a month, and Eugenia knew where she was sleeping. It wasn't in the gold villa; the two sons of the Count slept there. The sister was sleeping at the Count's house, the broken-down Guzmán palace in San-lúcar. Eugenia had found out by accident one weekend over a month ago when she had had a day off and had gone to see Pepe Luis. It was the greengrocer there who told of the blond girl's visits, and of her driving alone early in the mornings, back to the hotel. Then the girl would come to Sanlúcar again in the afternoon—or sometimes the Count would come to Suelo and they would have lunch on the hotel terrace with the Count's two sons or the girl's brother. Though the subterfuge was unnecessary, because the Count's wife was in Madrid, and nobody in the south could stand La Condesa de Guzmán anyway. Most of the poor people loved the Count and would say nothing against him: he had many friends among the workers in the province of Cádiz. Still, nobody around the hotel knew the whole truth, and Eugenia had not said anything to anybody. She knew about many of the guests' private habits—more than most of them had any idea of. There was the young American man in the pink villa on the other side of the blue villa—the one who had a weekly visitor from Madrid. When his rich friend had gone back after each weekend, the young man went driving in his car along the coast, and often he would bring back a shepherd boy or a young mechanic to spend the night. It was against the rules for anyone who was not registered in the hotel to sleep there, but Eugenia had seen him take the mechanic away in the early morning and she had known from the state of the bed sheets while she was changing them what had gone on during the night.

The sexual habits of the guests were of no particular interest to her, but if they had been, as she said to Enrique, she could have written a book. Or rather spoken one—she had never learned to read or write very well. But every summer it was the same. In her opinion it had something to do with the heat that made foreigners strip their clothes off in a place where they had nothing else to do, except look at each other's bodies, naked and oiled all day long. Then when the *foreño* came they couldn't even do that because the wind filled the water with jellyfish and made the beach impossible to lie on. So what else had they to do but play games with each other? She knew what the big American from Texas, on leave from the naval base, did with his spare time when his wife wasn't looking, and she knew, many afternoons, who was in whose bed all around the hotel. She knew how Alonso the young lifeguard supplemented his pay and she generally knew who he was supplementing it with. She knew who took certain kinds of drugs and who had certain other addictions. She just didn't say anything. It was her business to see that the maids in the hotel all did their jobs as well as they could and kept their mouths shut. That was what she was paid to do; she was a believer in keeping to her duty.

The only person who really worried her in the hotel was the boy named Will. She didn't like the way he had been looking—as if the invisible cloud that hovered over him was an unwanted dark spirit that nobody but him could see. He didn't talk much. But he noticed things, that boy. You couldn't help but be concerned about him living in the strange hotel. It wasn't that he couldn't take care of himself. It was that there were just too many things going on. . . .

She stopped in the gravel at the back door to the main building and looked out to sea. The fog was nearly gone. The purple blossoms and the waxy vine leaves on the hotel were moving sluggishly now in the wind. There was a figure swimming out there, not far from shore. She knew who it was because the same figure was out every morning, before the jellyfish came in, when the water was only murky from the air. It was the blond mother of the boy, she was alone taking her morning exercise. Eugenia knew something about her too—something the woman thought nobody was aware of. The blond woman was odd. There was a quality in her that didn't go with her hair or her manners, something that had been familiar to Eugenia the first second she saw it. The blond woman looked like one sort of person, and she was quite another.

Still, it wasn't any of her, Eugenia's, business. She had enough to think about with just making a living. Then Pepe Luis in Sanlúcar had not yet saved the money he needed to be married, though he would be twenty-eight next winter. She had not liked the look of him either when she saw him last, almost five weeks ago, and she had not heard a word from him since. His *novia*, Lupe, the woman he was to marry, had left him and married another man last April; it was a bad sign. Eugenia had never liked Lupe and was just as glad; but Pepe Luis had loved the woman—and Pepe Luis was a strange silent thing who, ever since the early paralysis, almost never let on to what was really troubling him. Eugenia was worried about not having heard from him. She would still have done anything for his sake, but he had never been the sort of man that people harmed. It was Life that was pushing down on Pepe Luis, just as it was pushing down on Enrique. So Eugenia had to worry about that too—

that more than anything. And if that wasn't plenty, there was enough to do just getting out of each day and into the next. Yesterday there had been a valuable camera stolen from one of the villas and it was going to be up to her to find out who had done it. Holtz, the owner of the hotel, had taken the matter seriously. He had ordered her to question the staff and to produce the thief within twenty-four hours; Eugenia had sent one of the maids to ask questions last night and report to her about it this morning, though she didn't have a clue to go on. *Por fin* they were all rich foreigners and whatever they did it was all the same to her. She was not a part of them.

She opened the kitchen door and stepped out of the rising wind onto the tile-cool floor. Four cooks were getting the breakfast things laid out in preparation for the hysteria that would come anyway when all the guests woke up and wanted their coffee and eggs at the same time. It was the hour to begin work, to leave off silly thinking, to start the day and survive it. The strangers with other problems, they could have them. They could afford them—they were safe from everything but themselves. The thing was to keep herself working and her family alive. For the rest, *una mierda . . .*

Then in the kitchen she saw the young woman sitting in the straight-backed chair in the corner. The woman was waiting for Eugenia, and she had been crying. She was very well dressed, dressed for the street, but her yellowish face had an even sallower cast than usual and her eyes looked red and swollen.

The woman was holding onto her purse and twisting it in her hands.

Eugenia stopped moving. She recognized the woman instantly and was not pleased to see her. She stood waiting for her to speak, though she could not imagine what the woman had come to say. "Yes?" Eugenia said.

Lupe, the ex-*novia* of Pepe Luis, rose and took a breath and held it. She stood awkwardly, more tears starting from her eyes—her shoulders raised and the brand-new patent leather purse bent shiny and tight in her hands, as if she were afraid it might get away from her. For a moment they faced each other and Lupe seemed at a loss for something to say. Then the invisible barrier between them broke, and Lupe threw the purse down and sprang forward.

She reached out, half-clutching, and threw herself, like a monstrous child, onto Eugenia's hard arms.

Twenty meters from shore, lying on her back, Helen kicked smoothly at the water and felt it rush like sheets of cold silk over her neck and shoulders. The salt water felt like crisp elegant linen between her breasts and over her flat stomach. Swimming this way, parallel to the beach, she had seen the heavy old woman in black enter the service wing in the main building of the hotel. She turned over and swam breaststroke for a while. She was a good swimmer and she held her long neck poised out of the water. She didn't need a bathing cap; her hair never got wet. When she went swimming she kept it tied up with a yellow ribbon. She didn't like the old woman in black, though she wasn't sure why. Cleaning her villa in the mornings the woman sometimes glanced at Helen with a sense of hidden familiarity, as though they shared some secret. Then there was a blank gutted look of ruthlessness about the woman's face that took Helen back to other times of her own life, times she could live without. She knew that particular look—she knew it very well. . . .

She kicked hard again at the water, frog-fashion, thrusting forward and catching herself by pushing back with her arms. The sea wasn't very choppy yet but you could tell from the sky that it would be soon. On shore the bushes around the main building and between the villas were beginning to wave ominously in the first of the day's wind. The plants looked comic from here, as if they wanted to uproot themselves and go inside. Without moving her face, Helen smiled to herself. She knew how they felt.

She turned and swam the other way, watching the trembling plants. She had five more minutes of exercise before she could tread water or just go in and take a shower before breakfast. Years ago she had disciplined herself this way: it kept her firm and trim. Other women her age made her laugh—the ones who went on a new diet every month, gaining and losing weight, puffing up and collapsing like so many balloons. Diet, Helen had always said, was a way of life—not a thing you went on when your clothes didn't fit. You either cared about your appearance or you didn't. And yet, swimming in the brackish cool morning water as the wind rose, she thought that all she had ever wanted out of life was freedom and safety. Just those two things. To uproot herself and go inside, like the plants. Only, unlike the plants she had done it: had ripped up her roots from the secret dirt they had been born in, a swampy treacherous soil where nothing was safe, and transplanted herself. The way she lived now at least she was free; and so, by the way, were her children. Whatever they thought of her, they had plenty of time to think it. They didn't have to worry about staying alive; they wouldn't eat stale bread, or rice and red beans. Or rice and ham hock or rice and catfish. Or rice and anything. Just the thought of rice turned Helen's stomach. Her children wouldn't ever have to see human beings shrivel into self-burning bones; see people who, when even the rice was gone, metabolized their own flesh instead, using themselves up by just breathing, coping with poverty and other parts of hell as familiar to them as trees in a landscape. There would be other trees in the lives of Helen's children, but not *those* trees. No skeletons. No gaunt bony world of slow starvation.

Turning again, she scanned the shore with her eyes for signs of life. There weren't any. The hotel was still drowsing. The different colored suites in the main building and the painted villas looked from here like illustrations in a cheap fairy tale. The place looked like a vulgar daydream. They were all quiet now—even the green suite belonging to the Donahues, and the one next to it, the lavender suite that Mrs. Lawson occupied. Idling in the water, Helen let herself think about Lieutenant Donahue. Since he had seen that her daughter wasn't available he had gone back to flirting with her, Helen. Once he had done more than just flirt. He had stopped at her villa, on the pretext of bringing her some magazines from the American post exchange in the naval base, and after Helen had thanked him he had lingered on waiting to be asked to sit down. She hadn't asked; but as she went by to put the magazines away, Donahue had put his hand on her back and turned her around and kissed her. She had known he was going to do it and she had let him. The big Texan who was a body-builder in his spare time pulled her up to his mouth, slowly against his overmuscular bulk; he kissed softly at first, heating into it until his wide tongue forced past hers. Lots of practice, she had thought at the time. But that had been all there was; when Donahue slid her down against him Helen had gone on putting the things from the PX away and had said over her shoulder, "I think you'd better go now . . . I'm expecting someone." The lieutenant had believed her and left. It was a lie, of course. But the lie combined with her indifference had unnerved him enough that he wouldn't think of himself as a fast-service filling-station around her any more. If they had anything more to do with each other it would ease into a full summer affair with all the usual trimmings. The trouble was she didn't think she wanted all the trimmings with Lieutenant Donahue. He was fair game—easily seventeen years younger than she, from a rich Texas family, wedded to a middle-class English snob who had married him for his money. It was a setup for a summer affair and it was easy. Only, for Helen, there were two kinds of affairs: the kind that might lead to money and the kind that was just for fun. Lieutenant Donahue didn't fall into either category. He was a dull man and besides, unless something very special came along, she no longer had time just for fun. No, if she went to bed with the big Texan it would be for one of two reasons—because it was good for her skin, or because she thought she could take him away from his wife. Neither one was practical. Anyway he wasn't all that rich—he wasn't even as rich as his wife thought—Helen knew the signs. There was no old money in Donahue's face; it was all new money and it was probably rather badly invested, she guessed. Treading water and swimming gently she began to move in a long oval-shaped pattern through the sea. What would Lieutenant Donahue or his snobbish wife think, she wondered, if they ever knew where she herself came from? They thought of her as a sort of mature southern belle turned European socialite. They all did. Even her daughter. Though Alice did know that Helen's family had been poor. . . .

Only what in hell did people think of when they said the word, Poor? Most of them thought vaguely, as Alice did, of a sort of lower-class family that had to worry about mortgage payments and things. When your father had to shinny up the telephone pole at night while the neighbors weren't looking and use a jump-wire to reattach the electricity the company had cut off for lack of payments—that was what they thought of as Poor. Or when the Depression came, and some of the men in the family had to work at manual labor to get through it. Some plain foolishness like that. Nothing to do with really being poor. But then nobody who hadn't grown up with it could imagine it. Nobody knew about Helen—not even her children. There wasn't a hint of it in her appearance any more—she had checked her mirror for years and even she herself couldn't find it. The thing was gone from her eyes, the hunger, and nobody since she was twelve had looked at her with that tinged pitying look reserved for the . . . nobody, that is, until the old fat Spanish woman in black had glanced at her the first time. As if the maid knew where Helen's ritual elegance had come from, or why manners were so important to her. . . .

She shook her shoulders in the sea and reached down with one foot for the bottom. Her red-tipped toes touched the sand. She stood balanced on them for a while, her head and neck clear of the water. Then she scanned the main building again out of the corners of her eyes. This time a few people were up and moving. He was there. Donahue. He was standing on the balcony of his suite in a bathing suit watching her. But there was another pair of eyes watching her from one of the villas, she thought. She tightened the bow in her hair with two fingers and glanced sideways long enough to get in a look. Yes, she hadn't imagined it. Now that would be something else again. That man. She had flirted with him once on the tennis court—but only out of habit. She hadn't seriously thought he might be interested in her. But why not? He didn't fit into the money category, but there *was* the hint of something special about that man. Besides, she had another motive for being interested in him —a motive that had to do with Alice. The business of Count Guzmán was upsetting to Helen, and upsetting for a reason her daughter would never believe. That Alice had taken a man away from her didn't matter one way or the other— there wasn't anything Helen had ever owned that Alice couldn't have had for the asking. The affair disturbed Helen for a reason that had nothing to do with vanity. What bothered her was the danger to Alice inherent in the relationship. The Count was too old and too unstable, she thought. The truth was that Helen loved her daughter more than she had ever loved anyone in her life—she always had. Long ago she had seen to it that Alice would have money, before she had even worried about guaranteeing her own future. And it had always been the same stubbornness that prevented her from showing her love in any other way. She knew that her daughter didn't like her. Once a long time ago Alice had said something to prove it. It was the first disturbing thing Alice ever did. Count Guzmán was the second. Twice in Helen's adult life she had been badly shaken—both times by her daughter. Right now she preferred not to think about either time. But sooner or later she was going to have to teach Alice a lesson. . . .

She began to walk inside the water, tiptoeing toward the beach until the soles of her feet could touch. There were more immediate problems to be taken care of first—problems that had to do with money. There was the party to be considered first of all.

Until last month Helen had been planning to start things slowly—by inviting one or two friends down from Paris to meet Count Guzmán, and then using those friends to attract others. If Helen didn't know all the right people, she knew the people who did. She had been planning an aristocratic party this summer. It would have been easy with Guzmán as bait. Now she would have to go about it another way. Ever since the Second World War, Europe had been filled with new money; millionaires were a dime a dozen. Except for the oldest aristocracy, nobody knew who anybody was any more. Helen had been making use of that situation for a long time; she had in fact been using it to support herself. She had started years ago by giving a series of small dinner parties in Paris to introduce the wife of a Hollywood real estate millionaire to French society. In gratitude, afterwards, the lady had sent Helen a very expensive set of rare books. It was a nineteenth-century edition of the complete works of Molière, exquisitely bound in leather and stamped in fancy gold scrollwork. Helen didn't want the books and it wasn't easy to sell them for anything like what the Hollywood lady had paid. The second time, in Paris, when she gave a few parties to introduce a family of new-rich Marshall-plan Greeks to some poor but aristocratic French, Helen made certain that her fee was discreetly but simply stated early enough to prevent another set of rare books. She was safe in demanding a fee: she knew that her clients wouldn't talk, and she wouldn't talk. After that, one thing led to another. There had been parties in Rome, in Lisbon, in London. Generally the theme was the same. It was only in the last two years, after she had become known as a hostess, that Helen had taken to making arrangements with hotels in order to cut down on her living expenses. Though she took care never to accept cash from any of the hotel owners, she made enough demands on them—the best rooms, the finest food, champagne, chauffeured cars—that most of them would have found a cash arrangement much cheaper. What Alice hadn't ever guessed, thank God, was the actual current state of her mother's finances; for a second on the terrace that day, Helen had nearly told her the truth. She had caught herself in time. Answering questions so openly and directly before dropping the subject had worked—it was the one sure way to put Alice off the track. Alice just assumed her mother knew too much about money not to have plenty of it. The fact was that Helen had made only one mistake in her life about money, but the one mistake had been a knockout. Even so, she had enough left over to scrape by for a couple of years—if she wanted to live in a two-room apartment somewhere and pinch pennies, which she didn't. But she didn't want Alice's charity either. She wanted to live the way she was living now, independent and in comfort; she just didn't have the money to do it, and it meant living on the edge of things all the time. She was getting tired of making a living by giving parties—more tired than she cared to admit. If almost no one knew it was how she supported herself, that was because people didn't notice things like that. They didn't even suspect the obvious fact that she needed the large sums she won playing bridge and canasta and gin. That was the point of the morning exercises: she didn't *look* like a woman near the edge of anything. She looked the way she wanted to look, not the way she felt. The problem was to get on with this year. As she walked, the first shape of a plan swung into Helen's mind, cloudy in the first moment it appeared, then coming slowly into focus. There was a way to get past the summer; the plan was good. When her hips were out of the water she stopped long enough to make sure she was being watched by everybody. She looked fine in a wet bathing suit coming out of the sea and she knew it. Her body was rounder than her daughter's, fuller in the right places, still more sensual. She pretended to stretch and saw several pairs of eyes following her movements. Above her, the villas and colored apartments did look like a movie set for the cheapest kind of fairy tale—the kind about a poor starving girl who becomes a princess overnight. As if you didn't have to work hard for your dream, and then, after you had achieved part of it, when you had relaxed for just one second, have to see your daughter come down a flight of stairs and walk away with the last chapter. And not even know yet what you would do about that. Until you coped once more with the problem of living. Forty-four was a peculiar age, even if you didn't look much over thirty-six.

She paused again with the water just above knee level. It was her best angle—better than full length because her legs, though perfectly shaped, were a bit too short for the rest of her. Then she straightened her back and faced the main building, ambling lazily out of the low tide. From his balcony Lieutenant Donahue waved at her once, but she ignored him.

No, it was a silly place they had all come to, this fixed-up beach town. It bore no more relation to reality than the man in the moon. She was familiar with reality—she had had her nose rubbed in it at a very early age. And now she had come to this, a kind of vast doll's house—a place that looked as if it were made out of after-dinner mints and sugar cookies. Walking out of the sea, Helen threw her head back suddenly and laughed at the hotel.

If you were standing on it, the balcony of the green suite made the Mediterranean look queasy at this hour. Sort of bilious. Once the lady named Helen was out of sight, it was like seeing a reflection of what you had drunk last night. It made First Lieutenant George Gary Donahue swallow, and, worse, it made him turn back into the bedroom where his wife was smoking a cigarette and watching him from the bed. "Anything interesting?" she said.

"What? . . . No."

He took a few more steps into the room and hunched his shoulders, pulling his back muscles out; then he did a few quick deep knee bends as if in preparation for his morning calisthenics. He had already finished his calisthenics, but his wife couldn't know that. He mumbled, "I thought you were asleep."

"Did you?" she said.

Donahue eyed her and loped into the living room. He knew from her tone of voice that there was trouble coming, but he had never yet known how to avoid trouble with women. He heard her sigh as she shut the door.

Sylvia Donahue put out her cigarette in an ash tray beside the bed and smothered a yawn. When she stood up, her loose nightgown flowed away from her as if it were going somewhere. She was an angular woman in her late twenties with a sharp nose, a British voice that was slightly nasal and very bright brown eyes. She pulled the nightgown down around her neatly and puffed the sleeves. She had already brushed her hair and her teeth while she was looking through the bathroom window to see who it was her husband was ogling this early. She knew it would be one of two people—either the eighteen-year-old maid he was having a part-time affair with or Helen Locke. It was Helen Locke. Previously Helen Littlejohn, née God Only Knows. Sylvia disliked the woman thoroughly, which was one of the reasons she had first begun to look for signs of interest in her husband and had found them. It was a fairly good rule of thumb: if Sylvia took a strong dislike to a woman, sooner or later Donahue made a pass at her.

She opened the door and went into the living room, walking around her husband who was on the floor doing pushups. She sat on the green sofa and watched him for a while. He was extremely good to look at and that was all he was. Sylvia had come to realize this during the two years they had had together; there was no doubt in her mind that she had married a man with the body of a Greek god and the mind of a ten-year-old defective. Like most American men Sylvia had been exposed to, Donahue had sex on his mind twenty-four hours a day, and the only reason he bored her in bed was that he bored her out of it. It was Donahue's fate that though he often liked mature women, with few exceptions he bored most women over the age of eighteen. Sylvia knew this for a fact. Despite his body. Or perhaps because of it. There was a world of difference, she had found, between a muscle-man and a real man. A world of difference.

She waited until he was halfway through a pushup and said quietly, "Did you decide to do your calisthenics twice today, or did you think I was asleep the first time?"

Donahue collapsed in a loose pile of himself and looked at a green tile in front of him. "I didn't finish them all," he lied, "so I thought I'd start over."

Sylvia lit another cigarette and blew a flat shaft of smoke over his head. "Good show," she said.

"I want to get through them just once."

"I shan't talk."

"I had too much to drink last night. Never could drink stingers. I had four stingers, didn't I?"

"I'm not talking," Sylvia said.

". . . You don't like me, do you?"

"That's a silly question."

"It's a fact."

"Lots of things are facts."

"You should get a divorce."

"I should jump for joy."

"Calisthenics would do you a lot more good."

"They wouldn't do me any good at all," Sylvia said. "I'm pregnant."

She got up and went to the pot of coffee that was left from Donahue's breakfast and poured herself a cup. Then she went and sat back down on the sofa with the coffee.

Donahue frowned. He eased over onto his back and then turned, throwing all his weight on one thigh. "Is that true?"

"You look absolutely majestic like that. Like a thundering great statue dug up out of the sea or somewhere. Yes, quite true."

". . . Since when?"

Sylvia put the cup of cold coffee back in the saucer and set it on the green table. Then she flicked her cigarette. "Guess," she said.

"About two weeks ago?"

"No," she said. "That wasn't me."

"It was. It was two weeks ago."

"What we did two weeks ago wouldn't have made me pregnant."

"Why not?"

Sylvia leaned forward close to her husband and stared at him with precision.

"Oh," Donahue said.

"Listen," Sylvia said, "it's like this. Women in my family don't have abortions unless they're dying, and they don't have divorces at all. I hope I shan't die. I may do. I almost did that time in Florida, and it wasn't an accident; I'm built awkwardly. I'd have a struggle with a normal-sized baby, much less one of yours; I'm not looking forward to it but I expect I'll do it . . . I don't know how, but I do know why. Only I can't explain tradition to you, so don't ask me. It's not like the navy. Five weeks and three days."

". . . Was it that long ago?"

Sylvia sighed.

"Should I take you back to London?"

"The doctor at the base seems to think he can take care of me, if you're still stationed here."

"You told him about what happened the time in Florida?"

"I thought it wise to. You know. Thorough."

"You don't have to be sarcastic."

"I wish I didn't."

"I hope it's a boy."

"Why?"

"If it's a boy," Donahue said, "it'll make my mother happy."

Sylvia sighed again.

She had been looking at Donahue's neck while they talked. She turned suddenly away from him and put her cigarette out and went to the window overlooking the balcony. The sea was choppy and the sand on the beach was beginning to fluff. The sky was taking on the heavy leaden quality it had had nearly every day for the last several weeks. The wind had come.

Behind her, Donahue picked himself up in a lanky way and stood in the middle of the floor like a purebred stallion, not knowing which direction to turn. He put a hand over his neck. "I feel like I ought to do something special . . . to celebrate." Donahue sniffed. "Maybe I ought to get dressed."

Sylvia kept her back turned, facing the sea.

"I was supposed to check with Mr. Holtz this morning about my camera. . . ."

". . . Your what?"

"He said he'd find out about it. The owner of the hotel. My camera was stolen yesterday."

"So it was," Sylvia said. "I'd forgotten."

"Right out of the front of the station wagon. And all the film. Twelve rolls of exposed film."

"Yes. Quite. Twelve rolls of exposed film."

"Are you crying?"

"I'm not the type."

"You sounded like it for a minute. My leave is up next Thursday," Donahue said. "Sure hope they can get the camera back for us before then."

"I think I'd like some breakfast now. I'm not going back to the base with you," Sylvia said. "I'm going to let room service take care of me here. They have very good room service. You can visit on weekends if you like."

"I guess it's the right way. I mean, you won't have to keep house and . . ."

"Quite."

"I can get a maid to take care of me at the base."

Sylvia laughed.

". . . That isn't what I meant."

Donahue shuffled one bare foot on the tiled floor and changed his weight to the other hip. He hated conversations like this one and he was beginning to sweat. "All I meant was . . ."

"For pity's sake," Sylvia said, "do what you want. For heaven's sake. Just don't talk about it. Go and take your shower."

"Want me to order your breakfast first?"

"No, thank you."

"It's just that it irks me somebody should steal my Leica like that."

"Yes, I'm sure. It's an upsetting thing."

"Mr. Holtz says he's positive we'll find it."

"Good."

"Sure . . . I'm really glad about the baby. . . ."

"Thank you," Sylvia said.

He stood some more. Then he said, "It isn't true what you're thinking. I didn't give the camera away to anybody. It was stolen."

"I don't give a damn what you did with your camera."

"But I didn't . . ."

"I'm not your mother," Sylvia said, "you can throw it in the sea for all I care. I'm not your damn Texas mother."

"Easy," Donahue said.

"Why must you treat me this way? Why do all American men have mothers? Will you do me the most enormous favor and go and take your shower?"

"I just wanted you to know, see."

"Know what?"

"It wasn't like that; I didn't give it to the little maid. It was stolen."

Sylvia didn't answer.

". . . I don't see what you mean about mothers," Donahue said.

"I didn't mean anything. I'm about to be one, that's all. I didn't mean anything."

"It's no reason you should start on her. That's all right about my mother."

". . . I'm sorry."

"It's if I just look at one other woman. You always get so coltish."

"Oh my God," Sylvia said. "Coltish."

"That's all right," Donahue said. "That's all right, that's all. That's all right about my mother. Let's not get confused."

"Very well."

"You always make a scene."

"Listen," Sylvia said carefully, "please listen to this one thing. I don't care what you do or who you do it with. You don't have to sneak around me; I don't care. I do very much care about being alone now for the next five minutes. Would you go and take you shower?"

"Sure," Donahue said.

He turned angrily and went out of the room. In the bathroom he glanced at his neck in the mirror. Then he slipped his trunks off and turned on the water. When he had stepped into the shower and the water was sliding down, his anger began to let go of him. That was the way his wife was, he knew, and there wasn't a whole lot you could do about it. Sylvia was three years older than him. She got started on one subject and went right over to another. Except for her being English, she was a whole lot like his mother in her way when you came right down to it. That was what had made him propose to her. He soaped himself down all over and turned around several times. It was one hell of a muscular structure. The men at the gym in the base shook their heads every time Donahue came to work out. Men gaped at him wherever he went. What was beginning to get to him was that they looked at him more than women did. There were six men right in the hotel who stared at him

under cover, and a little kid named Will who watched him as
if he expected to read something written on Donahue's
chest. Then there were the faggots. There were always the
faggots. The one in the pink villa practically keeled over
every time Donahue walked by. That faggot sometimes made
him laugh the way he stared. But only two women looked
—two he cared about—two, that is, in the hotel. First the
lady named Helen he was pretty sure was interested. A few
minutes ago she had seen him wave at her from the balcony,
even if she had pretended not to. And she had liked his
kissing her that day. He could tell. Then there was the little
maid.

Her name was Marimar and he hadn't had it with her
but twice. He hadn't given her the camera either. It was
true about the camera; it had been stolen. And what would
anybody want with twelve rolls of exposed film? Unless they
couldn't read the labels that said exposed. He would be glad,
Donahue, when he was back in the States where people
could understand plain English. He stood for a while with
the water pouring down the channel between the muscles in
his back. Marimar liked to put her fingernails in his muscles,
and she liked to make black-and-blue suction marks in the
front of his neck with her mouth. She did that so that his
wife could see, and he always had to stop her. Except that
she waited to do it until the second before he came, when he
wasn't in much condition to stop her. That was what Sylvia
had been staring at just now on his neck. Oh well, it couldn't
last. He was going back on Thursday. But it was nice to be
admired, and he did have one hell of a musculature.

He soaped himself down again and raised his arms and let
the water have him. He could come here on weekends like
Sylvia said. It was nice about the baby—a baby would keep
her occupied a lot. He didn't much like Sylvia that way any
more unless he was drunk, and there were a lot of girls between here and the base. Enough to keep him busy. He
wasn't worried.

He was going back on Thursday.

The gold villa and the pink villa were separated by ten
meters of lawn and one voluminous bush. Both villas were
quiet now in the new morning. The sky was as gray as the
sea but the wind had taken the fog off the land. The bush
between the two villas was clipped and squat, with a stiff
trunk that seemed a little sad. It was a very expensive bush
with waxy leaves and a hard look of quiet exasperation.

In the gold villa one man sat in a chair and the younger

man lay on the gold sofa with his bare feet sticking off the end. They were the two sons of Count Guzmán and they had been awake over an hour. They were wearing robes.

The two brothers had had an argument. It was because the younger one, José Ramón, had done a silly thing yesterday and had not told his older brother about it until this morning. The thing he had done involved their father and it was dangerous as well as stupid.

Juan Alberto stood by the window now looking out at the sea. His robe was like their father's—dark blue with a very small gold crown embroidered on the lapel. From time to time he raised one hand and made a fingerprint in the glass pane of the window and then watched it fade. He was angry at José Ramón for what he had done, and José Ramón knew from experience that when his older brother was this way it was better to leave him alone until the anger subsided. It was certainly better not to talk. Juan Alberto though he didn't look it had a fierce temper and was often known to strike out at people when he lost control. Once he had heard two men at a party speaking ill of his father and had knocked the first man out and put the other in the hospital before he came to his senses and realized that what the two men had said was not that bad. He was known for the flares of temper concealed beneath his quiet exterior, and the wisest thing to do now was to let him calm himself down; by the time he thought of a way to undo what José Ramón had done yesterday, Juan Alberto's anger would have been turned into another kind of energy and it would be safe to talk to him.

In the meantime on the gold sofa José Ramón watched the ceiling and thought about other things. Though he was shorter and more bullish-looking than his brother, he didn't like fights. He would do almost anything to avoid one. The thing he had done yesterday wasn't important, but it could have consequences. It had seemed to him an intelligent move to make at the time—he had waited with pride to inform Juan Alberto of it this morning—but his brother was only shocked and disgusted with him. They had been arguing since dawn.

"I wish I could understand it," his brother said now.

"*Bueno.*"

"Don't tell me again it's good," Juan Alberto said. "It isn't good."

José Ramón sighed and looked straight up. "I'm not telling you anything," he said. "I'm not even moving."

"Better." Juan Alberto made a new fingerprint in the

glass. "Why couldn't you have done that yesterday afternoon?"

José Ramón lay still and didn't answer. He reached to the table beside him for a cigarette and then changed his mind and left it there. Next to the package of American cigarettes was an ash tray and next to that was a brand-new Leica and twelve cartridges of exposed film. The room was silent for a while and Juan Alberto came over and sat down again. He crossed his arms.

"*Juanito*," José Ramón said, "I watched him. He was taking pictures all week. Every time he saw them, he took a picture of them. On the terrace and in the hotel, he took a picture. Lieutenant . . . what's his name . . ."

"Donahue."

". . . took a picture of them doing everything."

His brother looked at him.

"Not that," José Ramón said, "all right, not that. Only he would have if he'd seen it. He was acting like a spy. I wouldn't have minded so much about the pictures of *papá* and Alice. It was when I saw him in Sanlúcar taking one of *papá* with those workers. You said yourself *papá* could get into trouble meeting with those workers. It looks too much like a political meeting. You said so . . ."

"Only if it's a large meeting. And if the police notice it."

"But don't you see? Donahue took a picture of it. He was all the way over in Sanlúcar."

"Because of the Guzmán palace, for God's sake. It's an official historical monument, all kinds of tourists go there. Donahue's taken pictures of everything there is to see along the coast, all the way up and all the way down. It's all he talks about. That and sex. The only reason he took photographs of *papá* was because he's never seen a count before. He's an *American*, for God's sake."

"How was I to know . . ."

"Know what?" Juan Alberto said loud, standing up again. "What was there to know? You didn't think Donahue would report the theft to the hotel? You didn't think Holtz would start an investigation?"

"I don't know what I thought. I was thinking about Donahue. I thought he worked for the C.I.A."

"But you are ridiculous. You are a comedy. Donahue? . . . The Central Intelligence Agency of the United States? The C.I.A. is bad," Juan Alberto said. "They aren't *that* bad. They employ ignorant people. . . . Not cretins."

"*Papá* says . . ."

"Never mind what *papá* says. . . . He thinks of the C.I.A.

the way he thinks of the Communist Party. *Papá* thinks both extremes are after him. The Fascists *and* the Communists ... *Papá* doesn't know."

"Aren't both extremes after him?"

"If they aren't, they will be by the time he gets through. I spend all my time trying to keep *papá* from talking, and while he's talking, you're stealing cameras. It's a joke, *por Dios.* Who would believe it? It's a bad joke. . . ."

"I'll go out now and put the camera back," José Ramón said after a moment.

"Won-der-ful," Juan Alberto said in English.

"Por qué no?"

"So someone can see you putting it back, and we can *really* be in trouble."

"Nobody saw me take it."

"You mean you hope nobody did. You don't know yet. You only took it yesterday, and you only told me about it this morning. The point is, what are we to do?"

". . . I'm thinking."

"No," Juan Alberto said. "Please God no. Whatever we do, if you love *papá* and if you love me and if you love Spain. Don't think."

Juan Alberto turned and went back to the window.

José Ramón sighed. He coughed once and then shut his eyes and rolled over, facing the back of the gold sofa. The sound of the cough was sharp, like a little pistol going off in the room. Juan Alberto did not turn again from the window.

After that the two men stayed where they were without moving like two figures in a painting, and for a long time the villa was quiet again.

Across the ten meters of lawn on the other side of the malignant-looking bush the young man who called himself Jim Lepard from New York sat alone on the wide pink sofa staring emptily at a plate of fried eggs. They were gelatinous and the waiter who had brought them had forgot the salt and pepper. The two yolks had been staring back at Jim Lepard for some time and it was from watching them that he had realized how bad his hangover was. The details of last night's fiasco had come back to him in a clear picture and his stomach felt like the hidden underwater place where the Mediterranean became the Atlantic.

Jim Lepard lifted his eyes away from the eggs and glanced at the empty sofa to his left, expecting to see twenty little men with pitchforks stabbing each other. He imagined a hangover from delirium tremens would look like that. He had tried once long ago out of curiosity to drink himself into a state of delirium tremens but nothing had come of it. He had never seen mice or rats or spiders or even twenty little men with pitchforks stabbing each other. When he was in shape he could drink a great deal, and all he ever saw when he was drunk was his friends. Only, life had treated Jim Lepard in a silly way, and those of his friends who didn't remind him of mice or rats or spiders did remind him of twenty little men with pitchforks stabbing at each other. The rich one in Madrid who was keeping him down here for the summer was a decorator who reminded him of all four. Jim Lepard had come to Suelo to spend the summer being healthy and getting a tan and the sun had disappeared the week he arrived, and he felt sicker this morning than he had ever felt in his life. The hotel concierge had taken one look at him the day he checked in, and—with a straight face—had put him in the pink villa. It had made him laugh at the time. Only he wasn't laughing this morning. One of Jim Lepard's projects for the summer was to see if he couldn't find one person who wasn't either homosexual or insane. He had it figured, he was twenty-three years old and those of his close acquaintances who were not out-and-out fags were potential ax murderers; so he had decided to stop drinking for a while and try to get along with some straight people who didn't know the gay life or anything about it. He had been on the wagon for a month up to last night, and except for his lover visiting him on the weekends, and once or twice a nocturnal fling with a beach boy, he had been circumspect in his behavior at the hotel. His lover always accused him of cruising—of casing all the men in the hotel with his eyes—but it wasn't true. Except for the American lieutenant and the Spanish lifeguard and maybe one of Count Guzmán's two sons, he hadn't noticed anybody. He had looked for straight people in the hotel, but most of them were middle-aged and dreary. Last night he had given up and ordered a vodka martini in the hotel bar, feeling rather alone and hopeless. On the third martini, he had started to talk to a French couple sitting next to him—and they in turn had begun talking to a Spanish couple. It had been magic. Both men and both women spoke English and all four were very nice good-hearted straight young people. He had bought drinks for them, they had all decided to dine together and they had sat at a round table and made him the center of attention. After the wine with dinner they had benedictine; then they had gone back to the bar and sat at a table there and tried a special vintage Spanish brandy. Jim

Lepard's heart had melted for these new friends and they all made plans to go sailing together when the weather cleared. He could tell that they liked him. When the brandy came, he had stood up to make a toast to his new friends and they had applauded even before he began. Then he had raised his glass, and while he was trying to think of something to say for the occasion that would express his great love, he opened his mouth and threw up on the tablecloth. Because he had been on the wagon, the rich food and the liquor had clashed inside him and there had been no warning in his system. As a child he had been given to projectile vomiting and when he threw up it happened with such thrust that it refracted like light from the table and spattered all over his four new friends. Without another word he had gone running, stumbling out of the bar, and had continued until he was half a kilometer west of the town in an empty field. He had pitched himself down in the field and beat at the weeds with his fists. He was so ashamed that he tore up two handfuls of weeds and buried his face in them. Then he ran all the way back to the pink villa carrying the two fistfuls of weeds, and locked the door. He had gone to bed drunk and angry and had sobbed himself to sleep. Now in the morning he sat on the pink sofa and looked at the two neat handfuls of leafy weeds beside him. He did not need to look at them to know what they were. When he had got up to brush his teeth before ordering breakfast, he had seen his face in the mirror over the washbasin and he hadn't even been able to laugh. It was too perfect to laugh at. He had come running back to the villa last night in a drunken tragic rage, crying as if his heart would break and clutching two huge handfuls of *fala* grass. It was the only thing in Europe he was allergic to and it had exactly the same effect as poison ivy.

He got up and went in the bathroom again and looked at his face. The red raised area included his nose and one cheek and half his forehead. His hands were red too and all of it was beginning to itch like sin. What was there about this hotel, he wondered, that he had had to come here; he could have perfectly well stayed in Atlanta five years ago. He didn't have to leave and go and live first in New York and then Paris and then Madrid and then come down here to Suelo in order to throw up on four strangers in a bar and rub poison grass in his face. He didn't have to live in a pink villa halfway between a pair of good-looking Spanish brothers who were straight, and a little American boy named Will who was at that age where he was attracted sexually to both straight and gay people and didn't even know it yet. You didn't need those things. You didn't have to be in a place where you sat on the terrace and watched an American lieutenant parade around in nothing but a pair of trunks looking like Hercules. And you didn't need to have a lifeguard come every day and ask you if you wanted skin-diving lessons, wearing a bikini with a bulge in front that made the blood drain out of your face. Life was easier than that. The day you were born you could just take a flying shit in the wind and get it over with. But why the Hotel Malage? And why had he come to Suelo?

Why?

He went back into the living room and sat down and poured himself a cup of tepid coffee. Then when the nausea had gone he called his friend in Madrid and told him not to come for two weekends until his face had cleared up. After that he began quietly to eat the stony-cold flat fried eggs.

THE MAIN thing he couldn't understand now was about her. How it had come to be the other way around. It was like he was the one who couldn't sleep now while she could.

He lay in bed every night waiting for her to come back from Sanlúcar and all the people in the hotel turned slowly in his mind like faces on this big wheel. The people he mostly saw on the wheel were Eugenia the maid; his mother Helen; the tall lieutenant with the big muscles; the Count's two sons; and the young man named Jim in the pink villa next door. And, always, Littlejohn and the Count. The faces flashed at him with different expressions as the wheel turned and it went on turning almost all night and into the morning.

He was sitting now curled in a chair in the blue living room waiting, but the wheel wouldn't disappear till she came home and he could let himself go and doze off during the day. But the strange landscape he had felt trapped in before—the one he had thought was ended when she came back that evening in the white dress—wasn't ended at all. That was only one picture in the mosaic he had seen. There were others. The mosaic of facts was going on around him now in August worse than ever, like a senseless mess with bits of color and events and jagged edges that didn't fit anywhere—and those faces staring at each other in his head.

He looked down at the dog sleeping at the foot of the chair. Sneakers was filled out and beginning to look healthy even though the short scrubby hair and feathery tail would always give him the appearance of a mismatched creature with one eye. The muscles of the eyeless socket were twitching as if a fly had lit on it. There was no fly. The dog was dreaming.

Will put his hands behind his neck and cracked it and then put his head back trying to figure out which of the faces on the wheel was the one that bothered him the worst. It wasn't only Littlejohn—though the thing between her and the Count had knocked him around in a way you couldn't put into sentences. It had shaken and thrown Will's heart back to earlier times that he hadn't ever been able to make sense with, so it went straight back to his father's body being lost before he was born. The other day he had gone and asked Helen for the old picture of his father in uniform, but she had left it in a trunk in New Orleans. Sometimes now, he imagined it in a stupid way, with his father's head at the top of the tall lieutenant's body. Why, he wondered, was there any point in looking some other way if you could have a build like Lieutenant Donahue? His father must have thought so too, he thought. Only it didn't seem to him his father's body had been clearly that big and massive in the photograph. When he considered about his father being spindly and thin like himself it gave him this sick twisted terrible feeling.

Once he had started to go up on the beach and ask the lieutenant if he had always had a build like that or if he had built it up on purpose, but the words had choked in his throat. It was like he didn't really want to know the answer. The whole thing threw him, the whole subject. Only he couldn't ever seem to quit thinking about it. Every time he quit, back came the mosaic and the wheel of faces. Then he always wound up like this, waiting for Littlejohn to come so the faces would go away.

His head hurt now thinking of it. Littlejohn was very late this morning; she had been coming back later and later every day. Sitting in the blue chair half asleep, he thought dizzily of himself in his father's uniform. It was too big on him and it was baggy around his shoulders. He looked loose in it and gawky. He made up a song in his mind about himself.

William Charles Locke Junior, on the earth between. Who knew. The song began like that.

Then it went:

The horror of walking between.

Always born between.

To sleep is still between.

Always—is—between. Then:

It's like this, listen. I will sing it in my sleep. Listen and I will tell it to you now. Carefully in my sleep, Father.

Out of death, into death.

By death.

But it isn't death.

It's the horror of walking between.

Called life.

Will scrounged down into the chair and stuck his knees around his head like pincers. The song didn't have any end.

IT WASN'T the way she had always imagined it. Not like soaring on a cushion of water or of air, like being a whale or a bird. Lying next to him it was more as if she were floating in his bones. Littlejohn wanted to stay awake. She didn't want to lose any of it and that was what was ridiculous—not having been able completely to sleep for two years, now that the nightmare was gone and she could, she didn't want to.

She tried to pull herself out of it, to lie and think of the days and nights since she had walked downstairs into the hotel bar—but it was no use. Her thinking was relaxed and lazy, flowing into a great dark tunnel of unconsciousness. They had made love most of the night. Dimly in the distance now she heard someone walking on the roof over their heads. One of the workmen probably. Tomorrow, today, she must ask him. Morning footsteps over their heads. Who would walk over them?

She sank hard into her sleeping. Not wanting to. Remembering.

The last time they had made love he had stayed inside her.

He touched her now, his hand down flat over the arch of her back onto her buttocks, and even in her sleep she could feel the movement. She woke again lazily. She moved against him thinking Yes. Show me. No words. She moved against him nuzzling and felt him growing. Then there was the burning of the bones. It was as if the rest of him were melting away from the heat inside him and there was nothing left but the fire of the bones.

Yes, she thought, I will use the words.

Then she could feel the wild bones. A skeleton's a lie. No cock.

No death. No cock. No life. Just the plain burning of the bones.

Afterwards, he took it out and this time cupped her face with the bones below his neck and she lay there floating.

157

With the great deep heat and no need for cold, but safe and wild there in his bones. The leftover fire. The burning out of structure. Why don't skeletons have throats? Why don't skeletons have cocks?

She lay there drifting in his bones.

Then she felt herself sinking again, and this time she yanked her mind out of it. She flipped over and backed up to him, folding one of his arms around her onto her breast. She was facing the window; through a space in the draperies she could see the blooming pale color of the early day. The distant white was stretched like something that could wrinkle or tear, like new tissue paper over the sky. It reminded her of the white dress. The dress she had put on when she had become somebody else: the old-new white dress she had never worn before that day, though she had carried it with her for two years. At the beauty parlor that afternoon she had seen her own eyes in the mirror while they were washing her hair. She had known there was no point in running away. That had been the full extent of her thinking about it. After the beauty parlor she had gone back to the empty blue villa as if it were the most natural thing, and unpacked the dress and put it on, and ever since then she had not been the same person. Something in her had withered and flowered again from wearing the white dress, from walking down the staircase of the bar to the table where he was. She could think now—she was awake enough. Drowsing lightly and holding onto his arm, with him behind her she could remember that other morning. That very other morning. The one so long ago.

The morning after she had first put on the white dress.

She lay there thinking in his bones.

Helen hadn't been in the red villa that morning.

It was the day after the night in the bar and Littlejohn had been sure it would happen that day. She was even sure how: it would happen without his knowing. He would wonder afterwards why he had done it—had ever had the blindness to do it. There would be some very bad moments afterwards for him and she would have to get him through them. Because of his innocence, his blindness, she had thought (but never thought of the white-blind bones), and because he didn't know.

That morning she herself was the only one who knew that they were going to be lovers. Except for Will. And except for Helen.

But Helen wasn't in the red villa.

Littlejohn had gone to see her mother early in the morning and found the villa empty except for the maids. Normally Helen wouldn't be gone so early. Unless she didn't want any more confrontations and had guessed Littlejohn might come. Because all that Littlejohn and Guzmán had done in the bar the night before was to look at each other—a flat hard look. He hadn't even touched her. Helen knew that too.

The door of Helen's villa was open and the two maids, Eugenia and the young one, were mopping the red tile floor. The room had a faint sharp odor that was a mixture of coffee and soap suds and sun on paint. Littlejohn pointed to the bedroom door, but Eugenia shook her head.

Littlejohn tried a few words in Spanish. *"Donde . . . está . . . mi madre?"* she asked.

Eugenia didn't laugh. She nodded and took Littlejohn's hand and led her out of the red villa. Then she pointed to the main building and said too loud, imitating Littlejohn's American accent, *"Terraza del juego."* She was pointing at the terrace where games were played. *"Gracias,"* Littlejohn said.

"De nada. Con Dios, Señorita," Eugenia said.

Littlejohn found Helen playing canasta on the terrace with Mrs. Lawson. She was sure then that Helen had been expecting her and only wanted to avoid being alone with her: Helen never played canasta before eleven, and nobody could take much of Mrs. Lawson in the morning.

Bird beak was by herself in the far corner of the terrace pouting into a magazine. You could see she wanted to make peace and join the game—she hadn't spoken to Helen since she had stalked up to her room that time.

Helen was concentrating hard on her cards. She didn't look over as Littlejohn approached.

It was a clear day, the only day of blue sky that had interrupted the *foreño* at all, and you could see it wasn't going to last. Littlejohn breathed deep in it.

"Good morning," she said.

"Hello," Mrs. Lawson said.

Helen said absently, "You've taken to wearing white . . . that's a pretty linen dress. You looked lovely in the bar last night; everyone thought so. Have you had coffee? Your draw," she said to Mrs. Lawson.

"Pretty white shoes too," Mrs. Lawson said, "get them here?"

"Yes—in town."

She sat down.

"You must have been in town a long time yesterday," Helen said, drawing a card.

"I had my hair done and did some shopping."

". . . William thought you were leaving."

"Yes," Littlejohn said. "I changed my mind."

Helen and Mrs. Lawson went on playing cards.

"May I talk to you for a minute, Mother?"

"Certainly," Helen said. "Go right ahead; this isn't like bridge. I can listen and play at the same time. Is William up?"

"He's at the bungalow, getting dressed. He's coming with us. We're going for a ride. . . . Guzmán's going to show us the palace."

"Guzmán," Mrs. Lawson said. "She calls him Guzmán."

"William *too? . . . Is* that wise? . . . I still can't see if those are five sixes or six," Helen said to Mrs. Lawson.

"I'd like to talk to you alone," Littlejohn told her.

"Oh heavens," Mrs. Lawson said, ". . . don't mind me. I'm a grave. You call him Guzmán?"

"Even William calls him that," Helen said. "He asked us to. It's his name." Smooth as silk.

Littlejohn got up. After a while, when Helen saw that she was not going to leave, Helen got up too, on the pretext of finding a clean ash tray, and paused for a moment beside her. "I only wanted to make sure," Littlejohn said.

Helen waited.

"That you weren't . . . you know. I mean that you and he. . . ." She stopped. Helen had not spoken.

"No," Helen said. "We're not sleeping together." She turned away and sat down again.

Littlejohn watched her. "All right," she said, "I'll come talk to you later."

"I think . . ." putting a card down, ". . . that might be the best time. . . . Yes. You can't take that pack, it's frozen."

"I didn't see the joker," Mrs. Lawson said.

"Yes, when you come back from your ride with the Count we'll talk if you *like,*" Helen said. "Then maybe we'll have something to talk *about.* It's still frozen."

"I wasn't going to take it," Mrs. Lawson said.

Littlejohn waited. "Juan Alberto . . ."

". . . is in the lobby," Helen said, "I know where he is, I can see him from here. Have a nice day." She looked at Littlejohn. "And take care of yourself."

Littlejohn stopped. It was like a brick wall. "First time you've ever told me to take . . ."

"Yes. There's a first time for everything," Helen said, "that's what I mean . . . do take care. You'll want to know you have later."

"That's kind of you."

"No it isn't. Run along."

"Sometimes I don't understand a word you two are saying," Mrs. Lawson said. "I swear you both talk some kind of special language I don't talk. . . ."

Helen said, "It's called English."

Littlejohn laughed.

"Another first," Helen said, without looking up. "I don't as a rule amuse you. You look lovely. I can see why. Did you really think you had to come and tell me?"

"No. But . . ."

"Or ask my permission to go for a ride," Helen said, "or my permission for *anything?* I might accept rudeness from you—even cruelty. But not impertinence. Don't you think I know when things are done? You're not the sort of person who needs a make-believe lecture, and I don't give them. The only one who's seriously involved is the mother of the boys. . . . Think about *her,* it's worth it. If *I'd* had any personal interest, if I'd been seriously involved, it might be different. . . . But then it would be up to me to come and see you . . . not that I would; it's not my style. Those are just the rules of the game. As it happens I wasn't serious at all . . . game's over, I'm going down . . ."

"Damn," Mrs. Lawson said.

". . . so have a nice day."

"What are you going to do?"

"I'll think of something," Helen said.

"See you later."

"Of course. Just take care. It's your shuffle."

Littlejohn left her and went through the lobby. The forty-color tile mosaics along the walls and on the floor of the main building had been washed. They sparkled like stones under water. She could see Guzmán now. He was standing waiting for her with Will on the outside of the main building on the lawn. His eyes looked like the day.

She walked faster but before she was halfway across the lobby Juan Alberto stopped her—standing behind a pillar looking at postcards.

"Going with my father to visit the palace?" The kind of smile they call engaging. Shorts and a tennis shirt; carrying a tennis racquet. White teeth and dark skin. Born under the sign of a toothpaste commercial. An annoying man.

But she liked everybody today.

"Yes," she said. "You playing tennis?"

"Yes." Juan Alberto sneaked a look. Quick empty eyes down her skirt. Not like his father.

"With your brother José?"

"No; José's going with William and my father and you." Smile. "José Ramón often goes horseback riding out there, at the palace."

"Why have you three been living here at the hotel if the palace is so close?"

"We wait for the plasterers to finish. My father forgets to take care of it . . . it's in disrepair. This summer it is being fixed and painted, so for a while we stay here." Half-smile. "I had thought to ask your mother if *she* plays tennis. . . . Would you see that Father eats, please?" Juan Alberto said, low. Automatically—not in a special voice or even especially to her. Just anybody who was going out with Guzmán.

"I'll feed him," she said.

"Good." Good-bye smile. Still Eight by Ten Glossy. Repeat chorus: Stay glossy in color. Brush with Pep So Dent.

She walked into the day.

So this is the way it's going to be, she thought. Radio announcement: The fearless feeding of the fathers is an institution in the western world, from church to zoo, family to family, mother to daughter. . . . Do not throw peanuts. Feeding times are posted. Wean your child and save your teat. For where it counts.

Stay happy. Un-radio.

Then they were at the palace. That morning was the very first time she saw it. It was hard to remember now that there had been a time when she hadn't known it.

They went through it following him, room by room. The official tour: Guzmán leading the way—she walking behind with Will and José Ramón. All of them pretending there was nothing else in the air. Just a walk in the palace. If you could call it a palace. . . .

It had been declared an historical monument by the Spanish government. He explained as they went along. The Guzmán palace had been in Sanlúcar since the fourteenth century and it had always been called the Guzmán palace. It was one of the drabbest- and plainest-looking buildings she had ever seen. Most of the original bricks were covered by thick plaster. Twice in earlier centuries it had had to be restored, and now it badly needed repairs. It was white inside and out and it looked dirty. But most of all it just looked plain. He, the present Count, was not the kind of man who noticed when things around him needed repairing— or when a stone wall began to fall apart slowly down a hill. After his wife and he had drifted apart (he had not noticed either when it was that she had actually left him) he had let the palace go, until the damp cold winters and the scorching summers had turned it into a cracked-plaster thing, two wings of many rooms that lay spread out on the hill like a big broken bird. The view was the only attractive part about it. The palace was built on the highest hill in Sanlúcar, a kind of cliff overlooking the town and the mouth of the Guadalquivir River. From any one of the three long terraces you could see the slow rushing of brown and quick green where the river slipped into the sea. The cliff was on the east bank of the river, and across the water you could see the province of Huelva—white sand and silver-colored brush that went on endlessly into a game preserve that had once belonged to the Guzmán family, until one day when the nineteenth count, three counts back, Juan de Guzmán's great-grandfather, had got drunk and gambled it away on the turn of a card. The game preserve in Huelva belonged to someone else now, not a titled family, just a family that had had a great-grandfather who was lucky at cards. But the family had tended it well and it was stunning to see from the terraces of the palace, the endless drifting sand and the dull silver bushes of the preserve that was said by some to have belonged once to the lost continent of Atlantis. When the wind shifted hard or winter rains were strong, the sands moved; sometimes strange bits of pottery and coins of unknown origin, worn flat and unreadable by time and the weather, were found there. But here on this side of the river the palace stuck up brokenly in the air, big and awkward, cool in the summer, with walls of stone and falling plaster, and under it, an unkempt little woods of tangled trees. There was one huge tree just outside the main patio on the cliff—a tree that was as big as an ordinary house—umbrella-shaped and top-heavy, more than a century old. You could see the great tree from many windows of the palace. It was almost too top-heavy with green. The tree looked like a held breath. It spread out into a vast protective growth of green beyond the stone and some of the longer branches scraped the ground. The people along the coast called it the Columbus tree, because the seed it had grown from came from other trees like it that had themselves grown in the small woods below—and the seeds of those trees had been brought back from America by Christopher Columbus.

The second Count Guzmán and Columbus had been close friends; that Count had stood here, on a terrace of this same palace, and watched when Columbus took his ships out of the Sanlúcar harbor for his second voyage to the New World. Then as a gift to that Count, Columbus had brought back certain animals and plants, and these seeds, the ancestral seeds of this great tree. So the story went. But the people along the coast did not think of the tree as a descendant. For them, the great tree, the Columbus tree, had grown from a seed that was itself brought back by him personally. Columbus, they believed, had planted it. You could not convince them otherwise. It was true that the tree kept on growing even when one of its branches rotted and dropped off. The tree was considered in Sanlúcar to have strange properties and it was said that the spirits who lived inside it could grant requests for poor people if they had a mind to. Some said the tree had a certain grace that could work as magic, for good or for evil. People did not often come to see it, because, combined with their reverence, there was awe and a kind of fear of the tree in the town. It was rumored that its leaves were unhealthy and it was said that they had been used, in an earlier century, by former members of the Guzmán family, to do away with other members who were not wanted. The story may or may not have been accurate but it had the ring of truth; it was in the great Spanish tradition for members of the same noble families to do away with each other, for political reasons or because of jealousy or just for money. . . .

So Guzmán told it that morning, while Littlejohn and Will wandered in the palace, through the rooms that were full of shadow and summer dust. The white gloom, the white plain walls that echoed now with their own footsteps and voices and the loud buzzing of flies. There was the odor of olive oil from cooking somewhere inside and the dust and the sea on the terrace. Room by room they saw it, the white broken-plaster dream, the two wings, his own and the guest wing where his sons slept when they stayed. The servants were a family of three that grinned and then peered suspiciously as Littlejohn and Will walked through. Then Guzmán showed them the Columbus tree with its huge majestic branches of leaves; he showed them the bedrooms and the Ambassador's Room and the other big *salas* that had been used for occasions of state in other times. Then finally he showed them his private family archives, as a gesture of trust, the rows upon rows, shelves after shelves, stacks after stacks of letters his ancestors had written and received:

the diaries and business accounts and wars and memoranda and threats and love notes and menus and diets and plots and charts and maps and the other infinitely varied, infinitesimal jottings that were all that was left now of nearly ten centuries of living, of birth and death, of sex and money, of dullness and violence, of pettiness and purpose, of being and not being year after year after year.

Then that morning they, Littlejohn and Guzmán, walked alone along the cracked tiles and scattered plaster of the third floor terrace beside the room where the piled-up archives were kept. They stopped at the terrace ledge. The sky was clouding and the wind came in thin short bursts off the sea. Guzmán stood on her right, partly behind her.

Underneath them in the east corner of the garden Will and José Ramón were mounting two saddled horses. Littlejohn smiled down at them.

The garden below was as plain as the palace, ragged and burnt by the sun except for a rectangle of short flowers the cook cultivated. The cook's husband worked as groom in the four-horse stable; he was holding the horses now for Will and José Ramón. Will waved up at Littlejohn and she waved back. Behind her Guzmán had been talking.

". . . like that. Every year she would come still to see me once or twice; though she knew I could not make a life for her. With things as they are in the world, who has time to believe in something and still have that kind of life? You see?"

She nodded.

"*Es así.* Some think to be a duke or a count you must only be born. But it is not. Even as small as a count, you must *be* a count . . . you are liable for those who are not. There are many, and the way things are they have no lives— but even worse than that, they do not know they have no lives. But some *know.* It's for those one fights. She cannot comprehend this; it is not my wife's way of thinking. She also was born a countess but she is like the others. So every year she would come to see if I had changed. Do you know what I am saying?"

Littlejohn nodded. "Your wife doesn't understand you," she said.

". . . That is a part of it."

"It's the part I'm familiar with," she said, "the lyrics are a little different, but the music's the same. I had to come three thousand light-years for a man who makes love to me by talking about his wife."

"Am I making love to you?"

"Yes."

"Oh," he said.

The horses were prancing like live chess pieces back and forth below in the overgrown garden. Will's had a high pretty step. Will waved again.

"Nice arch."

"Excuse me?"

"The horse."

"Oh."

"Should they ride all the way back to the hotel?"

"It is not so far as it seems to the hotel, straight across the fields; José Ramón is a good horseman, he will be careful with your brother. Are you aware that I am old enough to be your father?"

"It's the other part of the song. Yes," she said. "Or grand-father."

"We should leave with them now."

"No."

Guzmán said, "I think so."

José Ramón waved and Littlejohn waved. Guzmán waved.

"Harder."

"I cannot press against you like that."

"Why not?"

"I cannot explain. I am in bad conditions."

"Yes," she said. "That's what I want. The bad conditions."

"You are not good."

"No. Lord no."

"This is most bad."

"Yes," she said.

"You must not lean back, they will see."

". . . Show me."

The horses were trotting now; José Ramón's broke into a canter and Will's followed him out of the gate. The gardener had turned and was looking up at her and Guzmán, watching them. It was the drabbest-looking garden imaginable. The air was turning gustier from the sea. When Guzmán stepped back from her she nearly fell.

"Please show me."

"Are you very sure?"

"I don't have to be sure."

"I should say to them we are working in the archives . . . they mustn't think you are that kind of woman, the servants . . ."

"I don't care what the servants think."

"I am not so much an aristocrat as that."

"I'll teach you," she said. "Show me."

". . . I think it is the first time for you."

"It's never the first time," Littlejohn said.

"I will hurt you?"

"Yes."

"We will stop this very silly talk now and we will go back to the hotel with the boys."

"If you start that again, I'll turn," she said, "and I'll scream."

"You would not do that."

She turned.

"All right," he said.

Then they were in the bedroom and she stood near a chair by the white curtains. He stood across the room from her near the door. She could smell the heavy draperies. The room needed dusting. Reddish brown. One ugly tapestry. Dark wood and old blood. "Lock it," she said.

"I think not. This is most wrong."

She unbuttoned her blouse.

"You will not convince me . . ."

She took her blouse off and unzipped her skirt.

"All right," he said.

He waited while she stepped out of her skirt and he pushed the door back and shot the bolt. He stayed where he was, across the room.

"Please," she said.

"Please what? I have not kissed you yet. How is it I have not even kissed you? This is a strange way to begin a love affair. You make it seem on purpose that you are seducing me. You are very young to make me seem so young."

"Listen," she said. "I don't know how. Show me."

He made one step forward and the muscles down his legs went hard inside his pants. Then he said something to her but a pulse had begun to beat in her ears and she couldn't hear him.

She waited.

"This is not the way—I know how two people begin. It is not like this," he said.

She waited again.

"Without kissing you first I will take you to bed in the daylight?"

"Yes, if you want."

"I'm not sure," he said, "what I want."

"Yes you are."

"Yes," he said. "I am."

He stood there and took his hunter's jacket off, and she took her slip off. She took all the rest of her clothes off and put them on a chair. He went on undressing and he watched her.

Then they were both standing all the way across the room from each other. He looked silly: he still had his socks on. The skeleton with socks. He stood there—in his bones and his muscles and his socks. "I have never seen anything like you," he said. "In all my life. The women I have known are not like you."

"Am I too thin?"

"Yes," he said. "We are too thin for each other."

"Please show me now."

"Don't keep saying that; I'm going to hurt you a great deal, probably."

"When?"

"I don't know. I have never talked so much about it . . . I shall walk across to you and hurt you now."

"Take off your socks first."

"Yes?"

"Please."

"You don't mind my not kissing you—you don't mind my hurting you. But you mind the socks?"

"Yes," she said.

He took the socks off and still looked like some bones dressed in heavy muscles. Huge bones. Flat sheaths of muscle and a linked-together body. He looked at her. "I've never made love this way."

"I've never made love," she said.

"Am I ugly?"

"Probably."

"We make a strange couple."

"Any two people," Littlejohn said, "make a strange couple."

He started to walk toward her slowly. "Do you know what you are going to do when I touch you now?"

"I'm going to die," she said.

Then there were the days and the nights of it. At first they were careful about the servants and they made sure Littlejohn was seen every morning early at the hotel; but little by little they stopped being so guarded. It was all they could manage to keep from doing it wherever they were—outside in the garden, on the terrace, even under the Columbus tree. After a while she began to feel very wise and at the same time stupid—a sort of old-new woman, but old and new at the same time, like the white dress. At the palace the three servants had become used to her—María, the cook, came to her at all hours with questions about what they would like to eat. She was careful only to suggest meals—never to order them. But still it was strange to think of a time when she had not lived here, even though officially she was still living now back at the beach hotel.

So far—aside from being with Guzmán—she had done only one thing. She had composed a long letter to E. J. Williams breaking their engagement and explaining her position in a way that he would understand or at least accept; she had written and mailed the letter, but apart from it she hadn't thought a lot about the future. She had not had time to examine the new person she had become. She couldn't catch her breath long enough. There were never enough minutes to be alone, and when they were they couldn't keep their hands off each other. Once in the middle of lunch in the palace dining room in a silence they had looked at one another and had just stood up. They left the food and she had run ahead of him all the way into his bedroom in the other wing, undoing her skirt as she ran.

She knew that it was time now to think and plan with him. The life of an aristocrat would take some getting used to, even if she wasn't expected to be completely a part of it. Guzmán spent his mornings alone upstairs in the family archives, translating old letters and documents from early Castilian or Arabic into modern Spanish. Apart from the politico-historical newspaper or magazine articles he sometimes published outside of Spain, with the help of the archives, he was writing a book about one of his ancestors—a man who had been a kind of eighteenth-century rebel whose thinking had been something like his own. The Guzmán archives had never been fully collated; they were carefully locked and guarded in one section of the palace attic. Officials of the current regime had several times asked to come in and organize the old documents for him. In the process, he knew, they would destroy any documents which disproved or disagreed with their own political philosophy. The regime had long been known for its whitewashing of Spanish history; a distorted version was now taught in the schools. Officials had already visited and censored several family archives belonging to the old nobility; the owners didn't seem to care one way or the other. Guzmán cared, and no one was allowed to visit the room where his archives were kept—including the occasional foreign historians who came especially to see them—unless he accompanied the visitors.

But the archieves were only the smallest part of his daily routine. In the afternoons he received visitors from all along the coast—old friends and new ones—poor people who needed advice and who knew that Guzmán could be trusted not to report them to the government. He had become a kind of symbol of freedom to men who otherwise might have been afraid to act. He had been instrumental in the forming of two *cooperativas,* cooperative organizations that forced a raise in pay for fishermen who had been working for less than survival wages. Guzmán had many friends along the coast; some even considered themselves his followers, though he had never pretended to any political ambition. He received them just as in past centuries his ancestors had received tenants with complaints about crops or taxes or neighbors; he listened to their problems gravely and gave what simple advice he could; it was not always much, but at least it made them feel better. It was said that people who left the palace always left with a greater sense of freedom than they had when they came in.

So his life went, and Littlejohn was now a part of it. Now lying with her back to him, she again took his sleeping hand, long and warm, and held it against her thigh. She liked his heavy bones against her shoulders. It was well into the morning. She could still hear the footsteps over them. There was something wrong about the sound she couldn't put her mind on—something almost frightening.

It was past time now for her to leave for the hotel. The light from the window was pale and crushed-looking and it was getting thicker.

It was time to get up, she knew. It was day.

FOUR

Eugenia

WILL yawned. The wheel of faces slowed down in his mind, and stopped.

He stretched in the chair and began to think now of the horseback ride. He thought: Sometimes I have to wonder what is happening right this moment in China.

It was like him and José Ramón that day galloping. Leaving the palace. Not letting José Ramón know he was crying —wiping it off on the back of his arm, thunder under him, a clear sky. Guh-*shuck* guh-*shuck* guh-*shuck* in the high green fields and riding the earth away, but leaving her. Leaving them alone. Leaving in the earth and crying but not thinking what was happening to her in the broken-plaster palace. Just guh-*shuck* guh-*shuck* guh-*shuck* guh-*shuck* in the goddamned grass, he in his part of the earth, her in hers. But he in his alone. Not daring to think. Thinking:

What is happening right this moment in China?

And now: Why do they make me have to know her dreams?

He frowned and rubbed his forehead. Then he remembered.

Littlejohn had told him last night that she might not come back this morning, and he had forgotten it. He hadn't liked the idea and he had pushed it right out of his mind. But she had said if she wasn't back by breakfast to catch the coast bus later and come to Sanlúcar for lunch. They would all take a picnic from the palace and go for a drive.

He sat up in the chair and blinked. Then he shook his head hard and stood up. Sneakers clomped his tail but stayed where he was on the blue tile floor.

Will went in the bathroom and put on a pair of pants and a T-shirt. The thought was still in his head what was happening right this moment in China. It was one of his usual morning thoughts; it wasn't new. It scared him a little, but everything scared him a little. He was no longer a tourist. It was as natural to him as breathing now to get up and find himself in Spain. But now, while he was doing these ordinary acts like brushing his teeth right here, somebody way on the other side of the earth in China was doing something else in a place where Will didn't know the language, where it was night. They would never see each other, him and this other person, and yet they were doing different things, standing with the soles of their feet pointing toward the center of the earth from opposite directions. It gave him a crawly sensation inside, as if he had swallowed a spider. Another of his usual thoughts was that every single instant of the day, somebody, somewhere, was having sex. All the time it went on. Sex never stopped, it was just a question of who was having it. The sensation that gave him wasn't a completely bad one, and he sometimes wondered if whoever it was in China that was pointing his feet at him had ever thought of the same thing.

The day was going to be another hot one; the sky looked choked from the bedroom window. He let the dog out the back door and waited, scratching his left calf with the top of his right foot. Sometimes he thought the real way of putting the feeling into words was this: he didn't have a root like other people. He hadn't said it to anybody out loud, not even to Littlejohn, but he sometimes thought it. A person who is growing ought to have some kind of root or he might stop growing, he thought. What he didn't like to consider was it might have already happened to him. It could be the very reason he had this spindly thin look and was so short. He wondered what it would be like to be back in the States, living in some small town where he would recognize everybody and everybody would recognize him. First off they had lived in New Orleans or New York, he and Helen—but as early as he could remember they had taken every vacation in Europe. Then the vacations had got longer—until now he was going to school here. But what about his personal root? He didn't feel like he had one in New York or New Orleans, but he didn't feel like he had one here either. Once he had read about the Sargasso sea where millions of weeds floated free with the tides and it made him think. It was hard to tell this to somebody. He felt like a Sargasso person. Helen thought that his speaking other languages would be good for him—and he didn't mind learning them, they were easy— but they only made the nameless feeling worse. He didn't even have enough root in one language to have an accent in another—right now he could speak three languages just about like a native. Up to now his only personal tie had been Littlejohn. But though he worried about her more than ever it was different and he knew it. It was another unsaid thing between them. She even smelled different now.

Sort of musky. Anyway it looked like he would have to find another root-person for a while at least. He thought he might prefer a man for a root. Littlejohn after all had never had that much of a root either. She had gone from Louisiana to Pennsylvania when she was nine. They were a rootless kind of family when you came to think about it, and Helen didn't like questions—certainly not about *her* parents. She was from New Orleans, and Will's father was born in Biloxi, and that was about all you could get out of her. Helen was a distant person; she always had been, ever since Will could remember. It was Littlejohn who had explained to him about sex—though it was true that once he had discussed sex with Helen too. It was in the middle of the night one time in Paris when he was thinking about this same problem, and he had got up and gone in to Helen who was reading a magazine in bed and had started to ask her about it—but he couldn't find the words and instead he had done a crazy thing. He had asked his mother what position she and his father had used when they had had sexual intercourse and made him. He hadn't known he was going to say it until he heard the words come out of his mouth. Helen had looked down at him from her bed, as startled as he was, and it was the only time in his life he had ever seen his mother laugh without planning on it. The question had caught her off guard; she hadn't laughed long, but the quick rumble had seemed to come from some place inside her he didn't know about, some hidden covered-over root of hers. It was only a short gut-giggle—but he never forgot the sound of it. Then she had straightened her face and said that she didn't remember the position they had used, but he could tell she was lying. She asked him why he needed to know but he couldn't explain. He had just gone back to bed. There wasn't a way of telling her. It all sounded like something else the minute you said it.

Anyway right now there wasn't anybody to say it to. Will hadn't ever made any close friends—he and Helen had always moved too fast. Besides, you couldn't talk to the people you loved about the things that didn't have words for them, let alone to strangers. Except maybe . . .

That was what he had gone to bed thinking last night, and this morning the idea was still with him. Maybe after all it was strangers you should talk to about certain things. He hadn't ever tried. But maybe that was what the wheel of faces was doing in his head all the time. One of them might be a listening person. It wouldn't be such a wonder. Sometimes very simple things happen in very out-of-the-way places. He needed a few facts to be simple—the complicatedness of living was what he minded most about it. He had decided last night that he would get up this morning and go out and just talk to somebody, and even if the words came out wrong he wouldn't care because he wouldn't know the person. Something might come out anyway that would take away some of the crazy feeling that was like being trapped in a mosaic, like being full of nameless things you couldn't say, enormous facts you couldn't touch. The empty hollowness that made you think of subjects like your father's body and wheels of faces. That. Empty and at the same time mingled with big piles of nothing—with clouds and wind like the sky.

Sneakers came back wagging his tail and sat down as if he expected something. He was looking for Littlejohn, Will knew; the dog had grown used to her feeding him his breakfast. Well, he would just have to get *un*used to it. Things were changing for everybody.

Will went onto the porch and opened a can of veal stew he had bought and put it in front of the dog. Sneakers sniffed at it and then nibbled a little, but he kept looking around. Will watched the dog nose the food in a tentative way, and felt a new anger well up in him. It was an odd dark annoyance and it was close to outrage. Even though Littlejohn had warned him, there was something about her not coming back at all that was a personal put-down. It was the worst kind of put-down—the kind you don't have any right to feel—so it was the worst kind of anger, because there was nothing you could do with it but nurse it.

So the hell with it. If you were going to have to walk around all day like that, the hell with it. You might as well find something you *knew* was dangerous as sit home and be safe and be angry. . . .

Will put on his tennis shoes and laced them up fast. You didn't have to be alone. Anything beat that. Even a wheel of faces or talking to one of the faces on the wheel, and knowing beforehand it was the wrong one: even that.

He put a clean handkerchief in his pants pocket and took the dog and marched out his bedroom door and straight across the back lawn.

This time it was Will who left the door to slam in the wind.

The pink villa was unreal looking under the heavy sky. In the gray blowing air it looked as though it was going to fade off the lawn. Will stood on the back porch and rapped with the brass door knocker. From up close you could see the pink paint peeling away in places. The dirty plaster showed through like stains in a shirt. He could feel a pulse in his head beating with leftover anger, and when the door of the pink villa swung back he opened his mouth to speak. What he hadn't bothered to think of was any single way to start the conversation. The man in front of him, Jim Lepard, stood looking down unbelievingly from behind the door; he squeezed his eyes in the air two or three times, apparently hoping if he did it often enough Will would disappear. Part of Jim Lepard's face was a funny shade, pink and blotched looking, as if he might be turning slowly into the color of the villa. He didn't say anything. Will cleared his throat.

"I was wondering," Will said, "if you knew . . ."

The man named Jim Lepard stared at him, and the words faded in Will's mouth. The words were as unreal as the look of the villa on the lawn.

"Yeah?" Jim Lepard said. "If I knew?"

Will sniffed. His mind went gray. He felt stupid, and he wet his mouth.

"I was wondering," he said, "if you could tell me the right time."

Jim Lepard went on staring and didn't answer him for a moment. Will could hear distant voices somewhere behind him and the slow folding wash of the sea.

"The time?" Jim Lepard said. "You want to know the time?"

"That's right," Will said. "The time."

Jim Lepard turned and looked behind the door at the clock on the wall. Then he turned back.

"It's seven-fifteen," he said.

"Oh," Will said. "Thanks." He shuffled his feet.

Jim Lepard didn't move. All at once the mystified expression in his eyes changed, and a strange, insulting look came into them. It wasn't the look that Will had sometimes noticed when Jim Lepard watched him on the lawn from the window. It was more amused than that, and there was something sly about it. It was a wise evil look, as if Jim Lepard not only knew that Will had lied about wanting to find out what time it was—but knew too what it was that Will had truly come over for. He couldn't have, because Will didn't know it himself. But it was that kind of look.

"You're welcome," Jim Lepard said.

"Well," Will said, "thanks again." He turned, his face burning, and went down the porch steps. He didn't hear the door close behind and he could tell that Jim Lepard was standing there watching him walk away. The anger inside him flared up again and he almost did another crazy thing. He almost turned around and yelled back at Jim Lepard. He wanted to make it clear that the man was wrong in whatever he was thinking, that he didn't know at all why Will had come to see him, that Jim Lepard was plain stupid, just that, *stupid*, for even thinking that he knew. It wouldn't have made any sense to turn around and yell it—"You're stupid" —but Will had a feeling that Jim Lepard would have known too exactly what he meant by it, without his saying anything more. So he didn't yell it; he just kept walking. He could feel the hatred in his heart and his whole face burned like fire. He thought that if he had had a pistol at that instant he would have turned around and shot Jim Lepard dead on the porch. He went on walking, the dog loping along beside him, and he stumbled once and almost fell. He caught his balance and he thought he heard Jim Lepard chuckle softly behind him. He would fix the man one day for that—just for that, for the chuckle. He went on with his heart pounding and when he got past the villa he could still feel Jim Lepard's eyes going right through the back of his skull.

He walked faster, around the corner of the villa; then he had to stop while the dog sniffed at the bush on the other side of it. It took at least a minute. Sneakers went back and forth over the territory and finally let a few drops fall under a branch. Since his wounds had healed, the dog had developed a way of being choosy. You wouldn't think he had spent his life outdoors scrounging for food. Now that he had a home he was snobbish about things; he was especially particular about where he urinated. He kept Will waiting while he made his mind up and the six or eight drops were given in grudging little spurts. After that he scratched at the lawn with his back paws as if to cover up the bush that was unworthy of him. Then he paused. He looked at Will, timid and intelligent, and wagged his tail. It was as though even the dog could see through to the thing that was in Will's heart. It wasn't only Jim Lepard. It was the one-eyed dog could see it too.

Will turned and started to walk again in the hot wind toward the gold villa and something happened inside him. It happened very fast and he couldn't tell the reason. The wish to kill Jim Lepard and the shame of the morning melted with the heat into an unnamed different sense, a big feeling that contained both the other feelings but wasn't either one of them alone. The anger appeared again inside him and grew bigger. When it touched the new feeling, something in his groin twitched and an awkward, almost painful shiver of pleasure ran all through his body. It was a cold knifelike twinge, a chill deep in his sex, but in a way he enjoyed it. He went past the back door of the gold villa and around to the front, and he tucked the new feeling into the back of his heart for future reference.

From outside, the gold villa looked better than the pink villa—at least it wasn't spotted. Will saw Juan Alberto standing motionless at the window and he slowed down. Juan Alberto turned to look in his direction. Will shoved his thumbs into the loops of his belt. He smiled. Juan Alberto waved and then a funny thing took place. Juan Alberto froze with his hand still up in the air from waving, and a sharp intense look flickered across his eyes. Will hesitated, one foot near the steps of the villa. He was absolutely sure, without knowing why, that Juan Alberto was about to ask a favor of him. It was the exact opposite of the cold look that Jim Lepard had first given; Will felt an eagerness rise inside him like a thermometer. For a third time today his pulse speeded up a little. Then, with no warning, the memory of the shame came back and he changed his mind. He decided not to stop at the gold villa after all. He quit smiling and looked blank. Purposely fast, he turned his back on the window and went on walking.

He walked hard now, the dog padding firmly at his heels. They went across the front lawn to the entrance of the main building and it wasn't till Will had reached the gravel driveway that he thought better of it. The instant his heel crunched on the gravel it seemed to him he had done the wrong thing again. He had come out with the purpose of talking to somebody, and clearly Juan Alberto had wanted to talk—the sharp look of interest across the man's face had been unmistakable. Will turned back and looked, but there was no one there now. The picture window of the gold villa was empty, skin-colored in the gray light, like a big closed eye. It was too late: it was wrong or it was too late. It was that kind of day.

The dog whined and Will led him around the main building toward the kitchen entrance to see if Eugenia was there. She at least was one of the faces on the wheel he *did* think he could talk to. He went around the beach side first and walked on the terrace. Then he walked under the many-colored balconies by the sea. The sea looked sad and gray. Walking next to it he felt good for the first time all morning. After that he began to feel sorry for himself in a professional movie way. It was like he was standing outside of himself, watching himself. He was just walking along alone by the sea in this tragic movie about a boy with his dog. He was so moved by the picture that tears welled suddenly in his eyes, and the ground ahead of him looked big and blurred. The picture of himself in his mind was stupendous. The sound of the sea was like background music and the tears spilled out of his eyes and ran down his cheeks. Just a boy with his dog, he thought, just a boy with his dog. He felt a sob catch at his throat. The whole world swam violently in front of him, mortified and tilted by the tears, and the half of him that was standing outside of him, watching his performance, nearly burst into applause. Then in the success of the movie he tried another one. The way it was this time he couldn't see anything; he was blind. He had been born like that. It wasn't just a boy with his dog walking by the sea, it was a *blind* boy with his dog, and it wasn't just a dog. It was a seeing-eye dog. He shut his eyes and was reaching down for the harness on the dog's back when he careened off a deck chair and fell sprawling into the center of Sylvia Donahue's breakfast.

There was a light popping noise from the orange juice glass on the tiles and then Will felt something thick and warm trickle on his hand. It felt like blood and then he looked down and saw the crushed egg yolk between his thumb and his first finger. Mrs. Donahue was by herself on the main terrace having her breakfast before the wind got worse; she pulled back as she watched Will. His face on the table was only six inches away from her knees. Sneakers was nosing the two strips of limp Spanish bacon that had fallen next to her and there was a piece of toast clinging to her blouse. Mrs. Donahue picked it off and held it away from her. She studied Will's face while he got up.

"Is it your eyes? Do you have trouble with your eyes?" she said quietly. Her voice was not sarcastic or hard, like it had been whenever Will had heard it before. She spoke in a warm way and there was a niceness in her tone that he would not have connected with her face at all. Her eyes were red from the wind and she wore a scarf tied over her hair.

"No," Will said. "I just didn't notice you."

Mrs. Donahue looked the length of the terrace in one direction and then in the other. There were no other tables on it and there was nobody else. There was only the deck chair that Will had stumbled on, and the one Mrs. Donahue was in, and Mrs. Donahue. She said slowly, "You were walking with your eyes shut . . . did the wind blow sand into them?"

Will started to say yes, and then the anger that he had tucked away inside came back and stopped the lie. "I was thinking," he said.

Mrs. Donahue watched him and didn't say anything more. "I could order you another breakfast."

"You could," Mrs. Donahue said. "Please don't. I wasn't hungry." She smiled quickly without her eyes. It was a flat smile, and for the first time since Will had seen her at the hotel she looked kind of pretty. The wind curled one end of the white scarf loose around her face. She sat still.

Will cleaned the egg yolk off his hand with his handkerchief, and then bent down to pick up the broken glass.

"I shouldn't touch that," Mrs. Donahue said. "You'd cut yourself; one of the waiters will get it."

"It's all right," Will said. He lifted the six pieces of broken glass and put them back on the table. Then he brushed his palms off and hooked one thumb over his pants.

Mrs. Donahue said, "May I ask what it was you were thinking about?"

"This thing."

"So was I. Which thing?"

"No root . . ."

Mrs. Donahue waited.

Will watched the tiles.

"No what?"

"Skip it," he said.

Mrs. Donahue eyed him curiously. "I don't think I understand. And your mother?"

"She's nice," Will said. "She isn't any root."

Mrs. Donahue went on staring at him. "That's an odd thing to say," she said. "A very odd thing." Then she crossed her legs.

"Would it be all right," she said, "if I asked a ridiculous question?"

"Sure," Will said.

Mrs. Donahue took the piece of scarf that was fluttering into her eyes and looped it under the top. "It's important to me to know. It has something to do with the way you're feeling at the moment. If you had your choice," she said, "of being born or not being born. Let's say you had your pick," she said. "Which would you choose?"

Will looked at the terrace and considered about it. There was a small pile of sand that had blown up from the beach. It covered some parts of the mosaic. You could hardly see the blue tile at all. "Who's giving me my choice?"

"I am," Mrs. Donahue said.

"Now?"

"Yes," Mrs. Donahue said. "This very second." Her voice had a queer tightness in it, and her forehead was stretched like a drum.

Will frowned at the sand. "I don't know," he said.

Mrs. Donahue sat straight and watched him without moving, her face pale as a dead person's. The air was coming warmer from the sea. She was staring into it and her eyes glittered in the wind. "You needn't answer if you don't want to," she told him.

The blue tile was gone. Will balanced the question in his mind. "I was wondering what it feels like."

"Feels like?"

"Not being born," he said, "it doesn't feel like anything. I'd want it to feel."

Mrs. Donahue looked like she had stopped breathing. She asked:

"No matter what?"

"Sure," Will said. "Even if it just hurt. I'd have to be born."

Mrs. Donahue swallowed and sat back sharply in the chair. The color came back into the skin around her eyes. "Thank you," she said.

"For what?"

"Oh," she said, "for passing by." She smiled.

Looking at her, all at once Will remembered the other time he had seen a breakfast ruined, when the Count had fainted, and what had happened because of it. He hoped Mrs. Donahue wasn't going to turn around now and fall in love with him. The way his luck had been running, it wouldn't have surprised him. "That's okay," he said.

"Yes," Sylvia Donahue said. "Oh yes. That is okay."

She looked as if she might be going to reach out and kiss him, and Will swiveled fast and started away. There was no way of telling why Mrs. Donahue suddenly liked him, but he could tell that she did. He wanted to get off the terrace before things went any further. The look in her eye wasn't quite like the look in Littlejohn's the day the Count fainted on her breakfast, but it was close enough. It occurred to him that there was something about falling on women's breakfasts that was pleasing to them.

The kitchen entrance of the main building was gray looking in the darkening light. The waxy leaves on the vines around it were meant to cover the kitchen from the guests. The door was open; Will left the dog waiting outside and went in. The kitchen was big and white, with dark tiles on the floor and a functional appearance. It was the only room in the whole hotel that didn't have any color in it. There were four cooks in white coats working around the stoves, their coats smeared with grease stains. The cooks were angry and sweating. The kitchen wasn't air-conditioned. Through the open windows was the parking lot of the hotel where the guests who lived in the main building left their cars. You could see all the cars. There were three waiters waiting for orders of food. The smell of food was high in the room but it wasn't like Spanish cooking. There wasn't any olive oil in it. The Hotel Malage specialized in dishes for all types of foreigners, and the room had a bland countryless smell to it, like American bread. The breakfast odors were as white and color-blind as the kitchen. Will stood inside the entrance waiting to speak to somebody, but the waiters and cooks were too busy to bother with him. Two maids came and went without noticing him, and then the little maid who usually worked with Eugenia came in with an empty tray. She set it on the counter and called an order to one of the chefs; while she was waiting, she took a safety pin out of her apron and tightened the string. She put the pin back and smoothed her skirt. Will went up to her.

The little maid didn't often talk to the guests. Her face was young and bright and she had a manner about her that was a combination of shyness with an odd, speechless, almost brazen quality lurking just under it. Will said in Spanish, "You know where Eugenia is?"

The little maid glanced up from arranging her uniform and her eyes touched Will. They were like shields over something. "In Sanlúcar," she said.

For a moment he didn't understand. "Sanlúcar?"

"Yes," the maid said. "She went a few minutes ago."

" . . . Is today her day off?"

"No," the maid said, "you need something?"

Will hunched his shoulders. "I wanted to talk to her."

"You'll have to wait till she gets back."

"When?"

"*No sé*," the maid said, "tonight or tomorrow. Her son . . ." The little maid stopped and chose new words. "She has a son there; she went because of something that happened to her son."

The maid stood smiling behind her eyes. There was a sort of secret and appreciative glint in the way she looked at men of any age.

"Me too. I'm going to Sanlúcar today," Will commented.

"Are you?" the maid said. "By car?"

"No," Will said. "In the *autobús*."

"If you go now," the maid said, "you might see her. At the bus stop on the highway."

"*Gracias*." Will turned to the entrance.

"Wait a minute." The little maid eyed him and then opened a drawer in the counter. She took out a grimy pad of paper and a pencil and wrote something down. "If you see her," she said, "give her this. About work. Something she needed to know."

Will took the note and grinned at her. The little maid didn't grin back. She went on looking at him with a certain knowledge. The knowledge was the thing in her eyes. It was one of those days when everybody in the world has loud eyes.

He ducked behind one of the chefs and got out without bumping into anybody. The chefs were going nuts with all the orders, and one of them had lost his temper already. It was only about a quarter to eight.

The dog stood up as Will came out. Will led him running across the parking lot and down the main driveway. The hourly Sanlúcar bus that passed the hotel going west didn't usually come till fifteen minutes after the hour, and it wasn't more than a third of a kilometer to the highway bus stop from the hotel. He stood a good chance of catching Eugenia; if she had just left she'd still be waiting. Will didn't weigh much and he skimmed over the surface of the driveway like a piece of straw, the wind behind him. His tennis shoes barely crunched in the gravel and he felt like something the sea had tossed up and was blowing inland. Sneakers was keeping up beside him, and they went past the colored villas so fast it was as if the villas were moving in the opposite direction. He didn't need to run that fast, but it felt good, and anything felt better than standing too long in the wind.

He turned to the left just before the highway and ran west along the shoulder of the road. He stumbled once and dropped the piece of paper the little maid had given him. The wind took it and almost blew it out of his reach into the street. Will put out one foot and stomped it against the earth; he held it that way till he could pick it up. The note came unfolded and he could see what was written on it in Spanish. All it said was "Don José Ramón. The gold villa." The words meant nothing to him and he folded the note into a strip again and went on running.

He was still on the sea side of the road and the town looked deserted. A few of the braver tourists were out in the *foreño* on the other side of the highway gazing at the shops. Once you were outside the hotel grounds, the town of Suelo seemed loose and put together wrong; you could tell it had stopped being a real town; it didn't have any center except for the stores and tourist bars, and even those were either spread out too far or bunched up together in one place. In the town square there was a brand-new fountain with rocks around it that the Ministry of Tourism had put up so the tourists could watch when donkeys came to drink; only, the donkeys didn't. The Ministry had had to order the mayor to keep a donkey tied permanently to the fountain, looking like it had come for water. The donkey that had been chosen for the job didn't even look thirsty. The shops were kept whitewashed and there was a new Ministry ordinance that said there had to be flowers grown in two small pots on either side of every lamp post. It was the only town in Andalucía that had flowers on its lamp posts. The tourists never seemed to notice them much. Spaniards from other towns along the coast sometimes came on Sundays to watch the lamp posts with cold curious eyes. There were a couple of Spanish cars now, going east; between them Will could see the bus stop on the other side of the highway. Eugenia was there, with another woman. Eugenia had her back to him, and the other woman was saying something to her. The other woman was ugly, Will thought; her face had a yellow liverish look and she had long white hands that she kept jabbing into the air around Eugenia.

He came to a stop across the highway from them and waited for the honking cars to pass. Then he picked up the dog and ran across to the bus stop. Eugenia didn't see him coming, and he ran and stood beside the gesturing woman. For a second, neither one noticed him. Then the woman quit talking and they both looked at him. They had funny expressions, as if they had both been crying; Eugenia had a handkerchief in her hand, but her black eyes were bone dry and they flashed with anger. Her face had a set, almost vicious look about it like a bulldog. She looked straight at Will as if she couldn't see him; it took her eyes a while to recognize him. Then she spoke. "No," she said, as if Will had asked her something, "not today . . . I'm busy today." She turned away from him.

Will looked at the other woman, but she only pressed one long hand to her teeth as if she wanted to keep herself silent. Her lips were working. She was a silly-looking woman, Will thought.

"Be quiet," Eugenia said in a hard way without looking,

though the woman had not spoken. "Be still." She held out
her own crumpled handkerchief. The woman took it and
pressed it on her mouth. Eugenia watched the dusty asphalt
on the highway. "Crying doesn't help," she said to the woman.

Will started to turn away. Then he remembered and
turned back. *"Tome usted,"* he said; "from the little maid."
He pushed the note the maid had given him into Eugenia's
hand and backed off. Eugenia took it in her fist without
seeing it and held it at her side, one piece sticking out
high up between two of the fingers of her left hand. She
made no comment. She didn't even know she had taken it.
She went on watching the asphalt.

Will scuffed around in the dust and in a while the Sanlúcar
bus came. He didn't see much point in getting on—it was
way too early—but he didn't have anything else to do either,
and he couldn't think of anybody he wanted to talk to for
the moment. He waited for the other people to get on first
and then he picked up the dog again and followed them. He
paid for a ticket and sat down. The driver fought with the
clutch and put the bus into gear. It lunged forward, seeming
to hover in space before it caught its breath. Then it shuddered, and jerked forward again. The bus was old and it
felt out of control when it was between gears. It settled down
into a low moaning, moving fairly fast along the highway.
People and carts got out of its way quickly before the bus
got out of town; they could sense the lunging unwieldiness of
it. Twice the driver swore at other drivers. A man standing
on the curb with a bicycle turned and spat at the bus after
it passed. Out of town it was easier and there was only
the twisting highway to cope with and the vast internal rattle
of the motor.

Will set the dog on the floor between his feet and watched
the other passengers. There were no foreigners on the bus at
this hour. It was half empty. There were about eighteen
or twenty Spanish people, most of them poorly dressed,
going to work or to a market in some other town. Then Will
noticed that Eugenia and the other woman had not sat
together. There was an empty seat next to each of them.
They sat across the aisle from each other, each looking
straight ahead, as if they had never met. At first he thought
it was because they were angry, and then he changed his
mind. It was almost like they wanted to give the impression
that they weren't traveling together. It was silly because
Will was pretty sure by now that Eugenia was only going to
Sanlúcar because of something the other woman had told

her. He gave up wondering about it, and watched the coast instead.

The highway was only five hundred meters or so from the sea and there were patches of sugarcane growing between the bus and the water. The window was dirty. Each time the bus leaned against a turn it shook somewhere in its depths. The wood seats smelled of old sweat and there was a faint odor of chickens inside the bus. The earth outside looked dry, as though it would crumble under the wheels and break away in pieces from the coast; the grass was flattened in the wind. The weeds that held the earth together were gray-green, and the long sea beyond was lined white and frothed on the surface like lace. Will turned and looked at Eugenia. She was sitting in front, on the land side, staring rigidly at a corner of the window next to her. He couldn't see much of her but he could tell that her eyes were watering. She picked her right hand up disgustedly and swiped the heel of it across her face. She was angered by her own crying. The heel of the hand had a rind on it like a callus. It wasn't white and unused looking like the hands of the woman who had got on the bus with her. When she had finished wiping her face, Eugenia made a clearing sound somewhere in her chest. She put the hand back in her lap.

The bus was a number eleven; it didn't follow the coast all the way. It ran inland in places, skipping the city of Cádiz, cutting around the small loop of land straight to Puerto de Santa María. Then it turned in again traveling northwest through corn and alfalfa fields along a thin road that had deep gouges in the asphalt from past rain. There were sudden holes in the narrow road and the driver had to keep swerving from left to right to avoid them. In places the bus seemed to be moving from side to side more than it moved forward. The rocking of it and the fumes inside made Will's head dizzy, and for a while he lost track of time. He fell into a half-sleep and in his mind he remembered the expressions: Jim Lepard's, with the insulting smile, and Juan Alberto's with the curious flicker of interest; Mrs. Donahue's sad face turning to a happy expression, and then the swallowed knowledge of something that gave pleasure in the eyes of the little maid. Then he saw Eugenia's eyes flashing hard with a feeling that looked deeper than anger. The big wheel of faces turned sickeningly in his mind and still he could not make out the connection that bound them together. Then the bus fell hard into a rut and bounced him awake. They were in open country now, farmer's country. The wide green fields stretched on either side, flat and planted, and in the distance there were low hills and two or three white houses. After the fields some trees appeared and more dust. There was always dust and then they were in Sanlúcar. The town was too small to have any real outskirts. The bus had approached it from inland. The sea and the river were both on the other side of the town.

The driver made two stops in Sanlúcar, the first just inside, where a cobblestone road crossed the main street. The yellow-faced woman stood up at the first stop. Eugenia did not move, and the woman hesitated for a second by her seat. The pause was no longer than a heartbeat, and the woman strode ahead and got off the bus alone. Eugenia sat as if she was made out of rock and didn't seem to take any notice. When the driver started again Will looked back and saw the woman standing on the street watching the departing bus. She stood motionless; but when the bus turned a corner she was still there, reaching out with her eyes.

The bus stopped again in the center of the town and emptied. Eugenia was the first off. She seemed in a hurry. Will saw her step down and move forward to a *guardia civil:* a policeman standing near the bus stop. When she spoke to him, the policeman raised his arm in an uninterested way and pointed something out, his tricornered black patent-leather hat shining wetly under the sky. Eugenia walked fast in the direction the policeman was pointing, without looking back. She had not even noticed that Will had been on the bus. Then she was out of sight. Will put the dog down and began to walk in the town.

The trip had taken longer than he thought; it was midmorning and the outdoor bars were full of people drinking *manzanilla* wine or beer. People moved through the streets of the town in the suspended, lordly manner of Andalusians —or of all southerners the world over who move as if they had nothing to do but survive in the heat. Will had seen people move that way back in New Orleans. In all southern cities, he had noticed, it's a little ill-mannered to look busy, the way it's considered ill-bred among all southern ladies to admit to having slept all night; the people moved past him through the hot sleepy town with a certain indifference. Only the very old women who dressed in heavy black didn't bother to look as if they weren't busy, because they weren't. The others were. But they never showed it. Will felt them pass him by with unconnected faces. Except for husbands and wives and blood kin, they did not seem related to each other, or to the day, or to any pattern in the world you could name. It was like the faces on the wheel: you could not see their connection. They moved along the streets and sat at outdoor cafés and bars and in the town square. The unconnectedness of them made Will's stomach loose. He remembered a distant cousin of Helen's he had heard about once who had committed suicide, and he wondered if the cousin had got tired of trying to find connections in the world and had thrown the world away. Only the cousin had not. What the cousin had done was to throw himself away. The world was still there and you could feel it all around you, drifting and fighting, tightening and connectionless. It made you want to yell it into shape.

He crossed the main square and went past a street six blocks long with three bootmaker's shops on it and then into another street where the asphalt ended and the dirt began. The lower part of the town was full of the sound of bicycle bells and the drifting smell of spilled wine. Will stopped between two buildings near a pastry shop. He could smell the egg yolks in the batter. Below him was the town square and above him on a steep blunt hill was the shabby Guzmán palace, mottled against the sky. Will lifted his eyes and followed the gray outline. To the left of the palace was the Columbus tree and then the ordinary, drab-looking ruins of some old castle. The ruins were the only thing higher than the palace on the hill. Just the turrets of the castle were left and the wall that connected them. The wall was sunset-colored, the shade of worn brick. Once the castle must have dominated the town. Now it was empty. Its shell was all. Will wondered if in some other year of some other time somebody had stood like him and looked at the same hill and wondered about the connections of things.

He turned his back on the hill and went into a tobacconist's shop on the corner. He didn't feel like going to the palace yet; he had given up his plan of talking to somebody. Mostly for something to do, he bought a pack of black-tobacco cigarettes and a box of matches and paid for them. The man behind the counter took the money and said nothing. The shop was very small. Besides cigarettes you could buy lottery tickets. You bought the tickets singly or in blocks of ten. There was a printed list of this month's winning numbers on the wall over the counter. The man was clean-shaven and his face looked oily in the heat. He looked at Will to see if there was anything else he wanted. "A ticket," Will said; "a lottery ticket."

The man nodded. Will's accent was Andalusian, and the man didn't recognize him for a foreigner. He put a ruler across a block of ten tickets and tore one off. Will paid for the ticket and put it in his pocket. "For you?" the man asked. "No," Will said, "for my father." The lie came out smoothly because it wasn't entirely a lie. It was one of the things he hadn't known he was going to say till he said it. He wasn't sorry he had said it—it had seemed the right thing to do. He had never bought anything for his father. The man said, "Anything else?" Will shook his head and started to leave. With the door open he spoke to the man, knowing it would sound crazy, almost hoping it would shock the man, "*Una raíz?*"

"*Cómo?*" the man said, frowning.

The request sounded senseless in Spanish, even sillier than it would have in English, and he said it again: "A root?"

"Root?" the man said. "Root?"

Will waited.

"What kind?"

"Any kind," Will said. "Any kind of root." He knew that the shop owner couldn't possibly know what he meant by the remark and he kept his face straight, enjoying the craziness of the conversation.

The man watched him for a few seconds. "I don't sell roots," he said finally, "I sell tobacco and lottery."

Will pursed his lips and tried to look disappointed. The man studied his face with a look of alarm. Will ripped open the pack he had bought and took out a cigarette. He put it in his mouth and lit it. He had never lit a cigarette in his life and he pushed the smoke out with his tongue so that it stood in the air like a fat little cloud between him and the man. "Smoking causes cancer," he said in a dead tone.

On the far side of the cloud the man went and sat on a stool in the back of the shop and didn't say anything. He looked hopeless.

"*Adiós, buenas,*" Will said, in a crazy-loud voice. He walked out of the shop before the man could answer and went up the street. The aftertaste of the smoke was raw in his throat. Once he was past the shop he dropped the cigarettes. He couldn't think of anything else to do, and he began to climb the hill to the palace.

The wind was coming hotter, and then all the feelings of the morning went away and in an empty chamber of his mind a sort of decision appeared. It was an idea about what he would do when he got back to the hotel in the evening and he liked it. The decision was that he would go on trying to find somebody to discuss connections with. It was just one listening person you needed, and it was the same as buying a lottery ticket: you gambled because you thought you might win. To quit looking was like saying you would never buy another ticket—it was ridiculous. You just went on gambling. If it wasn't the pleasantest decision he had ever had, still it made sense. Then, content with it, his mind eased down and relaxed, and he missed Littlejohn so suddenly that it was like a pain. The wheel in his mind spun faster until all the faces blended into one white winter face and he saw her expression of yesterday when she had looked at him and said she might not come back to the hotel to sleep. She had looked happy, but there had been a blank look too in her eyes. She had avoided looking at him head-on. Will hadn't paid too much attention at the time but still he had noticed it. Something in it was like the last look on the tobacco seller's face—hopeless. He quickened his steps. The palace appeared moth-eaten on the hill, and watching it Will had a sense that something in it was wrong. He didn't have any real reason for thinking so.

He turned onto the worn cobblestone road that led up to it and he felt afraid. For no reason at all but the sudden fear in his heart, he started to run.

THE OUTER room of the *Jefatura de la Guardia Civil* in San-lúcar was like most other police offices in Spain. It was dank-smelling and dark. The overhead bulb wasn't on, and the room was lit only by the bleak gray light from the windows. Eugenia sat alone in a straight-backed chair, her hands still and her body motionless. After a while she reached down and pulled her skirt lower over her knees. The gesture was al-most demure; yet there was no one else with her in the room. Then she straightened again and threw her hands back into her lap as if they belonged to somebody else. Some of her instincts were those of a wild animal and the greater the danger she sensed, the more still she became. The danger was very great here and for minutes only her deep breathing stirred in the room. Presently, though by now she was famil-iar with it, her eyes took in her surroundings. The waiting room had wooden chairs, and with a professional eye she could tell that the walls had not been washed for at least a year. The three dirty windows were open and there was a single trailer of cobweb hanging from the ceiling. It swung like a long ghost tail in the air. On the other side of the door was a room in which the secretary had his office. Beyond that, she guessed, was the office of the captain. Eugenia had been waiting now nearly an hour for an interview with the captain. So far she had not seen anybody but the second assistant of the secretary. The assistant was a snappy young man with glasses who gave himself airs. He had told her to sit down and wait. She didn't mind waiting; she was just as glad for the time. Privately she was using the minutes like sandbags to hold herself in. She had needed them to stop the stream of panic that had begun to flow inside her when Lupe had brought her the news.

A fly came in the window and she watched it trying to find its way out again. It was looking for an escape the way her thoughts were. Thinking was important, maybe more now than it had ever been before in her life, and she couldn't use her mind for anything if her insides were turning to

192

water. To stop the flow she pressed her knees together. Then she thought about other times when things had been this bad and she had been able to deal with them. She couldn't think of more than one. It was the time when the paralysis had struck Pepe Luis; outside of that, things had been bad, but things had never been quite this bad. She would have to use the same kind of strength that she had used that day, when she had made the promise to the Virgin of Pilar and had known that she would keep it. Only she couldn't keep such a promise now. She had thought that over carefully on the bus, and she had come to the decision that facts are facts. She couldn't even walk all the way from Suelo to the shrine now, let alone crawl up a hill. Only, so far, she had not been able to think of any other way to use herself. It was all very well for people to say you were a strong woman. But strength of any kind in a police office was as useless as the thought of going up a hill on your knees at her age. So she was still thinking. The captain would expect her to behave like any other woman of sixty, and weep, begging for her son's freedom. She had thought that over too. Her two older sisters had both been weeping women; they had wept through most of their lives and they were both dead. By and large, tears only annoyed Eugenia—hers or anybody else's. Besides, both her sisters in chorus wouldn't have moved a policeman, let alone *this* policeman. Aside from what she'd heard of the captain's personality, he was already married to a weeping woman, and judging from Lupe's condition at the moment he had probably seen enough of it lately to sink a ship. Lupe was a wet jellyfish. Eugenia still could not bring herself to like the woman, though she was grateful to her and in a way admired her. What Lupe had done this morning, she knew, in coming to see her in Suelo, was as courageous a thing as setting out to sea had been for Cristobal Colón. Not only had Lupe gone out to get help for a man other than her husband —she had taken the chance that her husband, who owned a car, might catch her in the act. In fact, she had made enough of a scene in the kitchen of the Hotel Malage that word might get back to him anyway, though the chances were it wouldn't, and Eugenia had sat apart from Lupe on the bus just in case. But from the little that Eugenia had been able to piece together out of Lupe's first hysterical burbling, the police captain wasn't the sort of man you played tricks on. Especially not this trick. He wasn't a man to make a cuckold of. For if Lupe hadn't put the horns on him by law, she had by spirit: siding with the mother of an old boyfriend against her husband was, in a sense, as bad as giving horns to her husband by sleeping with the mailman. To cuckold a man was nearly the worst insult you could give him in any part of Andalucía. In Sanlúcar, where old traditions still held, it *was* the worst. If Madrileños didn't seem to mind looking ridiculous these days, that was because Madrid was a modern city. Here in the south things were different, and despite the influx of tourists, most of the old towns still kept to the old ways. So what Lupe had done was unthinkable. She had come to say that Pepe Luis was in jail, that the captain was having him beaten periodically, that Pepe Luis was probably not far from death. She had come to help him; now it was up to Eugenia to do the rest.

Only, now—what was the rest? For the last three hours—on the bus and in the waiting room—Eugenia had clenched her fists and thought until her brain ached as well as her fingers. So far she hadn't thought of a thing that would do Pepe Luis any good. She could feel the next flush of panic start again in her belly and she reached down and pulled her skirt still lower over her knees. She was secretly ashamed because her knees could not climb the hill to the Virgin's shrine. There wasn't a sound from the next office and the waiting room was quieter than ever. From the wall in front of Eugenia a big picture of Generalísimo Franco stared down at her knees in an interested way. The General in his uniform looked kind and fatherly in the picture. Now, now, he seemed to be saying to her, now, now. But now now what? Now this?—Now what is this?—Now you are a woman with bitch knees? Now you are a weak-kneed woman who can't bargain with God, who daren't make a simple promise because you know your knees won't keep it? Now that or now what? Or is it even worse than that? Is it just now you are an old whore?

There was the sound of a sneeze from somewhere inside the next room, and Eugenia took her eyes off the picture and put them on the door. She waited for another sneeze but there wasn't any. There was just silence again. First there had been silence, and then the big sneeze, and now there was more silence. It was a sneeze sandwich with silence for bread. Before you are born you are nothing and right after you are born you don't know that you have just been nothing, and then you are something for a while and you know that you are something, and then right before you die you have to sit in a police office and know that you are nothing again. So life is a sneeze sandwich, and it isn't even silence that is the bread. You are the bread. In the end, only you are the bread. Before the end. You are the silence.

The door opened and the assistant to the secretary came out and took a paper from a drawer in the desk and went back inside and closed the door. So you are already finished unless you can think of some way not to be the silence. Talking to the captain was not the way. No matter what you decided to say to him now, it would fall on the police captain's ears like nothing. It was all silence: you couldn't even offer him money. You could try, but what if he accepted it? You could go out and rob a bank and get caught by policemen and tell the policemen you were only stealing money so that you could bribe the police captain. Silence. A big wave of silence.

Silence: you could tell the police captain you had always been worried for Pepe Luis. Silence: you could tell him the truth. You could explain that Pepe Luis was stupid—that he, your son, thought anything bad that happened to him in the world was a mistake, and if he waited long enough it would un-happen. Silence: tell that to the police captain. And, worse, silence: that whatever Pepe Luis had done to anger the captain he had done in good faith, and had probably not even thought very much about the consequences. So silence: that he was exactly that stupid—that she, Eugenia, had tried to teach Pepe Luis about life and had not ever been able to. And more silence: that she had come back from the shrine that day years ago with bad knees in a state of exhaustion and that Pepe Luis had looked at her reproachfully for months afterwards, while she wondered why he was looking at her like that—until she had finally arrived at the answer, the one shocking, untenable conclusion: that he was reproaching her, not even for risking her own life, but for his brother's death. That Pepe Luis was so stupid he had actually believed at twelve years of age that his mother could take care of everything, so that if his brother had died, it must have been through a mistake his mother had made. That Pepe Luis was a man who had never really grown up. That. Silence. That people called him silly, and people were right. That he wasn't defective—he wasn't limited; he was just stupid. That he wasn't even bad. *That he was stupid*. That silence and silence and silence and silence and silence.

Or the other silence, that she, Eugenia, loved him—that she would do anything to help him, would use anything in her power, but that nothing was left in her power now but silence.

The door opened again and she heard two voices arguing. Another policeman in uniform came out and went to the

desk. He was older than the assistant. He was carrying the
same sheet of paper the assistant had taken, and he put it
back in the drawer. Then he rummaged through some other
papers looking for something. You could see he was the captain's personal secretary; his movements were stronger and
less snappy than the assistant's, and he had the sure look of a
man who carried authority. The right word to such a man
might do some good—he had the captain's ear. Only Eugenia
could not think of the right word. She couldn't think of any
word at all. She watched the secretary and the cold wetness
in her belly rose so fast it came into her chest, and she
opened her mouth and cleared her throat. It made a loud
sound. The secretary glanced at her sharply once and went
back to rummaging in the drawer. The inability to speak to
him made Eugenia feel strange—not angry—it was more
than angry. Her powerlessness now made her feel unattrac-
tive. She reached down like a girl and stretched her skirt shyly again over her knees. No, it wasn't age she felt—it was
like being a cripple. As if her main fault had gone and centered itself in one place. The defect in her willpower had
found a home in her knees exactly the way that the defect
in Pepe Luis's character seemed to show, if you knew him,
whenever he walked. The childhood paralysis had left one
leg a little shorter than the other. Enrique had a bad liver;
Pepe Luis had a limp; and she had the knees. They were one
big whore family. They were a weak whore family and she
was the head of it, and she could not stop being the head of
it any more than she could stop the thing that had happened
to her knees.

The secretary had found the sheet of paper he was looking
for; he held it up to the window. It had an X on top; he
carried it back into the other room. He left the door open
this time and Eugenia could hear him arguing with his assistant. The voices rose in anger and then they stopped
abruptly. A door had opened invisibly inside the room. There
was a pause and Eugenia heard a third voice. The third voice
had more authority even than the secretary's. It was quiet
and gentle, and something in its gentleness made a cold
glaze edge down her shoulders. It was the captain, she was
sure, and it was worse than she had expected. She had known
the captain would be bad trouble—but this was more than
just bad trouble. A man who doesn't raise his voice *at all* is
the worst kind of trouble there is. There was another silence
from the office inside, and listening to it, Eugenia knew all
at once what it was she had been feeling. Through two
closed doors and an office, she had been sensing the

presence of the captain. That was where the silence came from: from him. He was the whole story. It was *his* sneeze she had heard, through the open windows, and now before the end of her life she had come here to have a talk with the man who was her death. She had taken a bus to discuss things with the Teacher of Silence himself, personally. She could not hear him now. She strained her ears, but there was no sound in the next room for a while. Then the fly came back in the window. The heat was worse and the wind blew and the silence persisted. In the noiselessness of the room she could feel a few drops of sweat start down her sides like little cold insects. She held her breath. Then she clenched her fists harder but her fingers were strangely cold in the hot room, and her insides felt like ice.

When the assistant wearing glasses stepped into the open doorway it startled her so that she almost cried out. The assistant saw her discomfort and smiled slightly. You could tell that he thought it was his own presence that made her uneasy. From the window behind him she saw a quick dust cloud rise in the street and then fold over itself like a wave of air.

The assistant stepped back into the doorway and pointed to the office over his shoulder with one thumb. Then he looked at the thumb. He chewed a hangnail from it and examined it again thoroughly through his glasses. Eugenia stood up. She listened, but there wasn't even the sound of a typewriter from the office. She waited. There was only silence. The assistant frowned at her. He couldn't see her knees. Her knees were trembling. Her knees were putting on an act like whores.

The assistant sighed. "Don't you understand, *Señora*? You can go in now," he said.

A very long time later when it was all over, she thought sometimes about that moment, the instant when she stepped forward to go into the office. In her memory it was like a curious gaping split in time. The thing was odd. It was almost as if, at that moment, time had broken open for her, and all the other moments of her life had spilled into it. Up to then if she thought about her life at all, she had thought about it only as a whole thing, a long oneness that could not be separated into two parts. Any break in the flow of it, she had believed, was death. But walking into the office of the police captain, her life *did* break in two, and she did not die. She only went on walking. The air was like warm glue around her in the room. She could feel it happen, the

cracking open of time, and the moments of her living fell
into the crack and rattled at the bottom somewhere like cut
glass in a child's kaleidoscope; but the bottom of what? That
was all she thought, walking into the office. *Sí*, she thought,
time has broken and my life has spilled to the bottom. *But
the bottom of what?*

The first office was a large room with four desks in it and
three men. None of them looked up except the secretary,
who pointed to the door that led to the inner office. The
three policemen all had their jackets and belts on. The
jackets were deep olive green and the belts were black. Many
poor people were fearful of these men, who patrolled in
pairs along the coast. The color of their uniforms and their
stiff black patent-leather hats gave their faces a dead look.
The assistant followed Eugenia through the room to the
inner office. The gluey air was stifling; the assistant was
sweating so badly his glasses had slipped down onto his nose.
He pushed them into place with the back of his wrist. Then
he blinked the sweat out of his eyes. He knocked on the
open door and the quiet voice inside commanded them to
come in. Eugenia was walking into the captain's office when
someone hissed behind her. She turned and saw the secretary
holding out a sheet of paper. It was the sheet he had taken
from the drawer in the waiting room: it had an X on top.
She took it. Then she went on walking.

She walked on her bitch knees and she didn't stop till she
came to the front of the desk and then she stopped forcibly
because of the desk. The captain was looking down at something, and she couldn't see his face. She could feel the room
around her. This office was bigger than the secretary's, but
instead of four desks it was furnished for one man alone.
The windows were open here too and there was a small electric fan on a file cabinet. The fan was pointed directly at the
captain but it wasn't doing any good. It was blowing hot air
from the windows at his neck and the hair on the back of his
head was shiny with sweat. Eugenia knew how to fix the fan
so that it would blow cooler air on the captain, and for one
loose second her brain reeled with emptiness and she considered telling him. Above the captain on the wall was another picture of Generalísimo Franco in uniform, and next to
it was a sign. The sign was white cardboard with a single
word written on it in thick black painted letters. Eugenia
couldn't read it without spelling it out letter by letter; she
looked down from it back at the captain. Just then without
moving the captain sneezed again. After that he blew his
nose on a handkerchief. He was still making notes on his

desk. He was a wide bulky man. The size of him reminded her of her husband Enrique, except that Enrique's largeness was no longer powerful and the captain's was almost a definition of power. He went on making notes and then without looking up he spoke to her. "Yes?" he said. It was almost a whisper.

Eugenia didn't answer and the captain took a metal-and-rubber stamp from his desk and stamped the sheet of paper he had been writing on. Then he looked up at her in a quizzical way. His face was boneless and moon-shaped, and the little moon eyes in it were cold and lifeless. Then she knew where the captain kept the silence; he kept it in his eyes. Eugenia blinked.

"You wanted to see me?" the captain said.

She waited.

The captain sighed. He took the sheet of paper from her and set it in front of him. He read it. *"Bueno,"* he said, "yes. The political prisoner." He looked up at the assistant with the glasses. "Who is going to take notes?" he said carefully.

"Yes, Captain," the assistant said. He went out of the room fast and the captain waited. The secretary himself came in quickly with a pen and a pad of paper. The secretary sat down in a chair next to the desk. "Sorry, Captain," he said. "I wasn't thinking."

"You never are," the captain said.

The secretary looked down at the pad.

The assistant stayed outside in the other office and closed the door to the captain's office. The captain sat back.

"Usted es la madre?" the captain said to Eugenia: "You are the mother?"

She nodded.

"Yes," the captain said, "it's a great shame." He put the tips of his fingers together and touched his thumbs. "A great shame," he repeated. He waited for Eugenia to say something to him. Nobody spoke.

Eugenia stared at the captain's eyes; inside her brain the silence grew like a cancer.

The captain leaned forward and put his elbows on the desk. *"Señora,"* he said in a genteel tone, "please believe me that I feel for you."

The man with the pen wrote it down.

"Every man," the captain said, "has a mother. I got no longer any way to do anything for *my* mother. My mother, may she rest in peace, is with God. What can I do for you?" he said to Eugenia. He opened his hands and made a lifting gesture that was meant to indicate that there was nothing that he could do for her.

The man with the pen wrote everything down, except the gesture, which he had not seen. The gesture had been silent.

"Tell me, *Señora*," the captain said in a voice of concern, "what you want. I'm waiting for you to tell me. . . ." He sat back and went on looking at her.

The man with the pen finished writing and looked at her too. He held his pen poised, ready.

Eugenia swallowed. Then she wet her mouth. The man put the tip of the pen on the paper. There was nothing in Eugenia's brain now but three words that she could not say. The words were, *May you die. May you die,* she said silently to the captain, into his eyes, *may you die, may you die, may you die, may you die, may you die.*

The captain stood up suddenly and moved away from his chair. "*Señora,*" he said, as if he were reading a speech formally from a piece of paper, "let me tell you something . . . I got to tell you this," he said, "I swear by the glory of my mother that I know what you're thinking at this moment. There's nothing that you and I got to say to each other that we don't both know." He turned and faced the file cabinet. "I see by your face you're an intelligent woman," he said, dictating evenly to the secretary; "I'm only a humble police captain, but I also would like to help your son. I try . . . *Señora,* will you believe me when I tell you your son is a strange man. Pepe Luis won't do the simple thing he's got to do that will allow me to help him." The captain stood for a moment, waiting for the words to sink in and waiting for the man with the pen to catch up with him. "Am I going too fast?" he said to the man.

"*Momento, mi Capitán,*" the secretary said. His pen scratched furiously over the paper.

"Tell me, *Señora,*" the captain said fast, paying no attention to the secretary, "how did you know your son was here?" He wheeled and faced her.

Eugenia looked back at him with her mouth open. Since she had come into the room she had been breathing through her teeth as though she had run a race. She put out her tongue and tasted the sweat on her upper lip.

"Let's see," the captain said slowly. "You probably got today off from work . . . you went to the house where Pepe Luis rents a room . . . you asked for him," the captain said, "and they told you he was here. . . . Is it something like that?"

Eugenia waited. The captain smiled.

"Well now," he said in a jovial way, "I'm not such a bad man that I don't understand things. Isn't it true I'm not such a bad man?"

Eugenia held still and the captain stood by his desk looking at her. "Now *Señora*," he said, "maybe you understand that I'm doing my best for . . ."

The captain went on talking and Eugenia stopped listening. The captain was saying one thing with his mouth, and another with his eyes. With his mouth he was saying that Pepe Luis was all right and that everything was being done for him that could be done. But with his eyes the captain was saying that Pepe Luis was as good as dead, that nothing at all could be done and that they both knew it. She and the captain were communicating in two different ways, and the way that had to do with speech did not matter. What mattered was the other—the way that had to do with silence— and everything that had to be said between them had already been said in that way.

So there it was: the thing she had felt before. The thing she had sensed in the waiting room was just death. Death had got hold of her son in the little town and there was nothing that she could do about it. The captain was saying that. Just that: *that there was nothing she, Eugenia, could do about it. . . .*

Eugenia stood back from the desk and locked her knees. She turned her ears back on and listened. The captain had stopped speaking. You could tell he had asked her a question and was attending the answer. The secretary was looking at her too and they were both waiting expectantly.

Eugenia raised her eyes and searched over their heads. She didn't know what the question had been and she didn't know the answer. She could not speak to the captain's eyes and she looked again at the cardboard sign on the wall by the picture of Franco. While her mind swiveled for something to say, she spelled the sign out to herself letter by letter. There were eight of them. The letters were S—I—L— E—N—C—I—O. She didn't think about the word as she formed it, until she had collected it all in her mind, and then she did. It was then that she started to laugh. The river of panic in her belly flowed up until it flooded her throat, and when it spilled out into the air it had changed somehow into a river of laughter. The sign struck her as the funniest thing she had ever seen. She laughed and she laughed. She pointed at the sign and then covered her mouth with her hand and the laughter pushed out and spilled between her fingers. It came down her nose and it was so loud that for a time it almost sounded like the noises her sisters used to make when they were weeping.

After a while someone pushed a chair into her from behind. The lock on her knees broke, and she buckled into the chair. Somebody was holding a glass of water in front of her and she took it. The captain was standing by the window in a bored weary way, waiting for her to quiet down. He looked as if he had been through this kind of thing before. Eugenia held the glass the secretary had given her and she drank from it. She felt empty and lighter than she had been before laughing, and for a moment she didn't know why. Then she realized it was because the cold stream that had been in her belly was gone. The panic had been released under another name. It had flowed out of her as laughter, and though she felt weak, she was no longer afraid. It was as if she had reached the far edge of the split in time, and now, way at the bottom in a loose pointed pile lying just as they had fallen, she saw under her the bright jagged moments of her life. They were lying there like jewels. She looked down at them in her mind, and she asked herself the same question she had asked when she was walking into the office: they are there, I see them there, the whole pile of my moments, they are at the bottom—but the bottom of what? She still couldn't answer the question, though this was the second time she had asked it, and she finished the glass of water and put the empty glass on the desk in front of her. The captain turned back from the window and looked at her again.

"Se sienta usted mejor, Señora?" he said in a tired tone: "Feeling better?"

The captain didn't wait for an answer but strode to his desk and leaned over it watching her. *"Señora,"* he said, "today is a busy day here. You'll have to excuse me . . ."

He broke off as a knock sounded on a door behind Eugenia. The knock was followed by the opening of the door, and another voice said, *"Mi Capitán,* I brought the pills for your aller . . ." Then that voice stopped too. The captain was looking above Eugenia's head and his eyes were like arrows. He lowered them to Eugenia and then looked back at the man behind her. "Sorry, Captain," the voice behind her said. "I didn't realize you were busy."

The captain shook his head. "No," he said, "come in. I could use the pills; my sinuses . . . it's the dust. It gets in the wind . . . I've always had an allergy to dust . . . let me present you to a lady. This," he said, "is the mother of *Pepe Luis."*

nough to let you talk to him without seeing him. Maybe through the window . . ."

Eugenia moved her eyes to the space between the doctor nd the captain. She was remembering a weekend years ago when there had been a little money and she had taken the erryboat to North Africa with Enrique. In Tangiers she had seen Enrique bargain with an Arab trader for a souvenir bracelet of false pearls. Enrique had bargained for half an hour and in the end he had won out over the Arab. He had bought the souvenir bracelet for less than a fourth of the price the Arab had first asked for it. Eugenia no longer had the bracelet; the links had worn down and it had come apart long ago, though she still kept a few of the false pearls in a box next to her bed.

She spoke with precision into the space halfway between the doctor and the captain. "Listen. If I was to convince him, I'd have to go slow. You know how stubborn he is. It would be better for me not to see him at all than to see him only once. It would have to be at least twice."

The captain was silent. Eugenia could feel the two men ooking at each other across the area she was staring into. The captain didn't move and the air began to pulsate in ront of her eyes as if there were an invisible heart out there n the space.

"You understand, *Señora,*" the captain said almost inaudibly, "you could only *talk* to him. You couldn't *see* him . . . I ouldn't change the regulations by *that* much."

"Yes," Eugenia said, her eyes on the space. "And you understand that no one else would question him for the two ays I was talking to him; only me. If you saw him on the ame days, I would be useless . . ."

"Why?" the captain said.

"You already know why," Eugenia said. "It's like the gulations. I couldn't change him by that much."

There was another silence while the captain weighed what e had said. You could hear the wind outside and some-here in the town above a cock began to crow. The captain ew his nose.

Eugenia broke through the space with her eyes and looked the sheet of dust rising from the electric fan across the m. Watching Enrique and the Arab pearl trader she had rned that even if you are only bargaining for pearls made of paste you must know when the bargaining is finished keep your mouth shut for a while. Then if you can, must talk about something else entirely; something that nothing to do with the pearls. "The fan," she said.

He arched his voice on the words "Pepe Luis" and looked hard at the other man.

The man came around from behind Eugenia and set a bottle of pills on the captain's desk. *"Mucho gusto, Señora,"* he said: "A great pleasure." He put his hand out.

Eugenia looked at the hand. Then she looked at the man.

"This is the police doctor, *Señora,*" the captain said. He was examining the pills the doctor had brought him. He had opened a drawer in his desk where there were six other bottles of pills and he was holding the new one up against them.

Eugenia didn't move. The doctor dropped his hand to his side.

"The doctor," the captain said, counting the new pills, "can explain to you how much we want to help Pepe Luis."

The doctor coughed and said modestly to Eugenia, "We do what we can; I treat your son every day. . . ."

"When he comes in here for questioning," the captain said, "it's the doctor who brings Pepe Luis and takes him back. Pepe Luis has been in three times . . ." He went on talking in a patient way. The tone of the captain's voice was angled down, as if he were addressing a child or a very old lady. Listening, Eugenia knew that the only reason she had been allowed in the captain's office at all, let alone allowed to stay this long, was because of her age. They probably thought she was a good fifteen years older than she was. The realization made the empty space in her belly where the panic had been start to fill again with another substance. The substance was like an extract; it was purer than the panic, and it was as hot as the panic had been cold. The substance was pure rage. It was filling her drop by drop, and she could feel the drops burning like acid somewhere in her belly.

She opened her mouth and kept her eyes on the doctor. She had not spoken once since entering the room. Now, since the panic had left her, she could talk, as long as she wasn't looking at the captain. She formed the words in a trim exact way as if she were teaching them. "You treat him for what?" she said.

The doctor stepped to the side and glanced at the captain for help, and then looked at her again. "Of course you know, *Señora,*" he said, "your son was arrested for starting a fight in a bar?"

Eugenia waited.

"Yes," the doctor said. "In a bar. A disturbance. Then somebody in the bar hit him in the . . ."

"It doesn't matter where they hit him," the captain said. "Does it?"

"Exactly," the doctor said, "exactly. Only, Pepe Luis got hurt. So I've been . . ." He looked at the captain again, but the captain was busy with the new pills. The captain had sat down at his desk and was arranging the pills in neat little circles on a sheet of blank paper. Watching his hands and listening to the doctor's voice Eugenia thought, Can they think I am so old that my brain is gone? The doctor went on talking and Eugenia felt the drops of rage increase to a long thin squirt that felt like it was burning out through her belly. Then the squirt stopped and the drops began again.

". . . so I didn't realize the extent of the injuries immediately," the doctor was saying. "First I thought it was only the jaw, but . . ."

Eugenia watched the doctor and waited.

"You, not being a doctor," the doctor said awkwardly, "it's a little hard for me to explain. . . ." He grinned at her.

"Explain it," Eugenia said. She said it in a half-whisper.

Both the doctor and the captain looked at her, startled. Her voice had been as quiet as the captain's. The two-word request had come out more like a command. There was a pause. The doctor backed up a step from her.

The captain turned his head away to keep from smiling.

"Well," the doctor said, "it's . . . like a fracture . . ." He coughed. "You know what a fracture is? It's like . . . well, it's like this," the doctor said. "He's got several fractures."

"How many?" Eugenia asked.

"Several."

"How many is several?"

"Three," the doctor said. "He's got three fractures."

"How many times did you say he's been in here for questions?" Eugenia said to the doctor.

The doctor started to speak and decided not to.

"I was the one who told you that, *Señora*," the captain said quietly. "Don't you remember? Three times."

Eugenia kept her eyes still. From the heat in her belly she could speak quite freely, but only as long as she wasn't looking at the captain. "I'll go and see him now," she said.

The doctor looked down at one of his shoes. "I don't think," he said, "that would . . ."

"No, *ni hablar*. I thought you knew, *Señora*. It's against regulations," the captain said. "Political prisoners don't get visitors till after they're tried."

"When is he to be tried?" Eugenia said, looking at the doctor.

"Soon," the captain said.

"When is soon?" Eugenia said to the doctor.

"Well, as soon as . . . when we got the informatio[n] need for the record," the captain said. "Now, *Señora*, you to . . ."

"What is it you want from him?" Eugenia said, still t[o] doctor.

"Want? . . . We don't want anything," the captain "Just the truth that he's been holding back."

"And when he gives you the truth?"

There was a little nearly unnoticeable pause.

"Then," the captain said, "he'll get a trial, and the cha[nces] are, if he's cooperated and spoke the *whole* truth, he'll off. Now *Señora*, please . . ."

"Listen. I'm not a young woman," Eugenia said. She u[sed] a consciously pitiful tone, and the heat-level rose in her bell[y].

"I know that, *Señora*," the captain said. "It was out of [re]spect for your years I let you come in here . . ."

"Listen," Eugenia said, still to the doctor, "supposing if I could convince Pepe Luis to cooperate. Age is sometimes good for something. Would I be able to talk to him?"

The doctor and the captain glanced at each other.

"No," the captain said slowly; "the rules got to be kept. The regulations are too hard . . . they're very hard, *Señora* . . ."

"So is Pepe Luis," Eugenia said carefully, "harder even than the regulations. He has a head like a bull. If Pepe Luis makes his mind up to something, he can die before he'd change it. I think you know that by now . . . I thin[k you] know you won't change him. He has only one weakness."

No one spoke for a moment. Then the captain said, [". . . what] is that, *Señora*?"

"The same as every man's. Me," Eugenia said; "I [am his] weakness. And even *I* couldn't do it in one day. To co[nvince] him, I'd need to talk to him every day for . . ." she [looked] at the doctor ". . . five days."

From the corner of her eye she saw the captain sh[ake his] head. "There is no way at all I could allow that, *Seño[ra]*," [he] said. He cleared his throat.

Then he said, "If I could . . . scrounge around en[ough to] find a loophole in the regulations . . . let you talk to h[im] once . . ."

"Three times," Eugenia said. "Three visits woul[d be the] least."

"Once," the captain said. "*If* I could shift the re[gulations]

". . . Señora?"

"The electric fan," she said, "is only blowing dust and hot air from the window. I was thinking before . . . if you wanted the fan to work, you'd have to close the window and put a block of ice in a bowl in front of it. Let the electric fan blow across the ice and it might cool the room."

The captain and the doctor both turned and looked.

"Pues sí. Tiene razón," the doctor said after a second: "She's right."

"Yes," the captain said slowly, "I think she's right about the fan. See about it later," he said to the secretary.

"Yes, Captain," the secretary said.

The captain turned back to her. *"Señora,* you're a reasonable woman," he said. "Maybe you're even a practical woman. That was a clever thing to notice about the fan. What made you think of it?"

"The captain is allergic to dust," Eugenia said.

"You heard me say that?"

"It's my job," Eugenia said. "I'm a maid."

"I see," the captain said. "Of course. Twice," he added. "Only twice. It's no use your coming and asking for more time after that . . . I couldn't give it to you if I wanted to. If you can convince him to cooperate at all, you can do it in two days. You could talk to him a little today and once more tomorrow morning."

"Afternoon," Eugenia said; "I work in the mornings. Today and very late tomorrow afternoon . . . I can't afford to lose my job."

"Yes," the captain said, smiling, "a very practical woman."

"There's one other thing."

The captain waited.

"I would have to know what you wanted him to say," Eugenia said.

She could feel the captain frown without looking at him.

"No," he said, "it's a matter of politics, *Señora.* You wouldn't understand a matter of politics . . ."

"Neither would Pepe Luis," Eugenia said.

The captain watched her.

"No," he said.

"Captain," the doctor said. "Please excuse me for advising you. . . . She may be right."

"If word got out . . ."

"If word got out about what?" the doctor said in a smiling way.

The captain looked at him. "Oh," he said. "Yes. That."

"The thing is, I think the part around the jaw . . . I think their conversation might be a little one-sided."

"I see," the captain said. "Yes . . ."

He turned to face Eugenia. Then he shrugged. "Pepe Luis did a silly thing. He joined an illegal political party," he said. "He wasn't a member very long. I don't think when he joined he understood what he was doing. . . . But it isn't him we want. It's the head of the party. You got that, *Señora?* We think this other man is organizing people here in Sanlúcar. We just need the confirmation from Pepe Luis . . ."

". . . Confirmation?"

"Pepe Luis knows who the man is," the captain said. "He's got to *say* it."

"Is that all?"

"I swear," the captain said. "By the glory of my mother. That's all he needs to do."

Eugenia held still.

So there it is, she thought—just that clear and that simple. And if he doesn't say exactly what they want him to say, he'll die from the beatings, and they'll say he said it anyway. The way it's going, in a week he'll be dead. But if he does say it, then they'll let him die anyhow, so that he won't be able to talk about the beatings. And that way he'll be dead in two weeks—three at the outside. . . .

Pues allí 'stá, she thought in a long rush: So there it is. So either way he'll be dead, no matter what I do; and the only difference is whether it happens in one week or in three. So there it is . . . it doesn't matter who the other man is, it doesn't even matter about the political party, because the captain knows that nobody in Sanlúcar is going to organize a political party. Because people in Andalucía don't think that way—and the captain is from Andalucía. And even if they did begin to think that way, they wouldn't be dumb enough to give a position to Pepe Luis. And the captain knows that too. So he's only talking nonsense, and the man he's trying to catch isn't the head of a political party at all, and the captain only wants to make it look that way, and really wants the man for something else. So it's *all* nonsense. It's meaningless nonsense, and Pepe Luis will be dead soon no matter what anybody does, because that's what nonsense is. All I've gained with my big talk is to make it stop for two days; today and tomorrow. And unless something else happens in these two days, the nonsense will begin again, and that will be that. So there it is. So there it is. So there it is. So Pepe Luis who didn't die from a paralysis is going to die instead from an overdose of nonsense—and the Virgin knew it sixteen years ago. *Pues allí 'stá.* . . . So when She came to speak to me on the hill a little more than halfway up to the shrine, that was what the Virgin was saying, "I won't let him die from this, I'll wait and let him die from that. I'll save your son from the disease, and I'll give him to the nonsense." So that is what you get for trying to bargain with the Virgin. You get the bargain you asked for, and you don't know what the bargain means till it's too late to do anything about it. Yes, so there it is . . . and all bargaining is the same, and all you wind up with —no matter whether you dealt with the Virgin or the police captain or an Arab pearl trader—is a broken chain and a bunch of paste pearls in a box by your bed. So all the marketplaces in the world are one, because the world itself is only a marketplace—and no matter how well people like me bargain, when it's over I'm going to lose. No matter how you live. In the end your strength is going to go, and there are going to be people who bargain better than you do, and you are going to lose.

The captain was saying something, and Eugenia looked at him. It was different now—she had no trouble looking at his eyes. She could match them with the silence in her own. It was the same for both of them, and looking at him, Eugenia asked herself the question she had asked twice before—only now that was different too because now she could answer it. She was well over on the far side of the split in time, and below her she caught one last glimpse of the glittering pile, the jagged moments of her life down at the bottom, and she asked herself, *at the bottom of what?* —and this time the answer came loud and clear, and so simple it nearly made her want to laugh again. Only she was fresh out of laughter. The answer was that the moments of her life were lying where she had left them—at the bottom of the marketplace. It wasn't a chasm and it wasn't a pit and it wasn't a mysterious crack in the world. It wasn't a crack at all—it wasn't even unfamiliar. It was just what it was, and it was quite familiar. It was a marketplace, and she had left her life in it. She had walked away from it, and not because she was tired of bargaining, but only because—with the instinct that comes from a lifetime of bargaining—she knew that her life wasn't worth anything any more and there wasn't anything to do with it, or any place else to leave it.

So it was clear what had happened; and in her mind she turned her back on all the other moments—and in her mind, she went on walking. She had nothing else to bargain with, but she didn't want to look at the pile anymore, and she walked on in the marketplace because there was no place else to walk. *"Señora?"* the captain said. He had been speaking to her.

She pulled the focus of her vision out from the back of the captain's eyes and looked at him. "Yes," she said.

"Are you listening to me?"

"Yes," she said.

The fat face of the captain wrinkled, gathering to sneeze, and he lifted one eyebrow disbelievingly. "Tell me then . . . what was I saying, *Señora?*"

"That we've spent too much time talking, and you're a busy man. You were saying, if he admits to dealing with this one person, then everything should be all right. . . ."

The captain sneezed. "Right," he said.

"So I have two days to see him that you will let him alone. And after those two days, I'd better go about my business, because Pepe Luis is in your hands after that, and there's nothing I can do. . . . You were saying there's nothing I can do about it. . . ."

The captain nodded. "The doctor will show you the way," he said.

Eugenia walked to the door. Then she turned back, and once more looked at the captain. She had not left the marketplace and old habits are hard to break. *"Si fuese cosa de dinero,"* she said to the captain: "If it were a matter of money . . ."

In the silence that followed, she watched the three faces in the room. Money was a ridiculous thing for her to bring up—they could all tell by her clothes and by her manner that she had none—but she studied the three faces all the same. Two of them, the captain's and the secretary's, didn't change. But at the sound of the word "money" two little points of light glimmered for an instant somewhere deep in the doctor's eyes. It wasn't a purposeful answer—it was only the automatic response his eyes made to the word itself. As soon as the points of light had gleamed, they went out, and his face was no different from the others. But she had read the answer to her question in his eyes. So that was the way it was with the doctor. So, when you've left your life in a pile, there is still one other thing to bargain with, she thought. Life or no life. You should make sure that you always have money.

She turned from the three faces and walked out of the room.

On the way to the part of the jail where the prisoners were kept, the doctor walking beside her said, "You'll be able to talk to him all you want through the window inside the cell door. . . ."

Eugenia was quiet. She had bartered, without knowing it; and in the same market she had swapped everything else for the rage in her belly. It was with the rage that she had asked the final question, about money. Walking now, she felt another squirt of acid inside her as they came to the long buildings where the cells were. The doctor stopped and spoke to a man behind the door. It was the jailkeeper and they stood and waited outside while he went for some keys.

Eugenia kept quiet and she listened to the wind in the courtyard and made an effort to prepare herself. She pushed down with her stomach muscles the way she would have if she were giving birth; the strain made her face turn red. She was trying to expel the rage before she entered the jailhouse, but she couldn't. She knew what her job was now. She had to give Pepe Luis a kind of peace that he would need more than anything, and for that she ought to feel only a certain tenderness for him—but it was strange. For the first time in her life she could feel no tenderness for him at all. She had left that behind her with everything else in the captain's office, and nothing was in her now but hollowness and the slow dripping acid. She recalled the time when she had prepared Pepe Luis once before, just after his birth; when the midwife had handed her the red silly screaming bundle of sound that had the face of an old man and she had held it against her until it stopped screaming and it nuzzled like a dumb animal against the side of her breast. There had been an overwhelming tenderness in her then for the helpless yelling voice, the noise-making thing wrapped in the blanket, and she had shut her eyes and tried to prepare it for life. It was that same feeling she needed now, because now she was going to have to prepare him for death. She shut her eyes standing in front of the door of the jailhouse. She wondered calmly where the gentleness that she had once felt for Pepe Luis and where her love had gone. Then the big metal door opened.

The jailkeeper let them in; she followed him down a passage. The doctor walked behind her. Eugenia's rope-soled shoes made only a soft scuffling sound on the cement floor, but the shoes of the two men struck hard and echoed in the long passage. Their footsteps sounded like applause.

An hour later she stepped down out of the dank gray building into the hot wind and began to walk alone through the town toward the docks. The wind had risen higher and the narrow streets looked deserted. The *foreño* was the worst that she could remember. Worse than the morning two years ago when it had come unexpectedly and knocked flower pots and small wicker chairs off balconies all along the coast. It hadn't been unexpected today, so nothing had been left on the balconies to fall. But there were bits of paper and string and odds and ends of things blowing high between the buildings; all around Eugenia, doors and windows groaned on their hinges, as if the little town itself were creaking in the wind. She pulled the scarf from her hair and tied it loosely over her mouth and nose to keep the dust out, and then she cupped one hand over her eyes and walked like that, avoiding the dirt in the center of the street. Both her hands had cramps in them and they ached with tension. She hadn't relaxed them since leaving the hotel in Suelo hours before. Her fists were like tight claws, stiff and curved and dangerous looking, the fingers pressed tight with no spaces between as if they had grown together. Later, when she had a chance, she ought to soak the two of them in hot water, she thought. She ought to do something soon about her hands. . . .

Somewhere on another street a donkey was braying and on the road in front of Eugenia two or three people crossed hurriedly. A man passed her holding his jacket over his head and near the center of town a woman was fighting with an umbrella she was trying to use against the wind. Eugenia walked past her. The wind was peaking now, she could tell; in a few minutes it would begin to subside. Then it would come in bursts again, with short breathless spaces between, and by nightfall it would be back down to a steady even blow. The sea would rise a little, covering the beach to the edges of the salt grass. Tomorrow would be like today, only not quite as bad, and every day from now on the wind would subside a minuscule amount until one day with no warning it would just stop blowing. The *foreño* operated with a mind of its own and sooner or later if you lived on this part of the coast you got used to its ways. It was like an old odious relative—you put up with it because there wasn't much else you could do. Sometimes, if you knew how to use it, the wind could even help you think.

But not now. It was all over now: she had done something in the jailhouse so useless that all the brains in the world couldn't fix it. She leaned forward and pushed herself onto the blowing air. She tried not to think about the thing

she had done and she fought the wind. Then she came to a
stop and stood leaning into it, wondering whether she had
finally lost her mind. The air burned her eyes and all at
once she knew what it was that had happened to her—on
the empty street her brain cleared. It had been a voice belonging to someone else that had got into her throat somehow and done the thing in the jailhouse: made the promise.
It was a kind of terrible comedy. She had walked into the
place with only one purpose: to make plain to Pepe Luis
that there was no way out—that this time even his mother
could not help him, that he would have to resign himself
to the thing that was coming and make his own peace with
God. Instead, she had done the opposite—and now she realized that it had not been her, but an evil comic grace guiding her words. After not making a promise to the Virgin
simply because her knees wouldn't keep it, how else could
you explain making *this*—a promise she couldn't have kept
even in the days when her knees could carry her through
the first one? No, it was clear—a strange soul of some kind
had taken possession of her in the jailhouse, and made
her do a mindless thing. The rage she felt had attracted a
bodiless spirit, a *malangel,* that had no purpose but to ravage
a situation which had been hopeless in the first place—almost as hopeless before the *malangel* had taken it over as
it was now. The only difference was that Pepe Luis could at
least have died like a man, instead of dying like a child
who would find out at the last second that his mother had
lied to him. And she *had* lied. She had opened her mouth
and made a nonsensical promise that was a kind of double
lie. But that was the way all evil operated. It came into you
in a moment of emptiness; it used what was left of your
body to make fun of your life: a *malangel* was a jester from
hell—a malevolent clown that could, with one touch of its
breath, make you do things you had never done before, and
leave you with no way to undo them. It turned all feeling
into a bad joke, and it left you without a laugh.

Eugenia kept her fingers clenched and went on forcing herself forward. If she disliked the wind for making her think,
there was one reason she needed it now—at least it was
clean enough to wash the smell of the jailhouse out of her
lungs. If anything *could* wash it out—though she had her
doubts about that. It was in the bowels of the building that
the *malangel* had taken over—up to then it had only toyed
with her in unimportant ways, like showing her that the doctor was a man who had a certain greed for money. But
the thing had not possessed her until she had breathed in-

side the jail. As chief maid she had trained herself to be
sensitive to smell; she could walk into a room and shut her
eyes and know in five seconds whether it was clean or not.
She had detected many bad odors in the hotel that way.
But except for the time some workers had dug up the
cemetery in Suelo to make room for a gift-shop center, the
odor inside the Sanlúcar jailhouse was worse than anything
she had ever encountered. She had stood at the door to
Pepe Luis's cell and it had been a full thirty seconds before
she had been able to open her mouth and speak. The
doctor and the jailkeeper had gone quickly back up the
passage to wait for her, and during half a minute Eugenia
had stood in the awful air and tried not to know that she
was in hell. Then she had tried not to wonder what was
causing the stench—only, after her eyes grew accustomed
to the darkness, she didn't need to wonder because she could
see what was causing it. There was a cement ditch on one
side of the wall of cells and at least three weeks' worth of
feces and slops from the fifty men in the jailhouse had been
shoveled into it. The mess was waiting there to be carted
away. It was August and the heat was terrible. There was
no plumbing in the jailhouse, and no outside windows in
the passage. The stench seemed to have soaked into the cement floor and the brick walls—into the stone heart of the
building. Eugenia stood in it and breathed as shallowly as
she could. The infernal air seemed to be thickening around
her and she put her head close to the door of the cell and
spoke Pepe Luis's name. There was no reply, and she had
to take enough air into her lungs to repeat it, loud, four
times, before an answering grunt came from the darkness.
The sound of his voice made her heart feel suddenly empty
and it was at that exact moment that the *malangel* entered
and possessed her: "You don't have to stay in this place. I'll
buy your way out," she said.

There was more quiet and then another grunt and the
sound of a cough from inside the cell.

"You understand?"

The sound in the cell began as a grunt again. Halfway
through, it increased in volume, and then as if by itself
it twisted into a baby word with two "ah" sounds in it.

"Shut up," she said. "Shut up."

The grown man's voice began again and rose, and in the
putrid stench of the building it repeated the terrible silly
baby word: *"Mamá."*

"Shut up," she said violently, "I told you. I promised. You
understand? I promise . . ."

As if it would kill her, the voice rose into a sour moan that ended in the same wet cough and then was quiet.

Eugenia said, loud, "My God, shut up. I don't want your voice. You are to do nothing. You are to shut up. . . ."

The voice inside the cell began again and in the darkness, without thinking, she could feel the *malangel* stir deep within her body. She looked at the cement ceiling over her head and she said, "I shit on life. It makes me sick." Then watching the ceiling she said in a louder voice, "If life comes to this . . ." And then all the breath went out of her. Quietly, with no effort at all, she said, "I shit on God."

The voice stopped inside the cell, and in the sudden peace of the passageway, Eugenia tipped her head forward and vomited into the ditch beneath her. When she had finished, she stiffened again. Then she moved away and left the cell without saying good-bye. After having wanted so much to talk to him, she could not listen to Pepe Luis any more today. She walked rigidly, stumbling, up the passageway to the mouth of the jail.

The walls in front of her looked wet as she walked and the cement floor seemed tilted before her in the passage as if she was moving up a slant, though she knew that the building was on one level. She felt dizzy and strange. The doctor was standing in the jailkeeper's office smoking a cigarette. He had sent the jailkeeper on an errand and he was alone waiting for her. Eugenia watched his eyes as she approached him. They were the color of charcoal and they gleamed like silver.

When he saw her, the doctor opened his mouth to say something dull and soothing, and Eugenia stood still and let the *malangel* speak for her. It was then that she told the second part of the lie. She hadn't planned on it, any more than she had on making the promise of freedom to Pepe Luis—and later, walking in the wind, she realized that it was the very same *malangel* that went on to tell the other half of the lie.

When the second half came out, it was as if it had been sitting in her mouth for several minutes. She could hear the doctor talking in a pacifying way as he would have to an idiot, and the instant she opened her mouth to interrupt him, the lie fell out. She said, "I didn't even know Pepe Luis was in jail when I came to Sanlúcar. I came to bring him some news."

Then she reached up and tightened the bun on her hair. She leaned for balance on the wall.

The doctor quit talking and yawned. He saw that she was

dizzy and he pushed a chair toward her with his foot. Eugenia sat down.

"The news came yesterday," she said.

"Yes?" the doctor said boredly.

"Yes," Eugenia said, looking at him, "I only came to tell him. Fifty thousand pesetas." She dropped her hands.

The two pinpoints of light that she had seen once before flicked like tiny wings deep inside the doctor's pupils, and went out. "I don't quite follow you," he said.

"I don't blame you—it's hard for me too. . . . With everything happening at once. An aunt of mine in Madrid," Eugenia said.

Listening to her own voice, she realized that it didn't sound like hers any more. The tone was thin and old and silly, like the voice of an idiot. It was the sound of the woman the doctor thought he was talking to.

The doctor listened. "An aunt?"

"It all happened together," she said confusedly, crossing herself. "May she rest in peace. Fifty thousand pesetas. It's a lot of money. . . . Fifty thousand pesetas is ten thousand *duros*," she said.

The words were mumbled, but the lie was telling itself —she had never had an aunt in Madrid, but she was on home ground. She had not always been a maid. She was also an old fisherwoman. She tested the bait:

"What will Pepe Luis do with all that money now?"

"I have no idea, *Señora*," the doctor said. He stood with his back to the window waiting for the jailkeeper. The wind was hard behind him, and the thin hair on the top of his head floated upward for a second like seaweed. "Your aunt died?"

"Yes," Eugenia said. "The only family I had."

"I'm sorry for your loss," the doctor said formally.

"Thank you," Eugenia said, *"pobrecita:* poor thing."

"Well, at least she had a life."

"Yes."

The doctor coughed. "And left him . . ."

"Me. She left me the money for Pepe Luis. Fifty thousand pesetas," Eugenia said, watching the two points of light flicker and dim, "fifty thousand." The doctor stared at her. The points of light dulled slowly and began to fade out.

"And another fifty thousand for me," Eugenia said quietly.

The two little points of light in his eyes went on and stayed on.

"So in a way it was good news . . . a hundred thousand

pesetas," Eugenia said, seeing the tiny lights flare like coals
that were being fanned, "and Pepe Luis never even met
her—he's never been as far as Madrid. He didn't expect
any money. Twenty thousand *duros* is a lot of money."

"Yes," the doctor said curtly.

"Enough for down payments on two little houses . . . I
never saw a quarter of that in my life," Eugenia said,
rambling on like an old woman. "Not once."

"Is that what you're going to spend it on, *Señora?*" the
doctor said with the crisp practical tone of a Catalonian.
"Houses?"

"I'm not going to spend it," Eugenia said. "I didn't tell
Pepe Luis about it. I'm not going to tell him. I'm not going to tell anybody."

There was a short pause.

The doctor coughed. "No?"

"No," she said, "for what? Why would I tell him? The
way things look now . . ." She covered her eyes with one
hand.

"Now, *Señora,*" the doctor said. "Be calm. . . . I know
it upset you seeing the jail . . ."

"No," Eugenia said. "It isn't that. I was only wondering."

She waited. The dust out in the courtyard rose like powder.

"Wondering what?" the doctor said.

"You know. Wondering."

She looked. The doctor's eyes were ghostly in the dust.
The points of light were smaller, but they were brighter.

"It's peculiar," she said.

"What is?"

"I've never had money in my life. *Es muy raro:* It's a rare
feeling."

". . . What is?"

"I don't know. I don't want the money," she said.

". . . How is that again?" the doctor said, frowning.

"Not if he's going to . . . it's like a judgment on me. I'd
rather give it up—every *céntimo.* I'd pay it all."

The doctor wet his upper lip and trimmed his mous-
tache evenly on both sides with his tongue. "Pay it where,
Señora?" he said.

"Anywhere. I'd be happy to see the end of it, and never
tell Pepe Luis about it . . . just to see him out of jail . . ."

The doctor did not speak for a moment. There were
footsteps on the walk outside. The little winged points of
light in his eyes looked cloudy. "I don't think your husband
would be so happy about giving it up," he said. "Especially

with no questions. Of course it's none of my business."

"My husband doesn't know I have it," Eugenia said.

The doctor blinked.

"I wouldn't tell *him*, even if I keep it," Eugenia said. "It was my aunt, not his."

The doctor glanced at the gray courtyard. The dust drifted away. The two points of light in his pupils cleared slowly to the color of pure silver. Outside the jailhouse somebody was walking toward them. Eugenia could hear the rattling of the keys.

"If I knew," she said, sounding silly and half senile, "if there was just one person. But who'd know," she said as though to herself, "if there was a person like that?"

There was a little crash of metal outside the building. Whoever was carrying the keys had dropped them. She could hear them being picked up again.

"A person like what?" the doctor said.

"Never mind. You're too . . . you wouldn't know about the ones I mean. The men who aren't so honest."

The points of light turned to steel. "I don't busy myself with such things, *Señora*," the doctor said.

"Of course not, of course not. Of course not," Eugenia said in a flustered way. On the other side of the heavy door the footsteps stopped and a key moved in the lock. The doctor watched the lock.

Eugenia turned and made a show of following the doctor's gaze to the door as it swung back. The man on the other side was the jailkeeper. He was carrying a pack of cigarettes that he had gone to buy for the doctor. "Him?" she said. "*Him?* Should I offer . . ."

"No," the doctor said quickly. "Be quiet."

"But maybe if I . . ."

"He's not the one. Be quiet," the doctor said sharply.

There was no more time to talk about anything, and Eugenia left the doctor where he was standing. But it wasn't till she had stepped down out of the jailhouse and walked all the way out of the courtyard that the dizziness left her and she realized the full meaning of what had happened to her or what she had done.

Now in the town she pushed herself toward the sea and sniffed the air. The memory of the stench was still with her and she took another deep breath. Below, the cheap bars and short warehouses near the water were battened down and closed against the weather. The water was white and green beyond them and a few olive trees shook their leaves over it. Eugenia watched as she walked. Even the landscape looked expensive. the sea was money-green and the tops of the trees were silver. There was no doubt in her mind now that the doctor could be bribed, if you had enough money. Only she had none. So it was over. First she had met her death, and then she had gone into hell, and then she had been possessed by a *malangel* and it was all over now. She had promised Pepe Luis his freedom; she had lied to the doctor and both the promise and the second half of the lie had been as empty as she was. She could not bribe anybody and it was over and she who had been a thrifty woman all her life had bartered her soul today for nothing. There wasn't much left to do but sit down and wait to die, only she was not the sort of woman who could sit down. So she went on walking.

Now along the coast she could see the sand rise into long lashes of white that grazed the warehouses. The wind was turning gusty as she had known it would. A thin foam lay on the water. The beach was deserted. As she came near the main road, she could see three women in the window of a house on the opposite side, watching her progress. The women were probably making bets with each other whether she would make it across the road in the wind without falling. There were several cars moving carefully along the coast. A car horn sounded behind her and she pulled to one side to let it pass. The car turned east onto the main road and followed the other ones. The people in it hadn't seen Eugenia's face, but she had recognized them—the man at the wheel was Count Guzmán and next to him on the front seat was the blond American girl; in the back was the boy named Will sitting next to his mongrel dog. The car passed the other cars quickly, as if the people inside were in a hurry to go somewhere. It left a skirt of dust in the air over the road.

Eugenia stood waiting for the dust to clear. It was a meaningless omen that the car should pass her now, as if it were telling her that she ought to ask the Count for money. There was no point in asking him—he didn't have any, and everybody knew it. You might just as well ask the Columbus tree that grew near his courtyard. If you knew anything at all about the Count, you knew he wasn't a man to get pesetas out of—and not because he wouldn't give them, but because he would. He already had; he'd given a great deal of his money away to poor people before his wife realized what was happening and took the Count to court and got an injunction so that he couldn't give away the rest of it. The incident had been in the local papers and everybody had heard about it. So the car passing was another empty sign; so you just kept walking.

The dust lifted and Eugenia crossed the coastal road. She passed the window where the three old faces had been watching her. The women were sitting down and their eyes followed her curiously along the house. Yes, women, she thought. You're right—I'm damned and I'm still walking. We're all damned; but there's a choice. You can sit and be damned, or you can walk and be damned, and I am walking.

On the narrow road between the houses another swirl of dirt flared up at her; some of it got on her mouth, and she lowered her face and wiped it off. Then she crossed another smaller road next to the shore. She was ten meters from the beach—far enough to keep the sand from her face—and she walked along the docks past some bars until she came to a café. The wind was against her and she had to fight the door to get it open. It slammed after her. The hollowness inside of her burned and she was thirsty now from the vomiting. She went to the service bar and ordered a coffee and a glass of cheap brandy and some water. The bar-café was filled with fishermen. They paid no attention to her. On any other day she would have felt at home among them. The fishermen were waiting for the weather to clear. She had waited all her life with fishermen. The coffee was bitter and black and she ordered a second cup. The man behind the bar was Pepe Luis's age; he smiled at her. He ground some coffee beans and put the cup under the steam machine; then he inserted the coffee and turned the valve, forcing the steam down through the grounds. He took the cup and set it in front of her. *"Algo más, Señora?"* he said: "Anything else?"

"Yes," Eugenia said.

". . . Something to eat?"

"No," she said. "I'd like a hundred thousand pesetas."

The man laughed in a friendly way. "Go to church," he said. "Ask the Virgin."

"No," Eugenia said. She sipped the coffee and put the cup back in the saucer. "Not the Virgin."

"Who then?"

"I don't know," she said. "What else is there? The Columbus tree?"

"Claro," the barman said. "Why not? Go and ask the Columbus tree. It has an angel." He went to serve some other customers.

Eugenia finished the coffee and wiped her mouth with her

hand. That's what it comes to, she thought. If you can't ask the Virgin, ask the Count. If you can't ask the Count, ask a tree. Go and ask the angel that lives in the Columbus tree for a hundred thousand pesetas and then go cut your throat.

She paid for the brandy and the two coffees and went back outside. She stood for a while by the shore between the bar-café and the water. She would have stayed to tell the barman that she didn't believe in trees, but she didn't believe in anything else either. She didn't believe in God any more; she didn't believe in the barman. She believed in nothing and she stood near the building out of the wind. Then the wind dropped, and she went and stood on the beach close to the waves.

She had come as far as she could walk on the land. The coast stretched out in front of her, endless and thin and gray, like the edge of the world. She had always loved it, no matter what the weather was, and often she had come just to stand and look at it. But she could feel nothing for it now. It was only barren and bleak looking in the ugly light. The *foreño* was beginning to subside, and between the blunt gusts came odd flat pauses when there seemed to be no air at all. When it couldn't blow the way it wanted to, the *foreño* filled its lungs for another try—while it was filling them it got mad and didn't blow at all. The more it ebbed the angrier it would get until the day it finally stopped. It was a Moorish wind and you couldn't expect it to have much manners.

Eugenia stood on the newly quiet beach and watched a piece of driftwood that was half buried in the sand. It had blown ashore and the one end that was showing looked soggy and damp. The wood had a peculiar shape. It was shaped like a streak of lightning. She bent over and picked it up and shook the sand from it. It was like holding a broken lightning bolt in her hand. There was no place further to walk and she looked at the piece of wood. Then while she was examining it, the wind came back too quickly and the sand rose all around her. She lifted her arms against it, but not fast enough, and she felt the grains prick her skin sharply. The sand dug like a hundred thousand needles into her face. It was all over her at the same time, and she turned and struck out with the piece of driftwood. She stood there turning in a slow circle, striking at the sheets of sand with the piece of wood, hitting the wind as though she thought she could beat it back from the coast. Then, as the *foreño* kept on rising, she began to curse the coast

itself. In a loud voice she called out that she shit on the land
and on the graves of her ancestors who had lived on the
land. She went on turning and she closed her eyes and
raised her voice; she called the coast every horrible name
she could think of. Her hair came loose and then in the wind
her voice grew louder until the words blended together, and
what came out of her mouth was more like an animal cry
than anything human. She went on like that, twisting in a
circle at the beach where the earth ended, on the coast she
had loved once where she had grown up, and her voice
rose so that she no longer recognized the sound. She yelled
without stopping till the blowing air subsided and was calm
again. She snarled the wind down. Then when the wind
stopped, her voice went on by itself without the wind.
From a kind of rough scream it fell slowly in a long wail
and rose once more in a growl so deep she could feel it
rock her whole body. When it was over, she ceased turning. She bent forward in a violent contraction, and the
piece of driftwood flew out of her hand. It struck the coast
and she saw the wood break into splinters on the sand.

After that she sucked evenly at her cheeks until she
had a mouthful of saliva. She collected some on her tongue
and, straightening, she spit after the wood on the coast. Then
she relaxed. She had done the worst thing that it is possible
for a woman to do. She had cursed her dead—she had
soiled her own blood—and she had spit on it. Now she turned
her back on the sea. She stood with her broad shoulders
against it, and she looked up at the long line of bars and
cafés where the earth began.

A few of the fishermen were standing outside the café
she had just gone into. They were watching her, grinning,
and two of them were nudging each other. She ignored them
and brushed the sand from her clothes. Then she took off
the black scarf and shook it out. She wrapped it around
her head and began moving. She passed among the silent
men with her head held high; she kept her shoulders flat
against the coast. She left the men behind her, and she
walked back up into the town.

The gust of wind was gone and this time she moved without a conscious direction. It didn't matter that it was all over
now. Walking mattered and something was not over as long
as she was walking. She kept going forward. She went back
across the main road and through the heart of the town.
She passed many places. She passed houses, and a vegetable
store where strings of garlic and peppers hung over a stall
outside; she passed a store belonging to a maker of windows

and then a *zapatero,* a shoemaker, and a small cement fountain with a faucet where country women came to fill their pails. After that she passed a hardware store. She was not aware of time and she did not know how long she walked. Her ankles were swollen, but she did not feel them. She crossed the street to avoid looking at a shop window where infants' clothes and toys were sold, and watched the road ahead of her.

When she had arrived at the top of the town she went on past some other houses, and then past a small gray church with a white steeple. The church doors were open and inside she saw two women kneeling in front of the altar with candles in their hands and beatific looks on their faces. The candles they were holding were the perfumed kind, and as she passed the open doors of the church Eugenia could smell again the awful rotten stench of the ditch full of feces inside the jailhouse. She walked faster until the church was behind her and then she crossed under a long arbor of white jasmine—but the jasmine too smelled like the ditch filled with waste matter. There was no way to get rid of it because the smell of waste was in her nose, and she passed the Guzmán palace and crossed along the top of the hill with the town below her, keeping away from the flowers. The hill was lined with prickly pear and wild roses in bloom and under it the thousand little houses fell in cascading tiers down to the sea. Smoke was rising from a few of the chimneys. It floated in gusts from the wind like the shadows of birds over the red housetops. Eugenia crossed the hill slowly to the ruins that topped the town. Everybody along the coast was familiar with the ruins of the castle and twice as a child she had come here to visit them and had played in them with other children. *Gitanos,* gypsies, lived in the ruins now; they kept their children and their garbage in the central courtyard. Once a month they carted the garbage away to the town dump, but the rest of the time they didn't seem to mind the smell. Eugenia preferred it now to the smell of the flowers and she walked three times around the high stone walls without going in. There were children playing inside—she could hear their shouts. There were tufts of dry grass anchored into the rocky earth and there were mounds she had to walk over. The gray sky was swollen and bruise-colored and painfully bright, and the ground was dark. There was a bird soaring overhead. She walked a fourth time around the outside of the ruins watching the bird and listening to the children. The sounds of playing reverberated in the high walls and after the fourth time around she left the ruins and walked to the edge of the hill. Long ago the first Lord of Sanlúcar had built the castle here because it was the highest vantage point, and from it you could see the river and all along the coast. There was no place else to walk; the ruins were as high as you could go. She looked down for a minute at the land and the water under her feet. The cliff was steep, and one step would have sent her down more than two hundred meters like a big stone onto the jagged rooftops. She lifted her left foot and turned; and then she walked away from the edge. She picked her way back along the clean patches of earth where there were no flowers. She walked toward the Guzmán palace, watching the frayed little hem of trees below. There was another retaining wall beneath the trees and then the last houses of the lower part of the town; she walked along the upper cliff wall to a place she had skipped on her way to the ruins. Then she stopped walking.

The tree over her was huge and motionless. The falling wind had ceased again, and the branches and leaves were as still as the sky. The branches were in full leaf most of the year. The heaviest of them dipped down till their tips scraped the earth. The Columbus tree was incredibly large, and it was known for its moods—it often changed according to the color of the day. Children seldom went near it. Sometimes as a child Eugenia had see it from a distance when it was cheerful in the sun one minute, and the next second had turned its leaves the other way. In an approaching storm the giant tree seemed to take life from the wind and its tossing branches made outlandish gestures and monster shapes on the hill over the town. You could see it from many places along the beach, and some of the fishermen used it as a sort of weather vane; those who knew it well, the old people, could look up from below and tell at a glance when the sky was going to change, just by the mood of the tree. It was plain-looking now and it had a thick dull gloom; but its branches were stiff and the leaves were hard as silver in the bruised light. There was something vastly mischievous about the tree from where Eugenia was standing. As she watched, a breeze touched it and all its leaves moved. Gradually the tree took on a tinged look— a sort of affronted nobility, like a faintly ruffled duchess. It had got a whiff of her, she knew. The Columbus tree didn't think much more of her now than she thought of herself. It was a known fact that the spirits that lived in the tree reflected the mood of any person standing near its roots. Eugenia spread her legs and gripped the ground with her

feet as if she were growing in the same soil. She thought:
Now listen. Listen. Listen, she said silently to the tree.

Above her there was a quick whispering in the thick leaves,
and one heavy branch to her right moved a little away from
her.

No. Listen, she thought without speaking. Stand there and
listen. You shut up. Listen to me.

The tree grew quiet slowly. Eugenia moved into a space
between the tips of the heavy bottom branches and the
trunk, so that the leaves were like a dark tent around her.
She kept her eyes on the place where the spirits had their
home. The devil and the other angels took up a lot of room;
the trunk was so wide that five men could stand with their
faces against it and still not be able to touch fingers. The
voices of the spirits were high in the leaves, but they slept
low down in the ancient roots of the tree. Some of the
roots looked swollen and knotted, like Eugenia's ankles. She
waited until the leaves were still and soundless around her.
Now, she thought, I can't help thinking and I can't help
being what I am.

Listen: I come to you for help, she thought. I can't cry.
I can't lie down and get kicked by the boots of everything,
like my sisters, all the rest. I might have been like my sisters,
but I'm not like my sisters and I can't help that either. I
can't give up, I don't know how. There are women who are
not satisfied unless they have control of things, and I am one
of those women. I am the way I am, and probably Pepe
Luis is the opposite way only because I am my way. Maybe
he can't help getting into trouble any more than I can help
wanting to get him out, to control him, and maybe control
over my family is all I ever wanted, and all I have ever
lived for in my life. . . . Maybe there is a God, and maybe
He knew on the hill that day halfway up to the shrine
that I was trying to bargain with the Virgin for Pepe Luis,
as I would for a cabbage in the market, not because I cared
about the owner of the market, but only to fill my own belly.
But if it was like that, then I shit on God all the same.
Because if He does exist, then He was the one who made me
the way I am—and He made the marketplace and the jailhouse and the doctor and He made the captain too. . . .

So I shit on all of them; I shit on everything in the world
but two things . . . I don't shit on myself. And I don't shit
on you. . . .

Because I want something from you. There is only one
thing left on earth I still want, and it's this . . . I still want
my way. . . . Despite the captain's office and the jailhouse

and the doctor and everything else. It isn't even for love of Pepe Luis, because there isn't anything left in me to love with—I just want control. . . . And the only difference is that this time I want *more* of it than I ever wanted in my life. Because before, I only wanted it over my family. . . . . But now I want it over the world. Over the captain and the jail and the town and the whole marketplace: I want control over the whole goddamned universe because now I want *not* to be helpless. Now that I am the most helpless I ever was—*now,* I want control.

So, you get it for me, angel, she thought, tree-angel; and I will give anything you want . . . I will give myself . . . I'm still a woman who can make a decent bargain. And if you are an angel who has fallen, a thing of the damned, so much the better, because I am a damned thing too. I am ready for you now—the little *malangel* made me ready. And I am better than any woman you have ever found because there's nothing in me but readiness for you. I know now that you are The Demon. And if I am fat and bad-smelling and old, I'm still the best woman you will find, because I'm better than all the other weak-bellied sisters who come here to beg favors from you, and then go to church and kneel and pray to the Virgin. . . . I won't pray, and I won't kneel. I am the ripest woman you will find, and you know it. So come into me now and give me what I want. I don't want love. I only want force. . . . *Now, now, now I want control.* . . .

The whispering in the leaves over her head had grown furious while she thought, as if all the mischievous spirits of the tree were fighting over her—or as though they were bargaining with each other as to which one would get her. The branches all around her shook in a quick gust of wind. The shaking was followed by a silence so sudden and so complete that it seemed as if the world had stopped turning. She looked up from the roots and saw that not a single leaf was moving in the tree. It was the greatest silence she had ever heard—greater even than the one in the captain's office—and she waited to see what would come after it, but nothing came. The peace held, like the one they told about in the stories of the great wave, when the surf had drawn back from the land and no one had known what it meant until it was too late. It was like the peace that had made the deaf-mute scream. Standing under the tree, Eugenia thought: Now. It must be coming to take me now. Then she heard it.

It began as a sound that was so slight she could not be sure it was real. It started only as a distant hissing in the branches over her head—so delicate that at first it hardly seemed to exist. It was like the crumpling of dry tissue paper from somewhere high above her, and she listened, craning her neck and lifting her arms, and then in the distance she was sure she heard it. She stood quiet and waited for it, and she went on lifting her arms until both her fists were pointed at the topmost branch, and then for the first time since morning she opened her hands wide and straightened the fingers. They were stiff and it pained her so that she almost couldn't, and then the pain went away. She was standing with her arms stretched up and her hands flat as leaves, like a tree under the tree, and she felt it coming from the roots. It came first up her legs and her loins began to quiver and then, shockingly, it entered her and she shuddered. Her body shook as the leaves began to move, and she moaned in the thrust of it. The thing rippled through her and it would not stop and it was more than she had ever felt with Enrique and more than she had thought that she could feel. Her body opened to it like something under water. She grunted aloud and the great tree hissed louder and she felt its breath on her face. Then the hissing changed, and there was a single gasp, and then one long vast endless sigh of the tree, and the breath of it was strong on her hands and arms and face, and it was over. The long heaving sigh in the leaves faded. It became another sound, and at first she did not recognize it. Then she knew. The tree was laughing. It was the gentlest laughter imaginable high in the leaves, and she could feel the presence of the angel. The lightest breeze of all floated down and fluttered on her body. It seemed to be all over her, and then on her hands. Something on her left hand looked like a bright leaf. It was high up between two of the fingers near the knuckles and she lowered her arm and looked at it. There was nothing there. Her hand was full of knots and as dry looking as it had been before. She lifted it again slowly toward the place where she had been holding her arm up, but nothing happened; the new leaf was gone. Then when her hand was as high as she could reach, she saw it again. It was just a little piece of light that came through the shadows of the tree. It danced back and forth on two of her knuckles, so that it did look like a new bright leaf growing there. It looked like something else too. It looked like a paper fluttering between the fingers of her left hand.

Eugenia lowered her arm again. There was a kind of line tugging at her memory. Almost of its own volition, her hand went to her side and pushed into the pocket of her dress; there were some coins in the pocket and there was another object. When she pulled her fist out she was holding onto a very small damp crumpled paper. It was grimy, as though she had been sweating on it through her dress all day. It was stained and torn.

She touched it curiously with her other hand. She could not remember how she had come by it, but she recognized on it the fancy crest that was the trademark of the Hotel Malage, and she opened the sweaty scrap of paper and held it up. The light from the sky under the branches was too dark to see by, and the markings of the pencil had faded to an illegible scrawl, with damp gray smeared places and a dark smudge near the center. The leaf shadows were densest where she was standing. She moved between the branches and walked out of the tree.

She went a few steps beyond it and stopped. The glare was too strong; it was even worse than trying to read the note in shadow.

Lowering it from the sky, she cupped it under one of her breasts and bent slightly over, holding it almost like an infant. After a while she could see it better. One and a half words were still partly intact—the others were mixed into the big dark smudge at the center. She went through the letters one by one and put them together in her mind but they meant nothing; the first word had been "gold." The second was "villa." Nothing else on the note could be read, and she mouthed the two words several times silently. They contained no special meaning for her and she couldn't imagine what the words had been that were erased now by sweat. Then she turned and looked at the tree.

She could still hear the angel laughing high at the top, but she did not go back under with it. She stood outside watching and waiting. She belonged to it now and there was some secret meaning that was still owed her. It was part of the bargain she had made and paid for, and she waited for it to become clear, but the laughter only grew fainter. Then she knew that the meaning was not going to get any clearer, and she knew why. It was because she already had the meaning, just as she had already had the note in her pocket before entering the tree. While she listened, the laughter drifted straight up; it stood high above the tree for an instant and was gone.

Eugenia turned and faced the coast and the cascading houses of the town under her feet. Clearly the thing that had just happened was a miracle. The only part that remained was for her to understand it. But there was no doubt in her mind, it was as much of a miracle as the Virgin's speaking to her that day long ago on the hill leading up to the shrine in another town. She took a step forward and began to walk back down along the hill to Sanlúcar. The meaning of it only had to be thought through. Even now she had a dim idea who had written the note. She had some sense too of what the missing words were; certainly she knew who to ask. Then as she walked, something adjusted in her mind like a kaleidoscope coming into focus, and she knew that she would not need to ask much more than that. A sort of idea was forming itself in the air in front of her eyes. Behind her the tree was laughing again. She could feel it like a whisper on the back of her neck.

She went on walking along the hill. The hot sky was losing its brilliance now; soon it would burst into flame, and then in the sunset it would turn gold at the edges where twilight began. Sparrows would rise like hawks over the rooftops. They would swoop and chatter and shriek like witches in the air. Bats were going to fly tonight; there would be bugs for them to catch as the wind settled. Eugenia looked to her right. Evening was falling. There were radios playing now in some of the houses. The music wafted up and hovered softly over the town like the beating of wings.

FIVE

Evening

IT HAD been while Littlejohn was drying herself on a big white Turkish towel that morning, looking through the bathroom window, that she had seen Will start up the cobblestone road to the palace and had seen him break into a run. The day began that way for her. Even from a distance she could tell what had happened—when an idea got hold of Will it did broad jumps in his brain till it wore itself out or put him to sleep. Littlejohn smiled, seeing him begin to trot and then come streaking headlong, tripping over the cobblestones in the road with the dog barking beside him. Will never had been able to do things just sort of, she knew; he wasn't a halfway man. He still thought he was, but he'd have to learn the difference for himself—he wouldn't believe anybody else. She closed the window and unwrapped herself from the towel she had been using and began to dress.

There were two doors to the bathroom she was in—one on either side. The bedroom door was open and she could see Guzmán sitting motionless in a casement window smoking a cigarette. She watched him while she was buttoning the back of her dress. Littlejohn could be as fascinated by the angles of the man as she could by his eyes. Just sitting still he was a marvel to her—the body loose, not slumped, the long bones linked and collected like a sleepy cat. It was as hard for her to think that she had found him ugly at first as it was to remember she had once not lived in the building that belonged to him. The thought of the building disturbed her now as it had been doing for a week and she turned away. She picked up the hairbrush and looked at herself in the mirror.

Then she stopped, troubled, the brush halfway up and her eyes caught on the air. When she had finally got out of bed this morning it was with the same week-old sense of being off balance and she couldn't seem to shake it. It had to do with early dawn and a threat of some kind; it was connected to the sounds of the workman she had heard above them on the roof. With her vision unfocused Littlejohn felt again the knowledge of something unseen that had no right to be there, as if the mirror was holding the answer to a question she hadn't yet asked. She scanned the other things that were visible in the flat polished glass. There was the white tile-and-plaster wall behind her, and a small table; then the open doorway of the bedroom and Guzmán sitting in the casement, his back to her. Beyond him was the second casement window and the far wall of his bedroom. That was all. Except for the smoke from his cigarette as it drifted up, curling, toward the ceiling. Littlejohn watched the smoke. Then she dropped the brush.

She swirled and walked into the bedroom too fast; the hem of her skirt caught in the hinge of the doorway. It didn't tear and she lifted it off. She went on more quietly and came to a halt just behind him.

But for a slight movement at the tip of his cigarette she wouldn't have known he had heard her. The movement made a loop in the long stream of smoke. It rose in a twist and broke against a wood beam overhead.

Guzmán took another drag. ". . . You are watching something?"

"I was admiring the wood. . . . I love the beams in this room."

"You have not looked at them before?"

"I spend most of my time looking at them; I just hadn't noticed. . . . There's an attic above here, isn't there? . . . between this room and the roof?"

Guzmán turned his head and glanced at her. His eyes were smiling. It was the smile of a patient baby.

"We'll be late," he said. "William is waiting for you. He's on the terrace."

Littlejohn felt herself start to frown. She went to the table where she kept her things and put on some lipstick; then she ruffled the back of her hair with her hand. She dropped the lipstick and a comb into her purse. There was another mirror in the dressing table. Behind her, Guzmán's smile had changed imperceptibly. She could feel the change in the mirror. "Do I amuse you?"

"Yes," Guzmán said. "Do you mind?"

"Not much." Littlejohn put a tissue between her lips and blotted off the excess lipstick.

"I was seeing how you go to the marshes in riding boots and a white dress. When you were a virgin you dressed like a man. Now you are a woman, you dress like a virgin. Why do you always look at me in the mirror?"

Littlejohn smiled at him across the length of the white

room. Then she turned and led the way out of the bedroom and down the big hall.

The white walls in the morning light smelled clean and dry; from the far end, the life-sized twelfth-century figure of a saint stared blankly at her as she approached. Guzmán was close behind her. The hall came out into the wide Ambassador's Room and they walked under the faded ceiling on the old wood floor. Littlejohn stopped at the door to the servants' quarters. "You go ahead," she said. "I want to see about something in the kitchen."

". . . See about what?"

"Dinner," Littlejohn lied. She kept her face averted. When Guzmán had gone on out to the terrace, she opened the door and went through the servants' hall to the pantry.

The servants' wing had the faint odor of rancid olive oil and an empty feel about it. The three people who lived in it weren't enough to keep the palace in proper order and there was always a series of rooms that hadn't been cleaned for a week. The heels of Littlejohn's boots clicked on the tiles. She found María, Guzmán's cook, standing at the west wall of the pantry peeling a pan of potatoes in the sink. María was delighted to have her come and visit; until now Littlejohn had stayed out of the servants' wing despite the cook's encouragement. She sat down on a stool next to the sink playing idly with the potatoes and chatting with María in halting Spanish.

Over María's head through the pantry window she could see the east wing of the palace—the wing she had just left. The north windows were like slate in the morning light; she couldn't make out the inside of the master bedroom. The vertical space between the windows and the roof was large enough for an attic a man could stand up in. She traced along the roof with her eyes and found what she was looking for. The upper-story wall curved into a kind of small mansard window she hadn't noticed before.

She interrupted María's talk about the picnic food and asked her a short blunt question about Guzmán. The hands on the potatoes grew still and María turned to face her. The stillness in the kitchen was white and hard. María was a nice-looking woman of thirty-five with an open face and gentle credulous eyes. She glanced once gravely through the window behind her and then around the pantry to make certain that she and Littlejohn were alone. Then she put the knife down and began to talk.

As Littlejohn listened, the prodding sense of hopelessness she had been feeling for a week bloomed inside her and she began to think of her life at the palace in a different way. She heard the low childlike tone of María's voice and the quiet around it and the wind in the big tree outside. After a while she heard the sharp cutting tick of the kitchen clock.

While Littlejohn was with María, Will waited for her outside on the second floor terrace. He was watching Guzmán walk up and down picking up olive branches that had broken and blown up onto it during the night. The Count was limber for his age, Will thought, but that was about all. It was like watching a five-year-old play by himself with occasional looks in Will's direction for approval. You had the feeling all the time you had to keep an eye on the man or he would back up gracefully and fall off the terrace.

Maybe, Will thought, it was Guzmán's presence that he had sensed coming up the hill. You couldn't help but think every day something new was bound to happen. Whatever had looked wrong on the cliff against the gray sky of late morning wasn't apparent when you got here except in the figure of the Count himself. He wasn't Will's idea of what a real man even busied himself with, let alone looked like. Lieutenant Donahue could probably have swung Guzmán around his head in the air with one arm. And Donahue could answer a question or two, that was for sure. You could tell he knew things. He wasn't the sort of man who would go around gathering olive branches. Littlejohn had given herself up to Guzmán as if he were the biggest man in the world, and it was this very fact that made Will feel so disconnected from her these days. Except for the last morning or so, every time she came back after spending a night with the Count, she had the same peaceful look about her. It was hard to describe, but Will didn't care for it. It was like she had got a hold of this new way of relaxing or something. Every morning he noticed it. The same soft look. And those smug lazy eyes.

Will's left thigh had gone to sleep on the wall and he jumped down onto the terrace now and shook it. Guzmán had gone inside with the pile of branches and Will was alone. He put his weight on his other foot and gritted his teeth waiting for the tingle that would come as the blood seeped back. His thigh often went to sleep when he sat on a wall or a stone; the reason was that it didn't have all the muscle it needed to hold the blood in. It wasn't enough that you had to put up with the rest of the world—you had to have a body that upset you too. There was your private world and there was your public world and all there was between them was seventy-five pounds of embarrassment. Will couldn't gain weight no matter what he did; once in New York he had eaten six cheeseburgers in one day and got on the scale the next morning and weighed exactly the same. Besides that, he had more bones in his body than most people: the way he figured it, he was eighty percent calcium. One time he read an article in an American magazine entitled "You Are What You Eat," and it had made him angry. He was the living proof that it wasn't true. He had sat down with a pencil and worked on the problem all one afternoon. According to his calculations, he averaged four pounds of food and drink a day—or one thousand four hundred and sixty pounds of it in a year. This meant he had eaten eighteen thousand nine hundred and eighty pounds of food during his lifetime. And all he had kept was seventy-five pounds of it. The other eighteen thousand nine hundred and five pounds had been converted into pure shit. He was left with some joints and ribs with a little skin drawn over them. Standing on the terrace with the sharp tingle of blood trying to get back into his left leg, he wondered if writers like the one who had written that magazine article had ever been children. He doubted it. It was more likely magazine writers were given an anesthetic at birth and brought to in time to go to college. He shook his leg out again and yelped from the feel of it. Guzmán came out from piling the branches and watched Will standing with one leg in the air.

"You are having trouble with your foot, or you are practicing something?" Guzmán said.

Will sighed. "I'm waiting."

Guzmán frowned. "Waiting for what, may I ask?"

"Blood," Will said.

Guzmán was silent. One of the things that most irked you about the man was the way he listened to every single thing you said and took it all seriously. It would have been perfect in somebody you wanted to talk to, but Guzmán was the one person in the world Will *didn't* want to talk to. He was beginning to wonder if there was some connection between the two facts. If there was, if was a connection that missed him.

There were sounds from inside the Ambassador's Room and a door slammed; Will heard Littlejohn's boots, way inside at first, then louder on the wood. It was faster than she usually walked. Behind Will, the wind on the terrace had increased.

Littlejohn came out, her skirt slashing against the door.

She still had the lazy melted look from bed, and something besides—the worried expression was in her face.

"Hello, Will," she said.

"He is waiting for his blood," Guzmán said.

Littlejohn giggled. "Good," she said. Her eyes were funny.

". . . I thought we might go horseback riding before the picnic," Guzmán told her. "I should like to show William the backlands. . . ."

He went down to see that the horses were saddled.

Will stood on both his feet; the tingling had stopped in his left leg and he studied Littlejohn, but she kept her face pointed in the other direction.

"What's happened now?"

"Happened? Does something have to happen?"

There was a cat below yelling in the garden. Littlejohn's face was pale. Will didn't move.

"A man," she said. "I don't want you to mention it." She turned out of the wind and lit a cigarette. She sucked evenly at it and held the smoke in her lungs. "Somebody gets into the attic over his bedroom at night. I found out who."

"The attic?"

"Yes," Littlejohn said.

She sounded very matter-of-fact.

"A workman?"

"Hardly," she said, "not at night. Not a man with a gun. I kind of think they've sent somebody to kill him."

Then it was late afternoon and the others were there. Littlejohn and Will were sitting on a blanket near one of the salt piles. The Count was standing alone a hundred meters away on a small bridge.

Thirty of his friends, workers from along the coast, had joined them for the picnic; they had brought five liter bottles of red wine and four cold potato omelets and some had brought *bocadillos,* hard-roll sandwiches of *salchichón* and *chorizo* and veal. A few had brought their wives and children so that it would not have the air of a political meeting. A gathering of more than nineteen men for any purpose had long ago been made illegal by the government. Guzmán's friends had been careful to come to this place separately, meeting as if by surprise at the picnic spot in the salt field marshes. Manolo Ortiz and Carlos Méndez, two of the leaders of the fishermen's *cooperativas* that Guzmán had helped to form, were among them. So were twelve grape pickers from Jerez. Ortiz and Méndez were Guzmán's most active disciples; he had asked them to come and help him speak to the other men of their own experience.

The day was waning now, but for several hours Guzmán had lectured the grape pickers who had come to ask his advice. A problem had arisen in the sherry wineries of Jerez. The grapes that produced the sherry came from vineyards owned by families of Spanish and British descent, families that had intermarried over the years and were clannish in their behavior, Fascist in their beliefs. For the past two years the men who worked in the vineyards had not earned enough to live on. This year they had decided to demand a raise of ten pesetas an hour. Strikes were illegal in Spain, and their demands carried no weight. But word had been passed among the workers in and around Jerez that no one was to pick grapes in the vineyards until the demand was met. Most of the workers had cooperated in what had become an unofficial strike. Now the families that owned the vineyards were fearful for the year's harvest and had called in workers from other parts of Andalucía. The local grape pickers were ready to use violence to stop the visiting workers from picking the grapes, even if they themselves ended in jail. Guzmán was against violence. He explained carefully that there were other more effective methods—he asked Ortiz and Méndez to tell how they had gained a raise in pay for the fishermen and oyster luggers along the coast. Strike breakers could be talked to, pled with; often they would listen to warnings and would not have to be harmed. Ortiz and Méndez themselves had not believed in quiet methods of persuasion before meeting Guzmán; now they spoke eloquently on his behalf. The grape pickers listened, hostile at first, then becoming interested as the two fishermen went over the details of their own dealings. The men believed in Guzmán, and by the end of the day it became apparent that his methods had won.

The meeting of workers had taken place at a distance from Will and Littlejohn—on the other side of one of the streams the salt farmers let in from the river delta to dry in the sun. The presence of two Americans, even though they were out of earshot, had made the workers nervous at first, and had delayed things. Will and Littlejohn had kept to themselves and Guzmán stayed with the men until the picnic was over. Then he had joined them for a while, and after that he had wandered off by himself. Now he was on the bridge halfway between. The meeting was over and in the distance the workers were sprawled on blankets over the reed-covered earth, clapping and singing. They were mellow from the wine. The bridge was short. The air was hot. Little-john was watching Guzmán.

Guzmán was fiddling with a slat of wood on the bridge.

"Why would a man want to kill him?" Will said. "I don't see why anybody'd kill him."

He lay back and listened to the buzzing of the day bugs in the short marsh grass. It was the third time he had brought the subject up. Littlejohn had not been willing to discuss it all day.

"I don't know what's going on," she said after a few minutes, as if no time had gone by since he asked her the question. "The cook wasn't all that clear when I talked to her. She's never seen the man. Her husband has. He told her not to say anything . . . they're both afraid if Guzmán goes up to the attic to find out, the man might use it as an excuse . . . he . . . the man carries a pistol. He's a watchman of sorts."

"A policeman?"

"A plainclothesman."

"Guzmán doesn't know about it?"

"I don't know," Littlejohn said. "I'm not sure."

Will sat back on the blanket and hugged his knees. There wasn't much breeze around them and there were heat waves rising out of the earth around the salt water lakes. The marshes were far enough inland to be protected from the wind. The men across the stream were laughing loudly at something. Guzmán's figure on the bridge was shimmering from the heat. He looked like he was standing on the air.

"I think the police are just fed up with him," Littlejohn said.

"What are you going to do?"

"I'm not sure yet. He won't leave. I might have to trick him into going. I'll do whatever I have to."

"I wish I knew why you're so stuck on him," Will said.

". . . It isn't about being stuck."

"What's it about?"

"You'll find out one day."

"I doubt it," Will said. "I doubt it."

This time Littlejohn didn't answer him at all. She put her hand on the back of her neck and rubbed the stiffness. She hadn't moved since they finished lunch. The heat was swelling like a balloon around them. Will stretched.

On the bridge Guzmán turned and beckoned. "Come and see," he called.

Littlejohn got up. Will put Sneakers in the car and followed her along a dirt path to the bridge. There were birds wading and pecking all around in the shallow lakes, like the other time he and Littlejohn had come to the salt marsh. The stream Guzmán was standing on led straight to the river. You could see the river in the distance.

"Look," Guzmán said when they got to him; he was leaning over the low bridge staring at the water. "You notice," he said in an excited way, "here on the river side there is nothing in the stream. Lean down and see."

Will looked over into the brackish dark water. The stream was empty and not very deep. There were high reeds in the mud banks on either side. Two little crabs were darting in and out sideways among the reeds.

"Now look on the other side," Guzmán said. He pointed down at the stream on the land side of the bridge.

"God," Littlejohn said. "What are they?"

Will followed Guzmán's finger with his eyes. The water on the inland side was higher. Just at the base of the bridge in the water you could see them. There were dozens with slick dark heads and wriggling long bodies pushing at one small place in the wood. They were gathered together bumping against each other and butting their heads on the wood.

"Eels," Guzmán said. "You see what has happened?"

"No," Will said.

"The salt farmers make a dike here under the bridge. First they dig the stream to bring the river water in—then they trap it. When it is stagnant, it evaporates to salt."

"Is river water salty?"

Guzmán said, "Here we are not far from the sea. Delta water."

Littlejohn was bending over the bridge watching the frantic movement of the eels.

"You notice?" Guzmán said, "it is bad. The eels are trapped. It is almost too salty now for them to live in it. So they panic and try to get out."

"How can they tell what's on the other side?"

"There must be a leak there in the wood. A trickle of fresher water is all they need. Now look."

Guzmán stooped and reached through the bridge; he unhooked a thick slat in the wood. Then he pulled down on a piece of rope that was attached to the slat with pulleys. The slat was stuck in the mud. "I should not do this . . . the marshes don't belong to me. But I am going to do it."

Will stood up and pulled down with him on the rope. The slat of wood jerked up and fell back.

"More weight," Guzmán said.

Will leaned on the cord and the wood slat lifted about

an arm's breadth. There was a flipping deep in the water and a tumbled rush of bodies as the eels burst under the slat in a bunch. You could hear them knocking against the wood. The slat shook. "Push down now," Guzmán said, "quickly."

Will got on one side and Guzmán set his big hands over the slat. They forced it down back through the water to the mud.

On the free side of the bridge the eels were swimming toward the open river. They made a dark shadow in the clouded stream; they were swimming fast.

Guzmán straightened and brushed his hands. He looked tall on the bridge next to Littlejohn. "Always there is something," he said. "If you only want salt, you must kill something to get it. It is a great pleasure to make things free. Even eels." He watched the shadow disappear along the stream in the distance. "I like to make things free," he said. "But it is not."

Will leaned on the rail near Littlejohn. "Not what?"

"No es posible librar nada en el mundo," the Count said, *"sin librarte antes a ti mismo.* You know how to say this in English?"

"No," Will said.

"Try, please."

Will swapped the words around in his mind. "You can't free anything without yourself?"

"That is close," Guzmán said; "but not exactly. The word first is in it. Without *first* freeing yourself. You understand?"

"No," Will said.

"And you?"

Littlejohn was quiet, looking at him. The air on the bridge was muggy and slow.

"You must get rid of the panic first," Guzmán said watching the eels in the distance. "You see?"

"Not quite," Littlejohn said.

"I have been hoping that you would speak with your brother."

". . . About what?"

"About what was on your mind."

Littlejohn held still.

"You have been discussing the policeman in the attic," Guzmán said. "I think you are afraid that I will die. But I won't die. You should not worry about the wrong things."

Littlejohn held off a minute before answering. "María says it's not the first night the man's been up there."

"No," Guzmán said. "It is the tenth."

". . . Aren't you going to do anything about it?"

"I am already doing something about it," Guzmán said, "I am waiting."

". . . I don't understand."

"I know," he said. "You have been thinking, but you have not been thinking enough . . . would I have let you sleep in the palace if there were danger? The police would like for me to make a move. *El Gordo* would like it very much . . . but I will not. *El Gordo* knows it."

"Who?"

"They call him the fat man," Guzmán said, "the chief of the Civil Guard, the police, in Sanlúcar. He isn't a deep man, but he is shrewd. He takes his orders from Madrid. He gathers things to use. Each fortnight or so, he finds someone to make incriminating statements against me and others like me, and he makes lists."

". . . Incriminating in what way?"

"Apparently it does not matter," Guzmán said, watching the stream. "Any way. Anything illegal. . . . He has forced people to fill out forms and sign complaints. I don't know who he is interrogating at the moment, and I prefer not to know . . . he is a cruel man, but not an unusual man. He beats people. It would make me sick if I knew. I can do nothing about it. . . . It may be weeks before anything happens, perhaps months. When he has enough false information to use against me, then he will make a move. He is waiting also. We are each of us waiting. What else can we do?"

"I don't know how to wait like that," Littlejohn said.

Guzmán shrugged. "You are from another country. Here people wait. I think you have been sitting there all day trying to invent a way to ask me to leave Sanlúcar."

Littlejohn looked away from him.

"Then you must think," Guzmán said. "There is no point in my leaving. There is a police captain in every town in Spain. But this town is my town. You must learn to wait. It is not your fault that you don't know how, you are not Spanish. . . . The Moors taught us. We had them for eight centuries. They were our invaders and our lovers . . . now it's Americans. . . . We will be an occupied country until the day we have a good government; a few of us hope for such a government, but we do not expect it soon. So we do what we can, and when we are not able to do anything, we wait. No, there is no danger yet from the policeman. I shall let you know when there is. It will be something small and silly that tips the scale—some little mistake. It is often like that.

All the big things are balanced, and then a small thing happens and upsets the balance. That is the time to move."

Littlejohn said, "But how will you tell?"

"How, I have no idea. When the little thing happens I will know of it. So will the police captain. Then we shall see how it goes."

"Isn't it illegal to have a watchman enter your house without permission?"

"Yes. I could get rid of him in a second if I chose to, by making a formal complaint to the captain."

"Then why not . . ."

"Because the captain would only put the man somewhere else . . . I would rather have the man in my attic. This way I know where he is. When the time comes, if I am in Sanlúcar, I will know exactly where to look for the trouble."

"You mean the captain counts on your knowing?"

"Of course."

"But then . . ."

"And I count on *his* knowing. And he counts that I count on his knowing it. . . . There is a chain of knowing that leads to infinity, you must not try to follow it. It's more simple than that. The captain and I, we are enemies. We hate each other; we are countrymen; we speak a common language. And we count on each other. . . . We have learned to trust each other as enemies. It is a system that only puzzles foreigners. Shall I tell you what the system is called?"

"What?"

"Spain," Guzmán said.

He looked at the two silent faces. Then he threw his head back and laughed like a baby. He was laughing at himself, you could tell.

"When the subject of the police captain comes up, I cannot help myself . . . I am something of a lecturer. . . . Come. I'll show you another animal. . . ."

He led the way. The bridge creaked and Will followed after Littlejohn. They went across to the mud bank on the other side; Guzmán squatted by a small hole in the bank and Littlejohn knelt beside him in the reeds. Since Guzmán had begun speaking, her expression had changed, Will saw. She had lost the hopeless look. Kneeling next to the Count she looked nearly as happy as she had the first night in the American bar at the top of the stairs. Will stood to one side. So there was a watchman with a gun in the attic, and Guzmán had made her forget about it.

Will didn't like him, but you had to give the Count a kind

of credit, he thought; there was something in the man that wasn't as simple as he looked.

He was fingering an object in the bank now. He lifted it out with two fingers; it was one of the crabs Will had spotted going sideways earlier among the reeds.

"Watch," Guzmán said. He held it between Littlejohn and Will. The two black eyes of the crab stuck out on stems. "This is a male," he said. "The female does not have the big claw. It is with a movement of the claw that he attracts her. Now watch." Guzmán put the little crab back on the embankment of the stream. It stood high on its back legs and glided smoothly away from him, running fast through the reeds. Then it changed direction as if it were floating; it swooped and skeetered to the left. It ran along the mud near the edge of the water past several small holes. All the holes had a mud lip that looked the same. When it came to a place about two arms' lengths away, the crab paused; it dipped and slid delicately out of sight.

"It knows where it lives, you see," Guzmán said. "The female is there. She waits for him at the bottom of the tunnel. She does not watch him in the mirror the way you watch me."

Littlejohn's eyes crinkled. Guzmán's smile was as contagious as a baby's and for a second Will felt himself start to grin too. He put his hand up and wiped the grin off his face.

"The marsh animals tell us things," Guzmán said; "many people here are superstitious. They believe in animals and trees. . . . How do you call them in English, these?"

"Fiddler crabs," Will said.

"Eso, sí. The movement of courtship. First it digs the hole and then it waits outside and . . . fiddles?"

Will nodded.

Guzmán laughed childishly. "It is fine, yes; the fiddler crab. It is secretive. It waits all its life. I think you too are very secretive," he said turning sharply to Will. "I think that is why your sister feels free to discuss so much with you."

Littlejohn said, "It's all right. He won't say anything."

"I believe you," Guzmán said. "I have watched William with care. . . . He nows how to wait better than you. Already he is something of a Spaniard. William would not repeat a secret even if it were *not* important. . . . But the secret about the watchman in the attic *is* important. You understand that, don't you?" he said to Will, his voice level. "I would not wish you to talk about the watchman to anyone at all. Not even to my friends over there, the workers. They must not be involved—I have a reason. It matters as much to me that no one know about the man in my attic as it does to the police captain who put him there. *Comprendes?*"

Will nodded.

"Thank you," Guzmán said. "The heat makes me thirsty. I shall go now to get the wineskin."

He walked around Littlejohn and Will, back to the group of men sitting on the near side of the bank. His body swung together into one long section when he walked, as though the different pieces of it were fusing at the joints. It was in Guzmán's movement that he explained himself, Will thought. You could see him walk into the shape of a man. Then his feet disappeared in the heat waves on the other side of the bridge and he seemed again to be walking half a foot above the ground.

"Something else, isn't he?" Littlejohn said.

Will moved his head and looked at her. She was still standing on the bank and there was a flat proud look on her face. Her boots were muddy and some of it had got on her skirt. "You know what I do?" she said, "I look at him and pretend I've never met him. I like to scare myself. You remember that day in the car?"

"Yes."

"I was already a part of him," she said. "I wouldn't have got away. No, it's not about being stuck on him, Will. It isn't about much of anything . . . I think I love him, but it wouldn't matter if I didn't. I am made out of him."

Standing on the bank Littlejohn sounded softer than Will could ever remember her sounding; she was still watching the Count on the other side of the bridge.

Then she said, shyly, "Everything I just said was stupid. You know the only way I can tell I'm in love?"

"How?"

"I'm afraid of dying," Littlejohn said.

"How come?"

"I'm happy, that's all."

Will pushed a stone into the mud with the tip of a stick. "I don't ever want to fall in love," he told her.

Littlejohn drew her eyes free of Guzmán's figure, and lowered them to Will. "If I know you," she said, "you aren't going to have much choice. . . . Let's go look at the birds."

She started for one of the lakes and Guzmán left the group of workers and came to her. He and Littlejohn came together without looking at each other. Will saw them touch hands.

After that they walked from lake to shallow lake, Guzmán drinking sometimes from the wineskin and all three watching the birds. After a while Ortiz and Méndez joined them. Before it set, the sun broke out of the gray for a few minutes. The sun was as hard as an orange in the sky; then the crickets began in the reeds. Littlejohn stood with Guzmán's arm around her on one side and Will stood on her other side; they watched the day end like that across the marsh water and once he heard Littlejohn gasp. "Over there," she said.

A flock of pink herons had taken flight, exploding out of the water with their necks stretched out. They tucked their legs under them. All at once their feathers were fiery orange in the light and all the birds looked like one bird.

Will watched them. Flapping after each other they made a high long streak, orange and gray, like the color of thunder. They were hellish looking and they screeched as they flew. They were like the throat of the sun. "They sound crazy," he said.

Guzmán laughed. Then he stopped laughing. The birds were disappearing on the horizon. The daylight had gone with them, Will saw. Guzmán said:

"It is night."

In the still air the darkness around the gold villa had turned into an almost palpable substance. It was sticky looking in the heat outside the windows and from where Juan Alberto was standing it looked like tar. His back was hard, but the muscles around his jaw were beginning to relax. Evening had come at last in the wake of the luminous pale summer twilight that had lifted higher and higher in the dying of the wind until it appeared as though the sky would rise and float away. It was nearly nine o'clock. The distant yellow had faded to the thinnest film as Juan Alberto watched, and the blackness had seemed to emanate like a pool from somewhere deep out of the ground. It was close to dinnertime. Cars from other hotels along the coast could be heard beyond the villa on the gravel road that led up to the main building. Friends of the hotel guests were arriving; now and then a few voices drifted in across the lawn. Juan Alberto went to a chair. He sat and stretched his legs straight, snuffing a cigarette out in an already full ash tray.

His brother made a bored face and went to the gold-tiled bar in the corner. *"Señor mío,"* he mumbled. He was carrying a glass. He poured a splash of whiskey in it and siphoned some soda on top. Then he wiped a thin film of sweat from his forehead with his arm and went to the window. "Since sunrise," he said. "Shut in one villa. *Me cago en la mar.*"

"Never mind. When dinner begins in the dining room you can do it."

"You said this morning it would be all right when it got dark."

"I said when there's no one in the parking lot *and* it's dark. You remember how?"

"Yes," José Ramón said exasperatedly.

"If the car windows are locked?"

"I leave it all outside. On the hood."

"How on the hood?"

"Oh God. All spread out," José Ramón said. "Right where

it's easily seen. Leave me alone. When I'm finished, I'm
going out and get drunk. . . ."

"You don't get drunk. You meet me in the dining room.
We have dinner as usual. Is that clear?"

His younger brother took some air into his lungs and exhaled, snuffling out through his lips like a horse. "One day
you must tell me . . . why for God's sake have you made
such a fuss about a silly camera and some film? It was a
dumb mistake to take them, but I had a reason. He took the
pictures of *papá* and those workers—I saw him. So I was
stupid, *bueno, y qué?* Nothing's worth this . . . what are you
punishing me for?"

"To teach you a lesson," Juan Alberto said.

José Ramón threw himself hard onto the gold sofa and
crossed his arms. The heat was bad and his forehead was
glistening; the sounds in the driveway were growing more
sparse. Most of the guests from the hotel were in the American bar by now or in the dining room.

José Ramón raised his right hand with the thumb crossed
under the forefinger; he kissed the crossed fingers. "I take a
solemn oath," he said. "I'll never try to help *papá* again.
Never."

". . . I only wish I believed you."

"You think I'm a liar?"

"I don't think you are," Juan Alberto said. "I know you
are. You always were. That doesn't worry me. . . . What
worries me is that you're an indiscriminate liar. Just as *papá*
is indiscriminate about speaking the truth. It isn't either lying or truth that will bury our family. It's tactlessness."

"Where did you get your great tact? From God?"

"From *mamá* mostly," Juan Alberto said in a thoughtful
way. "She at least . . ."

He stopped in midsentence and rose to his feet.

José Ramón shifted on the sofa.

With one clean gesture Juan Alberto swept the objects
that were on top of the gold cocktail table into a drawer.
After that he closed the drawer. "This hotel," he said, low,
"this idiot hotel . . ."

The back door had opened and two voices were heard
chattering in the bright loud manner of Andalusian women.
There was a deep voice and a high voice, and the little maid
put her head in the kitchen doorway. "*Servicio,*" she announced.

José Ramón rose and took a step forward. "My brother
left orders. We don't want the villa made up today."

"That was this morning. We thought . . ." The pretty little maid looked with sullenness at the two men.

"It's all right." Juan Alberto looked at his brother. "Go ahead," he said to the maid. "Just make up the bedrooms."

The little maid went through with a mop and a pail.

"Let her be," Juan Alberto said in an undertone after she had shut the door. *"Qué más da?"*

José Ramón was silent and the little maid came back and went to the kitchen for a bar of soap she had forgotten. She was aware that the attention of the two men was on her and she switched her hips noticeably as she walked. When she had gone back into the bedroom, José Ramón spread his legs in a casual way. Then he got to his feet lazily. He stepped forward and hitched up his pants.

"No," Juan Alberto who had been watching him said.

José Ramón gave a sleepy smile. "I just thought . . ."

"I know what you thought," Juan Alberto said. "No."

José Ramón sank back into the gold cushions of the sofa and raised his eyes martyr-fashion to the ceiling. The brothers waited in silence for the little maid to finish. She left by the kitchen door.

"The girl was willing," José Ramón said. "She likes attention; I know the signs . . . didn't you see how she looked at me? All it would have taken is a little present."

"It would have taken a big present. The girl is Donahue's whore."

José Ramón watched his brother with his mouth parted. *"Dios vendito.* Is there anything around here that doesn't belong to Donahue?"

"Only Mrs. Donahue. And Helen."

". . . Helen?"

"She doesn't like him any more than his wife does."

José Ramón allowed his face to fall into a different kind of a smile. "You've had your eye on Helen for days," he said; "I'm not as stupid as you think. You were watching her from the window early this morning."

"I intend to do nothing about it. Keep out of my affairs," Juan Alberto said. He turned to the window and listened. Then he looked at the clock. "Get up now. It's time."

"I don't like the way you give orders," José Ramón said, sitting up.

"You have in common with most bullies that you're a coward. Never make the mistake of trying to bully me," Juan Alberto said. "It would be stupid. Play your games elsewhere from now on. I'm bored with them, and I'm bored with having to fix them. You'll do as you're told. Now get up and go."

José Ramón rose, white-faced, and confronted his brother for a few seconds over the gold cocktail table. When Juan Alberto didn't react, José Ramón's face took on a pouting look. He turned to the table drawer and opened it. He emptied the contents of the drawer into a white canvas beach bag and slung the bag under one arm. Then he marched in an angry way to the front door and threw it open, loud. He went out and down the porch steps.

Juan Alberto waited until his brother's footsteps had disappeared on the gravel before getting up. He glanced after the younger man despairingly.

Then he stretched. Taking a comb out of his pocket, he ran it through his hair once and started for the nearer of the two bathrooms to wash his hands. Apart from the sound of the sea, the quiet in the gold villa was as total now as the darkness. Juan Alberto listened to his own heavy steps in the floor under him as he walked. It was just after nine o'clock and a smell of sage was in the air and he realized that he was hungry. The villa was so soundless that two steps before he reached the end of the living room rug, a slight noise from the kitchen made him wheel and freeze.

He stood listening but the noise was not repeated. It had not been loud. It had been like the foot of a chair scraping over the kitchen floor. For a moment more, Juan Alberto did not move. Then walking with lighter steps he strode to the kitchen doorway and looked in.

The old woman was sitting on one of the four gold stools that surrounded the little table; her feet were crossed and her body was relaxed and at ease. Only her eyes looked tired. When Juan Alberto came into the doorway she was already looking at him. Her face didn't alter, and she waited for him to speak.

"Listening to the private conversations of the guests is a nasty trick. You never know when you'll be caught and reported for it."

Eugenia sighed. "I wasn't listening," she said.

"I don't believe that."

Eugenia leaned her head back against the wall behind her and closed her eyes. *"Señor,"* she said, "I've been up since five o'clock this morning. I'm tired. I wasn't listening."

"What were you doing then?"

"Waiting."

"For what, church to open?"

"The church is open all night."

"Waiting for what?"

"You," she said. Her eyes were dull and there was boredom in her tone.

"Couldn't you have walked inside and spoken to me?" Juan Alberto asked, sharp.

"You were with your brother. You weren't alone."

Juan Alberto straddled the doorway in a wide stance and frowned at the old woman. Something was strange about her, he knew. She was almost too relaxed in his presence, as if she didn't care whether he believed her or not. Her eyes were half open now, her head still resting on the wall behind her.

"What is it you wanted to see me about?" Juan Alberto asked.

Eugenia yawned, and cleared her throat. "My son," she said finally. "Your father and my son."

Juan Alberto shook his head, to clear it. He was due for dinner. He could make no sense at all out of the old woman who had come in and sat down in his kitchen like a visitor who was expected or an old friend. "*Señora*," he said, "there's some confusion. . . . My father has a reputation for listening to people's problems. Strangers often go to him with their troubles. . . . Was it *him* you wanted to speak to?"

"No," Eugenia said. "It wouldn't do me any good to speak to him."

In the silence, Juan Alberto turned and faced the wall. He was feeling lost, as though he had been caught up in an invisible undertow that was pulling him somewhere against his will. The old woman had something of the imperviousness of time, and the calm in her voice was much like the evenly spaced gentle folding of the waves on the beach beyond the villa.

Juan Alberto remained silent a moment. She was very old, he thought; she could have had a seizure of some kind and wandered into the villa by accident. Her voice was more dead than quiet—it had a leaden tone to it, like a person speaking inside a bank vault.

"*Señora*, I'm due elsewhere . . ."

"Go ahead," Eugenia said. "I can wait."

"I don't want you to wait."

Eugenia leaned forward. "I can wait all night. . . . It's important to wait," she said curiously. "I learned a lot of things today. . . . I learned how to bargain. And you know what else?"

"*Señora* . . ."

"I learned," Eugenia said, "that the man the police are trying to catch is your father."

When Juan Alberto shut his mouth, he could feel a thud hit him like a wave of blood. It stuck high inside his chest. For a moment he stared at the dull eyes in the bored inflectionless face.

Then he bent and sat down slowly in one of the other straight-backed kitchen chairs across from her.

"It took me a long time to figure things out," the old woman said, "the police started it. The police got my son in Sanlúcar. He's only there by accident, he liked the captain's wife . . . but now they want him to . . . how do you call it? They're collecting excuses to lock up the Count and my son is supposed to provide one of them. You see?"

"Yes," Juan Alberto said. "I see. . . . Go on, *Señora.*"

"That's all," Eugenia said.

She nodded and said no more. She looked as if she had lost interest in the subject and gone on to something else in her mind.

Presently Juan Alberto rose and walked to the stove. "I should have known; I was the one who was being stupid. I've been busy today with something silly. . . ."

Eugenia made no move to interrupt him.

Juan Alberto said, "It's not the first time it's happened. The police have made a game of trying to catch my father for a long time."

He waited, but Eugenia kept silent.

"I hope you won't be insulted," Juan Alberto said; "I don't mean it as payment . . . only as a sign of respect and friendship. I'd like to do what I can. Your son will need medicine and food. I've got a little over a thousand pesetas on me. If it's a question of money . . ." He broke off.

Eugenia sniffed. Then she giggled. After that she leaned sideways to her right. In a leisurely slow way, she rounded her lips. She spat between her chair aand Juan Alberto's feet. The opaque blob of spittle hung from her mouth for a moment in the air and then settled into a round spot on the floor. Lying on the gold linoleum between them, it looked like a newly minted coin of the realm. She settled back in her chair.

Juan Alberto backed up from the spot in distaste. "How much?"

Eugenia did not answer and Juan Alberto watched the stillness of her hands. Then he raised his eyes again to her face. A heavy shadow from her forehead slanted across her cheeks and there was a quality in the lack of expression that gave it a peculiar look of darkness. Juan Alberto could not get over the feeling that the old woman had some private knowledge she was not willing to disclose—a deformed hidden thing that she kept to herself. A faint coldness moved along his back as if a little piece of winter had blown in from outside through the sticky summer darkness.

The glow in the room rose, and dimmed again. Juan Alberto looked around him at the kitchen walls. "What's happening to the light?"

"The same as always. The electric current on the coast goes up and down in the evening."

"Yes," Juan Alberto said. "Of course."

He stepped forward away from the sink. "I asked you how much you want."

Eugenia arched her back and found a more comfortable position in the chair. "I'm not very good at arithmetic; it's going to cost me a hundred thousand pesetas to get my son out of jail," she said.

Juan Alberto went on staring. "That's a bad joke," he said at last.

The old woman did not answer.

"You must be dreaming. You don't imagine I keep that much money in the villa?"

"No," Eugenia said. "The bank opens at nine. I'll come back."

". . . You came here expecting to get a *hundred thousand pesetas?* . . ."

"No," Eugenia said. "Three hundred thousand pesetas. I'm keeping the rest for myself."

Juan Alberto moved away. "You *are* mad." His voice was loud and his head throbbed a little. "Nearly a third of a million pesetas? . . . You're a working woman. You know the value of money. You don't seriously think you'll get that much . . . or anything like that much. . . ."

"Yes," Eugenia said. "I think I'll get it."

"Listen. . . . Seeing your son in jail must have . . . been a trial. I understand that, *Señora*. I feel for you."

Eugenia smiled.

"Listen to me," Juan Alberto said. "I can give you a bit of money from my own pocket, from my own good will . . . nothing like the sum you mention. I don't have that much, but even if I did I wouldn't give it. Paying for your son's silence would make it look as if my father had done something illegal. He hasn't. I can't pay to bribe your son, *Señora*."

The old woman took a deep breath and let it out. "Yes,"

she said dully. "I know. I guess it doesn't matter why you give me the money. Pick your own reason. They want my son to say that your father is the head of some political group that doesn't even exist. Pay me because if you don't, I'll say it's true. You can even pay me because if you don't I'll report to Mr. Holtz that your brother stole the camera and film yesterday from the station wagon of the American naval officer."

Eugenia leaned back and patted the pocket of her dress and looked around her. "Any silly reason will do. Just pay me the money. I haven't had a cigarette all day," she said. "Do you have one?"

After a while Juan Alberto reached in his pocket and took out a crumpled pack of cigarettes. He dropped them in front of her on the table. When he spoke his voice came out high and soft, like the voice of a child. "That was a stupid accident," he said. "My brother took the film by mistake . . ."

"No," Eugenia said, "it was because of the pictures of your father, with the fishermen and with the American girl. He stole the camera to make it look like a theft . . . two waiters in the hotel saw the lieutenant taking pictures. Your brother's stealing would look bad if it were known." She crossed her ankles. "Unless I tell Mr. Holtz I found the camera and film under the seat of the car where the American lieutenant forgot he'd left them."

Juan Alberto looked down. "Even the American lieutenant wouldn't believe that," he said after a pause.

"The little maid and the lieutenant have an understanding . . . he'll believe what she says. They have an appointment in an hour . . . she's got no idea why your brother stole the film; she saw him do it, but she doesn't know his reason. She thinks he was drunk."

"Why would she think that?"

"She thinks what I tell her," Eugenia said.

There was a short pause.

"Maybe you should know," Juan Alberto said in a curt way, "my father doesn't have a large bank account. My brother and I live on an allowance we get from our mother. It isn't much. I don't have anything like three hundred thousand pesetas."

"I know," Eugenia said. "Ask the American lady called Miss Littlejohn for it. The concierge says three hundred thousand pesetas comes to a little over six thousand five hundred dollars in American money."

Juan Alberto leaned over the table, staring. ". . . What makes you think she'd give me that much?"

"She'd give more than that to keep your father safe. . . . Why don't you add a couple of hundred. I won't say anything."

Juan Alberto stretched his forehead with the fingers of one hand. Then he said, "My father and I have never done anything to you. You hate us this much?"

"Me?" Eugenia's head was resting on the wall again and her voice had taken on a musical tone as though something inside her were humming. "I was sitting here remembering all the times I've seen dollar bills lying around in the villas and never noticed them. . . . I touched one once. I was dusting. I felt nervous about touching it. . . . I thought it was a terrible sin to touch somebody else's money. . . ."

She giggled and her eyes drifted down easily over Juan Alberto's body. "No, *Señor,* I don't hate you. I don't care about you one way or the other. I'm just tired. I'd like to get something to eat soon. It's been a long day."

Eugenia stopped talking and Juan Alberto backed up to a chair. He stood pressed against it with the calves of his legs. He was beginning to feel short of breath—as if the strange current that had swept him along despite his will had turned into a giant wave of gold that was tumbling him in its midst.

He went on watching the dreamy old woman in the hard gold light.

AT THAT moment the lights in the red villa rose brightly once and fell again like a heartbeat. Will tucked his feet under him and spread his toes.

He was sitting cross-legged on the red sofa in front of his mother; he had taken his tennis shoes off and put them on the floor between the sofa and the short red rug. The dog was lying at his feet and Helen was alternately standing and pacing back and forth, her long eyes narrowed with thought.

Will listened to her and tried to keep his attention from wandering. Besides just talking to him, Helen was thinking out loud herself, he knew. Her face had a look he was familiar with: the look of a businesswoman. He could always tell when she was making a plan. The classic serenity of her features seemed oddly out of place. The last time Will had seen her forehead furrow like this was when Helen had made her mind up to come to Suelo for the summer. Now he could feel the waves of energy moving ahead of her again like a sharp magnetic field.

It was an hour ago now since he had come back home to the hotel; after the picnic Littlejohn and the Count had driven him to Suelo in the car and dropped him off. There had been a note on the door of the blue villa from Helen asking Will to come and see her and he had walked across the lawn hesitantly. He hadn't remembered to check with his mother in the morning before getting on the bus. The freedom of movement Helen allowed him carried certain well-defined restrictions and if Will ever overlooked one of them the least that happened was that the freedom was revoked for a while. Crossing the lawn he was sure it would be one of those times; but when Helen came to the door of her villa he had relaxed. One look at her face was enough. She only wanted to discuss something and she probably hadn't even been aware of this absence during the day.

She stopped now at the far end of the living room and turned back to the opposite wall. She had been talking steadily about the party she was planning; but even the ins

and outs of a cold business proposition couldn't lessen Helen's
loveliness. Nothing could; she looked more beautiful than
usual, Will thought. She had on a long soft housecoat that
buttoned from her throat in a line all the way down to the
floor. The housecoat was plain and one-colored and it was
shaped like a sleeve over her body. The skirt touched over
the red rug as she moved. Will had always liked his
mother's housecoats—her "thinking dresses" she called them
—she generally had two or three with her in different shades.
This one was pale, the color of dust. In the dark light of the
red villa the long housecoat looked as soft as feathers.

While Helen thought things out, Will reached down and
mashed his toes together; he tried to crack them soundlessly.
The air conditioner had been at the three-quarter mark all
day and the red villa was cool, like a blood-colored shell in
the night. It reminded him of an air-conditioned heart.

"Why do we wear masks?" he said.

Helen turned again in the corner and started back, leaving
a streak of cigarette smoke after her in the air. "It's the point
of it," she said, "that's what it's called . . . a masked ball.
Just like the Mardi Gras balls people give in New Orleans.
Don't you remember my telling you?"

Will shook his head.

"I used to show you pictures," Helen said, "some that were
taken at the Comus ball. Comus is the oldest of all the
Mardi Gras societies. Very hard to get into. It was the year I
was preg—" She changed a word in her mouth and
coughed. "It was the year you were born."

"How could it have been?"

"Seven months before you were born. I've told you about
it."

"Did everybody wear masks?"

"Of course."

"Why?" Will said.

Helen sighed. "Because no one's supposed to recognize you
until it comes time to take off your mask. Up to then you're
anonymous. . . . Isn't that clear?"

Will looked down at himself on the red sofa. You could
see half his ribs through the T-shirt, and his ankles looked
like sticks. If he was going to fool anybody in the hotel by
putting a mask on it would have to be a mask about four
feet high. "Who's going to think I'm anonymous?" he said
in a flat tone. "Franco?"

Helen came to a halt in front of the sofa and looked down
at him. "There's nothing wrong with your height; stop worry-
ing about it. You won't always be short. You're growing at

your own rate, that's all. Some people grow faster and some people grow slower. . . ."

Her voice was level, but she didn't sound completely convinced, Will thought; she walked back to the corner again, the housecoat drifting around her. "Your father was a very tall man," she added.

"Was he?"

"I've told you he was," Helen said, "several times. You've asked me that question at least once a month for the last year; it's getting to be an obsession with you. . . . He was six feet three. You pay too much attention to what you look like, and not enough to what you are."

Helen kept her eyes ahead of her and flicked her cigarette into a red ash tray as she passed it.

"I wouldn't mind paying attention to what I am," Will said. "What am I?"

"You're a young man who's going to be thirteen in a few weeks and you're going to have a spectacular party. . . . *If* I can make the arrangements in time. I can't make them if you keep interrupting me. . . ."

"Okay," Will said.

"It ought to be fun for you," she said. "When I was your age, I'd have liked somebody to give me a party more than . . . I just would have liked it, that's all."

"Nobody gave a party for you?"

"No," Helen said curtly. "Nobody gave a party for me."

She tilted her cigarette holder into the ash tray and scraped off the coal of the cigarette.

Will studied her. It rarely happened to his mother in public, but once or twice when she was alone with Will her voice ducked down a couple of notes, almost as if something out of the past had taken a swing at her. It gave him a feeling like he wanted to protect her. Most of the time taking care of Helen would have been like taking care of the leading general in a war.

Will sniffed and swallowed. He already knew that she was asking him to be her business partner. It was too simple to think that she was all that pleased at giving him a huge party just because nobody had given her one. Helen was behaving the way she usually did when she didn't want to uncover her real reason for something—she sent up a bright fake reason like a flare, and while your attention was fastened on that, the real reason went by unnoticed. She was standing still now making silence. It was her way of asking him to accept the given reason with no further questions. Sitting there, Will decided to go along with it, not because he was fooled, but only because of the tone his mother had taken when she said that nobody had ever had a party for her. Something about her voice when she mentioned that wasn't quite as businesslike as Helen herself had tried to make it sound.

"Okay," Will said. "I'd like a birthday party."

Helen flashed him a grateful look. "We'll arrange it like this," she said, "the children in the evening, the grown-ups at night. . . . Say we begin at seven. Seven to ten can be yours. The younger children can leave by . . . oh, ten. At ten-thirty the older people should start coming. We'll have an orchestra and champagne; we'll serve food at . . ."

His mother broke off at the sound of a knock on the door. She opened it to admit the hotel owner, Holtz, who bowed himself in with his usual apologetic stoop. He was carrying an envelope.

"Forgive the hour, Madame," he said, "I have been in Cádiz for the day. . . . I have returned to find your kind note saying . . ."

"Yes," Helen said, "I thought we'd better talk no matter how late. We aren't going to have much time. I've changed my plans. Instead of several small parties as we . . . as I spoke to you about earlier in the summer . . . I'm going to give one large one. . . ."

Holtz's face fell slowly into three folds. The obsequiousness dropped from his expression and his eyes turned hard. "More than two months have already gone by. Our arrangement, Madame, was for . . ."

"I don't care what the arrangement was," Helen said. "This is my field, not yours. I'm speaking of a formal ball. . . . The kind that gets a mention in the society column of every major newspaper in Europe and some in America. I think you'll find it's worth it. I'll need the cooperation of your staff. If you like the idea, you'll be here at ten o'clock tomorrow morning with a secretary. If you *don't* like the idea . . ." Helen lifted her shoulders slightly.

Then she smiled one of her dazzling smiles.

The hotel owner watched her a moment without changing his mood. "You and your son are my guests for the summer. You have not received a single bill, for your accommodations or for your meals. I had expected . . ."

"Yes," Helen said. She looked from Holtz to Will and back at Holtz, as if to indicate that these things were not discussed by proper people in front of children. She added, "You might place a call to the Ministry of Information and Tourism in Madrid before you come in the morning. We'll need their cooperation too, I think. Find out if they can put a man at my disposal who speaks English, will you?"

Holtz continued to watch her a few seconds more. He seemed to be making a silent decision. "I must rely on your taste, Madame," he said at last.

The hardness left his eyes slowly and the stoop came back into his shoulders.

After Holtz had gone Will asked, "Why the Ministry?"

"I may have to make reservations in other hotels," Helen said thoughtfully. "There'll be a lot of people coming from other places."

"Where?"

"Oh, France and Italy," she said vaguely. "Even America. There's your cousin Jimmy . . . and the Marquis de Vendime. The Nicholsons are in London, I think; just from all over. You know how far people will travel for a party if it's planned the right way—you've seen me do it before, just never on this large a scale. . . ."

Helen didn't speak for a time and Will considered about things. All at once, without knowing it was going to happen, he said something that had been coming into focus in his own mind for the last two years. It was more like he was asking a question of himself than of her—but he said it out loud.

"It's not just for the summer. This is how we live," he said, "isn't it?"

Helen was standing with her profile to him. She did not acknowledge by a flick of her lashes that she had heard the question. After a moment she reached into a red lacquer box and took out another cigarette.

"How long have you been thinking that?"

"Don't know," Will said.

Helen lit the cigarette.

"All right," she said. "I always knew you'd ask. I'm not going to lie to you. Yes, it's how we live. Just recently . . ." She hesitated and shuffled a thought around in her mind. "I'm middle-aged now . . . I sometimes get tired. A lot of my friends will be invited to this party," she said, flat. "Plus a few people I don't know. I don't think any of my friends will refuse. All of them know I have a son—even the ones who haven't met you. They know your father died in the war, and they know he died before you were born. I never thought of giving a party in your honor but I should have. I want you to get to meet as many of the right people as you can, and I want them to know you. They'll remember you afterwards—they always do. It'll come in useful when you're older. . . ." Helen stared at the red desk. "I'll tell you a secret," she said. "I've always had two private ambitions . . . I wanted your sister to have enough money never to worry, and I wanted you at least to be . . . oh, 'situated' is the word." She shrugged. "It won't mean much to you now. It might one day. It makes all the difference, who you know and who you don't . . . I found that out when I was your age. You remember that Mr. Warren from Chicago you met last year? I'm going to invite him too. I'm sure he'll accept. He . . . there was some question of his wanting to marry me once. It never came to anything . . . I wasn't interested at the time. He's not a . . . well, a cultured man. . . . But he's nice. Anyway, we'll see . . ." She turned to Will. There was a weariness about her, he noticed, and there was a plainness and an unaccustomed frankness in her manner. "You'll be a grown man soon," she said. "Then I'll be able to ask your advice about these things . . . meanwhile we have a partnership. All right?"

Will nodded.

"I'll tell you something else," Helen said. "I trust you. I always have."

Will didn't answer. His mother turned away. "It shouldn't take long to engrave the invitations. I could fly to Madrid tomorrow . . . or maybe there's a good engraver in Cádiz. I'll ask Mr. Holtz to look into it in the morning, I'm sure he knows."

"There might be one closer."

"Yes?"

Will said without thinking, "Guzmán would know about Sanlúcar."

Helen stroked the sofa with her eyes and walked to the corner. "Count Guzmán is busy," she said. "Besides, I'd rather keep the party a secret—the way I always do till the announcements are ready. It's better not to tell anyone. And about what you said before . . . about this being the way I support us . . . I'd rather you didn't tell that either. Will you give me your word that you won't?" She pivoted at the corner and started back.

Will nodded. He had a feeling he was turning into some kind of secret receptacle for useless information, but he didn't say so. He waited for her to go on. Suddenly, watching his mother's housecoat move across the rug, a picture crossed Will's eyes and dulled over immediately, like something seen by lightning. It was a sharp vision and it was gone before he could make out what was in it, but traces of it stayed on in his head. The vision was of a lot of people standing around

on this big mosaic and everybody was busy in it but him.
They were all doing something and he was trying to see what
it was. It was the same vision he had had glimpses of two or
three times before. There was a white object in the middle of
the mosaic, but he didn't have any idea what it was. Everybody around the object was trying to kill it; it was fluttering
there at the center as if it was trying to get away. Will raised
his eyes slowly.

Helen had stopped pacing again; she was watching him
from across the room. "It's time you went to bed," she said.
"You're sleepy."

Will got up from the sofa and picked up his tennis shoes.
The dog stood up with him.

"Come kiss me goodnight," Helen said.

Will stepped around the table and reached up. His mother
had her evening perfume on—the one he liked the best. It
smelled thin and dry, like freshly cut wildflowers, and it en-
veloped you when you went near her like a shell. Helen bent
down and touched his cheek with hers. Her cheek was cool,
smooth as an egg kept in an icebox. A quick flood filled Will,
and he reached for her neck.

Helen stopped his hands. "Gently," she said, "I'm expecting someone." She swung his hands in hers for a moment
and let them go.

Will stuck his thumbs in his belt and stood dangling his
tennis shoes. Sneakers moved in between him and his
mother, pawing at him in an anxious way.

"I don't much like that dog," Helen said, stepping back.
"I had no idea you wanted one. I could have bought you a
pedigreed dog with papers for your birthday." She moved
away.

"He's all right," Will said. "He likes me."

"Most anything would like you," Helen said, her back to
him.

Will didn't say anything.

"Trot along. I'll have a waiter bring you a glass of milk
and a sandwich."

"I'm not hungry," Will said, "we stopped for a sandwich
on the way back."

The remark was out before he realized what he was saying, and he bit the inside of his cheek and waited for Helen
to ask where he had been, but she only arched her back at
him. She was looking at a painting of a red cat on the wall.
She seemed determined not to punish him today.

"Goodnight," she said. "The day is over."

Will walked to the door. There were a few times when he

wanted to break through the shell around Helen, and this was one of the times. Something had happened between them this evening that had caused her to open up to him, he knew. They truly were business associates now. He turned and looked at her. In a way, his mother was kind of touching to Will, though he had never told her; she was a solitary figure standing with her back to him. In the uncertain electricity, the walls of the red villa pulsated around her more than ever like an empty heart, and one or two strands of her hair moved in the conditioned air. Will would have liked to say something that would let her know how he felt in a way she couldn't avoid hearing, only it wasn't much use. None of the things he ever wanted to shout to Helen were shouting things. They were all quiet things and she wouldn't let him close enough to whisper. "Goodnight," he said.

He moved out of the cool villa into the heat.

The dark air gathered him in as if it had been waiting for him and he walked across the lawn barefoot through the blackness. The grass was warm and spongy between his toes, and he slid his feet over it as he walked. The first haze of sleep had left him for a while. He didn't feel like going to bed yet. He changed direction and went to look at the sea from the lawn of the main building, avoiding the gravel paths. Without the wind the air had a muggy stillness to it and he could feel the villas all around him separately like watchers in the night. He had a sort of need to be alone; he kept away from the villas where he knew people. It was nearing the end of the dinner hour, and many of the villas were dark. The lights in the main building were blazing. The hotel was nearly full occupancy; only two of the villas had no tenants—the brown villa and the black one were empty except for the weekends. Will had a theory it was because they were the ugliest villas in the hotel. The black one looked like a funeral parlor, and the brown one looked soiled all the time, as if people had been throwing mud at it. The brown villa was the least popular of all, it was always the last to be occupied. He passed it now, dark and dirty in the night, locked and deserted. Its window shades were drawn and it looked stifling; the heat inside the sealed brown villa must have been unbearable even for bugs.

He stopped on the east side of the main building above the beach and squinted at the water through the darkness. You could hardly see it from there except for the glint of the waves close to shore. The waves were still a little high, he saw; the stopping of the wind had not been matched yet in the water. The beach looked white. It would have been a treacherous night to hide in. A three-quarter moon was sliding in and out of the clouds, fixing the landscape in a hard white glare and then fading it away again. It made you feel like you were constantly going blind. Will kept his eyes pointed at the sea and tried to make out the farthest thing that was visible from shore, but there was nothing. The darkness receded to an impenetrable area that showed no light of any kind—not even a single lamp on a fishing boat. There were no boats on the water tonight. The fishermen were still waiting. The dark area above the sea was so deep it didn't even look black; it was no color at all, like the color of death. Will stretched the skin around his eyes and stared straight out in a bug-eyed way, but it didn't help; there's a little death in the loss of any sense, and he felt as if his eyes were dying. He was conscious now of standing at the edge of a continent. He was near where Christopher Columbus had left on his second trip, and he wondered if Columbus had felt something of the same thing: as if he were going blind. He couldn't have been just looking for spices, taking off into a darkness like that, however big the boat was. Peering into it with the moon gone, Will had a sense that the explorer might have been looking for something he didn't even know he was looking for. You couldn't strain your eyes at the unseeingness of it without knowing that. It was like the thing everybody looks for, and Columbus had just used spices as an excuse. He probably never did find the thing, but he tried. You wouldn't set sail if you weren't going to try. Boat or no boat. It couldn't have been just spices.

Still, Columbus had gone in the other direction; he had gone west. Straight ahead of Will now was south. There beyond the water, a short distance away, was Africa. It was the hot continent—the oven of the world—you could feel it out there waiting. Early in the summer a door had opened in the oven and a hot breath had come across the sea, and now the oven door had slammed shut again. The waves would be flat by morning. After all the weeks of waiting, the fishermen would be able to go out tomorrow.

The moon slid out again and Will looked up at the top of the hotel. There was a line of flags around the roof like the United Nations. At the center was the Spanish flag. Next to it was a smaller flagpole. Will watched the little flagpole curiously. It was there to warn people when the weather was bad or a storm was coming, and by rights it should be empty now that the wind had stopped. A warning had been up for weeks while the *foreño* blew, to keep people from going out in their yachts. The big flag was gone, but there was another smaller one flying now in its place. It was a pennant, not too long, but very sharp under the moon, and it was drooping motionless now on top of the pole. It was the flag for small-craft warnings. In the stillness of the night and the leveling sea, Will wondered if it might have been put up by accident. The bigger yachts didn't need to pay it any attention, he knew—but none of the fishermen would go out while it was flying.

When the moon slid back under the clouds, the pennant disappeared in the night and Will turned and started back across the lawn. A second haze of sleep had touched him and he retraced his path among the villas toward the blue one. Sneakers knew where they lived and he seemed to sense they were going home. Will walked behind him past the orange villa and the yellow and the brown one. None of them was lit and there was a kind of comfort in the darkness of the land at this hour. The moon was mottling the lawn with bright shadows. You would step on a shadow and it would be gone. Then somewhere in the night a man laughed. It was a low short laugh and the waves covered it, and then somewhere else a radio went on. A little way past the brown villa Will came to a halt. He had seen an object out of the corner of his eye. He wasn't sure what it was and he turned and scanned the night-filled villas but there was nothing moving near any of them. The dog had gone on ahead, and Will began to walk again. Then he slowed once more and looked back. It wasn't a movement he had seen—it was a thing that didn't fit. It was as if something had slipped by his eyes and his brain had resisted it. Still nothing was there in the path behind him except for the three darkened villas and the main building; nearly all the hotel guests were downstairs in the American bar. The record machine could be heard thinly across the lawn and the rest of the main building looked empty. Then, with his eyes on the building, Will saw it again. It was one of those things you see only when you aren't looking at it, and it wasn't really strange at all. It was just out of place in his mind. It was that the unpopular villa, the brown villa, the dirty-looking one he had passed before, wasn't closed up any more. One of the bedroom shades had been raised a small space and the window was open.

The moonlight faded while he looked, as if the night had been inked over, and the open window of the brown villa was gone out of sight. Will stood watching where it had been and nothing moved on the lawn. The breezeless air felt tight around him and he wanted to turn and go on walking but it was like he couldn't. It wasn't the same as the darkness of the sea from the beach. It was another kind: a darkness that wasn't impenetrable. Something in his mind reached out through it and seemed to see the open window still there. He stood quiet a long time before his feet began to move. When they did, he didn't have to tell them where to go. He felt like he was following on top of his feet and he moved easily, quietly through the night, and then he knew that he was standing close to the open window. He was within touching distance of the brown villa. He couldn't figure why he had come to be standing near it until he heard the man's voice laugh again.

Then he knew that something inside him had recognized the owner of the laugh from the first time it had sounded across the lawn, before he had stopped or noticed the open window. In the pitch black outside the villa his heart jumped and the new feeling he had tucked away that morning came unfolded again inside him. The twinge in his groin was the same, only stronger—a chill like the touch of a long cold knife—and he wondered how he had been able to keep the feeling quiet inside him all day. The moon was still gone and he was holding his breath when he heard Donahue laugh for the third time. The laugh was deep and it was low. He waited in the darkness beside the open window but the laugh did not sound again. There was a different sound in its place, a soft terrible sound, and a bitter taste came quickly into Will's mouth, as if he had chewed into an apple that wasn't ripe yet. He wanted both to run and to step closer to the window, but his heart was pounding so loud he was afraid Donahue would hear it if he went any nearer. The bitter saliva filled his mouth and he could tell that the moon was coming back out and he could not even swallow. The sound inside the window was so low it was hard to make it out. It wasn't as loud as his heart in the night. He was standing in the shadow of a short acacia tree and it was happening not three feet away from him; when the moon came out, it was clearly visible in the four-inch space between the window shade and the sill. The dark head of the woman was thrown back on the bed, and the twinge inside Will was the sharpest thing he had ever felt, like pain and pleasure at the same time, so he almost had to lean for balance on the villa wall. The little maid's face was staring straight up at the ceiling. She looked stunned, as if she were dying. Her chin was caught underneath the man, between Donahue's neck and one bulging shoulder, and her arms were thrown open, straight out on either side of him. She

was biting the muscle of his shoulder. Her hands were opening and closing, clutching slowly at the air, and then she
raised them and reached for the naked moving back of
the man over her. Donahue's back was slippery with sweat,
and her hands slid off. The sound of the man's breathing
was going faster now and all at once the little maid began
to struggle as if she wanted to get out from under him. She
was moaning and she buried her face in Donahue's neck and
began to claw with her fingers at the twin mounds of muscle
in his back. Donahue would not stop moving. It was like he
was protecting her and hurting her at once, and Will wanted
to reach out and touch her face under the great surging
body. He wanted to be there with her with Donahue on top
of him holding and mashing him and maybe even hurting
him too. Then the moon went away, and there was only the
sound again, the awful plunging sound of the man's breathing. Will put his hand flat on the side of the villa and
pushed himself away.

He turned and walked back across the darkened lawn
and halfway to the path he knew that it was going to happen
and there was nothing he could do about it. He clutched at
the front of his pants with both hands, but it was already
starting. When it happened it shook him so that it took him
to his knees on the grass. He knelt in the darkness holding
himself there and it wasn't like any other time. It went on
happening and happening and happening until he thought he
would die there on the grass. When it was over he got up
weakly and stood rocking back and forth as if something
very important had fallen out of him. Then the moon came
out again. He could see his two tennis shoes lying in front of
him where he had dropped them. In the sudden moon the
tennis shoes looked like somebody else standing ahead of
him on the lawn. He picked them up and walked to the edge
of the path.

He could not think of the meaning of what had just
happened. The bitter taste was sharp in his mouth and he
turned and spat some of it out into the gravel. Then he put
on the tennis shoes and walked along the path to the blue
villa. The dog was waiting for him near the porch; Will
sat down on the bottom step and rested his chin in his
hands. He could hear the thump as Sneakers lay down next
to him. He sat for an hour and a half outside on the steps
of the blue villa staring at the lawn. The night went on
without him and several people went up the path past the
villa without seeing him. He watched them walking on the
gravel and three of them were drunk. Then he saw the

heavy short black figure coming and he did not even recognize her until she had passed. The figure was Eugenia. She was walking slowly away from the hotel up the main path toward the town, and it seemed to him for an instant that she was holding herself straighter than she usually did and walking differently than she usually walked. She moved away, crunching in the gravel, her back receding a little more at each step in a long rhythm that was as endless as the waves below on the beach. You could tell that she was going home. Soon the darkness took her. When she was out of sight, Will got up slowly and went inside.

He undressed in the dark and lay down on his bed with all the windows open and the hot darkness through the trees. It was a long time before he could sleep, and once across the short black lawn he saw Jim Lepard come to his own window and look out. The window was lighted and Jim Lepard's face looked swollen and solid pink, as if he had finally managed to turn into the color of his villa. He stood looking back across the dark straight at Will, as if he could see him. You cannot see from light into darkness and you could tell that Jim Lepard wasn't looking at anything, but he stood there staring anyhow. Then after a while he went away again. His light went out and there was nothing, and Will lay still on the bed in the hot dark night. He could not feel anything and he could not hear anything but the crisp dry folding of the sea.

SIX

Murder

AT FIVE O'CLOCK in the afternoon of the following day, the police doctor standing outside the captain's office opened the two top buttons of his shirt and fanned some air down his neck with the flat of his hand. The day had been windless and hot. Policemen had been sitting around the *Jefatura de la Guardia Civil* in Sanlúcar since morning looking bent and paralyzed; it was an equal effort both to breathe and not to breathe. The *Jefatura* like everything else in Spain was officially closed from one to four in the afternoon and the *Jefe*, the captain, had come back shortly before five. He was in his office now nursing his allergies and examining for the tenth time the bottle of pills the doctor had brought him yesterday. The latest pills were as useless as the previous six medications prescribed by the doctor, who spent much of his time locating any new form of placebo that promised to alleviate the captain's symptoms, which were half imaginary, by means of the potency of the placebo, which was wholly imaginary, and by its color. The captain was a man who was impressed by color. The doctor had banked on this notion early and in the course of a few months had presented the captain on different occasions with red pills, orange pills, three combinations of bicolored capsules, a yellow liquid and a greenish-purple powder. Each new medication had about the same effect; at the end of a few days the captain's symptoms would return, and the doctor would have to hunt up another harmless but colorful drug. Two of the five bottles in the captain's desk were filled with candy-coated aspirin. The other three were bottles of imported Swiss vitamin tablets minus their original labels. The doctor had twice gone as far as Seville to find a new bottle of pills, soak off the label and paste on one of his own; he had explained to the captain that the cumulative effect of all the medicines taken in sequence was a cure of his own invention, and the captain had swallowed this idea along with the pills. The bottle the doctor had given him yesterday in front of Eugenia would be good for two weeks; the label explained that the medicine had to be taken in light dosage at first, due to a powerful drug it contained which was given only in extreme cases. The captain liked more than anything to think of himself as an extreme case, and the doctor had calculated correctly that his patient would not notice anything missing in a label that told him everything except what he was stricken with an extreme case of. Unadorned flattery, in the doctor's view, was one of the more potent medicines of this world, and he hoped that the bottle would tickle the fat man's vanity enough to dry up his left frontal sinus until a week from Sunday when a new medicine was to arrive from Barcelona. The directions also advised that one pill must be taken two hours after each meal, and the doctor was figuring now that the captain had come back to his office at five minutes to five in order to take one. The doctor had a Catalonian's sense of precision in all things. He stood fifteen minutes outside the captain's office fanning his neck in the fierce dull heat before he knocked on the door and went in.

The captain was sitting motionless at his desk, a half-empty glass of water next to him and a frozen startled look on his face; he did not respond when the doctor entered the room. The doctor understood and sat in a chair. It was the captain's habit to remain quiet a few moments after the swallowing of any medication to see if he could determine by the feel of things which portion of his body was most affected. He sat now at the desk for some time, his eyebrows raised and his little eyes gazing into space as if into a great distance. The look was impressive and it was one that had been used to advantage over many centuries in Spain by prophets, martyrs, saints and other types of killers. Had the captain been born in the late fifteenth century, he might have had a corner on the holy market. As it was, he had both the fear and the respect of everyone he knew, including the doctor, who was much too careful a man to allow the captain's display of sheer foolishness to camouflage an equally strong and proven display of power. They were both practical men. The doctor's respect for the captain as a figure of potential violence was not in the least diluted by the doctor's ability to make him look like an ass. He waited now until he knew from a slight upward turning of the fat man's face that the captain had had a revelation. The captain shut his eyes and the doctor leaned forward attentively. The captain spoke. "The thyroid," he said.

"Right," the doctor said.

The captain opened his eyes.

"It's absolutely fascinating," the doctor said, "the way you placed that. I don't think I marked it anywhere on the bottle. Could you tell it was the thyroid right away?"

"No," the captain said, "not right away. There was a sensation. Like a twitch."

". . . A twitch?"

"A sort of pulse," the captain said, pointing to his neck, "a definite pulse."

The doctor leaned back. "Interesting," he said.

"Anything new in the jailhouse?"

The doctor put one foot up on the chair. Avoiding the captain's eyes, he said, "That old woman is here. It's a bit of a mess. Pepe Luis is dead. He died a few hours ago."

The captain looked at him a second. Then he shrugged. "You said that might happen when I told you to shake him up the first time. He didn't have much of a constitution."

"No, he didn't. I'm afraid, though, it wasn't the shaking up," the doctor said, "that killed him. It was cholera."

The captain put a hand to his neck.

"Some symptoms of cholera," the doctor said, "as I'm sure you know, begin with slight sequential constrictions of the pulmonary vascular system in the upper thyroid area. It seems I gave you that medication just in time."

"You told me these pills were for my sinus condition."

"I had to tell you something," the doctor said. "Didn't I?"

"You . . ."

"You might call it a vaccine," the doctor said. "Yes. A type of oral immunization. It wouldn't have worked if you'd touched him or gone in the same room with him yesterday, but you didn't. Some of the guards did, but I've inoculated them and sent them home."

"Cholera," the captain said softly. He pushed his chair back from his desk. "You mean there might be an epidemic?"

"There might be. Personally I doubt it," the doctor said, "it's just this one case so far. The problem is the kind of reaction that sets in when a word like cholera is mentioned. The whole damn coast would panic—it's not unheard of. It's a nasty form of mass hysteria and it's very hard to put down."

"What about me?" the captain said.

"You're almost immune now. You will be, after three more days of those pills," the doctor said. He spoke very slowly.

"Then there won't be any more cases here?"

"Pepe Luis had been isolated for five weeks. The trick is to keep him isolated until the funeral."

"For what?" the captain said. "The way he looks? You told the old woman her son had got into a brawl, didn't you? So, if the body looks bad, that's why. Maybe his relatives get the idea we beat him up a little—*qué más da*? Let them prove it."

"I don't think you quite understand, Captain," the doctor said. "I'm not worried about the way he looks. Cholera's caused by a very tricky germ. The body stays infectious for several days. The old woman lives in Suelo, you know. And that isn't all . . ."

The doctor rose to his feet and stood facing the electric fan. "Diseases like cholera are brought on by certain unsanitary living conditions . . . such as, for instance, the conditions in the jailhouse. If anything happened in Suelo to affect the tourist businesss, Madrid could be very angry. The Ministry owns stock in half of those hotels. . . . I don't think they'd be too pleased at finding out where the infection started. . . ."

"I see. That throws a different light on it, doesn't it?"

"Yes, Captain," the doctor said.

"So," the captain said, "the funeral should take place right away. They can have the wake afterwards."

"I think that's very well put," the doctor said. "Yes."

"Somebody's got to talk to the old woman again. We'd have to make it worth her while in some way."

The doctor remained respectfully silent.

"I suppose," the captain said, "there must be something she wants that we can provide her with."

The doctor sat up straight. "You mean pay for the funeral . . . yes."

The captain didn't say anything and the doctor went on as if continuing a thought that he was receiving from the captain by mental telepathy:

"Or do you mean that we should buy a cheap plot ourselves in the cemetery here in Sanlúcar . . . and then cover all the other expenses . . . on condition the funeral be held right here. Then I seal the coffin myself today, and that's that. The body is never seen again. It never even has to go to Suelo. Is that it? Yes, it's good . . . it's very good. It's exactly the sort of idea I can't ever seem to work out for myself. . . ."

The captain looked as if he were weighing the facts together. "I guess that's what I meant," he said.

"Yes, I get it . . . and *I* should be the one to talk to her and make all the arrangements. . . . Not you. You're going to keep aloof from the whole business, is that right? If you came into it, it might look as if you were covering up for something. . . . Besides, you won't be immune for another two days. Yes, I think I've got it straight now . . . I take over as police doctor in a routine way, and I tell the old woman that arrangements are taken care of by us in cases where a man dies in jail. She won't know the difference. . . . She'd rather we paid the funeral, and she kept the money. You can take it all off the books. Yes, it's clear now. Thank you."

The doctor sat back. The captain was quiet, thinking about what had been said.

"How much," he asked finally, "do you suppose all this will cost?"

"I'll cut corners wherever I can; it shouldn't come to any more than six or seven thousand. . . ."

The captain opened his coat slowly and removed three individual green thousand-peseta notes from his wallet and dropped them on the desk.

"If I may be allowed to express one more opinion," the doctor said, "I think it might be good for you to put in an appearance at the funeral. Even though the coffin is sealed. It might look well. It's merely my opinion."

"Whatever you say," the captain said. "But three's the limit. It's all I can put on the books."

The doctor picked up the notes in a strict official way. Then he nodded stiffly and left the room. Outside, he closed the door and yawned. He took out his own wallet and put the three new notes together with the other hundred thousand peseta notes it already contained.

Then he walked off down the hall.

Above the *Jefatura*, on the high flat hill, Littlejohn dismounted from the horse in the overgrown garden. She stood rubbing its wide neck with her hand.

The day had made her cheerful. She had gone riding alone and she had been cantering the horse for the last hour across the brown fields lying fallow now behind the town and over the dirt trails that stretched out of sight north along the river. Of the four horses in the palace stable this was her favorite; it was a small chestnut stallion that had a special gait. At the lightest signal, the horse rose from his hind legs as if he were taking off, and the smooth canter that followed seemed to rest on a cushion of air. The stallion, Pájaro, moved over the earth as effortlessly as a sail. He satisfied something in Littlejohn that she did not understand herself: the need to float, to be weightless. María's husband who cared for the horses came out of the small stable now smiling at her. He took the reins from her and led the sweating stallion into the stable for a rubdown.

Littlejohn walked along the garden wall and glanced at the town below. The tiers of houses appeared more Moorish than ever in the heat waves, and she looked up from the garden gate at the Columbus tree just outside. She had come to love it along with everything else around the palace; she regarded it the way everybody did, as a sort of person, and it would have seemed almost rude to enter the building without a glance in its direction. The tree was lively and bright in the hot sun, and a green branch at the top dipped in the breeze, as if it had something to tell her that it wasn't ready to talk about yet.

She turned from the tree and entered the cool basement floor, her boots clucking on the unpolished marble. The door under the staircase was shut; it had a new padlock on it, she noticed. As she reached the stairs, she stopped. A hardly identifiable feeling of sickness had swept through her body in a feather-light wave. It was like a movement of invisible wings inside her and it lingered an instant before leaving her with an odd sense of emptinesss, like an idea that comes and departs immediately with only a sense of unease in its wake. She couldn't remember anything that had disturbed her during the ride, and she leaned for a few seconds on the bannister, puzzled by the new sensation. Then she realized that she had eaten almost nothing during the day, and she shrugged it off and ran briskly up the stairs. The trouble with the sense of freedom Pájaro gave you when he floated over the grass was the suddenness with which you had to readjust your body to the rules of gravity when he stopped. Littlejohn reached the top of the stairs breathless; she marched into the hall angry at her own stupidity.

She had begun to cross the Ambassador's Room when she heard the man's voice and slowed down. It was coming from the smaller *Sala del Loro*—the Parrot's Room—the one that contained a stuffed bird two centuries old on an ebony stand. Littlejohn rarely went into that room; she did not like stuffed animals, and the years had lent the sleek parrot a look of vast ugliness. Its beak was hooked in a way that made it seem more like a bird of prey, and the shoulders of its bony wings were raised in a shrug. Guzmán had left it there out of respect for tradition; the bird had occupied the same room for generations, and there were ref-

erences to it among letters in the Guzmán archives. He only
used the room himself in the afternoons when workers from
along the coast came to consult him and ask his advice.
When that happened the door to the Parrot's Room was
closed to give the visitors a sense of privacy. This time it
was wide open. The voice sounded loud and tense. Littlejohn changed her direction and walked into the doorway.

Juan Alberto, who was talking, ceased and stood facing
her. Guzmán took her in with his eyes; he made no move to
come to her in front of his son. The skull in his face was
starker than usual and the line of the jaw protruded. On
the terrace beyond, Ortiz and Méndez and two more of Guzmán's disciples stood drinking and waiting for him. "What
is it?" Littlejohn said.

She sat on the edge of an arm chair. The dusty draperies
were open and the room was still. A piece of late sunlight
fell across it like a patch on the floor. The furniture was
somber and the parrot was especially ugly in the late light.
Guzmán was standing beside it. There was a strange look on
his face. "Tell me," she said.

Juan Alberto glanced at his father for approval. Then he
outlined for her in a brief way the visit he had had the
night before that was more like a visitation. He told most of
the facts about the maid called Eugenia at the Hotel Malage,
and about her son. He left out a few of the unpleasant details. He added that he had already paid the old woman a
part of the money she had demanded.

"Why did she go to you?" Littlejohn said when he had
finished. "Why not straight to me?"

"Not in Spain," Juan Alberto said, "things are not that
way. A man of honor would never allow his mis—" The
voice crimped as Guzmán looked at his son. Juan Alberto
began again. "A man would never allow any woman to pay
blackmail money for him. . . . Eugenia knows my father
by reputation. He might have given her the money for no
reason at all, if he'd had it. He wouldn't be forced into
giving it, and she knew he wouldn't beg you for it."

"So she went to you instead."

"Yes," Juan Alberto said, "she was counting on my not
telling anybody but you about it until after you'd given me
the cash."

"She can't know much about your father if she thinks he
cares about money," Littlejohn said, speaking across Guzmán. "He doesn't. I'll pay it of course."

"Thank you," Juan Alberto said quietly. "I was sure you
would. . . . So was she."

"Will it help the man in jail?"

"He isn't there anymore," Juan Alberto said. "What I gave her was enough to get him out. My brother and I had a little over a hundred thousand pesetas saved between us."

"The request was meant for me. I'll replace that and pay the rest."

Juan Alberto bowed in her direction. "If you can simply pay the rest," he said, "it will be appreciated."

"Is that all?" Littlejohn stood up.

Juan Alberto looked toward his father again. Guzmán was standing at the center of the room staring pensively at the unpleasant-looking bird on the stand.

"It isn't all, is it?" Littlejohn said.

"No," Juan Alberto said. "Not all."

Littlejohn perched again on the arm of the chair and waited for him to speak. The quietness of his tone had made her feel weak.

"You see," Juan Alberto said, "it wasn't all she wanted; she made other conditions. . . . Her son is named Pepe Luis. It may be a problem your staying at the palace now. She wants . . ." His voice trailed off again as his father looked at him.

He went out and joined Guzmán's friends on the terrace.

Littlejohn waited and Guzmán turned and faced her over the stuffed bird. He seemed to be reexamining her face as though he had not seen it before.

"Stupid," Littlejohn said, "that they should both think the money would matter."

"Yes."

"I have no more feeling about money than you do."

Guzmán did not smile. "You have less," he said. "You have more money."

"What is it?" Littlejohn said slowly.

Guzmán stepped away from the ebony stand. He spoke in a plain way. "If you love someone," he said, "there are chances that you take. I am going to take a chance now. . . . You are a rich young woman, and you are more arrogant than my two sons put together. You are accustomed to having your own way. What you cannot make happen with your person, you can make happen with your money. As things go, there would come a day when you would try to control me too with money; I know the signs. I know them well. I think you must stop it now while there is time. Not for my sake or for our sake, but only for yours. I think you must grow up. . . ."

Littlejohn felt tears of anger start to her eyes and forced them back. She kept still and looked at the black wood stand.

"No," Guzmán said. "You can move me with tears but you cannot change things. You cannot alter what you are or what will happen, unless you make an effort. There are things I must do, and you must stay away from me while I do them. Money is no longer important; the old woman would not have demanded it if she weren't already sure you had enough and would pay it. You have it, you can pay it, and that is the end of it. Her other demand is more difficult."

"What other demand?"

Guzmán watched her.

Littlejohn said, "Her son. He's in the basement, isn't he?"

"Yes," Guzmán said.

". . . in the room under the staircase that has the new padlock. How did he get there?"

"He was brought in a truck this afternoon. A garbage truck. He has been beaten. The mother wants him to stay here until he can travel. He cannot go back to Suelo where friends might recognize him; it has been announced that he's dead. He will be here for as long as it takes him to recuperate. Then he must live in another province, where no one knows him. Meantime he is under my roof and my care. There is no place else for him but here; the old woman was right."

"Why is it a problem for us to . . ."

"You don't need an explanation. You already understand."

". . . I'd rather hear it from you."

Guzmán crossed the room and stood in front of her chair. He reached out for one of her hands. "You can visit me during the day," he said. "Not at night. Not till my new guest has left this province. You may not interfere, and you must not try to help me unless I tell you. You must be still and do as you are told now; the balance of things is upset. I will have two strange men in my house—one in the attic and one in the basement. It is important that they do not know of each other's existence. For this I have to be careful. As careful now as I have ever been in my life."

"Careful of what?" Littlejohn said.

Guzmán slipped his long hands up to her wrist. "I said that I would tell you when the time came. The captain is becoming careless. An extra house guest. You see? The little thing," he said. "The little thing has happened."

The funeral that took place in the mortuary of the San-lúcar jailhouse was a drab affair, notable for its lack of show. The usual sense of communal grief—the acknowledgment of a collective doom that gives most Andalusian funerals a kind of agreeable release—was missing. A working class funeral goes by certain rules. Normally, friends of the deceased would have dropped in at odd moments during the day for a piece of a cake and a glass of *anís* or brandy, or a cup of coffee. They would have stayed to share in the grief as well, accepting from the bereaved mother those possessions that best expressed and symbolized her position in the universe: her food, her liquor and her loss. The coffin would have been placed in a separate room, surrounded by women in mourning who would sit all night in chairs placed all the way around the wooden box. The women would remain there during the next day until it came time to carry the box to its final resting place—or what was said to be its final resting place—though everyone might know that the grave had only been taken on lease for a period of twenty years. After that (because the earth had still not been purchased) the coffin would be removed and chopped up to make room for the next tenant. If the family were middle class enough for the grave to have been purchased free and clear (as if anyone could own the earth he is going to be buried in: as if the dead could own anything besides the living. As if even the middle class could ever be anything besides the middle class) things would be about the same, except for a pompous air derived from the sense of ownership and discreetly presented in the form of better drinks and a better cadaver, proven by the superior containers of each. But the extreme upper and the extreme lower classes of Spain have in common, among other qualities, a certain snobbery and distaste for the class that is emerging between; the funeral of a fisherman, like the funeral of a great aristocrat, can be an event of great dignity. There will be no question of ownership, for the sense of loss will be the first thing shared. The bereaved mother will talk to each person who enters the room and she will give freely of herself and of her sorrow. It will be acknowledged that the deceased has gone to a better world and there will be a quality of glory in the proceedings.

This was not the case in the funeral of Pepe Luis.

The funeral took place in one room. The bereaved mother declined the use of a second room for the presentation of the coffin. She sat alone beside the sealed plywood box, a stark figure in mourning, her hands crossed in her lap and a black veil covering her head to her waist. Each friend presented his formal *pésame,* or sympathy, to her, and each waited in an embarrassed silence to be asked to sit down for a few minutes and partake of the refreshments. There was a small tray provided by the police containing some glasses and bottles on a table at one end of the room, but nobody made a move to offer a glass of brandy to a guest. This was because no other relative was present. The father of Pepe Luis, it had been announced, was too ill to attend his son's funeral, and the mother was forced to carry things out by herself. She managed by doing nothing; she sat motionless in a straight-backed wooden chair. When sympathy was offered, she nodded her head a fraction, enough to indicate that she had heard the speaker, and retired back into the privacy of her grief. The coffin was closed and there was nothing to see and not much else to do in the room. People who wished it helped themselves to the liquor and drank alone. The fishermen of the town came and left in a group. While they were there, the room was packed and the white walls were susurrous with whisperings of sympathy sent out and left unreceived in the air. The bereaved mother had taken to bobbing her head in a general way every few seconds whether anybody had said anything to her or not. This lent an anonymous air to the day that was not looked upon with favor. People who had only come there to be released a little from their own private sorrows left with a dim feeling of frustration. It was not a popular funeral. It was a dull one. The prospect of seeing an old woman, alone and childless, agonized at the death of her only remaining son, did not pan out. In fact the woman herself was more to blame for the drab quality of the event than the condition of the funeral's taking place in the jailhouse. Beyond a peculiar stillness she remained undemonstrative and at times she was stoic to the point of showing no emotion whatsoever.

Yet, years after the funeral, a strange thing was to happen. The impression of the lonely mother seated in silent grief beside the simple coffin was stronger than people thought and was to be talked about for a long time in the town. The pair had the starkness of a medieval Pietá. The woman's veil seemed both to bring out the paleness of the face underneath and at the same time diminish its years. Some people even said that through her thick veil the old woman looked exactly the right age for the Virgin—which, in Andalucía, is taken to mean that she didn't look much older than Christ. What was lost in the dullness of the funeral was more than regained in its memory. After only a few years the memory was to take on stature and, finally, fame of almost legendary proportions. From then on the coast had its own Dark Pietá—an image etched in colors of murk and midnight. The darkness of this picture—its inherent lack of light—might have been symbolic of a certain lack of spiritual or moral light. But the fact, simpler than the plywood box itself, that the coffin was empty could not interfere with the legend it created because it was never known.

It was the arrival of the police captain accompanied by his young wife that did more to enhance the legend of the fisherman's funeral than any other factor involved. At the time they appeared, the old woman was sitting as still as before, a special silence seeming to seep from her every pore. The unpolished plywood coffin had a classic purity in the dull light and the scene was banked by a large basket of white flowers sent by Mr. Holtz, the owner of the Hotel Malage in Suelo. When the police captain entered the room, those who were present stepped to either side and made a kind of channel for him to walk, leading from the door straight to the head of the coffin. As the couple approached it was noticed that the captain's wife was wearing a black veil that was equal in thickness and length to the veil worn by the deceased's mother. A few friends remembered that the captain's wife had once been acquainted with the deceased on somewhat personal terms. That she should wear a black veil to his funeral was proper. That her veil should be equal to that of the deceased's mother was considered, by some, to be too much—but only a fraction too much—as though she had slightly overshot the field. This was not widely commented upon due to the thing that occurred when the two women confronted each other—a thing that took the attention of every person in the room and held them spellbound for the short time it covered—a period of about three minutes. The police captain stood, cap in hand, his head bowed, solemnly facing the head of the coffin between the two women. Then almost as if some secret signal had been given, the older woman, who remained seated, and the younger one, still standing, reached down slowly at the same instant and lifted their veils to the top of their heads, revealing both their faces. It was the first time during the proceedings that the mother had shown any sign of life at all. The two visages—the sallow complexion on the younger woman's face and the white stark look on the older one—stared at each other in total silence. Two pairs of black eyes seemed to glow out across the coffin, as if each pair would bore holes in the other's forehead; the fixed expres-

sions of the women, brave in their sorrow, were engraved
on the memory not only of the other mourners but of the
captain himself, who chanced to look up at that moment
and find himself stuck between them. The joined glances
shot across him like laser beams and burned like black fire
in the air above the plywood box. Two events then took
place. First, the mother stretched her hand out as if to
touch the captain's wife; instead she lay her palm flat on
top of the coffin. The younger woman responded. She too
reached out, holding her hand horizontally just over the older
woman's knuckles. The two hands did not touch. They were
withdrawn so fast they might have been singed by some
unseen flame contained in the coffin itself. The second thing
that happened was that the captain dropped his cap. This
was an event of no particular importance, except that it led
to his stooping over to pick it up, which in turn, due partly
to the captain's obesity and partly to his nervousness, caused
him to strike his head on the coffin's edge with such force
that the sound reverberated in the room like an echo from
hell. The noise of the bump had a strange hollowness to it—
an empty quality that might have been caused either by the
wood or the captain's skull, or both—and the police captain
reeled back three steps from the coffin as if he had received
his mortal blow. The police doctor went immediately to his
rescue. Then, as though the sound of the bump repre-
sented another private signal between them, the two women
reached up as one and drew their veils back over their faces.
They remained the same, facing each other across the box.
The blow the captain had received was not serious, and the
police doctor took over and pronounced the wound a mere
scratch, which should nevertheless (he said) be sterilized.
He retrieved the cap from under the coffin where it had
rolled, and gave it back to the fat man, who murmured a
rudely hasty *pésame* to the old woman and left the scene in
a disheveled manner, his wife behind him. Just before the
younger woman left, the mother of the dead fisherman made
a final gesture. Putting her arm behind her, she took one
of the long-stemmed white roses from the basket that had
been sent by the hotel. She held the white flower away from
her nose and averted her head, as if its perfume were dis-
tasteful to her. Then she raised it high above her son's coffin, the long stem pointing down like an arrow to the light-
grained wood. In one brisk motion she tossed the flower
straight across the coffin to the younger woman. The stem
struck against Lupe's breast and hung, dangling, its thorns
caught in the black lace bodice of her mourning costume.

Lupe took up the rose, cupping it in her hand, and lifted it to her face. She pressed the flower to her nose and sniffed once, not offended by the odor as the older woman had been. Then holding the white rose she turned without a word and followed her husband out of the room.

The remainder of the funeral—the procession to the Sanlúcar cemetery and the brief service spoken by the town priest over the grave—was not remembered afterwards. The old woman did not complete the customary week of mourning that was her privilege. The next day she reported for work as usual at the hotel.

A week after the funeral of Pepe Luis, Littlejohn parked her rented car in the driveway of the Guzmán palace and carried a brown paper package around to the garden entrance. She checked the cliff outside the garden wall to make sure it was deserted and then headed for the basement door. It was another warm day but the morning sky was gusty and chunks of cool air rolled in fresh off the sea. The water sparkled like glitter and there was no one in the garden or under the Columbus tree on the hill. The tree was brilliant green in the full sunlight. The top branches were moving all together in a swaying motion that made Littlejohn want to wave back. She felt giddy and light under the open blue sky, and she turned and saw Guzmán watching her from the second-floor terrace. He had one foot up on the terrace ledge. Standing against the sky he seemed like a part of the building. Littlejohn held the paper package up and he nodded. Then she went through the basement entrance and along the passage. She stopped at the padlocked door below the staircase.

Taking a key from below a potted shrub that stood next to the door she opened the padlock. After that she knocked on the door. There was no sound from inside the room and she knocked loudly twice more before she heard an answering grunt. Then she opened the door and went in. A thin familiar wave of nausea struck her and she walked across the room in a tentative way, waiting for it to pass. Littlejohn had indigestion. She disliked consultations about her health as she disliked pills, but if things did not improve within another week or so she knew that she would have to see a doctor.

The room was small and bare. From the trundle bed that had been set up in one corner, Pepe Luis pulled himself up to a half-sitting position and watched her come in. He had been asleep, and the entrance of the blond girl broke through his waking mind with a kind of newness—a feeling of dawn in his room. It was the fourth consecutive morning he had wakened to see her; short of opening his eyes to find Lupe lying next to him, he could not have thought of any better way to begin the day. The basement room was flooded with sunlight from the open window and the sea air was crisp and clear. After weeks of waking in the Sanlúcar jailhouse, Pepe Luis did not believe his luck in finding things as they were now. He was grateful to the blond girl. He waited for her to say good morning to him and he watched her move across the room. There was something familiar to him in the way she stood at the washbasin, one arm loosely over her stomach as if she was trying not to be sick. Pepe Luis had seen that stance before, though he could not at the moment remember where.

The blond girl straightened and set the package she was carrying on the table by the window. Then she saw him looking at her and smiled. She dropped her arm. *"Buenos días,"* she said.

Pepe Luis grinned. A sharp needle stung him in the left half of his jaw, and he winced.

"No," the blond girl said. She picked up the package again and carried it to the foot of his bed, and sat down. "Don't move your face," she said in halting Spanish, "not yet."

"No me duele ya," Pepe Luis lied: "It doesn't hurt me." He poked boastfully at his jaw softly with one finger.

"Leave it alone," the blond girl said. "Here," she added, holding the package up.

Pepe Luis watched her unwrap the medicine. She peeled the paper off and lined the tube of ointment and the cotton and soap and boric acid across the foot of the bed. "You look a little better," she said.

"De verdad?"

The girl went to the sink on the wall. She removed the small mirror from its hook over the sink and held it in front of her. "Look," she said.

Pepe Luis looked at the face in the mirror. It was the third time he had seen it and he didn't recognize it at all. The face was pathetically thin at the top and the skin was like dried paste. At the bottom the whole jaw was pushed to one side. The mouth was splotchy, set at an angle and nearly as bad as his mother's. He did not like the face and he looked away from it.

"No," the blond girl said. "The doctor thinks they might have to rebreak the jaw. It's when you're well. After it's set again you won't notice."

Pepe Luis shook his head hard.

"No," the blond girl said, "it's all right. They give you an anesthetic. You don't feel it." She spoke precisely, calculating each word as she said it in the manner of a foreigner who is still groping her way through a new language. Pepe Luis had never liked the exact, prim fumbling of foreigners when they tried to speak Spanish, but he didn't seem to mind it in the blond girl.

He examined her now as she replaced the mirror and washed her hands at the sink getting ready to apply the new medicine to his jaw. She paused, bending over the water, and put the protective arm back above her stomach. Just then Pepe Luis remembered who it was he had seen do that before. *"Se siente usted mal?"*

"No," the blond girl said. She went back to washing her hands.

"What's your name?"

"I told you the first day. Littlejohn."

Pepe Luis tried it. It hurt his jaw and he couldn't get it out through the pain. *"Lee-tay-yaw . . . No puedo."*

"You can say it when you're feeling better."

"I doubt it," Pepe Luis said, "I don't think I can ever say it. You don't have a real name?"

The blond girl looked at him curiously, drying her hands. "Alicia."

He thought it over. "Not bad," he said. "Alicia. *Puedo?*"

"Yes," the blond girl said, "if you want to."

"I think so. Alicia is your real name."

"All right; use it."

Pepe Luis said, "Can I ask you something?"

"Of course."

Pepe Luis said, "Alicia, are you sick or are you going to have a baby?"

The blond girl stopped drying her hands. The room appeared to grow still around her and the damp towel slipped unnoticed to the floor. She let it lie there for a time before she bent down and picked it up. She straightened slowly, looking back at him.

"What makes you ask?"

"The way you were standing," Pepe Luis said cheerfully.

". . . Standing?"

Pepe Luis said, "A friend of mine told me."

"Told you what?"

"About women."

"What did he tell you?" the blond girl said.

"It was his wife," Pepe Luis said. "She said it. When the

sickness sits down low it's the monthly thing. Not up high. Up high it's a baby."

The blond girl stood a while looking at him.

Pepe Luis shifted to a more comfortable position. "I think," he said, "it would be nice to have a baby."

The blond girl kept still. Then she opened her mouth and gave a short sound that was closer to a laugh than to anything else. She covered her mouth with one hand.

"Yes," she said. "It would be nice." She put the towel back over the sink.

Pepe Luis fingered his face. The blond girl came over to the bed. She squeezed some of the ointment on a piece of cotton and applied it to the raw areas around his jaw. "This is going to hurt," she said.

"No. No me duela nada."

"Don't lie. It does hurt. You can call me Alicia," the blond girl said.

Pepe Luis didn't answer, and she went on applying the salve over his face.

"I think you're right. I think you're right about everything. I think my real name is Alicia. I think I'm going to have a baby," the blond girl said.

Pepe Luis went to sleep and woke often, without any regard to the time of day or night. It was a habit he had got into in the jailhouse when it didn't matter whether it was dark or light outside, and sometimes he would sleep for hours and sometimes not. Sometimes when he woke, the square of light in the window was dusty blue, dull slate-colored, so that he would not know if the day was beginning or ending. He would lie still and watch the light and if it turned yellow he would know that the twilight was coming. But if the dust thinned until the patch of pale sky lifted away from the window, he knew that it was day. He would not care which it was, but would lie there taking it in, letting it flow over him. His body needed air and he did not think that he would ever get enough of it. He would lie still feeling the freshness and he would try not to think about the dank horror-smell that he had lived in up to last week, or the way that he had felt while he was living in it. He only remembered it in nightmares now when he was asleep, and after a while the whole time of the jailhouse receded away from him, separate and condensed, like a sick dream that he was able to hold in contempt, a dim thing of fancy and outrage. He could not afford to remember the pain so he did not remember it. His body was healing and the bones were knitting; every day they were a little better. Besides his jaw, the three other fractures—the left forearm and right thigh and ankle—were not nearly so painful now that they were immobilized in plaster and he didn't have to use them every day. In the space of one week he found that he could get out of bed alone and maneuver his way alone to the corner of the room and back. He practiced by himself, though Guzmán's doctor had instructed him not to for another ten days; but he was gentle, and his body responded to his efforts in a friendly way as if it wanted to help him out. The doctor had been brought down from Seville. He was an old friend of Guzmán's who could be trusted not to talk; he had said that Pepe Luis must gain back some of his strength before having X-rays taken to determine the extent of bone damage. Pepe Luis's body was too weak to resist an operation even if he needed one, and the orders were that he lie there and recuperate first. Pepe Luis already knew that his old limp was going to be worse, but other than that—and a certain proclivity to urine malfunction that he might have on and off for the rest of his life—he was going to be all right. He had been beaten too badly in the kidneys for them ever to recuperate totally, but they would make do as long as he was careful. It was a miracle that he had survived the jailhouse at all; in the final weeks he had not expected to survive, and he could not explain the miracle to himself. When the pain had been bad he had prayed that he would die, and the prayer was among the last things that he remembered about the whole experience. The day that Pepe Luis had prayed, the rat-faced man named Rafael who had spied on him in the docks had been sitting in front of him in the captain's office. The captain had given the order, and Pepe Luis had stood up. The two policemen had held him while the doctor turned the broken bone back and forth in his arm, and while Pepe Luis was screaming the doctor had taught one of the policemen where the kidneys were. The first time the policeman had hit him and missed the kidneys, it had not been so bad, but when the policeman had located the kidneys it had been something worse than bad. Pepe Luis had not been able to scream any louder than he was already screaming, and he had looked at the rat-faced man and the smiling fat captain, and he had petitioned God to remove the pain. Then the policeman hit too low and the thigh bone had cracked and he had petitioned God to take away his life instead. After that he lost consciousness and there had been only sporadic instants of it, slivers of awful light like bright new knives turning in an old wound, and all

the rest darkness. The first and last days of the interrogation
had melted like tar in his mind, a black and silver dream, too
sticky to separate even if he had wanted to. Only one
sequence stood out from the rest. It was before they had
beaten him in the captain's office. It was when his jaw was
still bandaged after they had hit him with the broken bottle
and after the first day of interrogation when he had fainted
for the first time. That morning they had dragged him back
to the cell; when he had awakened he was naked and they
were hosing him down. The captain had complained about
his odor, and three of the biggest policemen were standing
at the door of the cell. One held the hose on him, washing
him. Pepe Luis heard the policeman say that the hose had
made him clean as a new-born baby, and he looked up, and
he knew suddenly what the policeman was going to do before
he did it. He saw the other policeman turn off the hose and
then he looked back at the first policeman, and the first
policeman's fly was open. Then he did not remember the
pain but only the outrage when they took turns doing it, taking him that way, like an animal, and the laughter. The one
who was holding him down began to laugh when the other
one, the one he could not see, grunted aloud and exploded
inside Pepe Luis, and then the one who was laughing said
that now Pepe Luis wasn't a new-born baby any more. The
policeman said that now he could have a baby himself and
before they had got through he wouldn't know who the
father was. Then the third policeman had boasted that he
could give it to Pepe Luis and make Pepe Luis like it. The
rat-faced man had been there too, though the rat-faced man
hadn't taken part in it but had only watched with glowing
eyes from the door, and at some point during it when Pepe
Luis was not making any sound, the rat-faced man had said
that Pepe Luis was enjoying it now. The rat-faced man even
said that Pepe Luis wanted one of the men to kiss him. In the
pain and the exhaustion it was the remarks made by the rat-
faced man that outraged him more than any of it. But the
sexual humiliation was the only thing he remembered as a
whole, and the last days of the interrogation were gone from
his mind. He could not remember lying in the dark cell of the
jailhouse after the beating, refusing to eat or drink. He could
not even really remember his mother's visit: he had been unconscious, and he had responded to the sound of her voice
without being much aware of what he was doing. In his
memory it was merely a part of the long sticky dream. In
this dream he was a child and something bad had happened
to him and it had been his mother's fault. She had gone

away; it was her being away that allowed the thing to happen, and when she came back he had yelled *Mamá* twice at her but she had only gone away again. He had not even seen her at the cell door. They had been together for that one moment in the jailhouse, and they had exchanged voices, but that was all. Then the dream of pain had started again and there had not been too many more white slivers of the awful light before he had wakened here in the Guzmán palace in this room.

When he first saw the blond girl coming in with a tray of food Pepe Luis had not spoken. But the blond girl didn't know he wasn't any good at talking, and perhaps because she didn't know it, he found that he could talk to her easily. When she was gone he would invent things to take up with her. Till now Pepe Luis had always been lost when he had to take part in a conversation; now he forgot his own shyness in trying to teach the girl how to express herself in Spanish.

He liked the blond girl so much that he wished she could come at night too, but she had explained that it was not possible. She did not live at the palace. She was a sort of day person. He had asked her once why it was that she could not stay inside the palace after dark, but the blond girl had only raised her eyes to the top of the window as if she were remembering an object high above it over the building, and had said no, it was just not possible. For a moment Pepe Luis had imagined that there was something she was frightened of, but he had soon forgot about that.

But in the dark things were different and the second night he spent at the palace a very strange thing happened to Pepe Luis. His mother came to see him. The old woman sat in a chair by his bed for two hours, and, after the first ten minutes, Pepe Luis found for the first time in his life that he was uncomfortable with her. He had nothing to say to his mother and he did not like the look of her now. There was something dismal in her face; the odd angle of her mouth had developed a twisted quality to it. Pepe Luis had been accustomed to seeing the funny angle of his mother's mouth since he was a very small child—he had long ago ceased to think anything of it. Still, he had never seen it quite this way before. There was a dull reddish glow in her eyes and his mother's whole aspect gave him a bad feeling, as though her black dress were reflecting darkness up onto her face all the time. She was as much a night person now as the blond girl was a day person. She had explained that she could not visit him during the day, for fear of being seen—and she had come to the palace twice since the first visit, each time at night, each time so heavily veiled that nobody would have recognized her on the street even if she had been seen. Pepe Luis did not welcome her visits. It was as if he no longer knew his mother. He did his best to hide his distaste, to pretend that he was glad to see her, but after a while he began to realize that his mother was not fooled. He had thought she would be hurt by his lack of feeling for her if she ever discovered it—but she had already discovered it and she did not seem hurt in the least. On the second visit, the old woman pulled her chair up and stared for a long time into his face, as if satisfying herself that she was right about her son's new reaction to her. After that she just sat back and looked out the window. Watching her, Pepe Luis imagined for a moment that she was angry, but when he took a good look at her he discovered to his own amazement that he was wrong. Not only wasn't she angry—she wasn't even interested. She was, in fact, bored. Silly as this seemed, Pepe Luis knew that he was not mistaken. He realized then that the relationship had changed not only for him, but for her: she was as weary of him as he was offended by her presence. Worst of all, his mother had developed a noticeably unpleasant smell about her—as though she had left off washing herself. She had been known for cleanliness all her life. Yet when she saw that Pepe Luis was offended by her smell, Eugenia was no more upset than she had been at his other reaction; she just moved her chair away from his bed closer to the window. From then on when she came she did not make any pretense at conversation. She didn't even take her veil off. She sat by the window staring out at the Columbus tree on the other side of the garden for a couple of hours and then got up and went home. The tree was the only thing that seemed to hold any interest for her. In the last days she had come only once, and before leaving she had given some excuse about not being able to come back for a while. Pepe Luis made no comment about this. Without knowing why, he was relieved, and so was she. Something about the jailhouse had come between him and his mother for all time now. It was as if they no longer liked each other—as if each one reminded the other of something vile that both preferred to forget. Like two people who have crossed paths in a plague city, they only reminded each other of horror afterwards. Something about the jailhouse stood between them and would go on standing between them for the rest of their lives. Each knew it instinctively, and there was nothing that they could do about it; it was out of their control. From now on they would be polite whenever they met—

and they would both always hope that they would not have to meet too often.

Partly because of this new wall between them, Pepe Luis never asked his mother exactly how it was that he had got out of jail. Though it was clear that she had had something to do with it, Eugenia didn't want to talk about it any more then he did. Gradually he understood from things said by María or by Count Guzmán that the blond girl's money had paid for his escape, and it was to the blond girl alone that he was grateful: he did not like thinking that Eugenia had much to do with it any more than he had wanted to think the other time, when he had been cured of the childhood paralysis, that her pilgrimage to the Virgin had had much to do with that. Pepe Luis believed in God as much as the next man but there were limits to religion in his thinking. As a small child he had believed that his mother's powers were limitless and that with the help of God she could fix any situation she put her mind to; but he never got over the feeling of betrayal when she had been unable to prevent his brother's death. And now something new and mysterious began to take place in his heart. Little by little he began to think of the blond girl as his protector. Though he was older in years, he could not get over this new feeling, and the fact of her pregnancy only served to increase the illusion. As she had become a symbol of daylight for him, so she became now a symbol of motherhood that was radiant, soft, oddly virginal. There was a quality in the eyes of the girl that touched him deeply, and it touched other people as well. María the cook was almost as affected by it as he was. She never failed to extol the girl's virtues to him—an opinion that added to his own belief. The thing that finally happened was predictable. Pepe Luis, lying alone in his cot from morning to morning, rejected his own parents in favor of the blond girl and Count Guzmán; he found in them a chance to survive and a new life. His own father, Enrique, had not been told the truth about Pepe Luis's escape from the jailhouse. Eugenia did not trust her husband's drinking habits, which increased as his health declined; for this and for other reasons, she had included him in her deception, and Enrique now believed that his son was dead. Pepe Luis was never to see his father again. Officially, according to the police files, he himself did not exist. All he had to do when he got well was to leave this coast. Not one shadow of his former life fell across his path.

So he lay there getting better while the light changed in the window of the little basement room and he saw the mornings come and go. Count Guzmán had said it was important that Pepe Luis remain in the room till he was well, and he did so happily; the blond girl had asked him not to say anything about her condition and Pepe Luis kept to his word. He did not mind the room he was in. Sometimes late at night when he could not sleep he would pull himself out of the window and sit on the other side in a patch of garden earth sniffing the sea. Then he would think of the places he could go and all the coasts he could live on. It had been explained to him that he would have enough money to start his life again wherever he wanted, and he would look at the clamshell path stretching in front of him into the night like the path he was going to take away from his old life into the future. He would sit unseen under an oak tree outside his window and watch the white shells in the moonlight. Nothing was ever as clean as the smell of the sea, nothing as white as the clamshells that went straight ahead of Pepe Luis into the darkness. After a while it became a habit when he woke to sit there and keep watch over the path. His bones were better now and he could move without any sharp pain. Under the tree by the window were several smooth stones that he had found by digging. They were differently shaped and Pepe Luis pretended that each one stood for another place in the world. A stone with a triangular shape was America. One was the Mediterranean, one the Atlantic Ocean. There was a stone for every province in Spain and a stone for each of several other countries, and he would examine them one by one in the night, holding each up close to his face. Once when he was digging for them he found an old tin can with a sharp cutting edge, and from then on he used the tin can as a spade to find and bury the stones with. After that the game of the stones became a kind of ritual. He would put several into the tin can and roll them out into the night against his foot and see which stone would win. Time went on that way for Pepe Luis, and if it wasn't exciting, it was easier and pleasanter than most other times he had known.

One evening at dusk he had a new visitor. It was about nine o'clock. The yellow glow in the window was turning deeper, the way it did every evening a few minutes before night. María the cook brought the visitor in and at first when Pepe Luis heard the footsteps outside the door he thought it was the blond girl coming back. He believed she was making an exception about staying in the building after dark and was coming to say goodnight to him. Then María opened the door and let the visitor into the room and Pepe

Luis wondered how he could have forgotten that part of his life so quickly.

He pulled himself up and sat contemplating the new visitor. He could not see much of the face behind the black veil, but he did not need to see much of it. The woman stood awkwardly by the door. Her shoulders were tensed and her back looked stiff. Glancing down at her body, Pepe Luis smiled at the purse held with such unconscious grace in the elegant fingers of the long white hands. "*Hola,*" he said.

The visitor nodded, and remained standing. The dress she wore was covered with black lace and must have cost a lot of money. Pepe Luis could not see her mouth behind the veil, but after a while she answered him. She spoke quietly, the single word glazed and reticent but quite distinct, like an obedient muted echo of his own: "*Hola.*"

There was a silence.

"I came to see you."

"Won't you sit down?" Pepe Luis asked formally.

"Thank you."

Lupe moved forward in an awkward way to the chair at the foot of his bed. She sat, rigid, her thighs at right angles to her back, the purse was held exactly in the center of her lap, like an embarrassing prize she had won at a fair.

Pepe Luis looked at her. Except for her father's and her husband's houses, you could see that Lupe had never been in a man's bedroom before. Only her hands kept their grace, and even they were curled nervously now around the black shiny purse, all ten fingers crossed and woven together like reeds. She coughed.

Pepe Luis held still. Lupe had evidently come to tell him something, and now that she was here she couldn't think of anything to say. In their relationship before it had been Pepe Luis who was fumbling and timid; Lupe had been the one in control. This was the first time he had laid eyes on her since entering the jailhouse and Pepe Luis could tell now that some things in his life were going to be different. He pulled himself up further in the bed.

"I'm glad to see you," he said.

Lupe seemed about to say something, and then changed her mind and remained silent.

"Only I can't," Pepe Luis said.

"Can't?"

"See you."

After a moment Lupe released her hold on the purse. She lifted her long white hands to her neck and hesitated another second. Then in one quick gesture she flicked the black veil away from her head. The veil flew up into the air. After that she held it to one side hanging from her fingers as though she didn't know what to do with it. Then she lay it across the foot of his bed. She snatched it up again immediately and put it into her lap. She was frowning. Pepe Luis sat against the pillows looking at her. "Are you in mourning?" he said.

Lupe's eyes were focused hard on the piece of material in her lap. "No," she said. "The veil is only . . . I walked here. I could get into trouble."

Pepe Luis sat back farther and waited.

"I was in mourning one day; for your funeral."

"Yes?"

"Yes. I put on mourning for your funeral."

"Thank you," Pepe Luis said politely.

He was quiet for a while and Lupe made a tuck in the black veil on her knee with her fingers.

"Was there something you wanted to talk to me about?"

"No," Lupe said watching the veil. "I go for a lot of walks."

"Walks?"

"Yes," she said. "I was going along the hill. Then I decided to come and see you. I only came because I was feeling sorry for you," she added.

"Did you have the veil with you?"

Instead of answering, Lupe turned dark red, and Pepe Luis was instantly sorry that he had asked the question. He couldn't think of any way to repair it, and he sat there.

"I can't stay . . . I just had five minutes," Lupe muttered angrily. "I'll be leaving now. I was wrong to come." She stood up and took a step forward. Then for the first time since she had removed the veil, she raised her eyes and looked directly at him. Her mouth opened and the blood drained out of her face, leaving it pale and more liverish looking than usual. She drew her breath in fast. Then she raised a hand and set one knuckle against her teeth.

Pepe Luis grinned. A shyness overcame him and he stopped grinning and covered his jaw with his right hand.

Lupe stood confronting the bad-looking thing that his jaw had become; she did not move.

"I'm sorry," Pepe Luis said. "It's going to be fixed."

"Don't apologize to me," Lupe said sharply.

"You shouldn't have to look at it."

"I never in my life heard of anything as stupid as your apologizing to me," Lupe said, stamping her foot and losing her temper. "Never. It's the worst thing I ever heard. . . . I think you're the stupidest man I ever met. . . ."

"Yes," Pepe Luis said. "I am."

"You don't have to agree with me either," Lupe said; "*that* doesn't do any good." She spun on one heel and walked angrily to the window, tossing her purse and veil into the chair she had been sitting in earlier. The veil slid off and fell unnoticed to the floor.

"I'm sorry," Pepe Luis said again. He realized the second he said it that it was the one thing she had asked him not to say.

He closed his mouth and pushed back down in the bed. His weight was on the painful hip, and he grunted aloud.

"Go ahead and wreck yourself," Lupe said, hard, facing the window, "it serves you right. You look just awful."

"It's the jaw. I can't help it."

"I *know* you can't help it," Lupe said, "*I know*, don't I? Or go ahead and say it again—go ahead. My God; you're worse than stupid . . . you're totally ignorant. . . ."

Pepe Luis who was not doing well in the conversation decided to keep quiet and let things take their natural course. He was not sure what the course would be, but it couldn't be a whole lot worse, and he could not imagine what exactly he had said to make her so angry.

Lupe didn't offer any further comment, and Pepe Luis spread his legs under the bedclothes and relaxed a little. Then looking down at himself he noticed that the clinging bedclothes revealed an exaggerated long bulge just below his crotch. He folded his hands over it and tried to smooth out the offensive bulge, but he couldn't do it without being obvious, and he couldn't hide it either. He hiked his knees up and covered the bulge from view.

Lupe did not seem to notice; she kept her attention fixed on the darkening shadows on the lawn outside. "I suppose you'll be going away soon."

"Away?"

"Yes. That's what I said. Away," Lupe repeated annoyedly, "don't always make me say everything twice. Away from Sanlúcar. You'll have to go somewhere where people don't know you, won't you?"

"Yes."

"It's the best thing you could do. I approve of it," Lupe said. "You should leave as soon as possible."

"Yes," Pepe Luis said. "As soon as she says I'm well enough to travel."

"She?"

"Alicia."

"Who?"

"The American—a friend of Count Guzmán. She . . ."

"Oh her. Yes," Lupe said. "His lover . . . I've seen her driving around town. Everybody knows about *her*."

Lupe turned from the window and walked across to the sink.

"Knows what?"

"Nothing in particular . . . I just meant everybody knows what American girls are, that's all. Not that I don't understand. I don't blame men at all for liking girls like that. . . . I'm only saying it would be nice to talk about something else because I don't have much time. I'll talk about anything you want, though. . . ."

Lupe paused, and primped her hair with both hands in the mirror over the sink. Then she crossed her arms again and strolled back to the window, humming a little tune.

Pepe Luis bent to the right. His bad hip was beginning to ache from the position of his knees, but he couldn't lower them without exposing the embarrassing bulge in the bed-clothes. The bulge was innocent, but like many innocent things it made its owner guilty and self-conscious. A less innocent bulge wouldn't have bothered Pepe Luis so much but the innocence of this one appalled him. He turned over on one side, groaning from the effort.

"Where were you thinking of going?" Lupe said.

"Going? I don't know yet. I haven't made up my mind."

Pepe Luis pretended to scratch his knee and yanked secretly at the bedclothes. His hand slipped, and instead of smoothing anything out he made the bulge larger. "You . . . you were saying," he said, "about traveling. You asked me where I was going to live."

"Did I? Oh yes. Going to live."

"I was thinking about Mexico City last night. Or maybe New York. I heard a lot about New York from Ali— I heard a lot about New York."

"Oh? . . . *North* America? . . . I'd have thought South America was a better idea. . . . Not that it's any of my business. . . . Are you good at foreign languages?"

"No. That is, I don't know. I never tried."

"They speak Spanish in South America. . . . I saw a movie about Buenos Aires—it looks like a pretty city. I like the name too, don't you? Buen-os Air-es . . . that's where *I'd* go . . . I imagine you could start a whole new life there without people asking any questions. You could just change your name and get a job, couldn't you? You wouldn't have to take much from here. Just yourself and whoever else might be going with you. . . . Will you have any money?"

"Enough to get started. My mother is lending me some, and Ali—I'll have plenty money," Pepe Luis said.

"Your mother, yes," Lupe said, standing away from the window and dropping her arms. "Now *her* I admire. . . ."

Pepe Luis looked at his hands.

"It's wonderful how well she managed everything. And so fast. Just one day after I told her you were in jail, she . . ."

"I don't want to talk about her," Pepe Luis said. His tone was flat and commanding.

Lupe stiffened a little. Then quickly she relaxed. In the deepening light she regarded Pepe Luis from the foot of his bed with a sort of respect. She was impressed despite herself. For weeks now Lupe had had a suspicion that there was something in Pepe Luis she had never credited him with —a strength she hadn't seen in the time when she knew him —and her awareness of it showed in her behavior. Instead of taking offense at the sharpness of his command, Lupe's manner changed to a docile softness, as if she not only accepted the new relationship between them but liked it.

A silence settled in the room.

"He has a bump on his head," Lupe said suddenly.

"Who?"

". . . Him. My husband. Haven't they told you? He hit his head on your coffin."

"Did he?"

"Yes. It gave him a terrible welt. His forehead's all black and blue. He can't even put his cap on," Lupe said.

"Oh. I'm sorry."

"Sorry?"

"Well, I mean . . . if it makes a problem for you . . . I mean if . . ."

"It doesn't make a problem for me. It doesn't make any difference to me one way or the other," Lupe said evenly.

Pepe Luis remained quiet, contemplating her. The room was almost dark now; except for the soft reflection of the yellow sky outside, there was no light. Lupe's eyes were glittering, and there was a boldness in the way she was staring at him across the bed. It was a look that seemed to be trying to tell Pepe Luis something that she could not put into words. Pepe Luis concentrated. Then, because he had once before tried to interpret one of Lupe's mysterious looks and got himself into the jailhouse because of it, he decided that he was only imagining things this time, and he put the idea out of his mind.

"Anyway," he said. "I'm glad things go well at your house. . . ."

"Are you?" Lupe said.

"I mean it's good there's no problem for you."

"I wish," Lupe said without moving, "you'd seen his face that night."

"What night?"

"That night. He didn't know what to say. . . . He didn't even know what to do. . . . He tried talking to me about it, only I wouldn't let him. He said you'd stopped him on the street and told him he couldn't buy me. I pretended I didn't understand; I said he had no right to talk to me about such things . . . he stayed up till four in the morning, pacing the floor upstairs. . . . It was the funniest thing you ever saw. . . ."

Lupe stopped speaking and waited for him to answer her.

"Yes," Pepe Luis said slowly. "I remember now. I'd forgotten about that night."

Lupe stared at him. In the soft yellow light of the room, her face went deathly pale, as though he had slapped her. "You?" she said in a furious whisper, "forgotten?" All at once she doubled over and giggled, her voice rising to a high-held pitch as she lost control for a moment. "He's forgotten," she said as if to someone else, "listen to him, please, forgotten . . . after what they did. After what happened to him because of it. . . . Forgotten . . ."

Pepe Luis sat and tried to figure out what he had said that could have angered her again, but the thing was beyond him. There was only one fact he was sure of. Inconceivable as it was, in their new relationship Lupe seemed almost to be afraid of him in some way. Pepe Luis frowned. Though he would probably never see her again after today, he ought to be careful during the rest of her visit not to hurt Lupe by any more careless remarks. If it was he who had control over the conversation, it was up to him now to steer it into a more pleasant direction.

"Listen," he said, "can I write to you?"

Lupe had managed to choke her giggles, and she turned now and picked up her purse from the chair. She took a handkerchief from it and blew her nose. The saffron light from the window was nearly gone, and the sallowness of Lupe's complexion shone like pale yellow alabaster in the room. Pepe Luis thought it was the most fragile color he had ever seen and he longed to tell her so, but he was afraid of what her reaction might be to the remark, and he decided again that he ought to stick to safer subjects. *"Puedo?"*

"Can you what?" Lupe fumbled with the catch on her purse.

"What I said. Write to you."

"Do you really *prefer* writing to me?" Lupe's voice was hardly audible.

"Yes," Pepe Luis said.

"Or would you rather . . ."

Pepe Luis strained his ears, but he could not hear the end of the question. "I know how to write," he said. "I've been learning."

Lupe did not answer him.

"I practice every morning," Pepe Luis said. "I started first with a children's book, but . . ."

"Listen," Lupe said. "Can't you ever listen?" She spoke in a thick way and her voice came out in a harsh ugly whisper, as if her throat were filling with the words. "I sometimes go walking by myself. I never used to. But I go along the path by the road to Jerez. . . . Remember? It's where we . . . I like it there. I never went there with anyone else. . . . Everything you said was right. Don't you understand? I saw you, all those nights you stood in the doorway across the street. I would wonder what you were standing there for. . . . Then when *he* came up the stairs and told me, I wanted to laugh. . . . You did it. You told him how a church whore is like any other kind of whore. . . . I'm not what they think. Him or my parents. I never went walking there with anyone else . . . I never could. Don't you see? I wouldn't mind anything. I won't be any trouble. I don't care what it's like. Another province, or South America; I was only pretending to care. . . . Can't you understand? I like to take the path by the road to Jerez. Don't you understand? Nobody else ever knew me."

Lupe halted as though her throat had finally filled and she stood just beyond the end of the bed. Pepe Luis could hear her breathing, and outside in the garden a stray dog that María had found somewhere loped past the window chasing a bird in the darkness. He could hardly see Lupe. He did not even know if she was looking back at him. Some of what she had said had made sense to him, but most of it had not. Once on the docks in the brilliant sunlight he had sensed something about her without hearing it in words. Now in the night having heard the words, he was more confused than if she had not spoken.

He pushed himself all the way up on the pillows. One thing was clear: Lupe was a married woman now; you could see she had become accustomed to expensive clothes and a maid. Her husband was a man who would not be pleasant about it if he came home in the evening and found the house empty. The longer Lupe stayed out at this hour, the worse it might be for her when she got back.

Pepe Luis tucked his tongue over his lower teeth and wet them. "Listen," he said, "it's late. We could maybe talk another time. Shouldn't you be getting home?"

The shadow at the foot of the bed stayed where it was. For a while there was only stillness between them in the room.

When Lupe broke free of the wall, she came all the way to the head of the bed and stood close beside Pepe Luis. Slowly in the darkness he saw her white hand glide below him to the electric cord. The cord moved, and the plastic switch appeared like a small black egg in her palm. Lupe pressed her thumb over it.

Pepe Luis blinked in the bright light that filled the room. He was hard put to recognize the face looking down at him. It was a puffy dark red—the deepest blush he had ever seen—and the lips were contorted in anger. The eyes were hard and flashing and Lupe dropped the light switch to the floor.

Then suddenly she choked and stood sputtering down at him in speechless rage. She grabbed her purse and turned to the door. "Oh God, how stupid," she said. "How stupid it all is."

She stood there a moment as if she were waiting for something.

Then she flung the door back and rushed headlong out of the room.

Pepe Luis lay still for a long time without moving in the bed, watching the empty doorway where she had gone. At least an hour passed and nothing happened. At ten o'clock María brought him his supper on a tray and left it on the chair beside the bed. She closed the door and Pepe Luis heard the padlock click into place. Still he did not move but went on staring at the closed door. He did not touch the food. The soup that had been made from the day's meats and filled with tiny noodles for supper grew cold sitting on the tray. When another thirty minutes had passed he drank a swallow of the red wine from the glass next to the soup. Underneath the chair that held the tray, he saw something. It was the veil that Lupe had taken off and left behind her where it had fallen. He picked it up and drew it over his leg onto his lap. The veil was so thin it was like a delicate touch on his thigh. It reminded him of the way her hand used to feel there, and under the bedclothes he felt himself stir.

He continued to sit looking down at the veil with a puzzled expression in his dark quiet eyes.

It was six nights later that the thing happened.

Pepe Luis had been waiting for Lupe from day to day but she never came back to see him again. Instead, something else took place in his life that made him forget about her once more. The event was not expected by anyone; Count Guzmán alone had anticipated the possibility and he had done his best to guard against it. It was the first of a final series of happenings that affected not only Pepe Luis, but the lives of a few other people along the coast.

The night it happened, Pepe Luis was sitting in his usual place under the protective branch of the oak that grew outside his window. He had dug up the stones he had collected, and he was laying them out in a circle with the empty tin can at the center. The top of the can—the part he used as a spade—was sticking straight up, and its jagged edge, scalloped and rusted, reflected the moon in little silver glints like cuts of light in the darkness. It was somewhere between two and three o'clock in the morning. The night was a fairly bright one, seven nights short of a full moon, and full of stars. It was relatively cloudless. A breeze was up and from time to time Pepe Luis could see the moon shifting like an unexpected egg through the branches of the oak. He was feeling listless. He was playing the game he had grown accustomed to at this hour, naming each stone for a different geographic place; but the game was not the same any more. It had lost its freshness for him since Lupe's visit. Pepe Luis tried to bring back his enthusiasm by naming the stones for exotic-sounding places like Tahiti and the Amazon River, but it wasn't any use. The idea that he would not see Lupe again had spoiled some of his excitement about the future. He remembered, among other things, how much he loved *cante jondo,* and how long it had been since he'd heard any. It wasn't likely he would be hearing any more of it—it was well known that the true deep song didn't last long outside of Andalucía: like some old wines, once exported it lost its full flavor. Besides, Pepe Luis loved Andalusian food and he did not like the idea of never tasting another good *puchero* or mashing a crust of bread into the fat of another *pringada.* He was no longer so in love with the thought of traveling wherever he wanted to go in the world with enough money to start a new life—or he was no longer all that happy about being by himself. Whatever it was, the game of the stones was over.

He shrugged off the gloomy mood that hung over him and set his eyes for the tenth time in an hour on the white clamshell path stretching out from the oak. When he thought of the path as the road that he would soon walk into the future it never failed to give him a lift. The shells were especially white and clean looking tonight and the cold moonlight lay on them like water. The path was parallel to the main building so that it was sliced in half lengthwise by the long shadow of the palace roof; it was joined by another path near the cliff wall. The two met near the Columbus tree outside the garden gate, still white even in the distance, giving a sense of never ending, like two rails of a train track that seem to meet in infinity. Pepe Luis liked to think of the path near him as his life and the other as the life of someone else, as yet nameless, who would one day join him out where the two became one. Looking at them now cheered him up a bit. Ahead of him the sharpness of the white shells washed by the moonlight was motionless and hard and open—clean as dreams. In the surrounding night, the white had a violent look to it that lent it an extra dimension. The path was achingly white and black, the colors of purity—the ache in the heart of any man who would spoil it. Pepe Luis sat there wondering why he himself wanted to spoil it. Then the thing happened.

He saw it the first time out of the corner of his eye and when his eye flew to it the thing was gone. The path was just the same as it had always been, white and flat and plain, empty as ever. Yet Pepe Luis was sure he had seen something that flicked across the path—something quick and evil in the night. He searched the shells with his eyes from one end to the other, from where he was sitting to the place where the path ran out of sight outside the garden gate near the Columbus tree. There was not one object on it. Then he centered his focus on a spot halfway up the white path, so that he would be aware of anything moving in either section. The second time it happened, he was looking right at it. One minute the spot he was watching was clear; the next it was alive with a sharp black shadow that writhed along it and disappeared. There was no sound. The shadow on the path was coming straight toward Pepe Luis and it was coming from the direction of the Columbus tree. He kept his eyes on the shells and after a while he saw it again. This time it was just one edge of a shadow, round at the zenith but oval near the middle, like the top of a man's head. It disappeared again and Pepe Luis kept on watching the shells. When he saw it the fourth time, the shadow was larger, and he no longer had any doubts about it. There was a man crawling along the roof of the main building in the middle of the night.

Pepe Luis stood up quietly under the branch of the oak. Several hairs on the back of his neck and the top of his shoulders moved by themselves. His hackles responded to the oldest fear of all: the path was his territory and it was being threatened. He kept his body still and raised his eyes to the terracotta-tiled roof of the main building. He could not see anybody on it. The tiles of the roof stretched out in evenly rippled waves, the dull color of baked earth, like a dark red tide lying over the building. He scanned every centimeter of the roof but there was not one movement visible. Not even a cloud shadow changed on the tiles. Then next to the second chimney a hand appeared and he knew where the man was.

Pepe Luis stood still, protected from view by the oak branch; he could not be seen by anyone looking down from above and he followed the progress of the man along the roof. No part of his own body moved, but inside him the glands and fibers altered their secretions in accord with the progress of the intruder. By the time the man was close over him, Pepe Luis wasn't the maimed and crumpled-feeling person he had been a minute earlier. He did not notice the weight of the plaster casts clinging from his limbs as he stood under the tree; he felt capable of whatever action might be asked of him. He stood, his knees slightly bent, his broken body ridiculously gathering to spring. The man on the roof had progressed to a point above and just to the east of Guzmán's bedroom; he moved easily across the tiles, soundlessly in the night, in the manner of one who knows where he is going and is used to the terrain. He stopped at a mansard window in the attic and put a hand out to steady himself; then he stood up next to the window and sat on the ledge. Resting from his climb, with the assured air of an intruder who believes that he is alone and unobserved, the man sat in solitude facing back toward the Columbus tree over the garden wall. His feet dangled loose between the mansard ledge and the roof. Pepe Luis watched the rubber-soled shoes hanging high in the air directly above him, not very far over Guzmán's bedroom windows. He could not see any more than the man's feet. Then in a parting of the branch above his head, he saw and recognized the face of the man on the roof, and the life inside his own body moved forward. Pepe Luis was not aware of the change he himself had undergone; he had no time to think, but only advanced, almost floating within the shadows, as if he had been using his body that way all his life. Not a stick broke and not a shell moved under his foot. He walked in the garden with the stealth of angels. He observed the wall of the palace until he had reached the other end, and then he reversed his footsteps. Once back, he stooped over and picked up an object from the earth under the oak tree. Then smoothly and calmly, gliding like a killer into the protective covering above him, Pepe Luis seemed to melt out of the landscape, dissolving as a shadow dissolves into the dark stone wall by the building.

In the same night, three stories above the garden, Juan de Guzmán was awake on top of his bed smoking a cigarette and remembering another time. The bedroom was cool for summer and only a couple of horseflies disturbed the air. Guzmán was a strong man despite his age; his chest was tight and his legs were hard and lithe as the legs of a goat. He lay naked in the dark and in it he saw other places, other times of his life when events had converged around him with a suddenness that had taught him to be prepared.

And yet he was always unprepared, and he knew it. To be prepared was to be unprepared; he had learned that much in the Civil War when you did not know whether it was your own brother or an unknown Italian who would drop the next bomb. The Civil War, now almost twenty years past, was still much a part of him. He would never be able to forget about it and he did not want to forget about it. There had been another girl then, though he was already married and his two sons had already been born. That time it had been a French girl, a sympathetic Loyalist who had fought with him and slept with him—and finally of course wanted him to go with her out of the country. He had been reasonably young himself then, just over thirty, and he had been fond of the French girl, though he had never pretended even to himself that he had been in love with her. He had sent her away when the war had got bad. The French girl had made a dramatic moment of their farewell, waving to him from the back of a truck through heavy sheets of rain while bullets flew as the truck bore her away from him forever. A month later he had heard that she was living with a different Loyalist commander in Barcelona. Most French girls were like that, and so were many Swedish girls, and all English girls worth sleeping with were like that and most Dutch girls. Many Finnish girls were like that also. He had never taken to Portuguese girls, and since the war he had not wanted to sleep with any Italian girls. Tourists in general were like that, and American tourists in particular.

All foreign girls, Guzmán knew, had romantic notions about Spain—notions that were not borne out by the facts. Tourists brought their own notions with them when they came; their notions were a part of their luggage. Only, unlike other kinds of luggage, the foreigners' ideals remained invisible, like rays of light traveling in space, until there was a wall on which they could be projected. Spain was such a wall. It had long been such a wall, and many romantics and other kinds of idealists had used it as a screen on which they could see their own fine dreams acted out. Most of the dreams never became reality, and when that failed to happen, the foreigners either died of it or left Spain feeling bad about the Spanish people. Spain went on, heedless of all the foreigners—knowing in a somewhat heartless way that there would always be new foreigners to replace those who had left or fallen by the wayside. Foreigners were foreigners. They were all like that.

But Alice Littlejohn was not like that. Or was she?

Guzmán crossed his legs in the thin moonlight that tinted the room and lit another cigarette on the butt of the old one. The bedroom was filled with the quiet sounds of night. Crickets and tree frogs sawed the air outside and changed their rhythms in the semidarkness. Yes, Alice Littlejohn was something like that—but such an extreme case of it that it was the same as being different. In any case she was a special girl. If anything, she was *too* anxious to learn. Guzmán was sometimes concerned about what might happen when Alice Littlejohn finally saw Spain as it really was, uncolored by her own romantic ideas. Such discoveries were apt to end in a bad way. Only he could not afford right now to worry about that; there were other dangers to consider that had nothing to do with her. The way to prepare for them was to get some sleep. He had to be fresh to cope with whatever situation might arise, tomorrow and every morning until the new house guest had left the province. Guzmán put his cigarette out.

He shut his eyes and opened his mind to the darkness. Yes, she was a special girl; once or twice, early on, Guzmán's conscience had hurt him enough that he had tried to give her up; but not enough to do it. He couldn't do it—he had waited now until it was too late. At first he had thought she was only a spoiled rich American traveling in Europe, but shortly after meeting her he had forgot about that. If it was true, and in part it probably was, it no longer mattered. He was addicted to her now: he wanted her nearly all the time. He had to discipline himself not to think about her. The fresh taste that came to her skin stayed sharp as resin on his tongue. He had a taste for the girl. The morning was time enough to think about it; he would see her then, and he could do more than think.

In the quiet night sleep overcame him gradually. The sound of the horseflies had ceased. Through the cricket noises Guzmán heard a slow rhythmic series of thumps growing louder at first and then dimmer in the roof over his head. The thumps were oddly new. On the edge of unconsciousness, Guzmán smiled. The man in the attic was getting careless—it was past time for him to be in his hiding place, and he had never made so much noise coming in. The thumps had a harder sound than the watchman's rubber-soled shoes usually made. Something flared in Guzmán's mind like a single spark of danger in a great lake of darkness. But the spark was too small—it only flickered and went out. The great dark lake of sleep rose easily around him and he found himself floating at its center. The lake was clear and black. Way in the distance at the foggy edge he saw a crippled animal limping along the shore. The crippled animal was creeping up behind another animal that had come to the lake to drink. The crippled one had opened its torn jaws behind the other animal's neck, and was about to bite. Guzmán tried to see what happened after that—but the fog on the shore was too thick and the black lake under him was clear as crystal. He no longer had the energy to see. He spread his limbs wide in the dark sweet lake and sank very slowly to the bottom.

In the same night, in the attic just above and to the north-west of Guzmán's last bedroom window, the police detective named Rafael was sitting on a blanket folded double over one of the crossbeams. There were many crossbeams supporting the arch in the attic roof. The beam under him was hard and the blanket did not help much. There was hardly any light inside the attic; there was nothing at all to do in it. After a time the rat-faced man swung himself around the other way and rested his feet on a second beam. As he turned, the moonlight from the mansard window through which he had entered touched his high darting eyes; it turned to black over his hair, and in the dull light his small rodent nose twitched cleverly. He had heard a sound and he was listening to it. It was his nose more than anything that gave

Rafael the look of a rodent. Because of it, and because of his efficiency at his work, the men at the various police offices where he practiced had long since ceased to refer to him by his name; he was known as *El Ratoncito,* The Mouse. In the beginning they called him that behind his back but now the nickname was affectionately used to his face. Among his associates he was well known throughout the south of Spain. He had long ago acquired a reputation for being the best plainclothesman anywhere in Andalucía. Though his home was Granada, he often traveled from one end of the south to the other. Once on a case, he stayed and saw it through to the end. Rafael did not allow anyone to forget his specialized talents or his ability to unearth facts that nobody else could find. It was said of him that he could discover things about a man that the man did not know about himself. When the Sanlúcar police captain, acting under orders from Madrid, had first called on him to dig up something incriminating on Count Guzmán, Rafael had been finishing a case in Seville. He had come to Sanlúcar as soon as that case was over, and he had set out methodically with this one. There was no doubt in his mind that he could put enough in Guzmán's dossier to incriminate the man, if he were allowed to go about things in his own way. He was doing that now, and he was glad that the captain was not with him. He had been in the process of building up a case against the Count when the captain had interrupted him with the idiotic business about Pepe Luis. The captain had ordered him to follow Pepe Luis around the fishing docks. Rafael had disapproved of the interruption. He did not like the fat man or the fat man's methods, which seemed to him ineffectual and small-town sloppy. The fat man was one of those people who allow their personal feelings to enter into their work and that was always dangerous. Rafael had known after only one day of following Pepe Luis that nothing would come of questioning the fisherman. It was his business to know such things and he had reported his judgment accurately to the fat man. When the fat man had insisted that he follow Pepe Luis until the fisherman was jailed, Rafael had known that the captain had a private reason for doing it. There was no choice but to go along with the captain's orders, and he did so, but with a certain contempt for the fat man's amateur behavior. You did not need the refined talents of a trained detective if you were going to throw them away. Rafael had let his contempt show enough for the fat man to see it, without ever giving him grounds for official complaint. The detective knew that his substitute

—the local man the captain had put in Guzmán's attic while he himself was busy following Pepe Luis—had been an incompetent person who didn't even know how to walk on a roof without being heard. He had discovered this on his first night back on the job: there were long scuff marks across the tiles next to the second chimney, and a large piece of the brick at the base was missing. It was obvious to Rafael upon examining the area that his substitute had slipped and almost fallen—and in doing so had probably made enough noise to wake the entire neighborhood. With a degree of malice, and with his usual blank expression, Rafael had reported back to the fat man that Guzmán was sure to be aware of his presence now and that the job would therefore take at least twice as long. It was the second thing about this case that Rafael had foreseen. His other prediction had concerned the death of Pepe Luis. He had warned the captain very early that the fisherman had more stubbornness than stamina, and that his body would succumb to punishment long before his mind did. It was an unnecessary death in Rafael's opinion; it only confused the case and muddied clear water. Besides, Rafael had come to admire something about Pepe Luis. The day the three policemen had hosed the fisherman down and afterwards taken turns using him, Pepe Luis had shown himself to be made out of a fiber that was nearly unassaultable; you could do almost anything to it except change it. You could rip it open, you could crush it, you could rape it, you could kill it—dead or alive, he remained a man. He was more of a man than any of the three policemen who had raped him. It had been a kind of curiosity that had made Rafael say what he had said at the time, knowing the fisherman would hear it; he had accused Pepe Luis of liking what the policemen were doing to him because, if there had been the smallest chance that the fisherman's spirit would break, that would have· broken it. To taunt the fisherman further Rafael had said that Pepe Luis wanted to be kissed by one of the policemen; but then the fisherman had looked up at the detective and their eyes had met. It was a strange moment. Something about the scene of the three strong men humiliating the helpless broken man, who remained more manly than they, had aroused Rafael to a degree and in a way he couldn't afford to admit even to himself—and the fisherman had seen it in his eyes. Rafael had not expected to be disturbed—it was a scene he had witnessed countless times in other jails. Sodomy was a way of life in most prisons. Cruelty applied in the form of sexual humiliation was a common form of put-down among

prisoners, as well as among some of the long-term jailers
themselves. Up to now the detective had seen it as a dimly
interesting phenomenon that had nothing to do with him.
Yet this time he had been disturbed by it. He had not returned to the cell of Pepe Luis after that day, and he had
not gone to the funeral. He preferred to forget about the
fisherman. He did not like thinking about what he had seen
that afternoon in the cell, and he did not like what had happened inside his own body from watching it. The thing had
stayed on his mind for a week—he had even thought about
it in church the following Sunday. It had made him wonder
if the soldiers who witnessed the Crucifixion of Jesus on
Calvary had also been physically aroused—there was something sexual about the silent figure nailed to the Cross. No,
he preferred not to consider it. About the fisherman's death
he had no personal regrets. His nickname, The Mouse,
carried with it an allusion of timidity that was partly humorous: he was among the most skillful and most professional killers in Spain. He was in a hurry now—he had already been too long on this job. It was months since he had
seen his wife or his three children and he would not see
them again now until the job was done. The police captain
had wasted enough of his time; Rafael had a reputation to
uphold and no more days to waste being vague about it.

The air in the attic was stuffy, and Rafael sniffed. The distant sound he thought he'd heard had ceased. Lifting himself
off the crossbeam, he went to the mansard window and
stood looking out at the view. There wasn't much to see.
The garden was empty. People were right: the top-heavy
Columbus tree on the far side of the wall looked more than
ever as if it were holding its breath. In the bright night the
tree looked horrified. It had no reason to look that way,
Rafael thought—the garden had never seemed so peaceful.
Just lately, from time to time at night somebody he couldn't
see had taken to sitting out under the oak tree, rattling a
can for a couple of hours; Rafael assumed it was María or
her husband, though he wouldn't consider the assumption as
fact until he had checked it out. He had purposely permitted his own shadow to fall on the path on his way across
the roof tonight so that the person who played games under
the oak would come out. There was no point in the detective
entering the attic with his usual precautions—everyone in
the building knew he was there anyway; he had an orderly
mind and he did not like loose appendages of facts that had
not been examined and filed away in their proper places. So
he had let himself be seen. But the person was not there

tonight. The garden had the serene appearance of a place that had never been entered, let alone inhabited. The long clamshell path sliced through it like a burn, straight and sizzling-white under the moon. There was nothing at all out there except for the tree standing suspended beyond the garden in a fright over the cliff wall. Rafael shrugged at it and turned back into the attic. He sat down once more on the crossbeam, and settled himself comfortably with his head against the slanted attic roof.

Then he was still. The detective had taught himself to sit for hours without moving. He was a wiry agile man, hard and spare, as though his body itself had been especially designed for his work. Just what he was waiting for in the attic of the Guzmán palace now he was not certain; but there was something unusual going on in the building, that much he was sure of. The American girl no longer slept in the palace—and yet she came every morning and spent the day. So she and Guzmán had not had a lovers' quarrel; they were being careful for some other reason. Rafael did not know what the reason was, but he intended finding out. A lot of facts had to be collected in order to build up a fake dossier on Guzmán, and the information by and large had to be accurate. A dossier made up of false details was no good; false information could be too easily disproven. What was needed was a compilation of true facts, each of them small, and each distorted just enough to give a big false picture. Rafael knew very well how that was done. The trouble was, Guzmán knew it too, and he was taking care not to reveal anything useful. Madrid didn't want Guzmán dead—at least not for now—it wanted him discredited. It wouldn't have been an easy case, this, even without the intervention of the captain and the dangerously stupid business of the fisherman. Now Rafael was going to need a new approach, though so far he hadn't discovered one. He had thought out several plans and discarded each for one reason or another. Now in the night he searched his thoughts for a possible scheme. Then all at once he knew that he was not alone in the attic.

There was a scurrying sound in the floor at the far end of the crossbeam he was sitting on, and Rafael remained as he was without altering a muscle. His eyes focused on the movement among the shadows; he had heard it almost before it had taken place. Two of his fingers slid into his coat pocket and found a thin elegant jackknife. The jackknife was never far from his right hand. He flipped it open and held it poised in the dark by his leg. He watched the area between the crossbeams where the sound had come from. Soon the maker of the noise could be seen walking on the slats, examining the dust-filled cracks in the wood. Twelve little whiskers twitched and Rafael smiled watching his namesake approach him unaware of the danger it was in. When it came full into the light he saw that it wasn't quite his namesake; it was too large. The light slanted across its steel-colored body, and in the stale air the rat continued on its course. Seeing the scum-yellow teeth protruding in the pointed head, Rafael smiled harder. The rat had given him an idea: it might be that he could use Guzmán's awareness of his presence after all, and even turn it to his own advantage. That way a certain amount of fear could be generated openly in the building. Fear, Rafael firmly believed, was a great uncoverer of facts. Thinking this over he kept watch on the crawling rat. At the rate and in the direction it was going soon it would come near Rafael's left foot; long before it did it would be dead. There wasn't a better knife thrower in the country than Rafael, and there were few who could kill as soundlessly. Even a rat would make a dying noise—unless the blade entered its neck first and sliced through the esophagus at the same time as the jugular. Then there would be no squeals—no time for anything but death— and the knife, muffled in the flesh of the animal, would make hardly any sound when it hit. Rafael had killed rats many nights in the past. He held the knife easily by the point of the blade, the handle beginning to grow in the air like a stem rising out of his hand. When the knife was poised high he stilled it between his thumb and forefinger, waiting with his wrist turned back for the rat to come a handsbreadth closer to his foot. Always just before a kill, Rafael stopped breathing and counted the seconds in his mind. Then as the muscles of his wrist tensed for the flick that would touch the gray animal with death, a noise in the roof above, at the far end of the beam, startled both man and beast. Each froze in silence. At the same time and in the same way Rafael and the small four-legged creature turned their eyes in the direction of the itinerant sound. When it was repeated, two things occurred at once. The rat slithered back into the blackness where it had come from— and Rafael in one easy motion was on his toes, balanced like a boxer across a thick wooden crossbeam in the darkest corner of the attic, knees bent, palms facing each other, the jackknife ready in his hand.

He remained motionless with his eyes on the mansard window. Then his eyes widened in surprise. The noise outside on the roof had become so loud that it was ridiculous. It was not like anyone trying to sneak in without being heard. It was more like a group of unattended schoolchildren stumbling over the roof and dragging their lunch pails after them. Rafael stood still in amazement. Something monumentally awkward was moving across the tiles—a thing that thumped and went on that way in the dark, section by section, from one piece of roof to the next—rudely, comically following a course toward the arched mansard window. The closer the noises came the more they sounded as though ten or twenty small cattle were bumping against each other. Rafael did not believe his ears. Then the noises ceased and a stillness lay there like a sleep. Suddenly, with no warning, a large heavy object entered the window and stopped, protruding horizontally in space. Standing in the shadows Rafael looked away and shook his head in case the message his eyes had brought to his brain had been mistaken. It had not. The gawky white oblong thing in the window frame stayed, just as if it had every right to be there, as if every mansard window had one like it, as if it were not out of place or even uncomfortable in its present position. There was nothing to be said about it and nothing to be done about it. Rafael, holding the open knife menacingly under the pointed roof, found himself looking at a leg (just one leg: only it wasn't a leg like most other legs. It was oversized and solid white. It was stiff. The white was soiled here and there with bits of dirt and a few streaks of pink rubbed off the red tiles of the roof; but it was still a leg. You couldn't call it anything else. A leg. It was definitely a leg) in a plaster cast, stuck in the window.

Rafael froze—not now out of any instinct of self-preservation, but because he could not for the moment think of any reason why he should move. He was immobile in the darkness, and the plaster-covered stiff leg was immobile in the window. Then, with a slow progressively louder rumbling thump that threatened to take the roof off its hinges, the leg jutted in further; hung suspended a moment more; turned east, then west, as if adjusting itself to the rancid air of the attic; and then jerked forward again and fell clattering to the floor, dragging with it a body that looked, at first glance, to be dead.

Rafael gaped at the thing in front of him. The man lay face down on the wooden slats of the attic. His body looked as though it might have been left out in the rain for a couple of weeks and then towed underwater behind a fishing boat for the rest of the summer. The body was not in good shape. Rafael, who up to now had seen men in many different stages of life and death, none of them looking very well, thought that maybe this one looked less well than any he had ever encountered. If the man lying face down among the slats and crossbeams was not dead, he would be considerably better off dead. There was not much left of him in one whole piece. He had two other plaster casts on him—one that ran the length of his arm, the other attached to his thigh. The attic was quiet again.

An anger filled Rafael's brain as he contemplated the strange figure. It was not within the framework of common sense that a man with three plaster casts on his body had climbed, as Rafael had climbed, up the Columbus tree to the garden wall, and along the wall in a roundabout way to the roof of the stable; from there to the west wing of the main building; up the slanted red tiles to the first chimney and from it to the second; then down to the lower roof of the interior passage that led to the roof over Guzmán's bedroom, and from there higher still to the attic that superseded this roof—all in order to sneak in a window and drop dead on the attic floor. It was not a right thing to do. Watching the limp body, Rafael felt a sudden outrage at the very unreasonableness of the act he had just witnessed. Then, from a rapidly beating sequence of palpitations about halfway between the arch of the man's back and his neck, the detective saw that he was not dead after all. He was only lying there catching his breath with the wind knocked out of him.

Rafael approached him and stood straddling the two crossbeams between which the man was lying. After another couple of minutes the breathing of the man slowed to a more normal pace, though it was still a sound of exhaustion. The figure moved its right hand tentatively, and then its left. It put its hands ahead of it, gripping the crossbeams; then with painful effort it turned itself over on its back to face the ceiling.

Rafael looked down at the familiar features below him. What had been first astonishment, then amazement, and at last a kind of stunned disbelief on his own face, now turned into a great gaping wound of nothingness. From the detective's open mouth, as silently as a sound in a vacuum, a brand new scream that couldn't be released drooped uselessly in the air. The temperature of his mind rose with incredible speed, like a fever of attrition. Every thought he had ever had and a few that were not yet formed fled from his brain, leaving it as empty as the mind of an idiot. Below him the face of the man on the floor did not seem surprised.

The fisherman lay, his breath coming in even gasps, quietly returning the gaze of the police detective.

Rafael leaned dizzily against the frame of the mansard window through which Pepe Luis had come and tried to let the thoughts back into his mind in some kind of order. Piece by piece, straining every part of his own reasoning powers, he lumped together several facts. He did not believe in ghosts so he did not have that problem. He saw that the man before him was not and had never been a cadaver; that the funeral of the fisherman had been falsified; that the fisherman named Pepe Luis Sanchez had somehow managed not only to escape deprivation and beatings and torture and outrage and injustice and sexual humiliation and symbolic emasculation and rape and murder, but had also escaped his own death. That having escaped all that, he had not just gone somewhere to tremble and live out the rest of his life in fear, but that he had been saved from that too. That Pepe Luis had been the man playing happily every night in the garden. That he, Pepe Luis, had seen his old acquaintance and enemy on the roof. That the fisherman had followed Rafael up here, unprotected and unarmed, and crawled into the window and fallen on his face on the floor, where he lay now catching his breath and looking at Andalucía's greatest detective with a peaceful and speechless serenity as though nothing at all needed to be said because they both understood exactly why and how he had come. Rafael set his head back on the windowsill. Something inside him relaxed, and he felt a sort of soaring happiness. The sight of the fisherman on the floor gave him a kind of relief he had not experienced before. The fisherman was alive. He had survived after all. It was like the survival of mankind itself, against all odds, and in the face of every disaster.

Without taking his eyes off the face on the floor, Rafael began very softly to laugh.

Laid out between the two crossbeams, panting and motionless, Pepe Luis stared back up at the policeman. It was the third time since they had known each other that their eyes had met silently, and Pepe Luis was especially aware of it. The first time they had exchanged a speechless look had been in the dockside bar, on the night when the fat man had come to arrest him. The second time was in the cell of the jailhouse at the moment of his sexual humiliation when Pepe Luis had seen the detective's pair of black eyes glow out at him like lanterns in the dark. Now, in the attic, he saw the eyes a third time, small and round, the two dark pupils above him uncovered and focused on his own. He said nothing, but lay there, still unable to recover his breath, the other man laughing down at him helplessly.

The dust in the attic that had been disturbed began to settle. Pepe Luis sneezed. Rafael sat in the window and clutched at his stomach. Tears of laughter and joy seeped into his eyes and spilled down his face. The hand that held the knife hung with its point aimed at the neck of the man on the floor; but Rafael had no more intention of killing the fisherman now than he had of ever letting him get into trouble again. The detective sat, unable to speak, looking at the sweet dark eyes of the man below him. *Está vivo:* He's alive, he thought. The two words ran over and over in the detective's mind like a song.

Pepe Luis put his arms out again and levered himself up to his feet. His hands and arms were shaking and his face worked with pain as he rose. He stood at last facing the detective across the beam of wood.

For a while neither man spoke, and the spasms of laughter slowed and stopped in the detective's chest.

"Me alegro verte," he said when he could speak: "I'm glad to see you."

"Yes," Pepe Luis said. "I'm glad too."

The two men ran out of words and became quiet staring at each other.

In the new silence, the detective made a small lifting gesture with his shoulders. The gesture was timid and shy. It was the only tender gesture he had ever made in his life, for he had never before felt shy in front of anyone. He did not know why he felt that way now—but in this moment, for a space of fifteen seconds, something happened between the two men.

The thing was not easy to explain. For now, inside the dusty attic surrounded by dirt and vermin, the men were seeing each other in a world of opposites. Both had climbed up here to a world neither one had been in before. It was the attic that had become for them such a place. They could not speak because there were no words to match what they felt. The world of the heart is like the world at the bottom of the sea. It is an unseen unheard opposite place. At the surface of the water, things behave as you would expect them to, and even the smallest squid squirts ink to protect itself. But farther down, deep at the bottom of the oceans where there is only dark and cold and silence, there is also mortal fighting. And there, the counterpart of the squid does the same thing in a different way. It is a fact that the ink of the deep-sea squid is phosphorescent.

There, in the world of darkness, it is light that is used to confuse and even to destroy. It was there that the police detective loved the injured fisherman. And as secretly as that, somewhere without sunlight in the cold unspeaking place of unplanned things, in that world of opposites, with rage and violence and with the blinding light of his own heart, the fisherman loved him back.

It was Pepe Luis who broke the silence around them: "I came to kill you," he said.

"Yes," the detective said. "I know." He shrugged, a smile flickering shyly at the edges of his mouth.

The fisherman stepped forward, lifting his plaster cast over the crossbeam. He was still breathing hard, like any lover. He stood close to the other man and Rafael raised the knife between them, pointing it at the fisherman's chest. Their knees were almost touching now. Then looking down, Rafael saw the object that the fisherman was holding in his hand, and the laughter rose once more into the detective's throat.

"Did you carry that?" he said, pointing to it.

Pepe Luis looked down at his right hand. Then he looked back up. "Yes," he said.

"All the way up here?" the detective said unbelievingly. "A tin can?"

"Yes," Pepe Luis said. "It's to kill you with."

Rafael looked at the ludicrous vision standing in front of him, torn and broken, bleeding a little here and there, dirty and sweating from his climb with the laughable useless tin can held firmly in one fist. Watching him, Rafael wanted to say "I love you," only the words had never meant anything to him before and he could not pronounce them. Like a man who has been given the part of the beloved all his life, the detective sat, his knife pointed at the other man's stomach, unable to speak.

Pepe Luis, who was the true lover, took another step forward.

Then, with their heads almost touching, Rafael thought abruptly, insanely, for no reason at all, that the other man was going to kiss him. He did not know why, and he did not know what to do about it. The blood drained out of his face. With his heart beating hard as a trip hammer, surging like the pulse of a schoolgirl in love, the detective pulled the knife up in readiness as he saw the fisherman's face come closer to his. Of its own will the detective's mouth parted slightly, his face turned up. He felt the fisherman's warm breath on his face, and then he felt the man's lips touch his own. Gently the two men kissed. Something stirred in Rafael's heart; he knew something that he had not known before. The lips left his and Pepe Luis stood back from the detective. Rafael watched the fisherman stand away and felt a kind of yearning that he had not known existed. He whispered something inaudible; then he whispered, "Jesus."

"Yes," Pepe Luis said. "I knew it. It was you."

"Me?" the other said, low.

"You. It was only you. I didn't like it," Pepe Luis said. "I didn't like any of it. You were wrong to say I liked it. I wasn't the one who wanted it. It was you."

Pepe Luis raised his right hand.

Rafael could not imagine what the fisherman was talking about, and he watched the hand come up between them in the air. Then, in a sudden explosion of sense, he understood. He knew why the fisherman had kissed him and why the fisherman had dragged his useless body over three rooftops to do it. He knew why the fisherman wanted to kill him. He knew what the fisherman had proven; and he knew that the fisherman was right.

The detective did not try to defend himself. A sort of weariness overcame him in the wake of his understanding. He hardly felt the cutting edge of the top of the can as it entered the side of his neck. He was not aware of the slow gouging of the rusted can as the fisherman probed for the jugular, and he felt no more than a quick sinking deep within him as the vein ripped open.

Pepe Luis tore the detective's throat from ear to ear. His hand was still shaking and the cut he made was jagged and clumsy. Then he stood watching as the detective's body, already dead, swung backward and slid easily down the tiles. It tipped off the roof toward the garden below. A small surge of blood rose from the open throat, making an arc in the air like a fan. The body somersaulted once. It hit with a heavy muted thump somewhere in the middle of the white clamshell path. The fan of red spattered a second later, soft as rain on the shells. For a long time Pepe Luis stood in the window and looked down at the white path under him. His right hand was covered with blood and the roof where the body had slid was streaked with blood too. One or two single drops ran down the red tiles, red on red, as though the roof were bleeding. He watched them drip into the rain gutter.

SEVEN

Helen

. . . So it was."

"Clearly."

"So he did it because of that."

"I'm not sure."

"Because he thought the man had come to attack you?"

"No," Guzmán's voice said. *"I don't think so. I don't know. . . ."*

"Then why doesn't he say something?" Juan Alberto's voice said.

"He did. He just came to me in the middle of the night and woke me up and told me he'd done it. That's all he said; it's all he'll say now. He won't give his reason. He won't talk about it at all."

"Mira qué idiotez. He's sick in the head, this fisherman."

"Is he?" Guzmán's voice said. *"Maybe . . . I wonder if it's all the rest of us who are sick in the head. . . ."*

The angry voices drummed on in the garden behind her. The two men, Guzmán and Juan Alberto, were putting the duffel bag and ice chest along with the pile of canned goods and other things into the truck. The truck was next to the stable. Guzmán had purposely not called upon any of his friends. The two were being helped only by María and her husband as they worked.

Alice Littlejohn kept her back to them, standing next to the Columbus tree and holding the invitation she had received that morning in the mail. It was close to noon and she had not had time to look at it before.

The morning had been full of plans and alterations. She had been standing here for quite a while now while the men, father and son, talked. The sea air was lovely from the top of the cliff and nothing in the day or in the garden behind her gave any clue about the thing that had happened here last night. It might have been any house in Spain or any garden. It was strange, she thought, that a place could

323

look so usual, so everyday-plain, the morning after a thing like that had taken place in it.

She had known about it three hours and she still was not able to accept it. For the last hour she had had to keep reminding herself that what Guzmán had been afraid of had come about. The man in the attic and the man in the basement had met, and one of them was dead.

In the hazy day she looked out across the water. The surface of the sea was crumpled and splotched, as if somebody had been sleeping on it who hadn't slept very well. Soon she and Guzmán would be somewhere on it moving south. It was not Guzmán but Juan Alberto who had come to the blue villa at nine o'clock in the morning with the news. He had not explained his reason; only that something had happened at the palace, that they were both needed there and needed fast. She had dressed without knowing what it was and Juan Alberto hadn't said it till the last minute, just as they were leaving the villa. Will had been listening, but Will was as safe as a tomb.

Now they were taking the next step and she was waiting; there had not been time for her to know how she felt.

Alice glanced at the tree beside her on the cliff and tried to make out what mood it was in this morning. People who knew it best claimed you could tell what you were feeling yourself if you could describe the mood of the tree. Only sometimes it was impossible to know what the Columbus tree's moods were and this was one of the times. It just looked aloof, as if it wanted nothing to do with any of the things that were going on. The sky above it was bumpy with clouds. Behind Alice the four people were still placing various objects in the truck, speaking more sharply now, with angry words ("Not there!" "*Pero por Dios!*" "But are you blind?" "But are you?" "*Pero no ves?*" "But don't you hear what I'm saying?" "There, no?—*there?*"): the same centuries-old exclamations that true Spaniards of all classes have made and always will make when confronted with the problems of organizing anything at all, no matter whether it's a war or a picnic. Alice smiled, listening to the change in Guzmán's voice when he gave orders about the packing of the truck. She could tell that he was mismanaging and muddling the objects himself. He sounded like a father with three unruly children who were confusing him. You wouldn't think he was leaving Spain for an indefinite period, without a passport, in plain view of the police, illegally but quite openly—taking her, Alice, with him (so that it would look as

if they were only off on a fishing trip) and besides her a
load of fishing tackle, one small suitcase, a duffel bag, a
large ice chest and two food baskets. You wouldn't think
that he was doing it on purpose in the middle of the day,
renting a fishing boat at the Hotel Malage in Suelo so it
would seem that nothing important or unusual was going on.
You wouldn't guess the truck and ice chest held much but
clothing and food. You certainly wouldn't know the ice
chest contained a murderer or that lying under the pile of
canned goods on the truck, sewn up in a piece of oilcloth,
was a cadaver. That they were taking Pepe Luis to Morocco where he couldn't be found, dumping the policeman's
body into the sea on the way. Listening to Guzmán and his
son argue about which packet went where on the truck,
you wouldn't believe the facts even if you knew them. Yes,
she thought, a fishing trip was just what it sounded like:
preparations for a peaceful weekend on the water.

Waiting for them to finish, holding the invitation stiffly in
her left hand, Alice slid her right hand down and touched
the place where the baby was. It would not show for weeks
yet, maybe months. Some women didn't show till the last
two or three months, she had heard. Her own belly was still
flat and smooth; but there wasn't any doubt about it now.
After Pepe Luis had first made the comment, she had gone
to a doctor in Cádiz who had confirmed it. But even that
wasn't new any more. Things were building up outside her
body now faster than they were inside her.

It was for that reason that she had not told Guzmán
about the baby; even before last night he'd had enough to
cope with. Only, she was going to have one and the baby
was going to change things too. When everything else calmed
down, there would still be that, she knew: babies always
change things, that's why they're babies. To remind you that
the clock of your lifetime, the one you never thought about
before, is beginning to speed up. Because your space is
limited to this little earth, this little air and only this much
time to look at it. So even if you're an atheist living in sin in
a Catholic country you'd better find out about it while
you're still here. Or know what you think so you have something to tell the baby.

Turning away from the shade of the tree Alice looked
down at the card in her left hand. Of all the things that
were going on, this one was the most incomprehensible to
her—and the most fantastic. She did not believe what she
saw:

HELEN LOCKE

REQUESTS THE PLEASURE OF YOUR COMPANY

AT A MASKED BALL IN HONOR OF HER SON,

WILLIAM CHARLES LOCKE, JR.

ON THE OCCASION OF HIS THIRTEENTH BIRTHDAY

THE SEVENTEENTH OF SEPTEMBER, NINETEEN HUNDRED AND

FIFTY-SEVEN

IN THE GRAND BALLROOM OF THE HOTEL MALAGE IN SUELO

AT SEVEN-THIRTY IN THE EVENING (FOR CHILDREN)

TEN-THIRTY IN THE EVENING (FOR ADULTS).

DONATIONS WILL BE TAKEN IN AID OF THE UNITED NATIONS

CHILDREN'S FUND.

THE PURPOSE OF THIS FUND IS TO BRING HELP TO CHILDREN IN

EACH OF THE UNITED NATIONS.

KINDLY DRESS IN THE COLOR OF YOUR VILLA.

(IF NOT RESIDING AT THE HOTEL, PLEASE DRESS IN

THE COLOR YOU BELIEVE YOURSELF TO BE.)

HOTEL MALAGE

SUELO, CÁDIZ, SPAIN   R.S.V.P.: THE RED VILLA

The thing was engraved on an expensively simple white card with a raised border and small raised black shining letters, and it made everything else that was going on at the moment seem normal. Yes, Alice thought; even murder.

There was a noise beside her and she looked up. Guzmán had come around the other side of the tree. The skull looked sharper than ever inside his face but his eyes were calm. "Something important?"

She handed him the card.

Guzmán glanced at it. "She sent me one also. We must accept at the hotel before we leave."

"Accept it? . . . You mean because of Will?"

Guzmán handed the card back. "No," he said; "the seventeenth comes in two weeks; we should be back by then, but we might not be. It's better not to make suspicion. No, I don't mean because of your brother. I mean because of me. The coast guard will be watching."

"I see," Alice said.

"Are you calm?"

"I think so; is Juan Alberto coming with us?"

"No," Guzmán said. "For that he is angry . . . he would like to take the boat and do it for me. I do not permit him even on the truck. I don't want my sons mixed up with police matters yet. The time will come . . . at least for him. About José Ramón I am not so certain, but one day Juan Alberto will be something like me. For now he has to wait. . . . It's all right for you to come—an American isn't in danger. If we are caught, you know nothing. I will corroborate that . . . The most they can ask you to do is leave Spain and not come back. You understand?"

"Yes."

"The police won't be watching," Guzmán said. "Not yet. The detective cannot be missed until tonight . . . possibly tomorrow. We should leave with no problem. Coming back will be more difficult."

"They'll know it by then?"

"Something, yes. Not everything. The fat man thinks that Pepe Luis is dead. . . . That will be the problem. He'll think I did it."

"What can he do?"

"He won't be able to prove much. There will be no corpse and he knows I won't answer questions. The man who rents me the boat is one of my friends, he will do what I ask. If we are delayed, we can make up some excuse. The captain won't believe it, of course. Then we shall see how it goes."

"What's that you're holding?"

Guzmán dropped it quickly into his pocket. "The policeman's knife," he said. "It was near his hand. Are you truly all right?"

"Yes. Is that all he had on him? A knife?"

"There was a wallet in his coat pocket. I burned it in the coal stove."

"His identification?"

"Yes. And fifty pesetas. Pictures. He had a wife and three children."

Alice swallowed.

"We are nearly ready with the truck."

". . . Pepe Luis?"

"He has fever. I think the arm must have broken again when he . . . last night. It is bad around the cast. We will take him to a doctor tomorrow in Tangiers or Marrakesh . . . the ice chest is bigger than it seems. I explained it would only be until we are out of sight of the land."

"What about . . . ?"

Guzmán shook his head. "He won't talk at all. I'm not sure he remembers clearly. He may never remember it. . . . When he woke me up at a quarter to five this morning he was in a stupor. He looked drunk."

"Was he?"

"Not from liquor. He had not finished more than a glass or two of wine. I looked in his room later."

"In a stupor from what? You don't mean drugs, he wasn't on any."

"No," Guzmán said. "I don't mean drugs. He only stood next to my bed and said it. Like a man in his own nightmare. *'Le corté el pescuezo'* was all he would say. . . . He might have seen the policeman before. Perhaps at the police office. I doubt we'll ever find out. I think it was all he said because it's all he knows . . . I don't believe he remembers climbing over the roof or even much about the killing. Just the one fact, *'le corté el pescuezo'* . . . he said it fifteen or twenty times standing next to my bed. Not at all emotional. A man who tells you the time, or what day of the week it is."

"Pescuezo?"

"Gullet. 'I slit his gullet.'"

Alice shivered and turned away.

"No," Guzmán said. "It's better you forget it as one thing. Face it as he has done, once, then put it down."

Alice said, "I've seen him every day for weeks. . . . I thought Pepe Luis was one of the gentlest men. . . ."

Guzmán shrugged. "He might be. It would not be gentleness if it had no strength. He isn't a coward. . . . Partly he did it to protect me, but not entirely. . . . I can't tell what his other reason was but he had one."

"But . . . he's a murderer now."

"Eso somos todos."

"What do you mean?"

"Estás en España," Guzmán said.

"Speak to me in English."

"I keep telling you. I lie in my room with the murders I have forgotten, just as he lies in the ice chest. Only his murder is more recent. Once I killed a man by breaking his back with my hands. I bent him backwards over a barbed-wire fence. He was twenty-five or twenty-six years old and he was screaming. I had forgotten about it until this second. The man vomited when I killed him."

"That was in a war."

"Because it is sanctioned by the state, or even part of the state, you say it is no longer murder? Here we are too tired to spend so much time lying to ourselves. It is enough trouble lying to other people. Come, I'll start the truck."

"Does Pepe Luis know the man had a wife and children?"

"I told him."

"Will he ever talk about it? The guilt must be bad."

Under the tree, Guzmán stopped and turned back, half smiling. "Pepe Luis does not speak now because he did something last night that shocked his system. He will be better in a week—in two he'll be fine. In three he won't remember that he was ever upset."

"The guilt of . . ."

"What guilt? . . . You must drop your romantic notions for a day. We are Spanish. Please, we *are* Spanish. The most we have is shame. . . . I told him about the wife and children because I thought he should think more about it the next time he decides to kill a man. Not because I thought it would make him guilty. Guilt is an American specialty . . . you bought it in Europe and you wear it like a crown. You must not try to analyze Pepe Luis. He cannot wear the jewel. He does not have the crown. The weather is different here. Guilt stops at the Pyrenees. Are you ready?"

"Yes."

"*Te quiero.*"

". . . When?"

He halted again. "When what?"

"*Cuándo me vas a querer?*"

Guzmán smiled. His pale eyes dropped down to her legs and back up to her face. "Yes," he said. "Your Spanish is improving. Tonight. Wherever we are. On a beach or a field or in a hotel. In the boat, if there's nowhere else. . . ." He turned and went back to the truck.

Alice looked back over the water. She folded the invitation and put it in the pocket of her dress. The sun was very hazy now, like a dimming beacon over the sea.

She followed Guzmán under the tree to the truck.

THE SUN stayed hazy for another half hour before it began to disappear further behind the clouds. From the screened porch of the red villa Helen looked at it above the tortoise-shell rims of her glasses, over the flat piles of engraved invitations. Her desk was lined with addressed envelopes and Mrs. Lawson sat across from her to one side addressing others.

Helen pushed her glasses up over her hair. She walked to the edge of the porch, watching some children play near the beach. Then she glanced across at the gold villa. It was empty. "How many are we up to?"

"Four hundred and twenty-three," Mrs. Lawson said, "including the ones the secretary mailed. Check?"

She closed the address book with a loud snap and put it back.

Helen turned and watched her with mild annoyance. Mrs. Lawson was a rotund woman in her late fifties with flat heavy breasts and eyes like chewed lollipops. She had not often felt important in her life and she was flattered at being allowed to help with the invitations for the ball. Her husband had returned to New York; she was alone. She addressed the envelopes and answered the phone as if she were working in an office of critical information during wartime. "Four hundred and twenty-five with the Crawfords," she said, "check?"

Helen lit a cigarette from the box on the table by the window and sighed the smoke out. "No need to check everybody out loud," she said; "I'm not running a shooting gallery."

Mrs. Lawson giggled. "You are according to the Paris *Trib* this morning." She picked up a folded newspaper from the chair beside her and read from it. " 'In its usual swirl preparing for autumn, the Parisian air has been electrified this year by a stream of sparks from Andalucía. Helen Locke's charity masked ball, to be given in Suelo, in Spain's province of Cádiz, has infused the thinking of some local French politicians and wealthy visiting tourists as well as many members of Paris Society. The fancy-dress ball—the final and by far the most chic event of Europe's summer season—also marks the beginning of autumn; invitations, to put it mildly, are at a premium. Those who have already received theirs are able to breathe freely. Those who haven't (among them a well-known French surgeon and his Belgian wife) have made rapid plans to leave Paris for Parts Unknown during the third week in September. Rumor has it that towns on the Côte d'Azur are filling up with Mrs. Locke's rejects and so are several Greek islands. It seems nobody wants to be left in Paris when things are swingin' in Spain . . . the same is apparently true in London, and Rome's *Citá* reports that . . .' "

"I know what the newspaper says," Helen said.

She examined the disposable cigarette holder she was using, found it to be defective, and broke it in two in her hand. Then she sat down again at the desk.

"That column in the *Observer* says nobody knows how you were able to pull it off so fast. . . . Did you read that one too?"

"No," Helen said. "I wrote it."

Mrs. Lawson's jaw dropped. "Mercy," she said. "Check."

Helen shut her eyes. "If you're finished with those, you might want to drop them in the mailbox on your way through the main lobby."

"Right," Mrs. Lawson said. She gathered her things about her on the desk. "Is it true about your costume?"

"Is what true?"

"About ten people being needed . . ."

"Three not ten. . . . Yes," Helen said. "There wasn't much time."

"Blood-red India silk. And a hoop skirt. When is it going to be ready?"

"Not till the day before the ball."

"Aren't you afraid it won't get here in time?"

"The couturier is flying down with it from Madrid; he's on the list too."

"What if the flights are canceled?"

"He's coming by sea plane," Helen said.

"And if . . ."

"If the weather's bad he'll take the train down that night; he already has a reservation. He won't need to use it. The weather won't be bad."

". . . Did you arrange that too?" Mrs. Lawson giggled too loud and covered her lips with her hand.

Helen yawned. "It hasn't rained here during the second half of September for the last fifteen years. I had Holtz do some research before I decided to open the ballroom and dining room onto the main terrace. . . . Would you tell the concierge I don't want any more messages today?"

"Certainly." Mrs. Lawson stood by the desk for a minute, stalling for time.

"Well?" Helen said.

"It's those friends of mine you said could come . . . Mr. and Mrs. Carver?"

"Yes," Helen said. "I gave you an invitation for them yesterday."

Mrs. Lawson said, "It's . . . well, the hotels. Every last one. There're twenty-two hotels in this town, and not one room is available for the night of the sixteenth or seventeenth . . . I checked all over. The concierge says it's worse than Seville in Holy Week. Tourists are offering double and they still can't get a room anywhere. Even people who aren't invited are coming to look at the people who are. It's a terrible situation. . . ."

"I know," Helen said. "Things got out of hand."

"Well, it's not your problem . . . it's mine. . . ." Mrs. Lawson stood fiddling with her pocketbook in a ruminant way.

Then she dropped her pencil. She picked it up slowly and reopened the catch on the pocketbook.

"All right."

". . . Beg pardon?"

"They'll have a room," Helen said. "I'll take care of it tomorrow."

"I hate to put you to the trouble. . . . Can you really . . . ?"

"I'll manage," Helen said. "The Ministry of Information and Tourism can do it. We talk once a day."

Mrs. Lawson giggled nervously. Then she waddled through the living room and went out the front door.

After a moment, Helen moved to the sofa and lay down, setting her head back wearily on a square red cushion at one end. She lit another cigarette and put it in a holder. After that she picked up the red telephone and placed a long distance call to Madrid. The hotel operator said that there was a *demora,* one of the usual delays for all calls going into or out of the province. While she was waiting, Helen went to the icebox on the south side of the porch and took out a split of champagne. She popped the cork and poured into an old-fashioned glass with some ice. Then she took the champagne and the cigarette and stretched out again on the sofa.

The sun was masked now behind the clouds and the light on the red porch was softer. The laughter of the children playing on the lawn outside had increased, but not enough to disturb her. Helen let her thoughts sway out easily over some of the details that hadn't been fully attended to. A few of the invitations had priority. She had mailed them herself from a master list she kept locked in a drawer. Some things were better kept private. Such as for instance the invitation she had sent to Lincoln Warren—she had written a personal note on that one. Warren was a Chicago businessman, a widower in his fifties. When he wasn't talking stocks and bonds, he was telling bad jokes. He came to Europe twice a year but he wasn't one of the new-rich people who could be introduced to society. Helen had tried. She had given up on him one night in Paris when she took him to some distant cousins of the Rothschild family for dinner. Warren never listened to names when he was introduced. Twenty minutes later he had told the Rothschilds an anti-Semitic joke about the Rothschilds. Lincoln Warren was worse than a bore, Helen knew. But maybe being married to a rich man who killed dinner parties was what she needed right now. She was tired enough of giving parties to take on just about anything, she thought. Lincoln hadn't ever proposed to her, but then she hadn't given him any encouragement. The encouragement had just gone out with his invitation. Then there were the others. The strategically important invitations that had gone to the three important Spanish duchesses—Alba and Medinaceli and Medina Sidonia, who might or might not come—and the invitation to Generalísimo Franco, who wouldn't come, but who wouldn't deny having been invited if it appeared in the papers. The Ministry might even persuade Franco to send her a well-wishing telegram, she thought; she opened a drawer in the table beside her and added a note about it to a list, and lay back again. There was the invitation to the American Ambassador who would probably come; to President and Mrs. Eisenhower, who wouldn't; and to the Condesa de Guzmán—the Count's wife—who just might.

Helen exhaled a stream of smoke over her head. It curved like a thin long scythe above the red sofa. The children's voices were rising and falling like the waves. It wasn't very important whether Guzmán's wife came or not. Inviting her was only a reminder to Alice that the affair was going to have to end sooner or later. Instructing Alice that way, by means of a third person, was an old habit; by now Helen did it automatically. She had kept a guiding hand over much of Alice's education the same way. It made her smile now to remember. Behind the scenes she had dealt with a governess, with principals of schools, with tutors, with a college through the years. Alice's father, who had all the stubbornness of a weak man, had often objected; he had tried arguing with Helen on the phone as a minister and as an objective observer—neither had worked. Which wasn't surprising: twenty men stronger than he wouldn't have worked either. There was too much at stake—there was love. Alice Littlejohn had become a kind of obsession with Helen. Pride had kept her from showing it to anyone but Alice's father, and all he had been able to do in the end was to turn his own fortune over to his daughter and hope for the best. It was what Helen had hoped he would do. Partly it had been effective, as she had known it would be, because Alice wasn't obliged any more to give explanations to anybody about her movements or her behavior; but partly it had not been effective because Helen still knew how to manipulate events when she had to. She hadn't come up in the world just to see her daughter go to the devil. She could handle the devil too well herself. She, Helen, had been born in his domain. She was a back-of-woods girl—she wasn't from New Orleans. She had grown up in the marshes and bayous of southern Louisiana in a place so poor that she hadn't gone to school, not because she didn't want to—not even because there wasn't any school—but because she didn't have shoes to go in. Relaxing on the red smooth sofa she sipped some more champagne and wondered what the people on her guest list would think if they knew about her background. It might make one of those chic romantic parlor stories about poverty that people sometimes tell over dinner. Though the grubbiness of it would kill the romance if she were to tell the truth. Anyway she had never tried, and she never would. Instead she had invented a fashionably amusing story about her own beginnings that was enough of a cliché to be believed. The story was often quoted. About how her parents were poor southern aristocrats who lived in a big old ante-bellum plantation house surrounded by bougainvillea and how she had had to struggle up in the world with only a certain breeding to help her. It sounded very nice and it was pure horseshit. The fact was that her parents had never been married, and they had never had a house of any kind. Her father had been an illiterate Cajun who worked on shrimp-boats in the Gulf, her mother a waitress in a tenth-rate roadside diner. When the Cajun's wife had found out about Helen's mother, Helen and her mother had had to leave the diner in a hurry—or as much of a hurry as possible—her mother drank a good deal and nothing ever got done very fast. From then on it had been a series of diners and bars and worse places—begging where they could, stealing where they couldn't—finding a job wherever the boss didn't know about her mother's drinking and keeping the job until he found out. The two of them had lived that way all around the marshland, where money was scarce and the earth lay like a soft fringe into the water. They had lived always on the edge of things—of the land and of the law—until Helen's mother, by that time an alcoholic, had given up and passed out on the side of the road one day, waking up long enough to lift her skirt over her head and laugh at every car that passed by. She wasn't a pretty woman by then and none of the cars had stopped. At the end of three hours a middle-aged man driving a green truck had put on his brakes and leaned down to have a look, and Helen had helped to pick her mother off the ground and get her into the back of the truck. Her mother had kept flapping her skirt, and the man had laughed and said that they could go and stay for a while at his place. Helen had climbed up on the back with her mother, and then, at the last second—just as the truck started up—without even knowing why or what it would mean, she had climbed over the back and jumped down. She had stood there calmly in the middle of the road watching the truck disappear. It was the last thing Helen remembered about her mother. The truck that carried her off was old but it had been freshly painted; it was a nasty bright green, a color Helen never would forget. The human heart takes strange turns, and it wasn't her mother's leaving—it was only the color of the truck that deeply offended the girl. The back flap of the truck had been put up after her mother got in, so she couldn't see any more than the top of the woman's right shoe sticking up over it. She could hear her mother's laughter as the green truck moved away. Then the dirt road was empty, except for the dust that settled around Helen.

That was the way her life had started; Helen had been ten years old then, unable to read or write; she had never been to school. She had no money and no other relatives. But she was a beautiful child and she survived for two full years, going to school where she could, working as part-time help here and there in the bayou country until she could pay her way to New Orleans. After that she lived in the city and managed to go to school for three years more before she got tired of badly paying part-time jobs and made up her mind to sell her services another way. She did not have any difficulty finding men who were interested. She was young and her looks were better than good. At fifteen she puzzled her companions along Bourbon Street by spending eight hours a day, every day, in the library. At night she worked the bars from seven in the evening; but by two a.m. she was in bed alone with a stack of books fatter than she was. She had long been in the habit of reading until dawn, living on three hours sleep in twenty-four. She only had to work the bars for two years. When she was seventeen she had learned enough to quit the red-light district and get a job as a lady's maid; she had a minimal amount of overwork to look back on and only two abortions. When the woman who employed her left New Orleans to go north, Helen had already studied the ways and manners of the middle-class rich enough to double her own pay on her next job application. After that it was relatively easy. One thing led to another. On instinct Helen was able to calculate her assets, and from the beginning she knew that she had one factor in her favor. She had always been lovely to look at. Her features were aquiline and aristocratic. They looked like the triumphant flourish of generations of careful breeding. No trace of the swamps was visible on her and she knew it. Out of the mud had come a classic beauty. Over the years, her looks served her well: if she hadn't made a fortune, her divorce provided her with enough to get by for the rest of her life—or it would have if it hadn't been misinvested—and her daughter was rich. It might not have been a good track record for a girl who'd had even a fair shake in growing up; but for the ten-year-old who had stood on the bayou road and watched a bright green truck disappear in a cloud of dirt, it was a decent achievement. Helen had made one mistake in all the years, and it hadn't lasted very long. The mistake had been Will's father. She had met him just after her divorce, during a period when she was off her guard, and she had fallen in love with him before she knew what she was doing. Falling in love had not been on Helen's agenda; it was the one circumstance she hadn't foreseen, and because of it she had stripped gears for a while. William Charles Locke didn't have fifty dollars in the bank when she met him, but he had a hard sensual face, eyes that looked painful when he kissed her, and she married him a month later. What would have happened to that marriage or what she might have had to do about it was now a moot point. She hadn't had to do anything about it—the war had taken care of things for her. The marriage lasted six months. When William Charles Locke took a nose dive in a navy plane he left her with a photograph, four love letters, an unborn child and a folder of stocks (bought with the money from her divorce settlement) that would soon prove useless. Along with the first impact of grief at the news of Locke's death there came to Helen a quiet sense of release, as if she had been freed of an emotional commitment she hadn't wanted in the first place. If death is the ultimate rejection, it is also the least interesting, and it can have certain benefits: after Lieutenant Locke's death, Helen gave birth to Will; after that she began giving more and more parties, gaining a reputation as a hostess both in America and abroad. There were a few "serious" engagements but no more marriages. Except for being worn out with supporting herself this way—and except for her finances—just for the moment she had more or less everything she had ever wanted. Or had she?

The cigarette had gone out in the holder, and Helen broke open a fresh pack and put a new one in and lit it. No, she didn't have what she wanted—there wasn't any use lying to herself about that. She was on the verge of wondering how well she had handled everything through the years. She ought to have married again, she knew that; she had turned down three bona fide proposals since Locke's death. The three men in question hadn't seemed rich enough, or they had disappointed her in some other way; she had failed to consider that there would come a day when she was no longer so sure of herself. And the day had arrived. She had been living way over her means for too long—never sure from one month to the next how much she could earn—and the strain was telling on her. She had not felt this way since she was a child. She was back to living on the edge of things. She would have to do something about that. Maybe . . .

The telephone rang sharply and she reached over without sitting up and answered it. It was the call she had placed to the Ministry of Information and Tourism in Madrid. While she was waiting for the Undersecretary of the Department of Tourism or one of his associates to get on the line she took out the list of questions and requests she had prepared and put it on the table. The connection was a bad one. There was a series of dim clicks, and the voice of the *Subsecretario* came on squeakily. "One minute, please," he said, "I call you back." Helen hung up and looked at her watch. After a minute and a half the telephone rang again. There was no delay when someone from inside the Ministry wanted to place a call—the world for average citizens worked one way, but anything in Spain worked right for the right people. "Yes, Mrs. Locke," the *Subsecretario* said pleasantly, "what can I do for you today?" She recognized the voice, it was Eduardo Morilla, the key man they had assigned to give her assistance and advice in making reservations for her guests and in planning other things for the ball. Of the two officials of the Ministry at her disposal, Morilla was the one she preferred. He had a deferential manner and he was always easy to deal with. Helen held the list up to the light and read from it, making checks and sometimes small notes in the margin according to the answers Morilla gave her. "I look forward to meeting you," she said after thanking him, "I hope you don't change your mind about coming." She put the list back while Morilla went through a series of ritual protests, swearing that he would come to Suelo for her party if he were anything short of dead. "Don't die then," Helen told him. "I won't," Morilla's voice deepened, "I *have* to meet you." Helen said something innocuous and closed the conversation. Morilla had been flirting with her mildly over the phone ever since her photograph had appeared in the Madrid press. She encouraged him just enough to keep it going. A man in the government wasn't a bad person to know; he could come in handy one day.

Helen looked at the glass beside her. She had nearly finished the champagne. It was time to stop indulging in self-pity, and the party was the answer: get on with it and the rest would take care of itself. The ball would be a high point in her career, she knew. She had taste, and a large number of important people would see it. Taste mattered to Helen; it always had. Back in the early days, working for her keep in kitchens here and there on Bayou Teche, she had seen a couple of big living rooms—and despite her own situation she had not been impressed by them in the least. It was the best clue to Helen's nature that at the age of eleven, with no background, no education and no help for the future, she had despised everything about the genteel lower-middle-class women she worked for. Some instinct had guided her even then. Someday, she had been sure, she would meet other sorts of people—and not too many years after that she had done it. Getting to know the "right" people became a kind of game for her that went way beyond plain social climbing. The Mardi Gras ball she got herself invited to in New Orleans had been made up of members who wouldn't have allowed the Bayou Teche families into their houses as friends of their servants. One event only had spoiled her pleasure at being invited to the Comus ball. What her daughter had said, an hour before the ball began, had devastated Helen more than any other incident she could remember in her life. The remark Alice had made—about not wanting to be like her, not wanting to live with her—had hurt so much only because it was so familiar. It had been the way Helen had felt about her own mother. By then in Helen's mind there were three distinct layers: lower, middle and upper. Her mother had been the lowest of the lower class. Her own values were profoundly middle class and she knew it. Her daughter was to be something else. The remark stung Helen not because she didn't agree with it but because she did. Her saving grace, that night so long ago, had been in not showing what she felt in front of Alice. A kind of remoteness was the thickest part of Helen's armor. Refusing to admit to real feeling had saved her more than once, and it got her through that incident too. Nobody at all, including Alice, had any idea what that night had meant. Helen had gone to the Comus ball just as if nothing had happened. And then, as a mild tremor sometimes follows an earthquake, the ball itself had been a surprise. With their antiquated poses and pretensions, their talk of opera and the racing season, the New Orleans aristocracy suddenly seemed to Helen as boringly genteel as the Bayou Teche world had appeared to her when she was a girl. And when that Mardi Gras was over she had left New Orleans for almost the last time. . . .

She took the last sip of champagne and watched the patterns in the smoke from the cigarette change over her head. It was going to take an awful lot of good champagne for the nearly five hundred people who were coming to this party. Holtz had balked at the price of the champagne she had ordered, but he had backed down fast when she had threatened to give up the ball. Spain was an easy place to have this big a gathering. Where else would a hotel owner order what he was told to order, at his expense, for this many people? Then, too, Suelo had another advantage. Being a special kind of town, it was wide open to manipulation of almost any kind. It was a little like living in a world of special services: the town had many of the "proper" mannerisms and social arabesques of England, with the corruption of North Africa barely under the surface. In the last few weeks, Helen had discovered that there was nothing she couldn't have for the asking—or for the paying. Holtz had put the hotel staff at her disposal; and the least-expected member of the staff had made it plain to Helen that she needn't worry about the nature of her requirements. It was the chief maid who had made this so clear. Eugenia, who didn't at all look the part, was apparently becoming the center of corruption in the hotel. Helen herself had no expensive addictions—but it wouldn't have mattered if she had. It was obvious that Eugenia could have taken care of anything from dope to a difficult sexual requirement with discretion. In fact, Helen suspected, the old woman was already performing certain procuring services for some of the people in the hotel. Donahue's affair with the little maid had been miraculously covered up at the last moment, just at the point when it might have become too open. The little maid was occupied elsewhere now (some recent arrival, a gentleman from Seattle, had taken a shine to her) and Donahue was living back at the American naval base. Helen had seen Eugenia talking to Alfonso the lifeguard several times in the last week or so, and she had long been sure that Alfonso doubled at night in a different capacity. No, there wasn't much doubt about it, the old woman called Eugenia had taken over all such arrangements, and was evidently doing a good job. There weren't many comforts in the world that couldn't be provided for Helen's guests; and some of the guests, she thought, did have one or two special needs. George Tucker, one of the three largest shareholders in oil in the Middle East, was a well-known flagellant; and the Giroudets who were driving down from Paris had a taste for heroin and for sharing their bed with good-looking girls and beachboys, it was said. Helen had overtipped Eugenia in advance—and though she hadn't specified what the money was for, it was understood that the chief maid would keep Helen's guests happy during their stay.

Yes, she thought, she could afford to take the rest of the day off. There was no use getting overtired. Above all, she needed to look fresh. And if things went as planned . . .

A dull knock on the porch door disturbed her thoughts and Helen half rose with a sigh on the sofa. She relaxed when she saw who it was. "Come in," she said.

The door opened and Will shuffled a couple of steps across the floor. He was barefoot and he had a note in his hand. He held it up without speaking.

"Yes," Helen said, "I asked Mrs. Lawson to slip it under your door after lunch. I wanted to talk to you about your costume. . . . You needn't stand there like a man waiting for an executioner . . . the party is in your honor, after all."

Will shifted his weight to the other hip and stayed the same.

"All right," Helen said. "It's my party . . . but it's your birthday. And you do have to stick to the rules. If *you* and *I* don't dress according to the color of our villas, we can't very well expect anyone *else* to, can we?"

Will swallowed.

"I'm sorry about it," Helen said; "but you *live* in the blue villa, you *have* to dress in blue. Do you still insist on wanting that costume?"

Will nodded a fraction without looking up.

Helen sighed. "Well, do what you want. It's not my affair. You can please yourself. But who ever heard of it? That's all I'd like to know. Who ever heard of a blue devil?"

Will sniffed and cleared his throat. He kept his stance on the floor and did not answer.

Helen put a hand to the tension in her forehead and smoothed the wrinkles out. "I suppose you have a private reason," she said, "you usually do. All right, if it's what you want. I'll have the tailor take your measurements in the morning. . . ."

Will left the note on Helen's desk. He shuffled to the door without speaking and went outside.

Helen picked a piece of ice out of the empty glass and put it in her mouth. Though Alice took precedence, William was beginning to concern her too. There was a shifty look about him she hadn't seen before. Whatever might have disturbed Will up to now, he never had gone around with that doomed guilty expression. And his insistence about the costume was unlike him too. Something new was going on inside Will's head. He hadn't left yet, she saw now; he was still standing outside the porch of her villa on the top step. Then through the screen she noticed the look on his face and she got up quickly from the sofa and went to stand behind him inside the door.

A large truck had stopped five hundred yards down the gravel path, next to the villa where William and Alice slept. Guzmán was sitting behind the wheel and Alice was getting out of the front seat. Helen didn't like trucks of any kind —had not liked them since the day years ago when her mother had driven off on one. This truck was dirty looking and filled with dust. It wasn't freshly painted like the nasty-green truck she remembered with such distaste—it was only a dull colorless shade of brown. The paint was faded and cracked on the hood in several places and the back of the truck was loaded with four or five bulky objects; a sheet of heavy canvas had been tied over them, but you could see the corners projecting through. Helen pushed the porch door open and stepped out on the stoop next to Will.

Will looked up at her a second, and then went on looking at the truck.

"Your sister doesn't like me," she said on an impulse, "it's always been painful to me to know that. You knew it, didn't you?"

Will did not answer.

Guzmán saw them and smiled. He stepped down from the driver's seat and strode across the lawn to Helen. "We go fishing," he called as he approached. "Tuna, we hope."

Helen smiled. "Nice," she said.

Guzmán came to a halt below the steps. He nodded to Helen and then to Will. "How good to have your invitation," he said to Helen. "I'd like to come. Shall I accept formally by note . . . ?"

"Oh, this will do," Helen said, "is Alice . . ."

"She went to the villa for some things she will need. We are to pick up some friends of mine in the boat from farther along the coast. We may be back in a few days, or we may stay out for a while . . . it will be very large, this masked ball?"

"Large," Helen said.

"Alice will enjoy to come, I think, also."

"Will she?"

Guzmán turned to look.

Alice was crossing the lawn to the red villa. She was wearing bluejeans and tennis shoes and she walked with a gay step, bouncing across the grass. She joined Guzmán by the stoop. Her face took on a more serious expression as she looked at her mother.

"Thank you," she said simply. "I'll come."

An hour later they were gone and Helen was still standing on the stoop watching the boat disappear in the distance. Will was down at the dock watching too, his dog next to him. Will looked as if he'd been left with an unanswered question. He was leaning forward, Helen saw, staring through the spray as the boat disappeared. She wondered idly what he was thinking about. Whatever it was, she could tell that it had to do with Alice. She had seen her daughter lean down, her face shining, and whisper something to Will just before following Guzmán onto the boat. A happy secret had passed between them, she was sure.

And there was something else as well. Alice had made too careful a point of not asking Will to come with them on the fishing trip. Helen had drawn her daughter aside while the boat was loading and had suggested that they take him. They were getting too open about their affair—the whole hotel could see Alice leave with Guzmán. But Alice had not liked the idea of taking her brother, and she had not given any reason. Will had seemed to know all along why he wasn't being invited, and not to expect it. It was just possible, Helen thought, that it wasn't a fishing trip. It was possible that Guzmán and Alice had been lying to her. . . .

From the top of the stoop, she glanced once more at the gold villa. It was still empty. Juan Alberto and his brother must have gone off for the day.

She went back inside her porch and lifted another split of champagne out of the icebox. As long as she was taking the afternoon off, she might as well enjoy herself. From tomorrow on she'd be working steadily until the party. She popped the cork and filled a fresh glass with ice; after that she went back and lay down on the sofa.

She let the bottle stand open for a while before she poured half of the split into the glass. Then she swirled the liquid around in the ice a few times. It was vintage Moët and Chandon—not quite as good as Dom Perignon, but good. Helen liked her champagne *brut* and she liked it a little flat, over ice. She liked it served in a chunky old-fashioned glass. Long-stemmed champagne glasses, ever since they had first gone out of style with the war, seemed to her affected and faintly vulgar.

She opened her mouth and set the cold rim of the glass against it. Everybody needs fun now and then, she thought. The hazy sun was gone and a pleasant breeze from the west crossed the porch. You could see the summer was almost over. The air was cool and comfortable.

Thoughtfully, Helen leaned the glass up and let the gold bubbles just touch the tip of her tongue.

EIGHT

Will

So HE slept on the hill in the loud buzzing sunlight and half the world smelling of thyme.

Just a little more than three months had gone by since June the Fifth. It was the beginning of Fall. Sleeping on the hillside, the squeezed pieces of his livingness were so tight inside him it was like he could not breathe. His birthday was in one more day and the masked ball was to take place in the hotel tomorrow night.

Will's dozing mind grappled with it but there was no way to sort all of it out: thinking was no good. It hadn't been any good since Littlejohn had leaned over to him just before getting on the boat and said the six words: "I'm going to have one, Will." While Helen watched them from her villa. And then Littlejohn had stepped on board and disappeared in the spray. Since then, in his mind, he could see as if from a distance the lumpy landscape of events—the people; the big mosaic and the little one—the faces and all of the linked things that had started happening the day in June when Littlejohn had come to Spain. They were all smeared out in the same direction, toward some end, and you couldn't see them clearly. Distance didn't help. Not even this way, by himself on the high hill overlooking the town. He was half awake now. He could hear the cadenced itching sounds around him in the bug-loud air. The sun was lower—the heat of noon had lessened in the couple of hours since he had come up here and gone to sleep.

Will blinked the sweat out of his eyes and sat up slowly in the dust.

His body was drenched from the sun and some of the dust had caked on the back of his neck. The pungent smell of the wild thyme was stronger than ever in the afternoon. Below him now at the dock of the Hotel Malage he could see the seaplane anchored bobbing like a duck in the low flat tide. Squinting, he was able to make out the initials of the charter service printed on the side, between the wing and the propeller. It was the name he had seen written on his

347

mother's agenda pad on her desk. So he had been right: the passenger the plane had brought was the high-fashion clothes designer from Madrid, and with him was Helen's costume for the ball. The arrival of her dress had happened as Helen had said it would, according to her schedule. Preparations for the ball were getting tense now; guests and carpenters and caterers were bumping into each other all over hell and gone from one end of the Hotel Malage to the other. The other Suelo hotels weren't much calmer. The press was referring to Helen's party as the "Mid-Century Masked Ball" because it was supposed to represent the end of the halfway mark between the years 1900 and 2000. Will didn't see how it could, being seven years too late for 1950, but there it was. According to a society column in Madrid's English-language newspaper, the theme of the ball was "a celebration of the uses of the first half of the Twentieth Century—a breathing space in the nineteen-fifties before the end of the Century is upon us." It didn't make a whole lot of sense, but when Will considered about it he could feel his skin tighten. Outside of the ball's being given on his birthday, it reminded him he was an in-between person no matter what. From week to week straight through the summer the list of his in-betweennesses had been added to. He was not the right age for anything. There was just one advantage to the ball to his mind: nearly all the people he knew would be together in one place tomorrow night and maybe the connection of things might reveal itself to him. If it didn't, it would give his mind a new surface to lean on while he was having another look. So far his own nervousness was growing along with the tension that mounted from day to day at the hotel. Everybody in town felt it. Everybody except one person. Only his mother stayed calm no matter what went on around her. Helen's coolness seemed to increase each day, as if the hysteria that was sweeping through the hotel affected her in the opposite way. Her presence stood out at the center: quiet, attentive, simple, capable. No matter what the problem was—a last-minute confusion in hotel reservations, or a carpenter who had misread the measurements for the orchestra stand, even a fight between a headwaiter and the driver of a delivery truck over a broken case of champagne—Helen would be on the spot within five minutes, or if she wasn't somebody was there with a set of instructions from her that corrected the situation and put everybody's mind to rest. Well, not quite everybody's mind. It was like his mother was at one end of the thermometer of nervousness and he was at the other. And Littlejohn was somewhere at the center.

Only where?

Will leaned over the rock at his feet, and scanned the empty dirt path he had come up by. The mosquitoes were louder and he lifted his hand and swatted at the air. Of all the problems that were itching his mind, Littlejohn was the worst. She wasn't away on the boat trip any more—Will didn't know where she had gone after she had come back. She had stopped in the blue villa one night while he was asleep and left a note saying "Back. Am fine, but G not safe yet. Don't say I was here, see you when I can. Love, A" tucked under his toothbrush on the washbasin between the soap and the glass; it annoyed him. She should come to the party, he thought—Littlejohn could afford to give one night to her mother. Will had become peeved with her in the last weeks and her wanting to be called Alice was the last straw. He had flatly refused to comply with the request. Then the six words she had whispered to him on the dock had irked him even more: he had known ever since he was old enough to talk that Littlejohn wanted children. She used to say she would have a dozen babies, and after that, if she still had strength, she would run around the block a couple of times to catch her breath and have a dozen more. The only time the idea of babies had ceased to interest her, Will knew, was for the years she went to college; as soon as she graduated, having babies had come right back into her mind. Whatever had been going on at the Guzmán palace would one day take second place to that, he guessed; he knew they were clearing up the business of the murder first, though he could not tell much about it. He didn't know the killed man and he did not know the man who had done the killing.

He looked up. The sky was thinning to a cool September blue. It was distant and afternoon-colored. There was one black-and-white cloud arched like a middle-aged eyebrow over him and the hill.

He hunched onto his toes and squatted there, country-boy style. Then he stood up slowly and shook the stiffness out of each leg. For some minutes he jogged back and forth on top of the hill, bouncing in his thighs like a boxer and taking a few short jabs and punches at the clean blue air. He counted twenty-four lengths of the hilltop and on the twenty-fourth he continued moving; he jogged along the rock path that led down winding into the town.

Taxis and hired cars brayed their horns through the dust along the main coast road. The road was heavy with traffic

now, thick with tourists who had come for the party. Spanish
bricklayers in blue overalls and two burros stood at the side
of the asphalt watching the parade of automobiles with a
look of quiet amazement in their dusty eyes, as though
something were happening in front of them that they could
not believe, could not imagine let alone accept. Not far from
Will a fruit seller had stopped his burro to watch—neither
the man nor the animal turning his gaze to follow each car,
but standing stock still in a stunned and brutal stupor as the
chauffeured guests moved by. Will darted across the road to
the main gravel path of the hotel. Even the path was choked
with cars aimed in both directions. The Spanish drivers
yelled each other out of the way, their voices angered, and
on the back seats the tourists sat smiling, putting up con-
descendingly with all the overwrought hysteria which they
themselves were causing and which they all thought of as
Spanish. Halfway up the main path a delivery truck that had
mistaken it for the service entrance had stopped, stuck, its
motor stalled. The motor whined up and down, starting and
never catching, turning over: turning: the pathetic metal
screeching under the relentless foot of the caged man at the
wheel who had probably not been driving a truck for longer
than the six months he had driven this one. He was stuck with
it now as the truck was stuck on the path, the two, man
and truck, like the man and the burro on the highway beyond, paralyzed, stunned, shocked, outraged and annoyed.
Will passed them.

He stood near the main building of the hotel while the
hullaballoo around him proceeded like a kind of organized
madness. There were tourists on the beach, tourists on the
lawn, tourists weaving in and out of the deliverers and party
directors and codirectors and drivers, tourists walking everywhere like people who had somewhere to go. A man carrying a wooden crate over his head bumped into Will so hard
they both nearly fell. Will tilted sideways into a group of new
arrivals who were descending from a taxi exclaiming loudly at the colors of the villas. The paint on the main building
and the villas had been retouched in preparation for the
party and the pastel façades of the hotel shone out, fresh
and radiant in the day. Will went up the three steps and into
the main doorway, but there it was worse. People were lined
all along the reception desk and around the harried gray-
faced concierge. Some walked under the busy carpenters who
were hammering above the lobby, completing the extra
staircase and balcony that would lead from the mezzanine
down to the main ballroom. Helen had ordered the staircase

built a month ago; it was to be covered in solid black carpeting. On one side of the lobby six workers sat like doomed soldiers on a giant black roll smoking black tobacco, waiting for the carpenters to finish so that their work could begin. There was no place in the lobby to stand without getting in somebody's way and Will was mashed and ignored until it seemed as if the very people who had come for his birthday were going to kill him for having it. He made his way through the kitchen entrance and out the service door to the lawn again in time to avoid being mashed by the arrival of a grand piano that was approaching like a bulky abstract disembodied gin-and-tonic tourist nightmare floating drunkenly through the air on the backs of six men. There was nothing to do but go to the blue villa where it was safe and play solitaire till suppertime. He ran the long way around —circling the manicured cuticle-backs of the villa lawns.

There was another note from Will's mother on the door of the blue villa giving further instructions about his part in the proceedings tomorrow night. Sneakers was waiting (he had left the dog inside the villa rather than risk taking him out through all the traffic) and Will sat for an hour playing two different kinds of solitaire, winning at each kind (something that only happened to him when there was nobody around to witness it) and settling down finally with a couple of books he had taken from the hotel library a week ago and had not yet read. They were *Pride and Prejudice* by Jane Austen and *Sexual Behaviourism and Survival Tactics in the Adolescent Male Baboon* by Jules L. Berns. How either one of them had got into the hotel library he didn't know; but you could never tell what a tourist might leave behind. Both of the titles had caught Will's eye and both seemed to hold a promise. He began to read them now but the inside of the books was disappointing. The novel was full of tiptop words and the second book was full of graphs. He leafed through the second one but there did not seem to be a single description of sex. In fact there was no definition of sexual behaviourism in any form. There was not even a picture of baboons fucking. The empty book put him in mind of the feeling of something falling out of him that he had had on the night he had seen Lieutenant Donahue in bed with the little maid. The entire subject of sex was one that had a sort of terrible fascination for him and at the same time made him kind of jumpy. He got up and took his ball costume out of the box it had come in; then he unfolded it and tried it on. Sneakers took a look at him and crawled boredly under the bed.

Will stood in front of the mirror and examined himself as a whole in the costume. It covered nearly all of him except for his face. His body, he noticed, was not as badly proportioned as he had come to think. It was true you could see some bones here and there, but his shoulders were wide, and there was a slim-hipped cowboy look he wouldn't have believed about himself even if people had sworn to it. His thighs looked almost muscular. This was the third time he had tried the costume on by himself, and he definitely approved of it in the most part. The idea of dressing up as a devil had come into his head one night as the last of a dream. The dream had had something to do with the two men—Jim Lepard and Lieutenant Donahue—that kept circling for position in his mind after dark. The costume was navy blue and it was made out of shiny material that clung to him like elastic. He liked the look of the two blue horns that stuck up over his head. The color suited him too; his mother had been wrong about a devil having to be red. In fact, only two things worried him. One was the blue tail. It dragged half a foot on the ground behind him with a wide arrow at the end of it. He did not think much of the tail, and no matter what anybody said, it was too long, he knew. People were bound to step on it. He had tried tying the tail around his waist to make it shorter but it spoiled the line of the costume, and the blue arrow stuck out in the air behind him suggestively; it made him look as if he had been born with his piece in the wrong place. He could not get the tail to be the right length. He had tried shortening it by tying a knot in it or draping it over one shoulder, but all of the positions were wrong. He picked it up now in front of the mirror and hung it through his arm. He kept the left hand hooked on his thigh, his weight on the opposite leg; the result was not bad. There was a nonchalant quality. Standing that way he had the careless appearance of a man who is used to having a tail and does not wish to make much of it. The trouble was he had to keep his weight on one hip. He did not see how he could go around with his weight on one hip all night without looking crippled. He walked once sideways in front of the mirror and then up to it and back again; the walk, he knew, was the key to the whole thing. It should be cowboy-casual—low-slung, like the walk of a man with heavy boots and spurs that jangled dimly at every step; it was not easy with a tail.

The other thing that disturbed him about the costume was the feet. They were supposed to look like hooves—only his own feet were too big and he was walking on the hocks all the time. He looked like a devil with broken legs. The hooves were split at the ends and the only way Will could fit into them was to put his big toe into one half of the cleft and the other four toes on the other side. It was awkward.

The sounds of late arrivals on the lawns around the blue villa were getting louder: laughter and questions and complaints, chips of voices, the braying of automobile horns and the cluck and jitter of orders called at yip-yell level, high, darting like dragonflies from captain to doorman to bellboys, their voices soaring across the grass. The noises rang unmingled above the hotel grounds like the sounds of a record played at the wrong speed. Faster and faster people were converging into the freshly painted, trimmed and decorated buildings of the hotel.

Will swung the tail once more over his arm and began to walk back and forth across the length of the villa. He walked slowly, straining to achieve the high-toed casual step of a small but well-built fiend.

He thought that it would probably take him all night.

AT SIX-THIRTY in the afternoon of the next day the sounds
around the blue villa ceased suddenly and a new hush descended on the hotel. Will was arranging the elastic of the
costume around his face when he heard the silence and
paused to listen. At first he wondered if the material over his
ears was pressing so hard that it blocked out all sound. He
moved it with his fingers, but the hotel noises did not come
back. He went to the open window and listened. Now, an
hour before the first part of the ball, the ruminant cacophony
of garbled noises that had been building up for weeks had
ended as abruptly as if they had never existed. A sort of
dreamlike stillness had descended on the town. Standing listening at the window, Will felt an instant's sensation of
fright, like the vacuum-moment in dreams when you want
to cry out and are not able to make a noise. Then the feeling
went away and he walked back and put his mask on. The
instructions his mother had left him were clear. At seven
o'clock he was to go to the lobby and wait for her there; the
children who were coming to the first half of the ball were
sons and daughters of the older guests who were coming
later.

At a quarter to seven he went out onto the front porch.
The autumn days were getting shorter and the sky above the
hotel was already going black. It was as if the cascades of
multicolored lights that had been woven into arches over all
the paths in the hotel had drowned out even the stars. Each
villa had been trellised and roofed with a net of light bulbs
that matched its color; off each front porch there was a
canopy of lights attaching that villa to the nearest path. The
light bulbs were tiny and they made glittering streaks of
color. The central paths led to the canopy over the main
doorway where they joined to become a great spangled crash
of light at the mouth of the hotel. Will stood on the porch
with the villas close around him. A tinge of pink, of gold, a
gash of blood red flashed out sharp as separate beacons. The
blue villa shone among them like an incandescent sea wave

354

lit from within by a cold fire. A sea gull passing overhead paused in midflight. The hush that lay on the hotel had the effect of a trance. The sea gull looked down at the area below. There was no one to be seen on any of the lawns. The hotel looked empty.

Then the porch door of the blue villa opened. From it, a small navy-blue Prince of Darkness stepped out and tiptoed into the night. Tail over one arm, he proceeded forward lightly.

The silence held as Will moved. He walked high on his toes, holding his heels out of the gravel. If it wasn't the walk he had hoped to achieve, it was good enough for a beginning; with a little more practice he could find the right devil's walk before the night was over.

The rainbowed blaze stood over him in shining silence, doomed and fine, like a travesty of a church wedding. He moved in the sequin night and felt the colored villas shine by.

Near the entrance to the main building he slowed up. The sunburst around the doorway had the look of a volcano; you couldn't watch it without squinting. It was a panorama, sharp and blinding, terrifically bright, like the source of light itself. Will crept up the steps, tiptoeing now not because of his costume but in a kind of awe; then the lights were behind him.

He entered the main lobby past a single tall doorman who stood at attention. The doorman bowed to him and Will went on into the empty tile-and-marble cavernous room. The lobby had been cleared of all furniture. After the brilliance of the doorway it seemed dark inside. He continued to the exact center of the room and stopped. Around him liveried bellboys stood at attention every three feet, all of them with their backs to the wall and facing straight forward, staring like wax figures at a central point in the air just over Will's head. Will froze. He used his eyes in a kind of V-shape, scanning the room from left to right. Not one bellboy budged. The doorman stood precisely where he had been before, inside the entrance with his back to the room, quiet as a zombie. Will did not know what he was supposed to do next and there was no point in asking anybody in the room. They all looked dead. He glanced underneath his hooves and saw that he was standing on the biggest mosaic in the hotel. He moved from tile to tile over it, stepping first on one color, then another; the tips of his hooves made little sharp clicks as they struck. He walked in a long slow circle and came back to the point he had started at. The bellboys hadn't budged; then it happened.

Himself as motionless as the bellboys, planted at the center of the room as if he owned it, without a thought in his head, Will farted. The small noise that released itself from his buttocks ran the length of the room; in the total silence it sounded to him like an atomic explosion. In the elegant lobby he wished himself dead. Along the wall he was facing, at least six bellboys stood, tensed, just as rigid as they had been before—their stomachs shaking with laughter. The giggles spread contagiously; they leaped from the bellboy nearest the entrance over to the doorman to the bellboy on the other side, and went on traveling. The suppressed mirth possessed the room. Then Will too became infected by it. He raised his arms, palms upward, as though he were the conductor of the laughter. He was still the only one making any noise and when his mother came from the hall to get him, not one other person in the lobby had uttered a sound.

Helen moved across the tile floor and looked down at her son. She took a handkerchief from her sleeve and handed it to him. "My decorations amuse you?"

"No," Will said. He blew his nose and handed the handkerchief back.

"Keep it," Helen said.

Will tucked the handkerchief up his sleeve. Helen was wearing a gray and pink chiffon sheath that buttoned from her ankles up to her throat. "What about your costume?" he asked.

"Later. This is your part of the evening," his mother said. She led the way to the grand ballroom.

Will hitched his tail higher and followed her, avoiding the looks on the faces of the bellboys. Once he was out of the lobby he was safe.

Between the lobby and the ballroom a black velvet archway had been put up through two rooms. Helen moved ahead of him, a gray slim figure blocking his view. Then she was gone.

They had come out into the grand ballroom and Will was alone. Gradually the high space he was standing in took focus in his eyes. He could not believe it, but he could see it. Then he believed it.

The grand ballroom of the hotel did not look like a room. It was a hollow site in the universe, as plain and simple as a clear night sky, and it was a place of magic. Stunned, Will dropped his tail. The ballroom was black and silver. Overhead, a crystal chandelier looked like the square root of

sparkle; under it the dark waxed floor gleamed deep. At one
end, a black staircase swept down, narrow at the top and
wide at the bottom, its slender bannisters slicing the air on
either side. The walls of the room had been covered in black
velvet, and spaced across them, equidistant as the bellboys
in the outer lobby, were long heavy branches of black iron,
each supporting a plain wooden torch. The flames of the
torches jumped up to stab at the ceiling. Here and there
were sofas and chairs of black velvet on silver legs. The
south-wall French windows had been thrown open onto the
terrace overlooking the sea. The night sky above the Mediterranean, pinpricked now with silver, appeared like an exten-
sion of the ballroom, as though the room had spread out into
the heavens. The black and silver swam in Will's eyes and
he blinked it back into focus. Overall the room throbbed;
there was an aurora that stirred at its heart. The waves of
light were like a pulse in space. The ballroom was a winner.

Helen was standing talking to a waiter. She turned to note
Will's reaction. "You approve?"

Will nodded.

"Good," she said; "your guests will be here soon. I want
to show you something. . . ."

She went past him out onto the terrace. Will went after
her.

Five hundred yards from shore lay a United States Navy
training ship. It was anchored with one side facing the hotel.
Across its side a light-bulb sign had been stretched about
one third the length of the ship. The bulbs spelled out three
words. The sign said:

H A P P Y   B I R T H D A Y
13 13 13 13   13 13 13 13 13 13 13

W I L L I A M
13 13 13 13 13 13

Will went to the terrace railing and went on looking at the
sign. After a while he coughed.

His mother stepped beside him, the gray chiffon of her
dress fluttering around her in the night breeze. "Happy birthday," she said. It was almost a whisper.

"How'd you get them to do it?"

"It does look nice, doesn't it? . . . The navy? Oh, easily,"
Helen said. "I told them who you were. It looks better in
silver than it would have in colored lights."

"You told them what?" Will said.

"They were going to use red lights, but I thought not. William Charles Locke—Junior. The navy keeps records, you know. The date is listed."

"What date?"

"Thirteen years one month and one day ago," Helen said.

"Oh," Will said.

"There's going to be some fun on the ship too," she said.

"You told them he died before I was born."

"I told them it was your birthday, they worked it out for themselves. Later on they're going to shoot off fireworks toward the beach. It's time to go back inside. . . ."

Helen turned and swept past him. Her chiffon sleeve grazed the top of his head. Will waited until she got to the French window.

"You don't like people to touch you," he said.

Helen glanced back and threw her head up. "Yes," she said, "you're his son all right. A ball for a birthday party and at least fifty presents. A United States naval vessel with your name on it. And you want to be touched. It may not be logical, but it's familiar."

She came back and leaned over him. There was her cheek and the perfumed air and the chiffon. There was everything but Helen. Then she was gone.

After a while they were inside standing next to the bannister. Will stood beside his mother. The children were beginning to arrive. He did not know any of them and they came down the staircase.

They came singly, without their parents, most of them clutching wrapped presents in their costumed hands, suspicious and lost looking: pirates and shepherds and Indians, bandits and bullfighters and court ladies, all of them without faces, or rather all with the same face—the blank explain-it-to-me faintly nauseated this-isn't-what-I-thought-it-was-going-to-be unfathomable dismal and inextricable expression of all children at parties all over the world. There were children from seven different countries and they all looked like the same child. Will introduced himself to each one in English or French or Spanish or German or Italian, in whatever language was necessary, as each arrived at the bottom of the staircase. Then he introduced each to his mother. That was the way she had told him to do it. He did not care who they were and they did not care who he was. You could see that none of them had wanted to come, and you could see that none would want to leave, and between not wanting to come and not wanting to leave you could see that they would be busy wondering why it was that they were not having a good time. You could see, five minutes before the end of the party, that the tension in the room would break—so that when it was time to go they would all feel as though they had just got there and would hate the party's ending as much as they had hated it beginning. As much as they had hated the idea of it in the first place: but would go. Would leave at last, food-stuffed, their costumes bedraggled, remembering not who they had seen or who they had liked, but only where they had been, and only that for a short while until the memory itself was packed beneath the sediment of time, so that years later, when their parents reminded them, they would say "Oh, yes" or "When?" or "Whose birthday?"—the younger ones seeing only, remembering (after they were grown up) the chandelier as it looked from the top of the stairs, or who got sick, or who had a better costume—and then thinking *Yes, I'll have a birthday party for my children when they're born and see how they like it* with a kind of dull and heavy vengeance, as though they had missed something that their children must not miss whether they liked it or not: happiness.

"Thirty-seven," Helen said.

"What?"

"The latecomers will find their own way; it's time for the music."

She moved away from Will signaling to someone on the mezzanine.

Will pretended to scratch the elastic over his head; he sneaked a look at the children. Most of them were standing in the center of the room. None were speaking and most of them were looking at Will. They stood in groups and clumps and short lines, the boys on one side of the chandelier and the girls on the other. Helen had been strict about limiting the age group of the children; only those between twelve and fourteen years old had been permitted to come.

Will's eyes strayed over them. On the near side of the girls' group there was a shepherdess he liked the look of. When she had introduced herself to him she had curtsied. She was French but she spoke English too. Most of the children were taller than Will, he saw; he had not been around children for a while and he had forgot about that. He became conscious of his height and he raised himself more on his toes. He did not know what Helen had gone off to do. He found himself again watching the French shepherdess who was standing alone; her name was Lisette and there was something strange about her. Will could not place what it was. She was shy—but that wasn't it.

The terrace outside was beginning to have people on it, he saw; the parents of the children had come to watch them dance. They stood like expectant shadows between the ballroom and the sea. They looked as though they would be pleased enough if their children could move: they looked like parents. They weren't allowed to come into the ballroom during this part of the ball, any more than the children would be allowed in their part; those were Helen's rules. Will looked away from them.

The girl named Lisette had moved. She was standing by herself farther apart from the other girls. Yes, there was something strange about her; it was in everything she did. Will thought he saw her edge her eyes at him under her lashes—it was hard to be sure behind her mask. Before, when she had introduced herself to him, she had pronounced her name clearly and a thin veneer of color had come into her face. She had dark eyes and very dark hair and there was an amber tint under her skin, as though she had some Chinese in her.

Will looked around the room for Helen. He wished she had told him what to do now—the boys were beginning to nudge each other and shuffle. Only the girls stood still, accepting the delay without comment. Many of them were elegantly dressed. Lisette was not. She was a small-waisted, slight-boned girl, and in places she was almost pudgy. Somewhere in Will's mind he already knew what was strange about her. He chased it around with his thinking for a few seconds, but it escaped him. Then he saw the pupils behind her eyelashes move again; Lisette had glanced at him once more. It was like she wanted Will to know that she was watching him and at the same time didn't. Will was not fooled. He knew the scene too well. He had seen *Romeo and Juliet* twice in the movies and he had acted the part of Mercutio once in school and he had always thought it was boring that Romeo should meet Juliet at a masked ball.

He did not like the look of Lisette, he decided. She was too aloof. Will was beginning to be nervous again, but he did not know it. He did not know the dancing was about to start. He didn't even know that he was in love. Except for Littlejohn he had never been in love before and he had no idea what was going on. He believed that he was watching the discomfort of the children. Then there was a sound from above.

On the mezzanine floor a black velvet curtain was pulled away to reveal the orchestra playing behind it.

"Now," Helen said.

He turned to his mother and frowned. She had come back and was standing next to him.

"I told you," Helen said, "they won't start dancing till. . . . Oh. Well, at least there's *one* couple."

A very tall boy had broken through the invisible barrier and asked one of the girls to dance. The other children had stepped aside to make room. The couple was waltzing around the floor. The girl was smiling and the tall boy moved with smoothness in time to the music. The girl was Lisette.

"Go ahead," Helen said. "Pick somebody and start. The ice won't break unless you break it."

It was when he tried to move that he knew a little of it. He did not know all of it till much later that night. But in the minutes that followed, Will did as he was told—except that it could not be said that he *picked* a girl. He did not look at a girl. He merely moved forward and stopped by the girl standing nearest to him, and asked her to dance; he could not remember afterwards whether she was a pretty girl (or whether she was a girl) or remember what language she spoke that he could speak enough of to keep the conversation going (or whether he had kept it going) because he was too busy watching Lisette dance with somebody else. He had expected that the worst part of the ball would be dancing with strange girls and thinking of things to say, but it was not so. When the music stopped, he walked west across the ballroom fast, straight as a plumb line. Before he got to Lisette another boy had asked her. She smiled at the new boy just as she had smiled at the first one. Will thought he saw her glance across the room at him for an instant. He wasn't sure now that Lisette had ever looked at him at all. She had very heavy lashes for her age.

It took him three more dances to get to her before somebody else did. Lisette, it turned out, was not just one of the popular girls at the party. She was the *only* popular girl at the party. It wasn't her costume that did it; she was the least gaudily dressed of anyone there. Among the other costumes there were two Spanish noblewomen, and there was at least one Russian Empress in the room. The American Ambassador's daughter had come as Queen Isabella with her brother in tow as Columbus; their two costumes shone like fire. By contrast Lisette was covered up to the neck in a sort of drab brown material, as if she had gone out of her way not to call attention to herself. She had a very wide mask on, but even so it was apparent that there were prettier girls among the others. Nearly all of them had taken advantage of the ball to put on lipstick and rouge; her face did not have makeup of any kind.

Will's fourth dance was with the daughter of an Italian count and he took her to a spot within touching distance of Lisette. When the music stopped he thanked her and turned quickly to his left.

Lisette was standing with her back to him. She had taken a mirror out of the shepherd's sack that hung on her arm; she was arranging a piece of her hair.

Will tried to make his body walk around to the other side of her, but it would not; when he opened his mouth to say something, nothing came out.

Then another tall boy was walking fast across the floor straight to Lisette. Will could not do anything about it. When the tall boy was only three feet away, the shepherd's sack dropped from Lisette's arm to the floor. She bent and picked it up before anybody could help her.

When she straightened, she was not facing the tall boy any more.

Will worked his tongue around but there were no words in his mouth to say. Then he knew that he did not want to dance with Lisette at all. He did not even know how he had got himself into this position.

"Would you do a favor for me?" Lisette said.

Will waited.

"*Attends*. It's the second time he has come to ask me to dance. I mean, it's not. . . . *Enfin. Il est charmant*. It's not that. I can't tell what it is. Maybe I'm afraid a little? Would you?"

"Would I what?" Will said. He had already decided that he would do whatever she wanted, without ever coming anywhere near the girl again.

"You know. The favor?"

"What favor?" he said.

Lisette watched him.

"Would you dance with me?" she said.

Will cleared his throat and condensed the spit that had collected.

"Thank you," Lisette said. "You are nice to pretend that you didn't notice."

". . . Notice?"

She smiled. "That I was watching you in my mirror. He is gone?"

Will nodded. He put his arms out in a stiff bad way, the left one down and the right up by mistake. Lisette didn't seem to notice. She arranged them around her with no trouble. Then she took his left hand in her right one. The music did not start right away. The arrow of Will's tail was sticking up over his left wrist. Just as they began to move Lisette touched it gently.

The early part of the ball fused in Will's mind and when he tried to remember it later he could not easily separate one incident from the next. All the things that happened were melted together into one long stream, with only two events of importance. The first was the taking off of the masks. An hour after the music had started Will was dancing with Lisette again. He had danced with her by then four times. It was a pure mystery how she was always free. The other boys were lining up for her, but it was like she was waiting to see if Will wanted her each dance or not; he could not make it out how things worked out so well. Helen came up to remind him that there were other girls who needed attending to; she stopped in midsentence. Lisette dropped her eyes and Helen regarded her with careful scrutiny. When his mother turned to him again Will saw a new expression in her face.

"Well," Helen said; "you can't really dance with *every-body. . . .*"

She went away again and it was then she interrupted the orchestra to call for the taking off of the masks. There were a few seconds of silence. Lazily, Lisette reached behind her head and unsnapped the elastic. It was when the cardboard fell away from her face that Will saw how little use there was in his ever being interested in anybody else. It was not that she was pretty. It was that she didn't need to be pretty. He forgot to take his own mask off, and Lisette reached behind her head and unsnapped it; she didn't blush again. It was then that he knew that in some ways she was not as embarrassed as she gave herself out to be. Twenty minutes later they were sitting on one of the black-and-silver sofas. (The presentation of the birthday cake had happened without Will's being much aware of it.)

He was still sitting with her when the second event happened that was to stick in his memory in later years as one of the worst moments of his life. It began in a small insignificant way. It occurred to Will that he had to urinate. Having put it off for the last six dances it was this: he had to urinate worse than he would have thought possible. Sitting eating cake with Lisette he realized dully that he was in a kind of agony. This was his first awareness of the problem. The second awareness was that there was nothing he could do about it. He could not excuse himself and go to the bathroom. You do not leave a girl sitting alone to get up and do a thing like that. When Lisette raised her eyes to look at him above the cake he went cold all over. Between a man and a woman there are many things that take place—but the prime thing that takes place, the thing that takes precedence above all others, the thing called making love— is the thing that the man does *with that part of his body which is also used to urinate with*. The realization of it made a kind of deathlike chill settle over Will's shoulders. After the cake was served it had been expected that each boy in the room would sit with the girl he most liked, and the two of them had come together without bothering to ask one another. A few other boys had gathered around in a hopeful way and had been dismissed by Lisette with a glance. Will was alone with her. There was no one else on the sofa and no one anywhere near. He was doomed. He was no longer listening to her conversation. Crazy things went through his head. For the first time in his life he began to think that he would one day die. Up to now death had been a sort of far-off idea. Now he realized that there were a great many times more dead people on earth than live people, and he saw that he would one day join them.

The chill that had settled on his shoulders began to run up and down his body in waves. The balloon of pain sat inside him like a dank lake, bigger than a nightmare. It was the most swollen thing he had ever felt. Soon he knew it would burst and his heart would stop; there would be an autopsy to determine the cause of death. He hoped that the newspapers would not print the result of the autopsy. Lisette could think that he had died of something else—of love, or even of a disease. He would fall off the sofa in a heap. Lisette would see him. She would grow faint and her face would turn pale. She would stand tottering for a second. Several other boys would hold her up. Then she would kneel by Will, her face white, hands trembling a little, and she would wonder what kind of pain he had suffered; she would not understand why he had collapsed in silence. She would softly caress his dead face and his chest. She would not caress him any lower than his chest. He hoped to Christ that she would not caress him any lower than his chest. If she did, it would not matter whether he was dead or not; the pressure of her fingers on his bladder would make his very corpse rise screaming to its feet yelling in a voice of horror that would be heard by the entire human race. Stone dead, wracked and agonized, he would . . .

Lisette said, *"Écoute. Tu vas bien?"*

She was leaning forward on the sofa touching his wrist. She had probably been watching him for some time.

Will shrugged and nodded.

"I was worried," Lisette said, "I was talking to you. You do not seem to hear me. . . . Is everything all right?"

"Yup," Will said. "Fine."

Lisette leaned closer and examined his face searchingly with her eyes. "Something is wrong," she said.

"No."

"Tell me," Lisette said. "You are happy with me?"

"I'm happy with you." Each word as Will said it reverberated in his abdomen and produced a concomitant stab as though somebody was running white-hot swords through him. Lisette went on talking and in the prim silence of the ballroom listening to her throaty voice Will began to sweat. Only it was not sweat, he thought. It was the urine that was seeping out of him any way it could. Long hot beads of it ran down his face and dripped onto his costume; he could not understand why death was taking so long to overcome him. To keep himself sane while he was waiting for it he went through in his mind the possible words he could use as an excuse to get up. There weren't any. He could not pronounce a word like urinate to a girl like Lisette; to leave her without giving a reason was not thinkable. He thought of words in French but they were the same, and there was no way out. Only there was no way either of sitting still with pain that had become now greater than the bounds of human endurance. His breathing was getting shallow, off the top of his lungs—he was panting lightly and some of the sweat was running into his eyes. He would not mind death at all, if it would only come, but it did not come. Fate had taken him to the brink of unconsciousness and was holding him there teetering in a state of misery and awfulness that could not be borne. Then he knew if he could not say urinate he would have to stand up and say bathroom; he would have to.

Lisette rose to put her empty plate down on the sofa. Then she smoothed the shepherd's frock around her and turned to Will. She looked straight at him in a matter-of-fact, level way.

"Excusez-moi," she said. "I must make piss."

She walked across the room and disappeared under the staircase.

For a while (it was a minute) Will stared after her without moving. He could no longer feel the pain in his bladder. A sort of numbness had swept over him like a torpor. More than anything he just wanted to lie back on the sofa and go to sleep. After a time he got up and walked after Lisette past the high pile of birthday presents that were lying next to the staircase. His bladder bounced inside him like a wound and he walked dragging his tail to the sign that said Men's Room in four different languages. Standing at the urinal he thought at first that his insides were spilling out. When he was finished there was a hard ache down his back and his knees were weak. When he went outside, he found Lisette waiting for him by the door to the Ladies' Room. "I see you are gone," she said; "I wait for you here. I don't want to talk to those other boys."

Will didn't answer.

"In France," Lisette said, her eyes shining, "in the old villages they do never make the separation. It is the same toilet for men and women. It is much more better that way. Tell me, what do you do at the end of the ball?"

"I don't know," Will said.

"I don't know either," Lisette said.

They were standing close together near the wall under the staircase. Lisette's hand was hanging down by Will's leg.

"My parents are in Paris. I came without my parents," Lisette said. "It is against your mother's rules. You must not tell your mother. You won't?"

Will shook his head.

Then he thought, the hell with it.

"You want to meet me later and see the second part of the ball?" he said.

Lisette's eyes darkened. She scratched at his leg with one finger.

Three minutes later they were dancing again. Then in the backwash of costumes, moving ahead with Lisette through the skirts and swords and the other couples in the radiant silver glow, he knew without any warning at all that he was happy.

At nine-forty-five, two stories above the grand ballroom, Mrs. Lawson in the lavender suite struggled alone with her costume. Nothing on it worked—not a hook or an eye. Mrs. Lawson seriously regretted not having stuck to her original idea of going as Aunt Pittypat in *Gone With the Wind*. Instead she had picked an historical American figure. For six days she had been torn between Betsy Ross and Martha Washington. When she had not been able to make up her mind she had ordered a copy of the first American flag made along with the dress. Her plan was to wait and see. If she decided to go Betsy Ross she would carry the flag and if she decided to go Martha Washington she would wear it. She yanked the skirt down angrily now and set the bonnet over her hair and stepped in front of the mirror to get the general effect. She got it. She held the tears back and took off the bonnet. Then without hooking up any more of the dress she stepped out onto her terrace for a breath of air.

The music from the children's ball below had ceased and the hotel was quiet again, waiting. The ballroom and the main terrace were being swept and repolished for the main part of the ball. The training ship offshore with its birthday sign did look splendid, Mrs. Lawson thought. Then she turned to her right and cried out. She clutched the bodice of her costume around her throat. On the adjoining terrace an enormous man stood in green tights and a green top, a large letter *S* in red across his chest. He was posed in an attitude of flight. The blood in Mrs. Lawson's veins thinned as if it had been cut with water.

"Sorry," Donahue said.

Mrs. Lawson backed away from him into the lavender suite. She did not take her eyes off Donahue and she locked the terrace door after her.

Donahue chuckled. He flexed his arms a few times and shook his thighs loose and picked up his barbells. He kept a set of weights on the terrace in case he wanted to use them on his visits from the navy base. He did a dozen lateral swings now and after that a couple of dozen knee bends—not enough to work up a sweat, but enough so that the muscles would tense up and he would look his best in the costume. It had been Sylvia's idea that he dress as Superman. He had not suspected the bitterness in her suggestion and he was grateful to her for thinking of it.

Stretched on the green sofa wearing a bathrobe, Sylvia looked up from her crossword puzzle at her husband outside. Then she flicked off the light switch and sat in the semi-dark. Sylvia's face was full, but she looked drawn; the first months of pregnancy had gone easily for her; what made her look drawn, she knew, was not her own condition but her husband's. The fact of his approaching fatherhood had not altered Donahue's habits by one iota. What kind of dream was it to look like the manliest man in the world? What could possibly be the end of such a dream? . . .

For no apparent reason she shuddered.

Donahue was standing in the terrace doorway now with one arm high on the door. Silhouetted against the pale starlight outside, his muscled body looked like a cutout of Mr. America. "What's it called again?" he asked.

" 'Mother Courage.' "

Donahue squinted at the costume lying inside on the bed. "Just looks like a gunny sack to me."

"It is. I'm beginning to show quite a bit."

"What's the cart for?"

Sylvia said, "She sold old junk."

"You're not going to wheel a cart around the ballroom all night."

"I can't dance much. It's empty and it's only made out of balsa wood."

Donahue watched his wife. She was speaking with an odd quietness, he thought, and her eyes looked unusually soft.

"You're right to rest up," he said; "I got a feeling it's going to be one hell of a party."

Sylvia kept her head back watching him. She did not speak any more.

In the gold villa Juan Alberto sat frowning with a false gray beard on his chin and a partially empty bottle of Scotch in one hand. From across the room his brother approached him with a worried look.

The bedroom they were in was littered with tissue paper from the costume boxes. The door was closed. Juan Alberto wore golden armor with a gold spear and shield; he looked handsome as Don Quixote. José Ramón as Sancho Panza was wearing loose tights that hung down around his legs and a thin sash around the bulbous overly padded blouse with puffed sleeves. "Listen," he said. "Juanito."

Juan Alberto took a quick sip from the bottle without answering.

"I never saw you like this," José Ramón said, "I don't like it. You quit it now. Juanito, if *papá* won't see you, he won't."

Juan Alberto sat still, as if he had not heard. Then he took another sip.

"Listen, what good is it to act like that?" José Ramón said, his voice rising, "there's nothing more to do. Listen . . . you flew to Madrid; you brought the lawyer. . . . You cashed in all the stocks that were left . . . there's money for a bribe if he needs a bribe. What else can you do? Ah? Juanito?"

Without altering his expression Juan Alberto glanced at the closed door behind them.

José Ramón followed his gaze. "That's the point," he said, "to keep it from *mamá*. We'll go through the ball, like you said, as if nothing were wrong. He'll get out of it. *Papá* can get out of it. Believe me . . ."

Juan Alberto lifted the bottle to his lips and took another light swig.

"Is it so awful?" José Ramón said. "It's the same as before . . . he wouldn't let you go with them on the trip. If he's in trouble now, why should he see you? He's right to refuse —you *know* he doesn't want you mixed up with the police. When he gets help, he'll see you."

"Gets help from where?" Juan Alberto said, motionless.

José Ramón opened his mouth to answer. Nothing came out.

Across the short space of lawn, Jim Lepard sat outside on the porch of his villa drinking a vodka martini and taking in the scenery. A few other people had come out and were standing around on the lawn sipping drinks.

Jim let his eyes travel like a radar beam making bips from villa to villa; he was thinking that when he got too nervous there was nothing that calmed him down like an hour in the sack with a truck driver; only there weren't any truck drivers left to choose from around the hotel. Watching the villas he sipped his martini and went over his assets and liabilities. There were not many in the first category. The summer had been a disaster for him and he knew it; his affair with the rich decorator was over. The decorator had never believed Jim's story about having an allergic reaction to *fala* grass; he had suspected Jim of another reason for wanting to be alone. It was the poison grass that had ended their relationship. Like most good liars, Jim Lepard could not stand being accused of lying when he was telling the truth, and he had told the interior decorator to take his money and his prestige and his clothes and go fuck himself. He had spoken too quickly and the middle-aged decorator was now interested in another young man. Jim Lepard was left in a bad situation—his money was dwindling and so were his contacts. He had stayed on at the hotel only in order not to miss the ball. Afterwards he would have to go back to the States and find a job.

In the brightly lit night he put one foot up on the porch railing and crossed his legs. He had long perfect legs. They looked elegant now in the *traje de luces*. There was no doubt that he could get himself taken care of tonight if he could find somebody he wanted to trick with. The suit of lights, made to his measurements, was deep pink, with side panels and epaulettes of heavy silver embroidery. There was something about going as a pink bullfighter that amused Jim

Lepard. He had long had a theory that at least half of all Spanish bullfighters were gay—and half of American boxers. He liked to make educated guesses about men's secrets. You could tell many things if you trained yourself to be observant, he felt; the most common beliefs about homosexuality were untrue. You couldn't know nearly as much from a man's movements or speech as you could by the thing that happened in the fraction of an instant when he first looked at you. Sometimes it was as if the knowledge were looking out from behind the man's eyes against his will. Like the stocky one over there, he thought—the man who had glanced across twice in the five minutes since Jim had come out on the porch. Jim Lepard had seen occasional signs of interest in several people in the hotel who didn't know it about themselves.

He had for instance seen it in the boy called Will—only he couldn't see doing anything about it. Will was even younger than the age referred to among homosexuals as "chicken." Tipping the scales at his age could easily knock the boy for a loop, and besides, curiosity about men wasn't going to be a permanent state in Will's case. Certain natures ought to be let alone, Jim believed; he was not an overly moral man but he did have standards. It might have been fun to give Will a couple of lessons, but it would have made Jim uncomfortable knowing what the boy would go through later. It wasn't worth it. Or it hadn't been worth it so far. His not seducing Will was one of the nicer gestures of Jim's life —he had never been aware of having a conscience before, and it pleased him. The trouble was it also aroused him, and badly as he wanted it he did not feel like paying for sex tonight. Alonso the English-speaking lifeguard had turned out to be available at a price, but what Jim wanted tonight was in another category.

There were a few more people on the lawn strolling around in their costumes. There were no attractive men. Eugenia the maid walked among the guests like a figure in mourning. She had put on a new black uniform. Seeing her, Jim drew back involuntarily in his chair. The twisted side of her face was exaggerated in the bright canopy of lights over her head. She stopped by one of the porches to talk to a costumed guest. Jim didn't know the person but he thought he could make a good guess as to the subject. Eugenia only talked about one of three things: companionship, relaxation, goods for sale. That is, sex, dope or contraband jewelry. She had made a fair name for herself in the last weeks as a dealer in almost anything of an illicit nature; she usually had

Alonso the bilingual lifeguard or the pretty little maid in tow, like walking advertisements, or in case she needed to speak English. The lifeguard was waiting for Eugenia on the main path, Jim noticed—and the little maid was standing only a few feet away. Her uniform was pushed out in the bodice by a brassiere that was padded to make her smallish breasts seem larger. Alonso was dressed up as an American cowboy; he was straddling the path and he looked very much as if he had rolled up a pair of socks and stuck them inside the front of his pants as a codpiece. Jim leaned his chin on his hand and chuckled. There wasn't a single thing in the hotel that was what it looked like, he thought.

Or was there?

It was a night to wonder. It was a night to find out.

Two hundred meters away, in the deep light of the red villa, Helen stepped in front of her dressing table. She adjusted the midriff of the costume she had just put on, and stepped back again.

Over two stiffly starched organdy petticoats the red silk floated down over her body onto the hoop; the dress was as light as a bubble of blood. Helen turned around once in it. It moved perfectly.

She thanked the couturier and his assistant who were standing behind her.

When they had gone, she picked up a glassful of champagne that she had left standing beside her makeup kit. Then she decided against it. She had finished with her lipstick and she didn't need a last sip of champagne. She wasn't nervous.

She had started to put the glass back down when the screen door slammed behind her. She did not drop the glass.

The annoyance that filled her mind was not without a certain calm. She guessed without looking who had come in. She should have expected it. Once, years ago, before the Mardi Gras ball in New Orleans, she had heard a door slam like this and had known then too that her daughter had come into the room. You know certain things because you know them, she thought; because you can't help but know them.

Then she glanced in the mirror at the woman standing behind her. Alice looked exactly as she would have to look—dirty, scruffy, the bluejeans caked with mud and the face white and streaked with dust from the road. She looked edgy about something. She was waiting for her mother to speak.

Helen lifted a traveling clock from her dressing table and looked at the time. It was ten minutes to ten.

She did not turn immediately to face her daughter in the doorway.

At eleven o'clock the mezzanine floor of the grand ballroom was empty except for the orchestra playing lightly over the people below. There were thirty tables set in the curve of the mezzanine with chairs. All the chairs were empty now except one.

Will sat alone at a table watching the guests arrive. Below him the ballroom was filling slowly from the black staircase. There was beginning to be a disgruntled feel about the room. The more important guests were the latecomers; several of them looked offended that there was no one to meet them at the bottom of the stairs.

Half an hour later the ballroom was almost full and Helen had still not arrived. Couples were talking to each other and champagne was being served, but it was apparent that the party was not off to a good start. The coordinating force of a host or hostess was felt more in its absence than it would have been by being present. Helen was to have given the signal to the orchestra conductor for the start of the dancing; no one had given it for her, and the orchestra was still playing watery background music. In one corner, men with cameras and TV equipment stood awkwardly, not knowing who to take pictures of. Now and then if a face was well known, a single flashbulb would go off, but most of the famous guests weren't recognizable behind their masks. Through the sound of chatter there was a disappointed mumbling.

Twenty-five minutes later Will had risen from his chair and was looking down at a still-born party. He was seriously worried for the outcome. He had never known his mother to be late this way. He did not see how she—or anyone, for that matter—could do anything to revive the feeling of gaiety. The forced chatter that drifted up from the crowd to the mezzanine had the flat sound of boredom in it; several people were yawning. No one was laughing. He saw the party dead.

Then he saw Helen.

She had come in from the mouth of the black tunnel; she took the room in at a glance. You could tell that she knew how late she was. Her arms were straight out in front of her and she was pushing people out of her way with a minimum of politeness. She crossed the floor to the black staircase and started up fast. Several people turned to look at her, but she paid no attention. When she got to the top of the stairs, she moved along the mezzanine to the orchestra conductor and gave him an order. He lifted his baton. The music stopped. After a moment the orchestra struck the kind of blast given before a speech. Below, people shushed each other, and the entire room turned slowly to face Helen, who was standing at the top of the staircase with her hands raised. A silence settled over the guests. Will held his breath.

Helen waited another few seconds.

"Dinner will be ready shortly," she said. "My apologies for being late . . . I've been on long distance. My father died in our old plantation home in New Orleans. I know you all feel for me. I'd rather not speak of it. I want you to have a good time . . . I'll feel better for being with you. . . ." She paused.

Then she took her mask off and in one easy sweeping motion she started slowly down the black staircase. When she did so, the orchestra began to play dance music above her. Helen continued to move without hurrying into the center of the waiting people. In the wide red dress, her own hair encased in a soft dark wig, she looked as beautiful as Will had ever seen her. There was a certain sadness in her smile.

Flashbulbs popped and the room responded as one person. People pushed forward to the bottom of the stairs to Helen, their hands held out. She walked straight into the crowd.

From the edge of the mezzanine, Will watched his mother stroll among her guests; she carried a sort of gentle warmth with her, touching a hand here, nodding there, soothing important people's nerves. She looked like the hostess of the world, Will thought; she didn't stop until she had acknowledged the couples and groups of people all over the room. On her way, she passed the cameramen and made a few discreet suggestions to them. Within minutes, more flashbulbs were going, the klieg lights for the TV cameras were lit, and many people were dancing.

As soon as his mother had come to a halt, Will joined her below. It was as if the room had been given a jolt of electricity, he saw. There wasn't any doubt that the party had been brought back to life, and Helen had done it. The guests who weren't dancing milled together happily; the ones around Helen were watching her. "What a wonderful woman," Will heard one whisper.

Helen introduced him and he shook hands several times. Helen did not stop smiling. She looked so startlingly beautiful that even Will was amazed. It was another fifteen minutes before they had a moment alone.

"Is your father dead?" Will said.

"I don't know," Helen said, nodding at another couple, "I never met him."

"What made you late?"

"Your sister had a problem. *Bon soir, Claire* . . ."

"Isn't she . . ."

"No," Helen said. "She won't have time . . . we'll get along without her. Don't you have a date?"

Will flushed.

"It's all right," Helen said. "It's that girl, isn't it? . . . the one you liked. I expected you'd ask her to come later. Run along. And have fun." She touched Will's shoulder with her hand.

As he started away, Will saw Juan Alberto step up to his mother through the crowd. The man's eyes were glazed and it was apparent that he had been drinking. "You look . . ." Juan Alberto shut his mouth and stood speechlessly in front of her. "You are very handsome," he said finally.

Helen turned to him as if in surprise. Then she smiled.

"I have a message for you," she said.

Will went back up to wait for Lisette. He was wondering why she hadn't shown before now; but when he got to the top of the stairs he saw her waiting for him in the shadows of the mezzanine. He grinned; then within a few feet of her he stopped grinning. He stood across from an empty table from Lisette and all at once he knew what it was that was strange about her. He had had it somewhere in the back of his mind all along.

Lisette was no longer wearing her shepherdess costume; she had changed into some kind of court lady. She had on lipstick and a brocade dress and she wore a small rhinestone tiara. "*Je t'attendais.* Until after your mother had come," she said. "I knew you would have to be with her. Do I look all right?"

"Yes," Will said. "You look all right."

They stood across from each other with the table between them and Will watched her.

"We dance now?" she said.

"No," Will said. "Not any more. You know some other people here?"

". . . One or two."

"Special?"

"Yes," Lisette said, glancing over the railing. "One of them is special."

"Why did you lie?"

Lisette didn't answer.

"How old are you?"

She blushed a little.

"Sixteen?"

"I'll be nineteen in three months. I'm sorry I had to say I was younger. It was the only way I got my invitation. I was not the age for the children's ball and . . . I was not invited to this one. You understand? I had to come, you see."

"The special person?"

"He is the main reason," Lisette said. "Yes. I did not want him coming to the ball without me. We are . . . how do you say . . ." She shrugged.

"How old is he?" Will said.

"Twenty-six."

Will didn't say anything.

"But I am pleased to be with you. I can look for him later. It is like finding a brother; I can't tell you how nice it is. I always wanted a brother. Shall we . . ."

"I have a sister," Will said.

Lisette dropped her eyes. "You are angry . . . I can tell."

Will kept still.

". . . Maybe later we will meet and we will dance?"

"Maybe."

Lisette came around the table. As she passed him she kissed him quickly on the mouth. Will could feel one of her breasts pressing against his arm. Then she was gone.

He did not turn around to watch her go down the staircase or join the crowd.

For a while he sat down again at a mezzanine table watching the costumes below as they moved in time to the music. He did not consider about anything. After a few minutes the view of the ballroom became the vision he had had once before: a great many people were standing at the bottom of a big mosaic and everybody was busy in it but him. Again all the people were attacking one lone person in white who stood at the center. And again he could not see who the person in white was. He leaned over the railing and focused his eyes as if he expected the vision to become clear from watching. When the vision faded away from him again he was still looking at a swaying lake of costumes.

He saw Donahue and the two Guzmán brothers and Jim Lepard. There was Mrs. Lawson, old and disheveled-looking in a new American flag. Twice he caught sight of Lisette dancing with a tall man who had big shoulders and a shock of blond hair. There was Helen, the skirt of her red silk dress pumping up and down like the heart of the crowd, never dancing with the same man for more than a minute before another cut in. Mrs. Donahue walked at the edge of the dance floor pushing a little balsa-wood cart in front of her, and there was the Spanish woman who sometimes played bridge with Helen, made up as Marie Antoinette. Holtz moved among the crowd alone. He was dressed as a circus trainer and he carried a whip. The Guzmán brothers did look like Don Quixote and Sancho Panza from above. Will watched, but none of the people seemed to matter. The couples were hooked together; when the music stopped they unhooked and rehooked into different couples. They looked very intense about the whole thing, as if by coupling they were doing something very serious.

When some of the guests began to come up to the mezzanine to rest from their dancing, Will left it and wandered down; he walked among the people on the main floor. For some reason he did not want them to know that he was alone. He set his face in an important way and he kept moving. A group of people called him over to talk, but he explained that he was on this errand and he walked away in a straight line until those people were out of sight. He kept it up like that for an hour. Twice he passed the Guzmán brothers in a corner talking to a lady in a solid gold dress with a gold mask and silver hair. The second time he realized that the woman was their mother. So it was just as well that Littlejohn had not come to the ball, he thought. Or maybe it would not have mattered anyway. Maybe nothing of the things he had always thought mattered, mattered. Maybe this was the way it was: you talked or you danced, and life was a question of not looking as if you were by yourself. He went out on the terrace.

There were people there as well. Mrs. Donahue had come out and was standing near one end of it watching the navy ship over the water. She noticed Will and smiled the way she always did, without her eyes.

Will passed her and started back the other way. From the darkness on the water there was a snap and then a hard bump of air. A single point of light fizzed up the night and burst into color. The people on the terrace turned to see it. Will stood back against the building. The fireworks were in his honor: he had to get off the terrace, or people would make a fuss over him. He did not want to go back into the ballroom. He considered standing in the bushes by the side of the kitchen entrance. The first rocket was just an announcement of the rest, and for the time being the sky was black again. . . .

The dark terrace was like a flash of vistas one after another in which different people floated by. He stood or moved among them like a person apart. But he was not any longer a leftover person. He was an in-between man.

He knew it now. He was not the right age for anything, he never would be. He knew that it was nobody's fault and that it was his fate and his nature to be what he was.

And standing in the soft night air of the terrace without any particular thought in his head, he could tell curiously, as if the fact had been handed to him in a slick tight roll like a diploma, that no matter where he went or who he talked to for the rest of his life, he would always be in-between.

Donahue made his way through the people who were coming out on the terrace and walked toward his wife. Several women took him in with their eyes and dismissed him. He did not understand it. Donahue had a set party routine. He flirted with several women and made his choice toward the end of the evening—only it didn't look like he was going to have all that much choice this time. He would have to try a harder pitch soon. He would also have to find one of the men to cover for him—part of his routine was to get a buddy to say they were having a drink later in case Sylvia asked. He walked over the tiles feeling the first of the liquor settle into his legs. It was a good idea to pay attention to Sylvia at a party, though his wife didn't look upset this time, he thought; her face wore the same dreamy stare she had had upstairs before the ball started. "What are you looking at?"

"William," she said.

"Seems like a nice kid."

"Yes," Sylvia said quietly.

"How about another dance?"

Sylvia shook her head.

"All you danced was that once. With me. Why are you being so careful?"

"The last time I was pregnant it was after a dance that the trouble started."

". . . I almost forgot. Miami airport—time I turned on the jukebox while the plane was refueling. And then afterwards. You damn near died. . . ."

There was a puff of sound from the navy vessel, and another single rocket swam a slow wavering line up into the sky. It exploded into a blue spider.

Donahue put his right foot on the terrace ledge.

"A penny," he said uneasily. His wife standing so still facing out to sea was making him nervous. She had not lifted her eyes to follow the trail of the rocket.

"Pardon?" she said.

"What were you thinking about?"

"The future."

"Go on." Donahue leaned on top of his knee and grinned at her disarmingly. "Tell me about it. Tell me about the future. . . ."

Sylvia put a hand on the balsa-wood cart. "Do you want me to?"

"Sure."

"All right," she said. "I was thinking that you're not doing too well at the ball tonight. You'll get through it, though . . . in another two weeks, when your transfer comes through, we'll go to Germany."

"Will we?"

"Yes," Sylvia said. "We will. I'll have the baby there. I wasn't thinking about that—I don't have to. It'll be a perfectly normal birth. I'm scared I might abort again for no reason, and I'm a coward about pain, so I'll do just as the doctor says. I'm practical when I want to be. There won't be any problems. The baby won't abort."

Another rocket slid up, and Sylvia stared at the reflection on the surface of the water as if she had been reading something that was written there, and was momentarily blinded.

"Go ahead," Donahue said. He was still grinning.

"By then you'll have gone through all the eligible women within a hundred miles or so of Berlin, on the excuse that I've been pregnant and unable to go to bed with you."

Donahue tilted his head. "Excuse?"

"Yes," Sylvia said. "Not that you need one. But you'll use one. Only you won't be using it as much from now on. Less women will be interested in you as you grow older, and the ones who are won't stay interested long. You'll have to work harder to go on proving whatever it is you're trying to prove. . . . I'll take it for a few more years and then I'll ask you for a separation. I won't ask for a divorce. I'll tell myself that I don't like the idea of divorce. That'll be a lie, of course, but I won't know I'm lying by then. . . ."

"Hang on," Donahue said.

"No," Sylvia said quietly, "you asked. So we'll get the separation. . . . I'll take the child and live apart from you a few months . . . until I see what's happening to me, and what's happening to you—and then, I'll take you back. I'll think I'm doing it for your sake. . . . So I'll go on lying to myself, the same way I did when we first got married. I don't think I ever told you, but for ages I thought I'd married you for your money. . . . I hadn't, of course, I married you because I loved you, but I couldn't face that. . . ."

Sylvia paused again, as though the words she had been reading on the water were being projected by a film that was not moving fast enough. Donahue who had stopped grinning kept still. There had been no more rockets from the ship. She said:

"By then, your father will have made two or three more of his awkward business deals and there won't be as much money. . . . Maybe that will be good for us, I don't know. I don't think anything will be very good for us. . . . Only you've never had to think about money, so maybe it will be good for you to think about it a little. . . . We'll try, and someday I'll have a few affairs and then I'll have those to think about. We'll never be very happy together, but we won't be very unhappy either, because we're not very serious people. So we'll just live our lives, and I'll go on imagining that I married beneath me. We'll be fine, and our child will probably be brilliant. Except that he won't love either one of us, because silly people quite often have brilliant children, but that doesn't make them love you. We may have two or three children, though I hope not. . . . I suppose we ought to have two at least, so there'll be someone there to protect the first one from us. We'll be nasty by then. We won't hate each other. We'll just hate needing each other. We're not a nice couple."

Sylvia took a cigarette from the piece of gunny sack she was using for a purse and tapped it on her nail before she lit it.

Donahue looked at her a long moment without taking his foot off the ledge. There was a line of men cheering on the navy vessel. Three rockets shot up from the ship together and flowered in the sky, the sounds of their explosions coming down like hard knocks on the terrace. Donahue laughed, short. Then he grinned again. "That damn dead-pan sense of humor gets me every time. . . . I wish you'd quit staring at the water. . . ."

He took his foot off the ledge.

"Hey," he said, "look. Joking aside. Don't you want to see the fireworks?"

Helen put her hand out to signal, but Will didn't see her. He was sliding behind the people against the back wall on the other end of the terrace. As the sky turned into a vibrating cascade of colors, at the first big climax of the fireworks display, she saw Will slink off the terrace and disappear into the bushes by the servants' entrance of the hotel. Helen shook her head. He was a hard boy to understand. There was no use chasing after him, she knew.

Behind her, Lincoln Warren said, "I been saving the one about this man—comes to a gas station in the desert? So he walks in, see. He just walks in . . ."

Helen closed her eyes and swallowed. It was not easy to remember what she had been thinking of last month when she had imagined marrying a man like Lincoln Warren. It was true she was tired of her present life, but there were limits. Standing in the uncertain light of the rockets, she thought that if she had her choice between facing starvation again —and Lincoln Warren—there wouldn't be any choice. Lincoln was a testament to something. It took a special man, she thought, a particular kind of human being to want to go on telling stories right through a firework display. Not the sort of man you could live with even long enough to divorce him. Lincoln Warren was rich enough to command a captive audience in several cities—probably in one or two countries. Helen had a second's horror of the effect of power in the wrong hands. Another rocket sizzled in the sky and Lincoln put four fleshy fingers in the crook of her arm.

"Listen," he said, "how about, after you get rid of all these people, we have a nightcap? What . . ."

Helen pulled back involuntarily from him and bumped into a hard flat stomach just behind her. "Mrs. Locke has promised to join *us* for a nightcap when the ball is over," a voice said; "I'm sorry we cannot ask you to join us. We always play one quick rubber of bridge after parties here. It is an old Spanish custom . . ."

"Is?" Lincoln Warren said. "Bridge?"

Juan Alberto leaned over the hoop of her dress and pressed forward against her for an instant before coming around to one side. "Unless of course you'd rather forget it . . ."

"No," Helen said. "Goodness no; I want to play." She smiled at Juan Alberto and emptied the last sip out of her champagne glass onto the terrace floor behind her.

"Would you mind getting me another drink?" she said to Lincoln after the noise of the next rocket had died down.

"Sure not," Lincoln said. "Be glad to. As the ten-year-old girl says at . . ."

"Thank you," Helen said. "The bar's right across the ballroom; or one of the waiters will get it for you. . . ." She turned away.

"An old Spanish custom?" she said to Juan Alberto when Lincoln had gone.

Juan Alberto laughed. "I don't even know how bridge is played," he said. "You would be surprised at what tourists will believe if you tell them it's an old Spanish custom. I saw you needed to be rescued."

"That's nice of you."

"No," he said. "It is not nice. Watching to see that you are all right is the least I can do after what you told me."

"I didn't tell you much. That things are better, that's all. Still not perfect, perhaps; but better. My daughter wanted you to know."

"It may not be much to you," Juan Alberto said. "It is much to me. I was . . . not happy. I had been drinking steadily."

"You looked it. You still do."

Juan Alberto grinned. "It is different. Before I was drinking to forget. Now I celebrate."

"Anyway, it was bright of you to know I needed rescuing. Good guesswork."

"You don't think," Juan Alberto said slowly, staring at her, "it was guesswork."

Another small series of rockets put an artificial pink into the sky. Helen lifted her shoulders. "I ought to be blushing," she said. "I don't feel like it."

"No. Nor I," Juan Alberto said, "I do not even feel like lying—I was not watching you out of gratitude. I have been watching you for six weeks."

Helen held his look without blinking.

A couple of people behind them laughed and a feeble trio of rockets fizzed out above the ship.

Juan Alberto stared at her. "Couldn't *we* have a drink later?"

"There is that possibility," Helen said.

"You have other plans?"

"I have other things to think about. Besides . . . there are some men who get drunk and just pass out. Then there are men it isn't safe to have a drink with."

"I am one of those?"

Helen smiled. "You think you are. You probably will be when you grow up."

"It is beneath you to dismiss me as a child."

"I didn't dismiss you," she said.

"What should I do then?"

Helen stepped around Juan Alberto and put her hand out to a French lady who had been left standing by herself on the terrace. "I have other guests—*hasta otro día.* You're not my only problem."

"Now you are insulting."

"I'm a hostess."

"I'll stop drinking. I'll wait all night."

"Will you?" Helen paused on the other side of Juan Alberto.

"I'll grow tired of waiting, but I'll wait."

The edge of a smile flashed again over Helen's mouth and disappeared. "I think so," she said.

She left him there and went to speak to the French lady.

By the kitchen entrance off the terrace Eugenia stood watching the first of the grand explosions that would become the finale of the fireworks. It looked as if the world had been blown apart, and all that was left of it was a maze of false color. She yawned.

There were several things left to do tonight, but not while the display was going on. Later she had to find Alonso the lifeguard and the little maid; they were busy now making up to people in the grand ballroom, but she had news for them. They had been hired as a team of lovers to perform later for the French couple that was occupying the white villa. The little maid wasn't going to like it, but there it was. Alonso wouldn't mind—he enjoyed being watched. The French couple had invited two other people as well. Then if the sexual exhibition turned into the sort of orgy that was expected, the performers' price would go up from five thousand pesetas apiece to ten thousand, of which Eugenia would get half. And it was almost a sure thing, she thought. She recognized the signs. She had obtained a quarter kilo of marijuana, at the French couple's request, an ounce of opium and three boxes of an English drug that was a chemical called amyl nitrite. Except for heart patients, amyl nitrite had only one use. She had just come from the white villa where she had ordered a king-size mattress put on the floor in the living room. The mattress was covered by a silk quilt, and she had seen to it that the white draperies formed a solid line on all the windows. No one could see in; the white villa was safe. The goods had been left in sealed boxes on the cocktail table, except for the opium which was in a plastic envelope in the dresser drawer of the first bedroom, under Madame's silk underwear. Eugenia had added a few sticks of incense as a touch of her own, to cover any remaining smells of drugs when the morning came. *Y ya 'stá,* she thought: So that's that. All that was left now was to tell Alonso and the little maid.

In the inverted cup of the sky a variety of artificial tones flared over her like a prism from hell. The noise was deafening; the earth seemed to have opened and gorged up everything false at one time. There were evil forces out tonight, she knew. She wondered how many of the guests were aware of the powers present among them.

Then she stepped back so suddenly that she almost fell over a bush. Her heart rushed forward within her and she could hear herself breathing. In the reflected glow of the fireworks she had seen something move. Her right hand went up as if by itself to cross herself. She jerked the hand back down to her side. She had not made the sign of the cross since the day she had spoken to the angel under the tree, and she did not intend to start now. The thing that was sitting there, between the two waxy-leaved bushes by the kitchen entrance of the hotel, would not harm her. Eugenia had been aware for some weeks that one or two invisible demons followed her wherever she went.

The sky blazed brighter and her heart slowed to its normal pace. Then she set her eyes on the pair of bushes where she had seen the thing. She could barely make it out, but it wasn't gone. It had been slinking along the kitchen by the steps. She saw its shape clearly through the two bushes in a burst of light. The chill that ran through her was left over from another time in her life. Then the small blue devil turned, and she saw its face.

She put her head back slowly and laughed at herself. There was a shout from the terrace and the sound of applause. Two huge images of the American flag and the Spanish flag appeared together in full color in the sky; the two flags marked the last flourish of the long display. As they began to fade, Eugenia turned and walked toward the terrace. She did not glance again at the devil behind the bush. Though she had been fooled this once, she knew that the bad angel was not far away; he was in control tonight and his forces were out in the world. She stepped up onto the terrace.

She was glad that she had not crossed herself. She grinned again into the bright tortured air over the hotel.

At five a.m., as the last of the guests milled about between the ballroom and the terrace, Helen stood quietly just inside the doorway. She was free to leave, she knew; there was no more reason for her to stay with these last few stragglers—

the important guests had already gone and most of the ones who were left now were disappointed drunks.

The ballroom looked as if a team of vengeful elves had been playing tag in it all night. Paper streamers were stewn about the floor in a thick layer from wall to wall. Confetti littered the staircase. The few remaining guests sat in window seats or stood on the terrace speaking in low voices as though they were afraid they would disappear with the night. Over the water, a cooling freshness had begun to take on a visible tone that was still too faint to be called light.

Helen put a fist into the ache of tiredness in her back. She glanced at Will who was sitting at the bottom of the staircase. The ball had been a success. By tomorrow the columnists in the Paris and London and Rome papers would be telling most of the other newspapers and magazines what to think. The party was "in"—Helen's life was going to be all the more tricky from now on. During the next week she had interviews with *Newsweek* magazine and *Paris-Match*. An Italian reporter from the *Corriere della Sera* had come up to her a while ago asking for an hour of her time. She would have to be sparing about interviews; too much coverage was worse than none: vulgarity would offend the right people. If she had to plan on doing this for the rest of her life—and it was beginning to look that way—she would have to be careful now. . . .

"*Señora, no sabe usted el gusto que me ha dado; espero que me va a permitir verla otra vez antes de marcharme.*"

Helen lifted her hand and gave it to the man to kiss. She applied a gentle pressure to his fingers afterwards, and she smiled. It was Eduardo Morilla, the *Subsecretario* of the Ministry who had talked to her so often on the phone. She had seen him several times since he had come to the hotel. It was Morilla she had called in for assistance just before the ball, when Alice had arrived with her problem at the red villa. He was in his early forties; not handsome but not a bad-looking man, she thought. Clean, anyway, and lean. She guessed from the way he kissed her hand that he had probably come up from a lower-class beginning to his present position; he didn't have the middle-class habit of leaving damp lips too long on her knuckles—or the aristocrat's trick of raising the hand all the way to the mouth and then not kissing it.

He was waiting for her to answer. She murmured, dropping her arm to her side, "*Quizás mañana.*"

Morilla eyed her acutely. He had just expressed a wish to see her again before leaving the hotel, and he had phrased it in the most formal manner possible—but she knew what it meant. In asking his help for Alice, Helen had had to tell Morilla at least one lie that put her own reputation in a doubtful light. She'd have to fix that before the *Subsecretario* left, and it wasn't going to be easy to fix. It would take some explaining.

"I shall go to my suite," Morilla said in English. "I shan't go to bed yet. I thought perhaps to watch the dawn. . . ." He allowed the sentence to trail off with just the tinge of a question in its tone.

Helen kept her smile. "I hope you enjoy it," she said; "I'll be asleep."

Morilla bowed. "Tomorrow then. Today, that is. Unless of course you find that you *cannot* sleep. You have had a difficult evening—especially before the ball. Such an unfortunate incident. There is an old Galician lullaby . . . I could sing it over the telephone."

"Goodnight," Helen said, a little sharply. Morilla was doing it on purpose now. Yes, she would change him before he left. A contact in the Ministry was one thing; but he would have to think of her as innocent, even if she had to go to bed with him to convince him of it.

Morilla withdrew, bumping into Donahue who stood wavering drunkenly behind him. "Hey, listen," Donahue said. He took Helen's hand in a double American handshake. "Some party," he said. "Just no kidding. Some party."

Helen looked at him steadily. He wasn't really drunk, she saw, just high and feeling no pain. He wasn't going to be trouble. "I'm glad you liked it, thank you for coming."

She smiled and turned away before he could make his usual fumbling pass. Holtz the hotel owner was waiting at her other side. He did not touch her. He only wrung his own hands together. "Madame, Madame," he said.

". . . You're pleased?"

"Pleased? *Gott*—I don't know what to say," Holtz said. "If there is anything . . ."

"No, thank you," Helen said, "you've already done it."

Holtz bowed. He knew what she was referring to. He too had helped her with Alice's problem. "Nothing at all. In me you will find that you always have a friend." He backed away and went off to talk to the assistant manager.

"*Bueno?*" a voice behind her said quietly.

Helen did not turn. "*Estás allí todavía?*"

"*Claro. Ya te lo dije.*"

"*Me dijiste . . . ?*"

"*Que te esperaba toda la noche.*"

"You say 'all night' as if it were such a long time," Helen said, turning to face him. "Is one night so long to wait?"

"I'll wait all year. Only . . . do you have someone to accompany you back to your villa?"

"Of course."

Juan Alberto's face fell.

"My son," Helen said; "I gave the ball in his honor, you know."

Juan Alberto's eyes sharpened. "Will he be staying with you long . . . ?"

"At five o'clock in the morning?" Helen said. "He should have been in bed hours ago."

"If I came to the front door in a few minutes, would he . . ."

"Yes," Helen said. "He would. So would the people in about three other villas. It's almost dawn. My villa faces the hotel. The back door. The shrubbery is high there, and there's a tree. Goodnight now." She added wryly, "And please give my respects to your mother."

"My mother has already retired." Juan Alberto bent over her hand.

He didn't kiss it. He brushed his lips over it, and returned it to her like a napkin he had borrowed. There ought to be a study made of hand kissing, Helen thought. Juan Alberto's would improve with age. He hadn't learned enough yet, that was all. His own hand had been trembling.

She turned from him and went to Will who was sitting on the bottom step of the black staircase.

On the way up the gravel path to the red villa, she asked, "Have a good time?"

"Sure." Will's voice was hard.

She glanced at him. Probably he hadn't hit it off with the French girl, she thought. Well, it was his first girl—and it was his private business.

"Anything you want to talk about?" She stopped in front of the red gate.

Will shook his head no.

She leaned down and kissed him.

"Thanks for the party," Will said.

She curtsied. "I like you," she said when she straightened. "You're turning into a very attractive young man."

Will hunched up his shoulders and walked away in the gravel. Yes, he was unhappy about something. Further up the path she saw him arch his back and stiffen his spine. The gesture touched her so that she wanted to call out to him to come back. She did not call; she watched him disappear around a car.

Inside the villa, she freshened herself in the bathroom. Then standing in the bright lights of her dressing room she paused. Something new had come about: she was sleepy. The time it would take to go through a ritual seduction scene with a new lover was suddenly not worth it. Nor was the time afterwards that would be spent talking and smoking and waiting endless boring moments until the new lover could politely put his clothes on and leave. Nothing was worth it—not compared to the cool fresh linen of a quiet bed and going to sleep. It was the first time in Helen's life that she had felt like this, and she pondered over it for a moment. The masked ball had been a triumph, but the strain was showing at her age. She did not need to see her face to know that her eyes looked puffy and her mouth looked hard.

All at once she felt stupid. The evening as a whole came back to her and she knew that it was not going to end the way she had planned it.

She lit a cigarette, and automatically repaired the line of her left eyebrow in the mirror. After that she wandered slowly into the living room. She continued into the kitchen and unhooked the back door. She hesitated a moment, still thinking, before she opened it.

The man slipped past her, shadowlike, and Helen closed the door and latched it loosely. She turned to avoid him and walked back into the living room. She stood between a table and a wall.

The room was dark, with only the edge of dawn like a champagne glow in the window. Juan Alberto stood in the center of the room. He had taken off his armor and his Don Quixote beard. He was standing with his legs wide apart and his face shone with excitement.

"I have an apology to make," she said. "The answer is no."

Outside, another tired guest crunched up the gravel path.

"I don't understand," Juan Alberto said, low.

"It's simple," Helen said. "I was hoping it would happen; I was wrong. I'm not going to bed with you."

Juan Alberto's forehead wrinkled finely. He was far from sober, but he held his liquor well, she saw. His big hands lifted a few inches and slid down the hips of his costume. He repeated the gesture twice; he was looking for the pockets of his trousers. "If I've said something to . . ."

"Oh no," she said. "Not at all. It has nothing to do with you."

"Fifteen minutes ago . . . you seemed to think . . ."

"I hate these conversations," Helen said. "A thing works out or it doesn't."

Juan Alberto looked away from her at the wall and then at the floor. His face was angry and young. Helen waited.

"I want you," he said, "very much."

Helen watched the lithe hard figure, the young man straining at her through the dawn, and knew that he was not lying.

"That makes no difference," she said. "I'm sorry."

After a few seconds Juan Alberto moved away from her to the doorway. He watched her for a moment more. Then he opened the kitchen door and went outside the way he had come in. The door flapped shut behind him. A silence followed.

Helen reached up slowly and closed the curtains of the red villa.

Juan Alberto kicked at the gravel path and took the five steps leading to the main terrace in two quick bounds. He strode on hearing the surf and noticing, with some remote and angry part of himself, that he was being watched from the beach. He was not the only one, he saw, who had returned to the main building from the red villa. Helen's son Will was sitting by himself in the sand, his profile to the terrace. He had his arms clasped over his knees and his tail stretched out behind him; he was only looking with the edges of his eyes, but he was fully aware of Juan Alberto's return. Juan Alberto stopped at the first terrace corner and returned his look. The boy's face went red and he moved his head and stared out at the sea.

Juan Alberto turned the corner and walked along parallel to the beach. He went slower, taking in the people on the terrace with quick scrutiny. There were three couples; he could see through the windows of the ballroom two more, as well as four or five single people. Donahue was standing talking to a very pretty redhead.

It took Juan Alberto exactly ten minutes to take her away from him.

Half an hour later in a magenta-colored bedroom on the second floor of the main building, the redhead said, "I'm scared."

"Because?"

The redhead, whose name he didn't know, crossed the

room uncertainly and kicked off the slippers of her ballerina costume. "Maybe it's the sort of . . . the way you look at me," she said.

Juan Alberto could not think of an answer. When the redhead came back, he put an arm behind her and drew her to him slowly with his legs spread.

Walking down the passage to the suite where his wife lay asleep, Donahue thought he could not understand it at all. He had taken careful stock of the people at the party; with no close second, he had been the best-looking man there. And still Juan Alberto had taken that last broad away from him. It wasn't a thing you could explain.

The liquor in his legs was singing gently through his whole body. He let himself into the green suite and went to look at Sylvia in the bedroom. She was sleeping in a peaceful way, one arm thrown over her face.

Donahue went into the bathroom and undressed and took a cold shower. It didn't help. There wasn't any explaining a failure like tonight. Standing in front of the full-length mirror, he lifted the towel away from his body. It was an indisputable fact—he was good looking. His sun-tanned skin had a luminescent tone, a deep tawny shine that made the muscles appear tense all the time. Straightening, he stroked the hard ripples in his belly down to where the hair began. What woman wouldn't want to get her hands on a hunk like that, he thought. Under his hand, his cock stirred once as if it agreed with him. Donahue turned quickly away.

There wasn't any use thinking about it; in town he knew a bar that would open soon where you could get a whore at any hour of the day. He put on a T-shirt and a pair of khakis and shoes.

Cutting across the empty lawns toward the coastal road, he thought that it must be the hotel that had brought him bad luck. Maybe it was just that kind of party—older people, or society people, or what the hell.

But no. Hell no.

No, damn it, he thought, just no. It didn't matter what kind of people they were. He struck out at a thick branch of a bush beside him. The branch broke off in his hand. Look at that, he thought—make sense out of that. So you're a little drunk, so what? You are still the best-looking big sonofabitch anybody ever saw in their goddamn life—how the hell did you get left alone?

Behind him a quiet voice said intelligently, "I think you're the best-looking man I ever saw in my life. Don't tell me you got left alone."

For a moment Donahue thought the voice had spoken out of his own head. He stopped and looked behind him. The lawns were deserted all the way back to the main building. There was no one in sight.

Then just beyond the bush, perched on a low stoop, he saw the sleek elegant leg and the dark flat bullfighter's slipper.

The beach in front of the hotel was clean and sparkling by eight a.m. Will did not mind the feel of the sand under his costume. He liked the empty look of the coast. Everyone else in the hotel had gone to bed; the sun was up and the Navy ship had long been gone. Will thought about the fireworks for a while. Then he snapped a piece of driftwood in two. With one end of it he scratched in the sand:

> AND THE ROCKETS RED GLARE
>
> THE BOMBS BURSTING IN AIR
>
> GAVE PROOF THROUGH THE NIGHT
>
> THAT OUR FLAG WAS STILL THERE

but he could not get over the feeling of something left unfinished. He erased that, and wrote a list.

> IN BETWEEN
>
> IN BETWEEN
>
> IN BETWEEN
>
> IN BETWEEN
>
> IN BETWEEN

Then he yawned and added something to each pair of words. When he was finished the message read:

> IN BETWEEN WARS
>
> IN BETWEEN SEXES
>
> IN BETWEEN COUNTRIES
>
> IN BETWEEN LIFE AND DEATH
>
> IN BETWEEN A CENTURY

He smoothed over half the sand and tried adding other words to the same first pairs. The possibilities were endless.

Sea gulls were calling now over the shore as the sun rose higher. After a while in the morning silence a fishing boat could be seen. The air was fresh.

The in-between man got up and brushed the sand from his costume. He walked up the beach to the deserted terrace. Of all the clefts in his life, the worst was the split between the kind of person he was and the kind he would like to be. He wished he was an intelligent person, and he wanted to look like a Greek god. At the rate he was going, he wouldn't be either, he thought. He would be the sort of person who spends his life watching other people live.

The hotel was deserted in the bright morning sun. Nothing stirred on any of the lawns or paths. Walking up the steps of the blue villa Will thought that he did not see how much longer things could go on jockeying for position in his mind. His brain itself would split if he let it go too long. He would become a crazy person: a schizophrenic. When he heard the laugh, it was almost like he was expecting it.

It wasn't like the other time—the night he had watched at the brown villa. This time, when he heard the voice, he went back outside and stood on his own back lawn. He did not mean to spy on anybody. He just recognized Donahue's laugh and wanted to know what Donahue was doing in the pink villa.

He didn't knock. He didn't go in. The shades were up and the living room was empty; so was the first bedroom. The dressing room was not. The shades were pulled down in front of it, and he walked around to the second bedroom and looked through the screen. The bedroom door opened into the dressing room. He could see at an angle about a third of both. At first he did not believe what he saw, and when he did believe it, he thought it was a trick the light had made. Then he squinted at the view. Donahue was standing in front of the wall-length dressing-room mirror. He had taken a stance and his arms were lifted high, the muscles bulging, in the pose of a Greek god throwing a spear; he was admiring what he saw in the mirror. Jim Lepard was kneeling in front of him. When Will saw what Jim Lepard was doing, he opened his mouth and something broke inside him that was never repaired. It did not need to be repaired. For a few seconds he couldn't move. Then he heard the voice.

"Yeah," Donahue said. "Suck it, baby."

Will turned and began to walk back toward the beach.

After a while he picked up speed; he did not stop to think and he did not hesitate.

In the clear blue day he walked along the coast out of the hotel. By the time he passed the last of the villas, he was running.

NINE

Alice

ON THE DAY of their departure from Spain Alice had felt a surge of lightness as the motor started and they left the hotel dock. She watched the bright colored buildings and the land disappearing in the spray and it seemed to her that Guzmán had got away and that she had been a part of his escape; she looked back at Will standing alone on the dock and she waved through the fan of water that rose in the wake of the launch.

Then she turned and joined Guzmán at the wheel in the inside cabin.

The air smelled clean and the boat was large. As soon as they were out of the docking area of the hotel Guzmán put one arm around her and they stood for a time facing the horizon of gray-green water.

The haziness of the day was pleasant on the surface of the sea. Two gulls flew squawking ahead and then fell behind and hung suspended like paper kites crisscrossing over their wake; the breeze was cool. It was nearly an hour before they saw the coast guard boat approaching from the east. Guzmán did not say anything when it appeared; his arm hardened around her. Then the arm dropped away.

"Let them see you," he said. "Go back and wave like a tourist."

She took one of the fishing poles—the largest she could find—but instead of going back, she walked the thin gunwale of the launch up ahead to the prow. Guzmán slowed down, as if to make ready for trolling. Alice stood in front of the cabin holding the fishing pole in front of her with the wind molding her dress hard against her body. When the coast guard boat drew near she raised one arm over her head. After the boat had passed she went back into the cabin. Guzmán was grinning. She had almost never seen him grin before. "I don't think they noticed our direction," she said.

"No," Guzmán said, "they will not notice anything for at least an hour. *Que sinvergüenza eres.*"

"A what?"

"A shameless. You are often full of guilt, but you have no shame. You are the opposite of Spanish. I'm fond of you."

"Is fond all?"

"No," he said.

"I don't always like it when you talk."

"There is not much breeze out here. The water should be calm off the coast. We may have to spend the night on the beach. I won't talk," he said.

When they were another half hour out he cut the motor. They floated a while in the wash of the open sea. Guzmán stood in the stern and scanned the water. For three hundred and sixty degrees the sea was empty. He opened the ice chest. There were airholes in it. She helped him undo the padlock and lay back the lid. From the flat cushions inside Pepe Luis blinked up at the sunlight. Something behind his eyes tried to smile, but it was too weak and sleepy.

"Can you lie there with the lid open till dark?" Guzmán said in Spanish.

Pepe Luis gave a nod.

"We may have to close it again. If the coast guard comes back. Or the Moroccan coast guard. We'll be lying off a cove inside the coastal waters. Are you familiar with the shoals there?"

Pepe Luis stared up at Guzmán as if he had not understood the question.

"No," Guzmán said slowly. "You never fished that close to Morocco."

He left Pepe Luis and went to the pile of canned goods. "You can speak to him," he said in English. "I have something to do."

"No," Alice said.

"It would be better. You won't like watching."

"I'd rather help."

"It will make you sick," he said.

They went to work. The unpiling of the cans and boxes was nothing; she did not look at the body wrapped in oilcloth. She helped push until the box that contained it stuck out over the stern. Guzmán held it and pulled at the cloth. The body did not move. Then it came unstuck and the oilcloth opened at the wrong end. It was not supposed to open at all.

"It will be done in a second," he said. She held the box steady while Guzmán pulled but it was no use. He took a knife and pried the oilcloth free of the dried blood at the bottom of the box and held it up so that the body slipped

back inside the cloth. By then she knew it was the wrong
end and she tried not to look but she saw it anyway. The
eyes were half open. There was a look of mild doubt in
them, dull and glazed, as if the man had found out something too silly to be believed. Then she saw the two mouths
—one in the face and the gaping mouth below it where
the second pair of lips had opened across the man's neck.
The head dipped back into the water; a tinge of red colored
the green surface for a few inches like a sudden decoration
in the sea. She almost had to be sick and then she didn't.
Guzmán got the body back inside the sack of oilcloth and
tied a rope around the head of the sack.

"Supposing it floats?"

"No," he said, "we put stones inside." He stood it straight
up and hit the bottom of the box hard a few times. The
body tipped forward. When it was vertical it hesitated for a
long moment in the air, as though it were thinking. It made
more of a plop than a splash. It disappeared quickly, as if
the sea had been expecting it. Guzmán took the box around
to the side of the boat and cut it into pieces and let it
float away. Alice waited for him, standing stiff with her arms
at her sides, and when he came back her stomach was all
right again.

Guzmán washed his arms in the sea and touched her
neck. His hand felt like wet iron. He set the fishing poles
out behind the boat to look as if they were trolling; then he
started the motor again and they continued south. For a long
time he peered speechlessly at the rim of the sea. After two
hours they began to see it. The vast continent of Africa
loomed low and small like an unimportant rain cloud on the
horizon.

Guzmán altered his course and they went on till they could
see the low cliffs and coves and the dense dull green of the
land. There was a curved fringe of surf along its throat like
a ruffle. He cut the motor again and they sat waiting for
dark. Alice had been taking care of Pepe Luis who was
wrapped in a blanket, his head on a cushion, in the open
ice chest. He had not complained of the pain but the swelling of the right arm on either side of the cast was large and
it had turned a mottled sickening purple. He would not take
food. After Guzmán had stopped the boat she went over and
whispered a few words; Guzmán bent down and looked close-
ly at the cast. Then he took a fishing knife and knelt beside
the trunk. He rested his eyes on Pepe Luis's face for a
second. The fisherman did not respond but he braced his
body against the walls of the trunk and looked up at the

sky. Alice knelt and wet a cloth in the salt water and put it on his forehead; she took his other arm between her hands. Pepe Luis did not resist when Guzmán began to cut off the cast. His eyes took on a troubled look as if he did not understand where the pain was coming from. The plaster was thick and it took Guzmán ten minutes with the knife.

"Yes," he said, when the cast was half off, "I thought so. He broke it again when he killed the man."

"Maybe when he climbed onto the roof."

"No," Guzmán said, "he could not have done the killing with a broken arm. It must have been then. I have to hurt him. It might be better if he fainted."

Alice took the other arm tighter but Pepe Luis did not move at all; he made no sound. When the pain got worse he closed his eyes. He sighed once but you could not have told from the sound itself whether it came from pain or from pleasure.

Guzmán stood up and Alice wiped the angry flesh of the arm with cool sea water and tore a piece of a clean shirt into a sling. There was a burner in the cabin and she heated a little soup out of a can. This time when she tried to make him eat he did not resist. He could only swallow four spoonfuls of the soup but he kept them down. After the fourth spoonful he spoke his first word. He said, *"Gracias."*

They waited there close to the rocks but the Moroccan coast guard did not appear. It was just after nightfall, when the sky had turned a strange opaque blue, dim over the water, that she heard the voices. She was in the stern of the boat behind Pepe Luis and she turned, frightened, but Guzmán did not seemed disturbed. He was busy with a small flashlight examining a map of the coastal declivities. "What is it?" Alice asked, loud.

Guzmán glanced up at her over the map. "What is what?"

". . . Don't you hear them?"

He strode to her and stood listening. "Hear what?" he said.

The voices were thin and high, calling out of the darkness. "What are they?" she said.

Guzmán turned and examined her face seriously. "Tell me what you hear."

"Them. The. . . . Them."

"Seals maybe?"

"It's stopped now. . . . It couldn't be seals. It was human."

Guzmán chuckled. "The water bitches," he said. *"Esas . . . las hijas de puta del mar.* I never heard of a woman hearing

them. They sing for men. Sailors used to follow them onto
the rocks."

"No," Alice said.

"What then?"

"I don't know, but it was friendly enough. Like a friendly
warning."

"A warning of what?"

Alice could not say and she did not answer. Guzmán went
back to work with the map. She didn't speak about it again,
but twice more she heard it. After the full darkness came
she couldn't tell which direction the voices began in or where
they ended. They were like frail cries made when disaster is
seen; then they were over. She strained her ears in the darkness but there was no noise but the wash of water and
the rhythmic distant lumping of the surf on the Moroccan
coast.

Guzmán started the motor and made it into one of the
coves before the quarter moon rose. The surf was high on
the outer rocks; they could hear it on either side of the boat.
Alice sniffed. The smell of the rocks was dark and green in
the cove. Guzmán dropped anchor close to a deserted
beach. In the early evening he got the packs ready and
stripped down to his shorts. When he lowered himself out of
the boat the water was up to his chin but he could stand.
Alice helped Pepe Luis get up and then she helped him sit on
the gunwale, his legs dangling above the water. *"Te va a
empujar,"* Guzmán said to him.

Then he spoke to her over Pepe Luis's head. "Push," he
said.

Alice put her hands against his back and pressed. Pepe
Luis fell with much less resistance than the cadaver. He
made a louder splash, and Guzmán caught him under the
water as he fell. He folded Pepe Luis's arm around his chest
and floated the fisherman from his back. Taking his time he
half-swam and half-walked with him in to shore.

Later while Guzmán slept Alice lay wrapped in a towel
on the beach. She watched the faded patterns in the sky.
The night was clear and full of stars. The moon shed enough
light to see by and there was a dense white halo around it.
There was a slight south wind, soft and warm, a whisper
off the earth, and she wondered if it could be this same continent that had produced the harsh ugly violence of the *foreño*. Guzmán lay beside her at right angles, his head on
the edge of the sleeping bag. Pepe Luis was rolled up in an
old quilt three hundred feet farther up the beach. They had
not dared to make a fire to cook supper, but they had eaten a

cold potato omelet María had made for them that morning
and some hard rolls filled with thin veal; they had opened a
bottle of red wine. Guzmán had only taken two sips of the
wine before lying back on the sand. "A good man would not
be sleepy now," he said. "I am my age. . . ."

He was asleep before he had finished the words. Alice
knew that the night would be long. For a while she thought
about the distant wailing she had heard in the boat off
shore. She wondered if she was becoming as superstitious as
the fisherfolk who lived along the Spanish coast—now she
believed in omens and signs, animals and trees and voices.
Though her own trouble was dead: the old nightmare, the
white shape of emptiness that she had once seen whenever
she closed her eyes, had not stirred since the first of summer. Guzmán's life and his problems had taken over her
dreams. Watching him in the warm open night she wondered when things would be quiet again—enough at least for
her to talk about the baby; she wondered what he would
say. She would have to take a house somewhere near the
palace when the pregnancy began to show. The baby ought
to be born along the Spanish coast. She thought she would
rather have a boy. After a time she slept without knowing it,
her hand on his hair, her face turned up. When she woke it
was still dark but several hours had passed—the patterns in
the sky were different and the moon was on the other side.
For a minute she did not know why she had wakened and
she lay still feeling the softness of the night. Then she heard
the chugging.

She put her hand on Guzmán's shoulder.

He sat up fast and peered through the darkness. It was on
the other side of the cove and it stopped for a time and
started again.

"Fishermen?" she asked.

Guzmán nodded.

Alice looked up the beach to see if Pepe Luis had heard
the boat, but the moon was too low and she could not make
out more than his shape in the blanket. The chugging went on
for ten minutes more and grew fainter. Then in the spaceless
night they could not hear it any more.

"They went," Guzmán said. "But they must have seen our
boat. We should start early in the morning. They may report
us to the authorities."

But the fishermen did not report them, and when she
woke again before dawn even the surf had grown quiet.
The sky was not yet beginning to pale. The earth had
paused and she could feel the day holding back. It was the

breathless moment when air stops flowing—the hour of odd twisted dreams that are tinged with light. She dropped the towel and stepped into the still water of the cove.

She swam underwater for a few yards taking mouthfuls of it and spitting them back, swiveling her shoulders in the flat low waves; then she swam breaststroke along the beach toward the boat. When she was tired of swimming she walked inside the water, pushing it with her arms. She felt safe in it. She liked the feel of the sandy ridges under her feet, and she liked the shells and tiny stones. She did not see the man until he touched her.

Then she nearly screamed. Standing with the water past her breasts she struck out blindly at the slabs of muscle in the chest, tearing at his arms until she heard him chuckle. Then she fell against him and gripped the big shoulders with her hands.

Guzmán stood in front of her in the water laughing quietly down at her and holding her. It had lasted only a few seconds, but she leaned against him and felt weak all the way down to her ankles. Suddenly for no reason at all she wanted then, in that second, to tell him about the baby. It was the right time and she knew it. She did not say it.

Something stopped the words in her mouth and she only wanted to stand there, the two of them against each other in the water. After a second she could feel his hardness prodding under the surface. She took it in her two hands and then sprang lightly up onto it, floating against his chest. She wrapped her legs around his thighs and Guzmán gripped her waist and speared her deep on the hardness, moving her hips up and down with his hands, entering her in long slow wise thrusts, keeping it up until her moans grew into cries and then the softness dropped from them and the cries were buried hard in his neck. Alice shivered. She tangled around him, writhing. Then she shook in a long shuddering wave but he would not stop and she could feel it all through her. Her breath caught and she struggled to get away. "Stop a minute," she said.

"No."

"Just a second . . ."

"Not now."

She felt like something in the surf and she could not get her mouth away from his. Guzmán said harshly:

"Stay close."

"I can't."

His movements were rhythmic and violent and she could feel that he was almost finished.

"I can't breathe," she said. It was a whisper.

"Tell me. Is it absolutely necessary?" Guzmán said. "That you breathe?"

While he rolled up the packs on the beach, she dressed and saw to Pepe Luis. The fisherman was still sleeping. He was weaker than he had been when they had arrived; his eyes were dull and the color of the skin below them looked sickly pale.

Alice went back and opened a can of cold soup. In the dawn they lit a small fire and she warmed it. She spooned some of it into his mouth but Pepe Luis did not swallow. He watched her in a stupefied way. He did not resist when she put the spoon to his lips. The soup ran against his teeth and out the edges of his mouth. It was like feeding an infant that had not yet learned to eat from a spoon.

"How is he?" Guzmán said.

She did not look up. She glanced at the boots beside her in the sand and shook her head. She did not know why, but she felt responsible for Pepe Luis's condition, as if she had given birth to a child that would not take food from her.

"When are they coming for us?"

"That is the problem. They may not come," Guzmán said.

Alice stood up beside him. He was watching the entrance to the cove. The land was beginning to be visible, as though it were being printed under a developing solution. The air was thick with mist and there was no horizon line; the sea and the sky were the same color. Guzmán searched the entrance with his eyes but there was nothing moving. Yesterday one of his friends, a fisherman in Sanlúcar, had sent a cable to a friend in Tangiers giving the approximate time and place of their arrival; the message had had to be cryptic and Guzmán had not known within a hundred kilometers of the coastline where they would land.

"If they don't come?"

"We will get help," Guzmán said. "We will walk. We can find a place to hide him inland from the beach and come back for him."

"No," Alice said. "You can go."

"It may take hours."

"I don't care," she said. "I won't leave him here."

She could not have said the exact reason Pepe Luis mattered so much to her and she did not try. Guzmán went to put the fire out and continue packing. Alice watched him for a time, and then she knelt again and made Pepe Luis stand up. He did not seem to know why. He gazed at her placidly. She helped him walk a few feet to a patch of saber grass; she turned her back while he relieved himself. In the pale light she helped him back to the blanket and tucked the quilt around him, the blanket folded under his head. Pepe Luis let her do what she wanted with him, as if whatever happened now was no longer his business. She felt his forehead but he had no fever. He was in the same stupor he had been in ever since the murder.

When no one came Guzmán got ready to walk to the nearest road. He did not want to call attention to himself by wearing a pack and he filled his pockets with things he would need. He had already said good-bye when they heard the chugging again. Alice heard it first and by the time Guzmán turned to look she could see the boat moving in the cove entrance. It did not hesitate but came across the cove to where they were standing. "It's the same one as earlier," she said, "it has to be. But are they . . ."

"I don't know," Guzmán said.

They could not run with Pepe Luis. She could feel Guzmán stand taller. There was no one visible on the boat. But when it came close, they made out the fisherman in front, smiling and waving. He was wearing high rubber boots. He jumped into the water and waded in to shore.

"We have got six boats out looking for you," he called. "One, he saw you early this morning, but he did never report it till now. We got always to be careful of the guard. . . ."

The man was young and darker-skinned than most Spaniards; he spoke Spanish with a funny lilt, as if the words were part of an old song and he was not sure of the music. There were four other men in the boat. When it had anchored they all jumped out and waded in. Each shook Guzmán's hand and embraced him awkwardly. Three of them were Moroccans and one was a Spaniard who had left Spain like Guzmán without a passport. Two had relatives still living along the Spanish coast. They were friends of Guzmán's friends and they had already helped twelve people who had come to Morocco to get away from the Spanish police. They stood on the beach while Guzmán explained what he wanted. Alice waited to one side. Pepe Luis showed no interest in the new arrivals, but only lay in his blanket watching the color of the sea.

It took nearly ten hours to get to Marrakesh. First, the fishermen helped them leave their boat in a protected cove. Two of the fishermen went with them—both Moroccans. They traveled by boat and by car. They were careful not to be stopped by the Moroccan police because neither Guzmán nor Pepe Luis had identification. The drive inland was long and dry; the two Moroccans sat in front and the three of them in back. The Moroccan fisherman who was driving kept behind a string of trucks for an hour and a half because he would have had to break the speed limit in order to pass them. Guzmán and Alice and Pepe Luis slept intermittently in the flat desert heat. Alice sat up when she sensed the air change color.

Marrakesh was green and lazy and lush—as hot as if it were still midsummer. After the baked earth it looked like an emerald growing inside a topaz. They parked inside town and the two Moroccan fishermen went to look for accommodations. Guzmán and Alice sat and waited with Pepe Luis in the hot air of the parked car with the windows open. Just when Alice thought she could not stand it any more, the driver came back. He had found a *pensión* where Pepe Luis could stay without a passport. The other man had found a doctor willing to visit and treat Pepe Luis without questions. When they took Pepe Luis to his office, the doctor examined the arm and then drew Guzmán to one side. The swelling had gone down since the day before. The doctor said that the arm had to be rebroken. The longer they waited the worse it might be for the patient. Guzmán and Alice stood on either side of him and Pepe Luis was given a whiff of an anesthetic while the doctor struck and broke the bone with a heavy mallet. Pepe Luis only cried out once and then was silent till it was finished. The arm was reset in splints and a looser cast; the doctor said that in two or three weeks the jaw would have to be broken too and reset. They walked Pepe Luis out to the car and took him to the *pensión*. It was run by a family of Moroccans who spoke Spanish and were sympathetic to Spanish refugees; the owner's brother had married a girl from Seville. Pepe Luis was given a small white room with a single bed and a bureau and an armoire. They left him sleeping.

Guzmán and Alice decided to stay in Marrakesh until Pepe Luis was well enough to fend for himself. They were given space in a private house belonging to an English woman who let rooms. The woman was away but her *mayordomo* was a friend of one of the Moroccan fishermen. The two fishermen left them and went back to the coast. Alice did not want to sleep. She took a bath and Guzmán showered and shaved. They went for a walk in the town.

The light was beginning to thicken to orange and with the coming of evening the air was slow with smells. They walked in the narrow streets of the Moorish quarter and came out on the other side on wide smooth cobblestones.

At the square of Jama 'Lasna—the square of Nothingness, of Nonexistence—they stopped for a drink at an outdoor café and sat down to watch the darkness come. Heavily veiled Arab women drifted past on foot and men in long flowing burnooses. Alice did not see how they could bear the burnooses in the heat. She sipped a glass of sweet *anís* and thought of her first afternoon on the south coast of Spain when she had sat with Will in the outdoor bar on the day that the car had hit the dog. It seemed a lifetime ago. There were fewer people on bicycles here and no foreign sailors; the air was richer and it smelled of spice. The hard odors of the trellised flowers over the streets was laced with the odor of cloves.

Alice watched the people. All at once she loved the place. The sidewalk they were on was lively; she liked the fluttering trees and the air that was moving so slowly over the hot cobblestones. Before dark, single sparrows appeared from the eaves of the buildings and flew together. They screeched and played tag over the city, whole clouds of them that moved as one, sailing high and making chitter noises from tree to street to tree. Alice laughed and put her hand in Guzmán's arm. The *anís* made a buzz in her body. Guzmán was preoccupied, she knew. He was worried about getting back—about all that would happen in the next days and weeks—but she could not bring herself to think about it with him. She was content. After a time they walked to a little restaurant in the next street; there was a beaded curtain over the entrance and six tables inside. Chicken couscous came on two steaming plates and there was a decanter of not very cold, not very dry white wine. Then they got up and wandered some more in the city. A pair of men wearing brown burnooses followed them wherever they went; when one of the men smiled Alice knew that Guzmán's friends had left a bodyguard. She and Guzmán walked for another hour in the dark through long needles of light that fell from shutters and then they walked back to the English woman's house and went to bed. Guzmán opened the windows and came back and lay down across her body. In the distant clatter of the night he touched her again, running his mouth up and down her with a strange new urgency as if she were going to leave him. He buried his head between her thighs. After a while he moved it up until he held her with the point of his tongue, the tip inside her like a tuning fork so that her whole body rang with it. He went on moving up, his open mouth against her belly and then up between her breasts until he entered her, subjecting her to torsion, making love always slowly, his body nailing her hard to the bed. It was like the first week of their being together when they could not have enough of each other. In the eight days they stayed in Marrakesh, they made love often. They were more relaxed than they had ever been and when they were not making love they spoke lazily. "I am not the right age for this," Guzmán said once in an aftermath, smoking a cigarette. "Not since I was twenty. It's surprising."

Alice lifted the cigarette from his lips and took a short puff and gave it back. "Who was the girl when you were twenty?"

Guzmán laughed softly. "All women ask the same question. Think of another question."

"How," Alice said, stretching, "would you like to go to hell?"

Guzmán's laugh was low and obscene. "Now I'm always . . . how is the word the American sailors use? Horned?"

"Horny."

"Like a cuckold?"

"Like Pan."

"Oh, him. The one with the pipes. Is he American now?"

"I don't know. If you touch me I can't talk."

"Do you want so much to talk?"

"Yes. No . . ."

"Someone must be celebrating."

"It's me."

"I mean on the street."

"It's an awful racket. Shut the window."

"Yes?"

"Oh lovely. Oh yes."

"Make up your mind."

"The hell with the window."

"Once I had a period of impotence—when I was forty. It won't always be like this."

"The hell with that too."

". . . I'll be too old soon."

"Just," she said, "so you're not too old now."

"Tell me not to stop."

"Don't stop. Don't . . ."

"Now."

"Don't stop . . ."

In the mornings they walked the smaller sidestreets drinking cups of thick black coffee in the shade of the city. They walked for two hours in the heat. Always before noon they visited Pepe Luis at the *pensión* and went to see the doctor who was taking care of him. The bone in his arm was setting well, and Pepe Luis was sitting up in bed once more and eating. From his window he could see two of the alleys in the white-lined Casbah; the alleys were walled on either side and the walls converged where they ran out of sight behind a building. Pepe Luis seemed fascinated by the two white walls. Alice had a feeling that they reminded him of something. One morning he began to talk. Guzmán had gone to make arrangements for Pepe Luis's transportation to Tangiers when he was well, and Alice sat in a chair listening. Pepe Luis spoke for the first time of the captain's wife and of his early days in the fishing town. He talked about Lupe for a long time. He explained about her mysterious last visit to him at the palace. Alice listened carefully, and when he was finished, she nodded. Then she leaned over and whispered something. Pepe Luis smiled and his face lit up. He looked surprised. He did not answer her, but lay there quietly thinking about it.

After an hour, Guzmán came back and explained that Pepe Luis was to be taken back to the north coast in another month, after the resetting of his jaw. Alice had given Pepe Luis some money and Guzmán began to give him instructions now in some of the things he would need to know to live in Morocco. Once he was well, he would work with the fishermen on the coast west of Tangiers; they would know how to get him a passport. Few people bothered to falsify Spanish passports any more because they were worth so little, and the authorities were not on the lookout for them. Pepe Luis liked the idea of having a passport: he knew that one day he would be traveling farther. Since Lupe's visit he had not been able to get South America out of his mind. He expected that in a month, in a year, he would go there to live. Meanwhile as he grew better he began to live on hope, on the secret promise that Alice had whispered to him when he told her about Lupe's long visit.

The day that she had to say good-bye to Pepe Luis, Alice felt lost. She knew somehow that she wouldn't be seeing him again. She left him safe in his new room and she walked alone through the streets to the English woman's house where Guzmán was waiting for her. A gray veil began to cover her eyes and she blinked it away. Always it had been emptiness that frightened her and it was a kind of emptiness she felt now that Pepe Luis was safe. He had come into their life and he had left it. It was noon and Guzmán was sitting in a chair under the clover-leaf ceiling fan of their bedroom. He was in his undershirt and his face and shoulders shone in the heat. Alice undid the cloth belt of her dress and stood by the window. She wanted to talk, but there was something about Pepe Luis that was too much like a child they had given up and she could not bring herself to say it. It was silly and she did not understand it. "What is it?" Guzmán said.

Alice shrugged, and shook her head.

"Pepe Luis?"

She kept still a moment. "I hate to lose things. I don't know why I hate to lose things. It worries me. I'm not going to lose anything else. I'm going to have a baby," she said. The statement came out flat and cold, not at all the way she had planned it. She had spoken in anger and she ran through her mind for something to follow it up with to take the sound of anger away, but she couldn't find anything. After a while Guzmán came around and faced her.

"Since how long did . . ."

"I found out two weeks ago. It may have been eight weeks then."

"Are you glad?"

"I think so. Why not? I want a child of yours. Why shouldn't I be glad?"

"Why are you angry?" he said.

"It's not about that. I'm just angry, that's all. It's not about anything. I was fond of Pepe Luis."

"You'll see him again."

"No," she said, "he's gone. I won't ever see him again. Can't I be angry? Do all pregnant women talk like this?"

"I haven't known many."

"You must have known a few. You must have got some pregnant yourself, didn't you?"

"Not many."

"How many?"

"A few."

"How many is a few?"

". . . Is it important?"

"No," she said, loud. "It's none of my business."

"Three," Guzmán said. "Two besides my wife."

Alice stepped out of her shoes and took her dress off. "What happened to them?"

"It was taken care of."

"I bet it was. What a phrase. Taken care of. Everything is always taken care of. Pepe Luis was taken care of."

"You're not making sense."

"I know I'm not," Alice said. "We take him out of Spain and give him money and that's that. Good luck, Spain. Get lost, Pepe Luis. We took care of him fine. It makes perfect sense, I don't know why I . . ."

She turned away but the tears came too quickly, without warning, and she couldn't control them or hold them back. Guzmán put his arms around her and she wept hard for five minutes without knowing why. The sound of her sobs broke harsh and dry like something scraped out of her. When it was finished she stood weakly wondering what had got into her and what it was that she had been crying about. "I'm sorry," she said.

"It doesn't matter."

"Yes it does. I hardly know him, and he's a murderer and he's fine, and we helped him get away. Why should I cry?"

"You're tired. It has been a long trip. I never would have let you make it if I'd known."

"I love it here. Can't you tell I love it here?"

"Be still."

"Listen," she said. "I love it here."

Guzmán didn't answer and in the hot stillness of the room with the shutters closed and the breathless air he picked her up. He lay her on the bed. When he had undressed himself, his body glistening with sweat, he touched her with a kind of methodical slow violence in the lazy afternoon. They gave themselves up to it again. The room was dark and everywhere Alice looked she saw only his pale eyes, ice-blue around her, until they broke open and inside her she could feel the silent throbbing.

In the morning they left Marrakesh. The day was blazing, hotter than ever. The two men who had been their bodyguards drove the car; they went along a different route that led them through Tangiers. The road was full of dust; behind the car the dust rose and faded. There were chickens along the cracked countryside. Tangiers was raucous and gray, a fierce small city busily whoring on the sea, not at all like Marrakesh with its flowers and hot scented air. The four men were waiting for them in the cove with their own fishing boat and with Guzmán's rented boat. The rented boat had been guarded, not seen by anybody, and the men had partially filled the ice chest with fresh-caught fish. They drank from a bottle of brandy; two of the men gave Guzmán presents to take back to their families in Spain. After dark they led him out of the cove in their boat and waved good-bye. One of them saluted him. They would not take money.

It took five hours to cross the straits to the Spanish coast and then another hour to find the hotel; Guzmán was only a fair navigator and the first landing he made was much too far west, near Sanlúcar and the province of Huelva. The crossing had not been rough and neither of them was sick. Guzmán turned out to sea again and made a second landing farther east. They came to the Hotel Malage without seeing the coast guard. As they approached, a light began to flash on the shore beside the hotel. Guzmán thought it was one of the local fishermen who were his friends; but no one came for them and after a while the light stopped flashing. After they docked, Guzmán tipped the watchman on the pier to clean the fish for the next day, and Alice left a note for Will in the blue villa; then they walked back to the truck. They had left it in the parking lot by the dock. They did everything in a slow easy way, as they would have after a normal fishing trip. He drove smoothly, not very fast, out of the hotel. He expected the truck to be stopped at the gate for identification—but no one appeared. West of Suelo the coastal road was deserted at four in the morning; in a short while they were in Sanlúcar. Guzmán parked the truck in the patio outside the darkened palace.

It was a relief to be back and she touched his hand in the night; Guzmán used the carved door of the downstairs west wing. After he had got the heavy door open in total darkness he kissed her gently. Alice saw the other man's eyes before Guzmán saw anything. In the yellow shaft of light the moon face of the man was three feet away. She stepped back. Guzmán did not flinch and the fat man went on smiling. The six policemen were standing next to him. None of them spoke.

"Have you a warrant to be on my property?" Guzmán said.

His voice was flat and cold in the night like the wall of the palace.

The fat man chuckled in an admiring way. "You're a nice man, *Señor Conde*," he said, "you got a lot of style. You could give lessons. It's style all the way . . . but you forgot one thing."

"Yes?"

"Yes," the police captain said. "You even thought of the shells. You cleaned the path where he fell; you burned his identification and took the weapon with you. There was nothing left. But . . ." His voice trailed off and he lifted his shoulders.

"I don't understand a word you're saying," Guzmán said. He added, "But?"

"But," the fat man agreed pleasantly. He stepped forward

farther into the light. The naked yellow bulb from the passageway magnified the pores in his skin so that they looked like craters on the moon. *"Allí está,"* he said. "But."

Then he relaxed. He said, "But for the blood on the roof."

It was less than a week after their return, five days after Guzmán had been put under house arrest, that events began to move again. Alice was still in Sanlúcar; she was beginning to be calm. The early night was pale and balmy (it was the night of the party in Suelo); she went to the end of the second-floor terrace of the palace and looked down.

The small group of them was sitting silently, waiting for Guzmán. She could barely make them out in the dark. Some of the men were fishermen and some farmers; they were a self-elected group of his friends, all of them workers, and they sat on the earth under the branches of the Columbus tree watching the palace with hard wooden faces. They were so still they might have been parts of the tree. It was María who had sent word out the first day that Guzmán was being interrogated by the police and the men who were his friends arrived now early every evening, as soon as the twilight ended and the dark came. They stayed there till dawn. There were nineteen of them because a larger number would have been considered a political event: a meeting of more than nineteen men remained illegal throughout Spain. But this group came, representing the others, the fishermen and tenant farmers and the grape pickers from along the coast—all the men to whom Guzmán had given advice. Alice leaned on the ledge of the terrace watching them. She thought she recognized two of them. None of them could do anything to help—their coming itself could be a danger to them. Yet they would sit all night and in the morning some of them would be replaced by others who would sit as quietly during the day. There had been a group of them under the tree for five days. Whenever he wanted to, Guzmán could glance out and see them. They were there to show him that they belonged to him as the big tree and the space around it and the palace belonged to him. They faced the high east windows of the second floor.

Upstairs in the Ambassador's Room and the rest of the east wing was where Guzmán was living now—though how the men knew that, Alice could not tell. Lights were on in the rest of the building too. Maybe, she thought, they had seen the shadows of the policemen moving against the curtains; or maybe Guzmán himself had parted the draperies once or twice. She did not know. She had not seen Guzmán since their return. He slept at night in the Parrot's Room and not even María or her husband was permitted to talk with him; his meals were brought on a tray by a policeman and so was the linen he used and his clothes. The rules of house arrest were strict. Outside of family, no one could see him but his lawyer as long as he was being questioned. The captain came every morning with a fresh set of questions. The traces of blood that had been discovered on the red tiles under the mansard window of the attic provided enough evidence to enforce house arrest; something more definite would be needed to hold Guzmán. It was the something more the captain was trying to find—another piece of evidence or an admission about the death of the police detective would be enough to put Guzmán in jail. As long as this step was not taken the police captain was at least partly bluffing, Alice knew.

She lit a cigarette and kept her eyes on the men under the trees. Some of them were smoking too—she could see the orange dots from the coals of their cigarettes flare from time to time in their hands. She had a feeling that the men did not trust her, and she knew why. She was being treated in royal fashion by the police captain. She had only been asked to answer questions once; the questions had lasted less than half an hour. Afterwards, she had been told she was free to go back to the hotel in Suelo. When she had refused, she was allowed freedom even within the palace grounds. No explanation had been given and she could not make out why she was handled with such open respect. It was impossible that the captain thought she was ignorant of all that had taken place; more likely he had other reasons. For three days she had waited, but neither María nor her husband had any advice to give her about what could be done to help Guzmán. The nineteen silent men under the great hulking green branches seemed to be saying that they could not tell her anything either. Guzmán had had time to give only one order on the night the arrest had been made. In the doorway, as the police moved between, separating them to take him up to the Ambassador's Room, he had said (in English without looking at her) in an even tone: "Call Juan Alberto, tell him to get my lawyer. But tell him not to come himself. Tell him I will not see him. After that the important thing is to do nothing. They will not touch you. But do nothing. No matter what happens, *nothing*," and then in the same emotionless way he had turned and gone up the stairs without glancing back. Alice had known from the way he walked that he was not worried at the time. She made the phone call to Juan Alberto, who flew to Madrid the next morning and flew back that night with Guzmán's lawyer. Then the siege began. In the days that followed, Juan Alberto disobeyed his father's command twice by coming to the palace. He was worried and he could not keep away. The second time Guzmán appeared on the terrace above as he arrived and ordered his son to leave. Juan Alberto took a look at his father's face and did as he was told. After that Alice was alone.

Now for five days she had held onto her nerves, not knowing what was happening, but nothing further had occurred except for the arrival and departure twice a day of the nineteen men outside. Squinting through the darkness she saw that some of the men had turned slightly under the tree. Two had moved their heads—no, it was three. As she watched, another turned, then another. Man by man, speechlessly, all nineteen turned to face in a different direction. They did not stand up. But they were watching something new. Their heads were like stiff awakening roots and in the night it looked as if the tree had bristled.

Then she saw the six uniformed policemen marching under the brick arch of the east wing of the palace; the policemen were heading for the men under the tree.

The moon was low but the leaves expelled it. From the deepest shadow of the branches the nineteen men watched the gray file of police approaching like soldiers across the garden. No one under the tree moved, but one man spoke. He said softly, *"Me cago en sus muertos:* I shit on their dead,"* insulting the ancestors of the policemen, and he spoke for every member of the tight little group under the branches. The green-uniformed policemen came all the way to the tip of the outermost twig and then stopped. The first policeman stepped forward, his head framed by a halo of rigid dark leaves. In the night shadow of the great tree he looked as unimportant as a figure in a "TBO"—a comic-strip character. "Six of you come with us," he said. His tone was brittle and commanding, but it was not convincing, and it was not as coldly superior as he had meant it to sound; the policeman couldn't see under the tree clearly and he felt somehow diminished by the towering growth of green. Guzmán's friends seemed in some way protected by it.

There was a silence among the men, and the policeman repeated his order, raising his voice and adding, "But don't you hear me?—are you idiots or what?" He lifted his hands to indicate that in his own mind there was no doubt that they were all worse then idiots. The gesture was lost in the vast shadow of the leaves.

Another silence followed and one of the men in the group of nineteen spoke out of the darkness. "Which six?" he said.

"It's the same to me," the policeman said, "the captain wants to see six of you. The first six," he said, "the last six. *Es lo mismo. Son ustedes todos iguales.*" He said it to indicate that there was no difference among the men who were Guzmán's friends, any more than there would have been among a herd of pigs, but again the superiority in his tone failed him; he felt as if he were speaking not to the men but to the thick green gloom. He was standing against the light of the palace; the nineteen men were in darkness. He realized his mistake in not ordering them all out in the open first, but it was too late. The policeman stood his ground under the tip of the branch and said, *"Darse prisa:* Get a move on. . . . You think I got all night to wait here?" but for the third time his voice came out more surly than cold. He was a young policeman and he could not get over the feeling that there was a presence in the tree that was holding the men together.

A low muttering came from the shadows by the trunk. Six men stood up and formed a second group to one side, walking almost invisibly under the protective branches. The six said nothing but stood there waiting for the policeman to move. The policeman rapped out, "Follow me!" and turned. As he walked out from under the branch, the leaves above him swept across the top of his head and knocked his cap off. The cap fell like a stone to the ground. The policeman froze with his back to the tree. One of the nineteen men chuckled. Another followed and in a space of a few seconds all nineteen were laughing together as one inside the leafy darkness. The policeman stooped over and picked his cap up roughly before he realized that he should have made one of the men under the tree do it for him. Then he left the tree. After a moment the six men followed him out. Their faces were worn and weathered in the thin yellow light that fell across them from the windows of the palace. They walked behind the policemen across the garden. In front were Ortiz and Méndez, Guzmán's two most active friends—the fishermen who had formed the *cooperativas*. They glanced at each other now as they followed the policemen between the shrubs. Above, on one of the terraces of the palace, they could see the blond American girl watching their progress intently. It had been rumored among Guzmán's friends for some time now that the American girl had been changing the man—softening him in certain bad ways—and the two leaders, Ortiz and Méndez, nudged each other seeing her there. There was another fisherman behind the leaders in the group of six, and one tenant farmer and two grape pickers. The grape pickers owed Guzmán a raise in their salaries. All six men watched the girl on the second-floor terrace. Some eyed her suspiciously, as though she were in some way responsible for Guzmán's present troubles. Then the first policeman stepped onto the clamshell path and led them all into the light. The two groups, policemen and workers, six and six, entered the building by the archway that led off the garden. They marched upstairs in formation like a parade.

The Ambassador's Room on the second floor of the palace was an immense rectangular area that was sparsely furnished, with windows at one end and a circular sofa at the center. Chairs had been brought into it from several other parts. Policemen lounged or stood about in it in different places; they glanced over languidly as Guzmán's friends were told to wait inside the entrance. The six men took the room in, in a stiff way, without moving, only shuttling their eyes back and forth in their skulls. At the center, on the sofa, Guzmán sat alone. He was wearing a pair of old trousers and a clean white shirt with the sleeves rolled up. The captain sat in front of him in an easy chair and the police secretary sat with a pen and a pad of paper. The police doctor stood behind the fat man, his head raised toward the ceiling; he was looking at the faded gilt on the deep carved wood over them and he appeared to have let his mind wander away from the proceedings, as if he had more urgent things to think about. Guzmán did not look directly at any of the six men who had entered; he included them with his eyes and looked back at the captain. The captain noticed and glanced behind him. *"Pasen, pasen,"* he said to the men, indicating some straight chairs set up near the sofa; *"siéntense, por favor:* sit down." He added with sarcastic politeness, *"Señores."*

The six men shuffled across the long room bumping into each other vaguely. They sat. The two leaders looked at Guzmán as if they expected to receive orders from him; the others gazed into space or looked at the floor.

"Esos dos," the captain said, indicating Ortiz and Méndez with one finger, "they're familiar."

The police doctor looked over at them and then at the ceiling again. "The fishermen's *cooperativas,*" he said, "the leaders."

"Hombre, claro," the fat man said, "the half-Commu-

nists. Or maybe they're all that way. I bet they're all Communists."

"We aren't Communists," one of the leaders said.

"Listen," the fat man said in a different tone, a more quiet tone that appeared to carry in it the power of a country: "you speak when you're told. Not before."

The leader remained silent and no one else in the room said anything.

At the center Guzmán seemed to have forgot about the six men. He was watching the police doctor who was watching the ceiling. He was thinking that it was probably the doctor who had arranged for Pepe Luis's escape from the jailhouse. Guzmán was not concerned about his friends; there was no way he could incriminate them, or they him. They knew nothing about the police detective who had been hiding in the palace.

"Señor Conde, I see you're not paying attention," the captain said to him, ". . . I hope I'm not boring you. Am I boring you?"

Guzmán lowered his eyes to the fat man's face. "Yes," he said quietly. His expression did not change.

The fat man's smile congealed. One of the six men snickered. The captain looked over, but it was impossible to tell which man had made the sound. The six faces had a dull and impassive look, carbon copies of Guzmán's expression. "And *you,"* the fat men jerked his head at all six, "I might take the lot of you in . . . by the time I get finished with . . ."

"Take them in on what charge?" Guzmán said.

"Charge, hell. Any charge," the captain said.

"I don't think so," Guzmán said. He called, "Paco."

From a corner of the room where he had been dozing in a chair, Guzmán's lawyer rose and walked sleepily across to the sofa. He sat down on the sofa beside him. The lawyer was called Paco Fernandez; he was a middle-aged man with yellowish teeth and two tobacco-stained fingers. He held the two fingers always in front of him when he sat, whether they contained a cigarette or not. "Can he take these men in?" Guzmán asked.

"Según. What were they doing?" Paco said.

"They were sitting under my tree," Guzmán said. "With my permission."

". . . What else?"

"That's all."

"Just six?"

"I picked six at random. There's more out there. It's a political meeting," the police captain said.

"Can you prove that?" Paco said.

"I don't have to prove it," the police captain said, "I *say* it's a political meeting."

"How many of you in all?" Paco said to one of the men.

"Nineteen," the man said.

"That's it," Paco said. "It's not a meeting unless it's more than nineteen. . . . Surely the captain knows *that*," he said, speaking a little too respectfully in the third person. The respect carried with it a tinge of contempt.

"Listen," the fat man said very loud, rising from his chair. *"Aquí mando yo:* I give the orders here."

"No," Guzmán said. "Not in my house." His voice was toneless and it retained the same quality of quiet it had had before. He had not raised or lowered it a fraction of a note.

The fat man—who was being challenged, and who knew it—stared back at him in a level way. "Supposing then, we don't stay in your house. . . . Supposing we go to *my* house . . ."

"As you like," Guzmán said. "But just me. You won't be able to take any of these men with us. You won't even be able to keep me in jail long. You can't prove the charges you've been making. Paco will inform my other attorneys in Madrid. . . . And I'm not resisting arrest," he said after a short pause, with great clarity. "I'd like my lawyer and these six men to witness that now. I do not resist the arrest."

"Witnessed," Paco the lawyer said.

"Keep your mouth shut," the fat man said to the lawyer. "And you listen," he said to Guzmán, "I can book these men on suspicion. There's been a murder in this house."

"According to you there has. None of them knows that," Guzmán said.

"But *I* don't believe them," the fat man said carefully, "any more than I believe you. . . . I can book them any time I want."

"Is that true?" Guzmán said to Paco.

"It's a fine point," Paco said. "It's true."

"They'll be well known," Guzmán said to the captain, "within twenty-four hours. Paco will see to that. Too well known for you to harm them. Particularly if you're using them to threaten me . . ."

The fat man wheeled and brushed past the chair he'd been sitting in. "I'm getting tired of all this," he said, "it's just talk . . . *qué coño*. Just book them," he said to one of

the policemen. "The six and Guzmán. Maybe they'll like the
jailhouse better."

"Watch how you treat them from now on," Guzmán told
him.

"But we'd like to go with you," one of the two leaders said,
low; "that's why we're here." Guzmán looked at Ortiz and
Méndez and at the other men and said no more.

The captain turned to the sofa. "Anyway we'll see now,"
he said to Guzmán, "who wins. You or me." He sounded
relieved.

"Yes," Guzmán said. "Now we'll see."

The fat man led the way; the party of seven was backed
up by two lines of policemen. Guzmán's lawyer walked behind the policemen. They all went out into the hall. María
was waiting there. When Guzmán came out with the policemen she began to weep. The fat man came to a halt at
the top of the stairs.

"Buenas noches, Señorita," he said to someone else. He
spoke with deference.

Alice Littlejohn was standing at the other end of the hall
facing them. She made no reply and when she saw Guzmán
her face did not alter.

"Go back and wait at the hotel," Guzmán said in English,
"I'll be out soon."

The little group of men went out single file, followed by
the policemen and the lawyer. The building was left empty
and yellow. Alice came to the stairs and looked after them.
For some time she could feel the empty hall around her.
Then she turned and went back slowly to the terrace.

It was two hours before she was able to make a decision.
She spoke to no one. María had gone back to the kitchen.
The remaining thirteen men sat as before under the tree.
Alice understood that the captain had been unable to break
Guzmán with questions and that he had taken the six men
in as an alternate plan. She had seen for herself what Pepe
Luis looked like on the day he came out of the jailhouse.
Now for two hours she stood waiting on the terrace and
she could not think of a way to help. The calm she had
been feeling left her and her ears filled gradually with the
sound of blood. It was while she was watching the Columbus
tree that she got the idea. The light from the windows on
the outer leaves looked metallic and ghostly, like distant
sequins set in a sweeping green dress. When a breeze came
the dress moved, and it looked as if the tree had on a costume; it was then that she remembered about Helen's party.
The solution came to her standing stock still and it came as

gently as the breeze. She did not see why she had not seen it before.

Five minutes later she was driving on the coast road to Suelo. She drove tensely, unhurried; with a purpose. Her nerves felt pulled tight in her body and she darted in and out of the single lane of heavy traffic when she could, but without speeding. She could no longer hear the pumping in her ears. All the way to Suelo she seemed only to see the huge green tree in front of her, curtsying in a breeze, its wide branches billowing out as if they were held on hoops.

She parked the car in Helen's drive and waited outside the red villa for the couturier and his assistant to leave. When she opened the door and saw Helen standing in the wide crimson dress that moved at the bottom like the swaying of the tree she felt lost for a moment. She stood just inside the doorway without knowing how to begin.

For a while neither of them moved.

"We've had a scene like this before," Helen said quietly.

"Yes," Alice said, "I was thinking about it earlier this summer. Mardi Gras is in February. It wasn't seven months after that Mardi Gras ball that Will was born. . . . You knew you were pregnant when I came in that night and said I didn't want to be like you. It must have been a bad shock."

Helen waited and watched her.

"It was, wasn't it?"

"Look," Helen said. "This party's important to me . . . I'm due in the main ballroom in twenty minutes. I'm not pregnant this time."

"Of course not," Alice said. She looked away suddenly.

"Oh," Helen said. "I see."

She watched her daughter for half a minute and then shrugged. Her face looked tired and she turned away.

"You'd better sit down," she said.

Alice did, and Helen lit a cigarette.

In the sharp red light of the room Alice began to tell the story haltingly, stammering, stopping several times to go back when she had forgotten something, telling it badly and often getting the sequence of facts and even the dates mixed or confused. She had never gone to anyone for help in her life and it wasn't easy. Helen listened without comment, watching her with an inscrutable blank look, not speaking until the story was finished. Alice was not aware when it was that she herself stopped talking.

"All right," Helen said after a while. "Let's go over the facts. You're twenty-two years old . . . you're going to have a baby by a man who's married to someone else. You're in a country where it's illegal to get a divorce, even if he wanted one. The man is over twice your age—he's a potentially dangerous political figure and he's in jail. Now it looks as though they might kill him. Is that it?"

"Yes."

Helen nodded. "Darling, you do have a way of spoiling a party," she said. "You really do. So you left the country illegally. You disposed of a cadaver, and you went with your lover and a murderer into Morocco illegally. You left the murderer there. You returned with your lover and you got back into Spain illegally, and the only time your courage failed you was just now when you had to walk in here and ask me for help. Yes, I get the picture."

She moved back to the dressing table; the hoop of her skirt spread a path around her like a protective circle of air. "I don't believe he told you to come to me."

"He said I should do nothing."

"What made you decide?"

"I've seen how a jailhouse in Spain treats people. I'd do anything."

"So," Helen said drily. She lit a cigarette and went to the phone. "Let me get one more thing clear," she said. "You believe the reason the police captain's been treating you with respect is because he's afraid of offending the Ministry in Madrid . . . you think he knows you're my daughter. You're probably right. The local papers have been full of the party. Your name's been mentioned . . . I've been dealing with the Ministry from the beginning, I imagine the police captain guessed that. The Undersecretary of Tourism and his assistant are here tonight. I think they'd help my daughter if she's sure of what she says. You *know* the police have no evidence?"

"Just what I told you."

"Where were you when the detective was killed?"

"Here."

"Where is here?"

"In the blue villa. He wouldn't let me sleep at the palace while Pepe Luis was . . ."

"Who else knew about Pepe Luis?"

"Just the servants, and Eugenia. And Lupe. She's . . ."

"No one else?"

"No."

"Are you sure? Think."

"I'm sure. No, wait. There was a doctor . . . Guzmán called him down from Seville to take care of Pepe Luis. He's gone back to Seville, I think."

Helen said, "Can the doctor be trusted?"

"Yes, absolutely."

"How far?"

"He's one of Guzmán's oldest friends."

"But would he be willing to lie to protect him?"

"I think he'd say anything."

"You *think* he would?"

". . . I know he would."

"All right," Helen said. She picked up the phone.

"What should I do?"

"Try looking demure," Helen said. "We'll need it."

Alice watched her. Helen's voice was quiet and spare, without the glasslike overtone. It was a voice Alice was not familiar with—there was nothing fragile in it. It seemed to her as if she had never heard her mother's voice before.

The whole thing took Helen a little over ninety minutes. Alice had no part in the proceedings. She sat kneading her handkerchief invisibly in her fist and she listened. First Holtz came in. His abdomen looked larger than usual; he was already dressed as a circus trainer with the top hat and whip, and all forty colors of the hotel on his costume.

Helen began on a low key. She opened the subject as a worried mother with a complaint. Her daughter had been detained and interrogated by the police; she was upset. The only reason the international press had come to Spain to cover the party was because she, Helen, had known how to make it interesting enough to be news. If the press got wind of the police interrogation—or of Alice's relationship to the Count—there would be a minor scandal of the kind that would destroy Alice's reputation and it might reflect on her mother as well. Helen explained it all neatly—emotionally enough to make it forceful—stopping now and then to let it sink in. Holtz listened with a sympathetic air to all she had to say. When she had done, he explained that as much as he sympathized with her predicament, he could not interfere with any legalities. He was a foreigner in Spain himself and the first rule for a foreigner, particularly one in business here, was to stay out of police matters entirely. Helen had been expecting that answer and she allowed him to finish.

"Herr Holtz," she said curiously, "so many things go on in your hotel. The bar is open after hours, there's gambling in some of the private rooms; there are even other activities . . . I'm told Eugenia the maid runs most of them. I've given parties in so many hotels—I know how it is . . . there's no way you can run a hotel like this without paying off the police, is there? And you own four hotels between here and the Costa Brava. . . . Is that staying out of police matters . . . ?"

Holtz colored. He was in for a bad time and he knew it. He had learned early in the summer that despite her quiet ways Mrs. Locke was not a woman to be taken lightly. As she went on talking, it became clear to Holtz that she did not want him to cope with the Sanlúcar matter himself, but only to lend his presence and approval in dealing with the Undersecretary of Tourism who had come to his hotel for the party. He was relieved. After twenty minutes he went to the phone and called. Morilla and his assistant were staying in the black villa. Even though they were only the fourth and fifth in command at the Ministry of Information and Tourism in Madrid, they were useful and important men. Morilla did not come alone; the two came to the red villa together. They sat down and listened attentively as Helen repeated her story. This time she emphasized the power of the foreign press—and the impossibility of her own and her daughter's situation. Unlike Holtz, Morilla had heard no rumors about Alice's relationship to Count Guzmán. Helen spoke at first of a "close friendship" between the two, but she did not intimate anything more for the moment. Before she had finished, Morilla spoke up.

"Forgive me for interrupting you, Mrs. Locke," he said. "I don't understand. What is it you want us to do?"

Helen walked to the window in a helpless way, without answering. "I don't know," she said finally. "I can't tell what's to be done—I've never been involved . . . I've never been . . . caught up in politics before."

"Of course not," Morilla said. "I'm afraid there is no solution to this problem. . . ."

"Isn't there?"

"None that I can see."

"Wouldn't it solve things," Helen said, "if Count Guzmán were to be released from jail? There wouldn't be a chance of the foreign press finding out about *any* of it."

Morilla smiled. "I am afraid, Mrs. Locke," he said, "if the charge is what you say it is, there is no chance of that. The police can't release a man suspected of murder just because he might ruin the reputation of the very nice daughter of a very nice woman." He added, "An extremely charming woman."

"That's just it," Helen said, "he couldn't have committed any murder. The police have the wrong man. They can't have any proof, I happen to know he didn't do anything during those three nights they say it all took place. . . . I don't understand policemen acting like this . . . it's as if they're threatening *me* in some way . . . I only came to Spain to do some good . . ." She broke off and turned away.

Morilla didn't move. His face took on a hard look and he watched her for a moment. "You say," he said, "you know something about . . ."

"I only know he was busy on those nights," Helen said. "He was sick. All three nights. He had a fever and he never left his bedroom."

Morilla turned slowly. He looked at Alice, and then back at Helen. "You mean you have evidence because your daughter called on him?"

"No, I don't," Helen said. "I mean because she slept with him. All night."

In the short pause that followed, the two Ministry officials, Holtz, and Alice watched Helen with similar expressions.

Morilla began, "I must ask . . ."

"Please," Helen said. "Let's be simple about it. My daughter has been spending nights in the palace since the beginning of the summer. I've known about it since then. By now most of Suelo knows about it. . . . It may not be what I wanted for my daughter, but it's what she chose. The press will listen to me if no one else will. I'll tell them Count Guzmán never left his bedroom . . . I'll have to. My daughter's reputation is dear to me, but not so dear that I'd sacrifice a man's life for it."

"Mrs. Locke, I cannot . . ."

"All right," Helen said, "then forget I asked for help. . . . People told me what the government was like in Spain; I didn't believe them. . . . I hope the foreign press asks me how a single woman and her daughter are treated in this country."

"You can't," Holtz spoke up. "You can't talk that way to the press. My hotel. Don't you see, Madame, people would be frightened . . . tourists would . . ."

Morilla stood up. "Mrs. Locke," he said. "You must believe me, I am trying to be cooperative; I want to understand you. You believe that your daughter was with him?"

Helen said, "It isn't a question of believing. I drove her there myself."

Morilla eyed her carefully. "Just let me understand. You say he . . ."

"You don't have to trust anything *I* say," Helen said. "Ask somebody else. The servants. Or ask the doctor."

". . . Doctor?"

Helen sighed. "Obviously there was a doctor taking care of

him," she said. "My daughter has no medical training. I don't know the name of the doctor, but he can be found. Or call the police captain and ask what proof they have that the Count did anything. They *can't* have proof. He never left his room. My daughter will swear to it. And I will back her up in a court of law. If you still have such things in Spain."

Morilla kept his eyes on her long enough to calculate something. He said, "I would like to use the telephone in the other room."

Helen turned away again, taking a tissue from a box and putting it to her face.

Morilla tapped his associate on the shoulder and the two officials went out of the room. Helen did not move during their absence. Holtz and Alice stared at her back.

Morilla placed the first call, through priority, to the home of his immediate superior in Madrid. He explained that the situation was both delicate and unpleasant. When he had obtained permission to deal with it himself, he hung up and called the police office in Sanlúcar. He identified himself, got the captain on the line, and demanded to know what proof there was against Guzmán. The police captain said that one of his detectives had disappeared. He told of having arrested six men along with Guzmán on suspicion of murder. "Without a body?—do you know that there's really *been* a murder?" Morilla asked. The captain admitted that he did not know for certain. "For God's sake," Morilla said, "be more careful. Guzmán's not a peasant. You'll put us in an international scandal with your nonsense. Don't take him in again unless you've got something on him. Keep the six men if you have to cover your foolishness. But not Guzmán." He hung up and went with his associate back into the living room.

"It is taken care of," he said to Helen who was still facing the corner. "I'm sorry if this has caused you worry or pain. . . ."

Helen waited before turning, the tissue held to her face.

"You have our word that nothing you have said will go any further than this room," Morilla said formally. His voice went a shade more quiet. "This must have been difficult for a lady like you . . . may I say that I admire you for it. . . ."

Helen bowed her head to him.

The two officials and Holtz bowed to her as they went out of the red villa.

Helen moved to her dressing table and tossed the dry tissue into the waste paper basket. Then she took the dark Spanish wig that was the final touch to her costume from its box. She put the wig on and began to repair her makeup. Alice went on looking at her for some minutes. During most of the time that Helen had been speaking to Holtz and Morilla, Alice had not removed her eyes from her mother. She knew that Helen had taken a large chance in speaking as she had. If she'd carried through her threat of speaking to the press, the Ministry would certainly have used the very things Helen had spoken about against her. Her reputation would have been ruined along with her daughter's, and even if Alice had not been considered an accomplice to the murder, both women might have been asked by the government to leave the country. Yet Helen had handled the whole thing as if it had no more importance than a bridge game, and she had played it as well as she played bridge.

There was a silence between them.

"Where do you come from?" Alice said.

Helen sighed. "The swamp," she said. "Run along. I'm late."

". . . Just the swamp?"

"Yes," Helen said. "Just the swamp."

"How poor were you?"

Helen did not answer.

"I'd like to know."

"I've forgotten most of it."

"I liked the way you talked to them," Alice said.

A trace of malice crossed Helen's face like a smile. The hoop of her skirt sank lower on the floor and she curtsied lightly.

"I used to wonder why you always had to put on such an act. When I was little, I thought every part of you was an act. As if you made yourself up, from nothing . . ." Alice saw her mother's face and stopped.

Helen put the hand mirror face down on the dressing table and leaned on it for a moment. "Look," she said. "Poverty is not a sentimental condition. It's just bad. I'm finished with mine. I give parties now. Just get out of here and go find your own hell. I am late."

Alice opened her mouth and moved forward a step.

"Tell Juan Alberto things are all right," she said. She touched Helen's hand and left.

Then standing alone in the villa Helen did not move for a while. After the sound of her daughter's car had disappeared in the distance, she turned back to the mirror expecting to see her own face tired and her makeup in need of more repairs.

She found, to her surprise, that her loveliness was soft and gentle.

In the police office in Sanlúcar the fat man was sitting at his desk.

He had been there since he had come in with the men who had sat down opposite him like schoolchildren in a class-room—Guzmán in the center of the row. When they had first arrived, the fat man had made himself comfortable. He studied Guzmán and tilted his swivel chair back against the wall. *"Bueno,"* he said, *"aquí estamos."*

Guzmán and three of his friends on either side of him sat motionless and several policemen stood against the wall. Paco the lawyer sat off in a corner, his two tar-stained cigarette fingers held like open scissors in front of his stomach.

"Muy bien," the fat man said, *"de acuerdo.* You don't want to talk? We'll just wait here."

Guzmán's pale blue eyes touched the captain in a blank way. "I never said I didn't want to talk," he said, "I only said I didn't know what you were talking about."

"And the . . ."

"The blood on the roof is nothing," Guzmán interrupted. "If it's true you found any."

"I found plenty. A smear in the attic too. By the window."

Guzmán lifted his shoulders a fraction. "Also in the kitch-en, I imagine," he said. "María cut herself last month. She was peeling onions and the knife slipped. I cut myself shav-ing last February. There's probably some blood in . . ."

"All right," the captain said, *"Sin guasa, ah? Aquí esta-mos en mi casa.* Just watch your mouth."

Guzmán shrugged. "Make up your mind. You want me to talk or you don't want me to talk?"

One of the six men snickered and the fat man's eyes slid sideways in his head and singled him out. *"Ese,"* he said to a policeman, pointing to the man. "He's in solitary when he leaves this office. You can put them all in solitary."

Guzmán said nothing and the fat man watched the group of seven—the six workers and their strange leader, the stub-born aristocrat who had committed himself to standing by them. It was going to be hard to turn Guzmán's friends against him. In fact, it was going to be impossible—sheep are sheep, the captain thought; you could see the devotion in their eyes whenever the Count said something. The slight-est thing that happened to Guzmán would make him a martyr in the minds of these men, and there was no way to make it appear to his friends that Guzmán was not right in everything

—no way at all. Madrid would have to settle for putting
Guzmán on trial and removing him from circulation for a
while, if that was possible; the captain would be lucky if he
could find out enough for use at the trial. He wasn't at all
sure that he could. There was something invisible that was
binding these men together and it could not be scared out of
them in a day, or in a month, or in a year.

He put one leg up on his desk and eyed the line of men.
None of them was moving now except Guzmán. Guzmán's
hand was rummaging in his coat pocket. The captain watched
as the fingers straightened something in the pocket and lifted
it out.

"No," the captain said.

Guzmán hitched one eyebrow as if to say that it was of
no importance, and put the cigarette back into his pocket.

"I want them relieved of money and possessions," the captain said to the first lieutenant-policeman, his eyes still on
Guzmán.

Before the policeman could move, Guzmán put the same
hand back into another pocket and took out his wallet. After
that he removed a pen, and then he dug deep into his pants
pocket and took out some change. He tossed it all on the
edge of the desk with the cigarettes in front of the captain,
and sat back. The captain did not move. In the silence, all
six men followed Guzmán's lead, tossing whatever they had
up onto the desk. In the end there was a disorderly heap of
money, photographs, tobacco, keys and cheap billfolds spread
out like a layer of litter that had been left after a picnic.

The lieutenant-policeman gathered the objects together; he
dumped them in a sack and dropped it in one of the file
cabinets along the wall. His actions were brisk, but it made
no difference, the captain saw. Nothing effaced the gesture
the six men had made in throwing their own belongings on
top of Guzmán's. The captain remained motionless in his
chair and let his gaze go back and forth. His best move now
was to make no move at all, he knew; he had learned that
silence could be a weapon in the hands of the right man. If
there was enough of it, people impregnated a silence with
their own fears and grew their own nightmares in it. Once
at the beginning of his career in the *Guardia Civil*, the
captain had stood in front of a mirror and practiced staring
into space for minute after minute without blinking and without appearing to breathe. He sat that way now, his body
immobile, his head poised as though he were waiting for
something. After ten minutes, he saw with satisfaction that
three of the men were beginning to grow nervous. It was no

great step forward, but at least the captain, not Guzmán, had become the focus of attention in the room.

Two and a half hours later he was still sitting there. He had asked a mere half dozen short questions in all that time, though he had repeated some of them more than twice. The repetition of the questions had had no real effect, but the silence had. By now the six men were waiting for something—though none of them could have said what it was. Even Guzmán looked a little tense. The captain remained the same for some minutes more. No one had moved in the room and the captain was quiet when the telephone rang.

It rang first in the outer office and the fat man noticed with pleasure that the Count started slightly at the sound. It continued ringing without anyone else moving until it became clear that there was no one left in the outer office. One of the lieutenant-policeman's aides strode out and answered it. The aide's voice could be heard, questioning sharply at first, and then all at once his tone changed. He came back into the room and signaled to the lieutenant-policeman, who followed him out. After a moment the lieutenant appeared again in the doorway. His face had taken on a quality of extra alertness, almost of strain, and there was a childish look of awe in his eyes. "It's the Ministry," he said.

The captain looked bored. "In Cádiz? About that . . ."

"The Madrid Ministry," the lieutenant-policeman said. "He says they're in Suelo for the day."

The fat man stopped talking. He reached out and picked up the receiver from his desk. Then he thought better of it and went to answer it in the outer room.

The conversation was brief and they could hear the captain's part in it. They could tell from his tone that the man he was talking to was more than just a superior. The captain sounded apologetic and abashed. There was a pause. When the captain came back he stopped for an instant in the doorway, his eyes on Guzmán. *"Muy bien,"* he said.

The lieutenant-policeman stepped forward. *"Mi Capitán?"*

The fat man returned to his desk. "Just give Count Guzmán back his things," he said. "He's got an immediate release."

While the lieutenant-policeman went to the file cabinet, the captain glanced at the Count. In the center of the row of men, Guzmán was frowning. The men on either side were watching him with doubtful faces, and some of them were shifting uncomfortably in their chairs. The men looked vaguely troubled, as though something were happening that they could not get through their heads.

It was in that half second that the police captain sensed that things might not be as good for Guzmán as they seemed. It was obvious that the phone call had been as much of a surprise to the Count as it had to the fat man himself. On instinct, the captain maintained his silence.

Guzmán had parted his lips once and closed them again.

"You could have told me," the fat man said at last, shifting some papers on his desk. "It might have saved us time and trouble. . . . I didn't know you had connections in the government."

"I don't," Guzmán said. "I . . ."

"Oh come on," the captain said. "It's out now. I arrest you, the Ministry steps in. That was one of the ministers. At eleven o'clock at night."

"I know no one in . . ."

"Tell that to these idiot-sheep who follow you around," the captain said. "Not to me. You know where he was calling from? The blond girl's mother is giving a party. They came all the way down to Suelo just for her party."

"I know nothing about that," Guzmán said.

"Don't you?" the captain said. "Weren't you invited too?"

Guzmán didn't answer.

"I'll explain it then," the captain said. "I'm not permitted to touch you. It's forbidden to keep you here even on suspicion of murder. . . . I doubt they'd let me keep you if I'd seen you kill a man. It sounds to me like you're one of their most *respected* friends. . . ."

Guzmán's mouth twitched. His face had gone pale.

The captain watched the six workers. No one spoke. Then in the silence he himself had made, a little pocket of malice spilled like a quick bright fluid into the fat man's mind.

"In any case," he said to Guzmán, "you have my sincere apologies. You won't be disturbed by the police in this town again. Will you see," he said to the lieutenant, "that the Count has an official escort back?"

On either side of Guzmán the six workers, following Guzmán's move, rose to their feet.

"No," the captain said, "you stay where you are. You can settle down here for a couple of weeks. None of *you* is under the protection of the government. . . ."

The men did not reply. There was another silence.

There was no doubt at all in the captain's mind now, watching him, that Guzmán looked worse than troubled.

When Alice left the red villa she paused beside her rented car to watch the costumed guests. The last of the masqueraders were still straggling along the path in the general direction of the main building. She did not think that any of them looked as nice as her mother did. Then a dark figure walking among them caught her eye. Eugenia the maid was going from person to person, asking whether she might be of assistance. Alice almost went over to her. She wanted to explain that Pepe Luis was safe and that there was nothing to worry about. Then she remembered hearing her mother say that many illegal things went on in the hotel and that Eugenia the maid ran most of them. She decided against talking to the old woman.

She got back into her car and drove at a snail's pace out of the hotel. The central road was full of curiosity-seekers, all of them walking into her headlights and all turning as she drove by to see what kind of fool would leave such a party. The short distance from the red villa to the coastal road took her nearly thirty minutes, and she had to wait another ten to get through the line of traffic onto the asphalt. The traffic going west was almost nonexistent. Everybody in the world seemed to be traveling in the opposite direction. In town the line of cars, bumper to bumper, was moving like a slow endless stream toward the hotel. Alice drove away from it feeling light-headed and giddy, as if she were the only object in the universe that had settled on a course of its own. The sense of being out of orbit made her happy. The open country was cool and the night was clear. In the darkness, the distant fields on either side of the road were burning in low uneven flames. It was the time of year when the farmers set fire to leftover roots to enrich the soil for the next year's planting. The fires licked and trembled under the low night sky; the smoke from the flames disappeared upward into an intense blackness.

The field fires ended just before Sanlúcar, and the darkness made the street lamps of the town look cold and pallid after the deep orange glow. Alice took the shortcut—up a narrow bumpy dirt road between low buildings that seemed to touch at the top over the car. Here and there men stood chatting outside the bars, and in the town square several couples walked or stood close together. The younger couples were waiting to find a place where they could go and make love unobserved. Some glanced at the car as she passed, but no one paid any attention to it after they had seen who was at the wheel. Alice had become as much of a fixture in the town as a well-known grocer or the mayor or Guzmán himself. There was no criticism in the way people looked at her, as there had been when she first appeared in the town as Guzmán's lover; they acknowledged her right to be there now as one more proof of the Count's eccentricity. To be entirely original is the private dream of every Spaniard, as only every Spaniard knows, and apart from other things, Guzmán was a symbol of the dream's fulfillment. As Alice drove by, some of the townsfolk she passed even nodded to her; their growing approval made her smile to herself.

She left the car in the courtyard and hurried up the stairs. She was lighter than she had felt in a long time and at the top of the landing she saw María and her husband. They looked worried. Guzmán was at the far end of the Ambassador's Room by himself. He was staring out the window. Alice's steps made light thuds on the wood floor. She stopped next to him, out of breath and shaking with gladness. For a long moment Guzmán stayed as he was, though he must have heard her.

He said, "Do you know what you've done?"

The light from the chandelier made a cold glow in the room, and when Guzmán turned around Alice hardly recognized him. The face she was looking at was a face she hadn't seen since the beginning of the summer. There was no special expression in it. It was white, and the skull inside was more apparent than the skin. The eyes seemed to be looking out from some place she had not heard of—the sort of place where things happen that aren't accounted for in usual terms. He did not look angry. He just looked like a shell that something had died in, and he did not appear surprised to see her.

He did not say anything more.

Weeks later, when it was all over but the very last thing, she could not remember when she had started to move. It was as if her life was just a long walk she had taken and everything in it was connected to this walk. The first and the middle and the end of it were only different parts of one long seemingly endless journey on foot that appeared to have no beginning, as if all of her time were joined that way—moving forward step by step—though she knew it wasn't like that. The walk did not begin until quite late, and something else happened before it.

The month was September and the rain started without any particular warning. There had been no clouds over the sea; there was no thunder. It was more as if, one night, the water was just there. The rain began on a weekend and for days they could hear it outside all the time—a dull effortless plopping, as though something in the sky had torn open and spilled. There was no cloudburst and the nights were windlesss; it rained gently without ceasing for fourteen days. Alice began to walk on a Monday—the day after the men who had been Guzmán's friends came and tore down the Columbus tree.

The first time the rain stopped, the sky turned a bloated glaring gray that sagged flatly over the land. It was like a canvas that was being repaired; you could see that it wouldn't hold. People in the palace waited for the new rent in the cloth, and without meaning to they expected it to come each morning and evening, from one day to the next. Then one night it came. The sound wasn't loud. It was a soft tearing noise that ran fast overhead from east to west—ripping in the distance till they couldn't hear it any more—and they knew that the canvas had rotted away right over them.

Before the sound was finished they could hear the rain again.

It was when the rain began for the second time that the men came in the night, their movements muffled in the sound of the falling water, and destroyed the tree. No one heard them and no one could tell how many there were or how they did it. A couple of them must have had axes, and at least one a saw; the marks could be seen in the morning on the low jagged stump that had once been the trunk and on the giant fallen body of the tree itself that lay next to it. When Alice got up in the morning she knew nothing of what had happened and Guzmán was gone from the bedroom. She looked for him in the hall and then through the west wing of the building. It was not until she came to the high windows of the east wing and glanced over the terrace through the sluggish falling water that she found him. At first she could not believe it. She wiped the inside of the glass, but the rain sliding down the outside distorted the view. It was the rain, she thought, that made it look as though the tree was lying down. She went to the glass door and, after she had opened it slowly, she went outside herself and stood in the rain on the terrace. Guzmán was just beyond the garden wall next to it. He was not moving. The water fell in a listless curtain over him and over the big green body. After a moment Alice went down to him, but he did not look at her or speak to her. She saw that he wanted to be alone with the tree and she came back inside. He did not need to tell her what had happened. The day before, she had seen Guzmán in the marketplace go up to say hello to the grocer María dealt with—a man who had been Guzmán's friend for many years. She had seen the grocer look up at Guzmán; then, without smiling, methodically and insultingly, the man turned his back on the Count in public. It had not been the first incident of its kind. Since the jailing of Ortiz and Méndez and the four others, many of Guzmán's friends had shown him in one way or another that they were suspicious of him. They believed that he had betrayed them. Their reason was easy to understand: Guzmán's great appeal had been as an individual, a man who refused to knuckle under to the government in any way; now it appeared that he had been under the government's protection all along. Silent accusations are the worst kind, and Guzmán could not defend himself from them without sounding guilty. In the last two weeks he had been to see several of his friends, workers along the coast; each time he had been confronted by a man who was too busy even to listen to him. On Sunday, at the house of a fisherman in the lower section of town, he had been told by the man's wife that her husband was "out" and that she did not know where to find him. While the wife spoke, Guzmán was able to see her husband in the room beyond; he was listening to their conversation and making no move to come to the door or even to cover himself from view. It was known in town that the captain of police had kept the six men in jail for two weeks. He had only allowed their families to visit them. Guzmán had done nothing about it. Long before the men were let go, word had spread along the coast among Guzmán's other friends; there was little he could do to prevent it or to argue the story that was told. Ever since the day of the men's release he had been expecting that something would happen and now it had happened. Before, there had been nothing his friends could do to show how they felt but to sit down outside under the tree—and now there was nothing to do to show how they felt but cut the tree down. The men knew that Guzmán would not register a complaint about it, or even try to find out who had done it. When the rain quit for the second time a small crowd began to collect down along the beach to point up at the trunk lying on the cliff's edge, where it had grown. They pointed also at the man beside it. The sun came out and baked at the earth and the big dead body of the tree. It was from seeing it prone in the bright new sunlight, Guzmán standing next to it (he did not even seem to know that the rain had stopped), that Alice realized what she had done. Helen's talk to the Ministry had not hurt Guzmán; along this coast, the coast where he lived, it had ruined him. It was when she understood that everything that had happened during the whole summer had led up to this one moment in time, to the cutting down of the tree, and saw, too, that there was nothing that could be done to undo her own part in it, that she began to walk.

In the beginning she walked without having any goal in her mind; mainly, she did not want to see Guzmán standing like a mourner by the tree. She walked the afternoon in a roundabout circle through the top of the town, avoiding crowds and going carefully through the less busy section. She was self-conscious about being seen, though in the last couple of weeks her pregnancy had barely started to show and would not have been noticed by anyone; she walked steadily, passing the church and a flower stand and the same street several times.

After that she walked most of every day. She did not like being indoors. She could not sit through meals with Guzmán trying to make conversation. She just went on walking. After a while she knew that she was going somewhere, though she did not know where.

The walks took her to many different places. Once when she was going along the hill she saw at the near end of it a few curious people standing around the remains of the tree. Guzmán was not with them. Arrangements had been made for the trunk and branches to be chopped and carted away, but it had not been done yet. She walked from the castle ruins to the place and stood among the people who were watching it. That was when she noticed the smell. It had been drowned out in the rain, but now with the sun out it rose like fumes from the wood. Two of the people around the tree were holding their noses and pointing at the stump. Alice stepped forward and looked. There were things moving inside it. It did not strike her till then that the inside of the tree had been rotten. You could see it easily, a wide hollow space that ran up through the fallen trunk, with bugs crawling inside it and a few maggots. The stench was awful—the tree smelled like corpses—and it was apparent that its center had been decaying for some time, probably years. One of the men was pointing down to the new green shoots at the top branch and explaining that a tree that is rotten inside will send up a burst of shoots like that before it dies. So it would have fallen in a year or two anyway, she thought. Three or four at the most. They need not have torn it down. Only if it had died on its own it would not have meant what this meant. She thought about the men who had done it. It must not have been hard to cut down a tree with a hollow trunk.

The breeze turned, and a whiff of the stench from the hollow wood turned her stomach. She moved away from the tree and went on walking.

In the days that followed she did not pay attention to a great deal that went on around her, and she saw to it that nothing interfered with her strolls. One afternoon Will came to visit the palace. Helen had taken up residence at a new hotel in Seville for the autumn, and he was to spend his last days with Helen before school started in Madrid. During the afternoon, Alice had no time alone with him; she couldn't tell how much Will was able to gather about what had happened at the palace and she didn't ask. She let Guzmán drive him to the train station. Just before Will left, she knew that she ought to say something or other to him and she went to him on the terrace. No words came, and she only bent and kissed him good-bye. When Will looked up at her, studying her expression, Alice blushed dark red and started for the door. She had been blushing a good deal in the last week. At the door she turned and looked back at him. She spoke to him quickly, urgently, and the words made no particular sense even to her. "I'm a very standard girl, Will," she said. After she said it, she laughed.

Then she said, "I always used to think I was special. It was like a dream, Will. The whole time was like a dream. I wonder if that's all it was."

Will didn't say anything and Alice leaned closer and said something in a whisper. The whisper came out low and intense, as if she were explaining a matter of great importance. "I'm a very standard girl," she said, "I'm not much, Will."

Then she turned and walked off the terrace.

Will thought she might be losing her mind.

The next week passed slowly for Alice. After Will had left she walked more, visiting new places and sometimes skipping meals entirely. She did not like any of the times alone with Guzmán; the silences between them were getting worse. There was nothing to say and the dead tree was with them all the time. The garbagemen had finally carted it away, but still she did not walk along the cliff. She kept to the town and watched every object she passed with minute observation, as though each detail had suddenly become fascinating to her. People she was familiar with looked new, and places she had seen many times before began to look like strange places. Only Guzmán's face did not change— she avoided him because of it. The gutted dead look stayed the same no matter what he did or where he went. Sometimes, she knew, he went to visit some of the workers or fishermen who had been his friends along the coast. Most of them would have very little to do with him, and the ones that did receive him or allow him to sit among them only did so to make fun of him behind his back. They had felt passionately about him once, and there is nothing deader than dead passion. Alice could not stand his face when he came back from one of the visits, and when she knew he was going to see the workers she stayed out nearly all day. The conviction had not left her that the seemingly endless walk did have an end; sometimes she even believed that she knew already in the back of her mind where she was going.

One night at dinner Guzmán muttered something about starting over again—about explaining to other workers along the coast what they could do to insure survival wages. He was not very articulate (he hadn't spoken to her of anything that had happened to him since the tree had been cut down) but he made it clear that he was going away for a few days. "They won't want me, but why not try?" he said.

He left the room without waiting for an answer.

He was gone for three days and came back one evening to shower and change his clothes. Then he went away again. Juan Alberto accompanied him the second time. Guzmán had called and asked his son to come with him. Alice continued her walks during the days he was absent just as she had when he was there. Once she came back to find a strange car parked in the courtyard. She did not know whose it could be, and there was no one to ask. When she went upstairs she found that María and her husband had gone into the attic with the new arrivals and were rummaging loudly among the trunks and belongings that were kept there. After a while they came down carrying a small trunk and crossed the hall. María signaled with her eyes to Alice, who didn't understand what the signal meant or why María and her husband suddenly looked embarrassed. With them was the Count's younger son, José Ramón. Alice, who had been avoiding people she knew, was strangely glad to see him and she started forward to say hello and then stopped. Behind him was an older woman with a trim figure and a high sweep of gray hair. She stared at Alice as if she were seeing straight through her. She followed the three people who were carrying the trunk and went through the doorway into the hall. Alice could hear her footsteps going down the stairs.

For a moment she did not realize who it was. When the identity of the woman came to her, Alice went into the Parrot's Room and sat down on the sofa. She sat for a

long time going over the matter in her mind. Then she
straightened nervously. The footsteps were coming back. She
rose from the sofa and stood waiting as they grew louder.
After a moment the woman appeared in the doorway of
the Parrot's Room and stood looking at her. This time the
woman's stare was more focused, as if she were looking
for the answer to some question.

Alice said, "I'm . . ."

"Yes," the woman said. "You needn't bother."

She crossed the room and went to the windows that overlooked the garden. "They told me about the tree," she said.
Alice frowned. The Condesa de Guzmán spoke English with
hardly any accent at all. She stood watching out across the
terrace. "My husband's friends cut it down?"

"They thought he'd changed. He . . . something happened;
it wasn't his fault."

The Countess shrugged. "It would have died sooner or
later in any case," she said.

"Maybe. Not this way."

The Countess turned and faced Alice, examining her again
curiously with her eyes. She was not at all like Guzmán—
there was nothing ageless about her. She was probably in
her mid-fifties and you could see that she had once been a
pretty woman. The face sagged badly now and there was
something dull back of the eyes, as though she had been
suffering from an illness for a long time. "You're younger
looking than I expected," she said. "People have been lying
to me."

". . . Oh?"

"Oh yes," the Countess said. "People often lie to me. My
sons especially; I'm used to it. Some of the time I like it.
The only person in my life who never lied to me is my
husband, and he's the only one I never wanted to know
the truth about." She smiled. "Are you well?"

"Yes."

"But not much more."

Alice looked away.

"No," the Countess said. "Silly of me to ask. I can see
for myself. I noticed before in the hall. I'm sure it's his
fault, not yours. All of it. I suppose my husband has made
you believe, apart from everything else, that you have destroyed his life?"

Alice watched her and did not answer.

"Listen to me," the Countess said. "My husband is like
that . . . he can't help it. It's simply his nature. Sooner or
later Spain *will* go Communist, I suppose; only if my hus-

band is still alive, the Communists will persecute him for saying what he thinks just as the police do now. . . . He's a professional martyr, I'm afraid. I am different . . . in the Civil War I was a Falangist. Now I don't know what I am—a conservative, I suppose. What do the words matter any more? But what is he? . . . A man who speaks out against the government no matter what the government is . . . and what is that? You see, it's true that his friends don't trust Americans. . . . But then America supports the Franco regime. If it hadn't been for America, the regime could have fallen. The people might have knocked it down." She glanced behind her. "Like the tree . . . but that is not quite the point, is it? The point is, *you* haven't destroyed anything. Don't you see?"

"No," Alice said.

"But my dear," the Countess said. *"He* can't be hurt, don't be silly. Men like him are quite indestructible. There'll always be someone to believe him . . . if not here, on another coast, or in another part of the country. It won't take him long to find a new group of followers. I should think he's started looking already, hasn't he? It won't be so easy this time. He may even have to go into a different section or a different province . . . but if he has to, he will. He won't suffer much. He doesn't. It's other people who die, and other people who are destroyed—the ones around him. Not *him* . . . he is not used to suffering. You see, he *means* well. . . ." The Countess smiled again. "He always did. He's lethal, of course, but he can't help that . . . he's useless, and that's always lethal."

Alice stiffened.

"No," the older woman said, "I don't suppose you can afford to believe me. You probably think I'm trying to do him harm. Perhaps I am. He doesn't *look* useless—he looks as though he were accomplishing a great deal all of the time." The Countess's smile was like a tic. "I'm rather tired of picking up the pieces after he's finished. He doesn't even understand why so many people around him are destroyed. What has he accomplished in the time you've known him . . . a raise in pay for a few fishermen? He's not a revolutionary, thank God . . . he's more like Quixote; he is one of those people who spend their lives dreaming out loud. It looks harmless enough, but it's more harmful than being a revolutionary in its way. And *he's* never in any real danger, he is too well known. The police wouldn't seriously have hurt him. He's quite safe . . . he always was. It's you who aren't. . . . That's what I came back to say. I didn't like the look of you in the hall. . . . Are you sure you're all right, my dear?"

Alice nodded

"They told me you're . . ." The Countess's eyes traveled down again. "About April?"

"I think so, yes."

The ticlike smile came back. "Do take care. The new followers won't like his having an American mistress, much less an American baby. Of course, you can always keep the baby Spanish, but won't that be awkward in the long run? Tell me, when did he go away?"

"Three days ago."

"You can tell him we met if you want. It's up to you. He doesn't like me much . . . you can see why. I only came here today to pack a few of my things. . . . I heard he was traveling; I thought I'd take advantage of the time. . . . It never occurred to me that you wouldn't be with him. . . . They tell me he looks old for the first time. The tree, I suppose. He was always too fond of that tree. . . ."

The Countess went out without saying good-bye, her heels touching the floor like disappearing darts in the distance. Alice did not move after her.

Later that afternoon her head ached as if the sky were pressing down on her. She found a new street to walk on, one that was lined with dark green avocado trees on either side. Guzmán had sent a message that he'd had to delay his return by a week. She continued to walk every day, sticking to the upper part of the town. She spoke to no one on her strolls. It seemed to her that people looked at her with different faces; she no longer saw the approval in their eyes. She thought about many things while she was walking. The Countess's visit had made a strong impression on her and she went over it often in her mind, without ever arriving at a conclusion. She couldn't decide whether the woman had meant well by her visit, or if she'd had some other motive for coming into the Parrot's Room. It didn't seem to matter either way. Some part of Alice's mind had gone numb, and she let her feet carry her forward from day to day. One afternoon she took a completely new route, walking down through the town and then along the coast. From the beach she could see the palace on the hill with its garden and the gaping small space like a slice out of the air where the tree had been. She walked on the sand for a long while and then she turned her back on the coast. She went back up through the town.

In the dimming light she went to visit the ruins of the

castle and she walked several times around them. On this particular day it was as if she could not stop walking. After a while she knew that this was the day that she was going somewhere—though she still could not have said where it was. Gypsy children were playing inside the ruins. When she passed a break in the castle wall, a gypsy woman sent one of them out to beg from her. The child was a boy of six with a bad case of rickets and two teeth missing in front. His skin was olive colored and he held his palm out and mumbled something he had been taught to say. He was still too young to look sly about begging for money, but not young enough to think it was natural. He looked ashamed. Alice had only two five-peseta notes with her and she gave him one of them and then followed him back into the dirt-filled courtyard. She walked among the other children who were playing a game. She could not tell what they were playing. They did not seem very interested in the game. There was a baby of about three sitting on the lip of a well on one side of the courtyard. After a while she went over and lifted him off. The well was dry but deep; if the baby had fallen he would surely have been killed. The gypsy woman who had sent her son out came over and took the baby away from Alice; she put the baby carefully back on the lip of the well. "He won't fall," she explained in Spanish. "He knows; I train him. Some people come in to see him and leave money. Last week some rich lady wanted to adopt him." The gypsy woman giggled. "Me give him up? I told her, 'he makes good money. Adopt him? Adopt him?' "

The woman turned and went back into the ruins, and Alice walked behind her to a doorway. The room inside had been whitewashed. It was small and clean. There was an old woman inside; the black dress she wore was more like a rag than an article of clothing. She was sitting bent over, rocking herself back and forth in a straight chair. Next to her was a man working on a coffin. The old woman took no notice of it. Her back was covered with flies and she swore viciously to herself as she rocked. The younger woman passed her and went to a small stove where she was cooking something. She noticed Alice in the doorway, watching the old woman, and she grinned. "It's my mother," she said. "She's been trying to die. Won't eat, but she just can't do it. She won't even take a glass of milk . . . Well die then," she said loudly to the old woman, "if you're so set on it. Doesn't understand much Spanish," she explained to Alice. *"Solo caló:* Only the gypsy tongue. Used to speak

Castilian, till she got too old and forgot. Die, Mama," she yelled at the old woman, "can't you die?" The old woman did not seem to hear but only went on rocking angrily in her chair. Her son-in-law went on hammering on the coffin beside her and her daughter went on cooking a pot of white beans on the stove. Alice left the other five-peseta note on the edge of the coffin and walked out of the doorway before the young gypsy woman could say any more. She walked into the courtyard and once more around it, and then she went back outside.

She went twice more around the ruins. The sandy ground was hard and the topsoil was thick and chewy-looking after the long rain. At the other end of the hill she could see the palace; the stump of the tree was like a broken-off arm. She had avoided it for a time, but now it was as if she were being drawn toward it, and she moved forward. When she came to the stump she stopped and glanced down. The bugs and crawling things had long since gone. There was only an empty space and a hollow look. Around the stump, the roots of the tree stuck up out of the earth. The stump roots went very deep into the soil and some even reached down over the cliff. Standing there, Alice remembered something. She had whispered a promise to Pepe Luis that she had forgotten to keep. She made up her mind to take care of it today, and then all at once she knew where she was going afterwards; where all the walks had been leading her. Watching the tree stump, it was as if her mind had rested momentarily on the promise she had made —and while it was resting there, everything else fell into shape. The knowledge of her destination came like a breath of relief. She had been carrying it around for a long time without being able to see it—and seeing it was easier than carrying it had been. In the ease it gave her, she smiled at the stump in front of her. Then she left it and walked back into the palace.

She took a couple of things from her room and put them into her purse. After that she went out and passed the stump again; she walked away from it down along the slope of the hill.

She stopped first at the bank in the center of the main street and cashed three large traveler's checks. Some of the money she put into her purse and the rest into an envelope she had brought with her. The envelope was plain white with no name on it. She asked the bank teller how to get to a certain house, and she went outside and followed his directions. They led her to a street in the upper part of the town that she was not familiar with. It was a small white house surrounded by a garden of fruit trees. She was not sure who might be at home at this hour, and she waited in a doorway across the street for twenty minutes. Finally a maid came out of the house and walked down the street. There was no car parked anywhere near the house and Alice guessed that the person she wanted to see was probably alone now. She crossed the street and rang the bell. There was a long pause and then she heard footsteps coming down the stairs. A thin young woman with a long yellowish face opened the door and peered out. Everybody in town knew Alice by sight, and when the woman recognized her, she backed up a few steps, as if Alice had come there to do her harm. They had never spoken to each other. Alice could not remember ever having seen the woman before.

"May I talk to you?" Alice said in Spanish.

Lupe stared at her distrustfully. "What about?"

"Him," Alice said. "He sent me with this." She held out the white envelope.

Lupe looked at the envelope without touching it, as if it might have been alive. "No," she said. "I don't want to talk."

"I'd like to come in for a minute," Alice told her. "It isn't only this. There's another message."

The woman raised her eyes grudgingly to Alice's face and kept her body firmly against the door. For a moment she went on staring. Then she seemed to think better of it, and moved aside. Alice followed her into the house.

Half an hour later Lupe came out again and looked up and down the street. When she saw that it was empty she motioned with her hand. Alice slipped out from behind her and started out of the gate. As she went, the other woman grabbed her by the arm for a second and the two of them looked at each other once more. Lupe's look was different from her expression a little earlier. Alice nodded briefly and walked away.

She was on the west side of Sanlúcar now and she walked back to the palace from that side; but she did not go in. She took her car from the courtyard and drove down the road and out of the town. Traffic was fairly heavy and it took her longer than usual to get to Suelo. She left the car in the driveway of the blue villa and walked to the main building. Night was coming on and there was no one around. The summer season was over; nearly all the guests had left the hotel after the party. The main building was empty except for an elderly couple looking at a map in a corner of the lobby. Alice walked across the empty lobby and stopped at the desk of the hotel concierge. His face lit up in recognition and he looked pleased. "What may I do for you, Miss Littlejohn?"

Alice told him what she wanted to know.

"Not today," the concierge said. "Nearly everyone is off today. We're less than a quarter full. Tomorrow morning she'll be here . . ."

He stopped as Alice pulled a bank note out of her coin purse and left it lying on the counter in front of him. "If it's urgent," he said slowly, "I can tell you where to find her."

He took a pad and pen from the counter and jotted down an address. Alice folded it and put it in her coin purse where the bank note had been. The concierge put the bank note in his pocket. "You go straight over that way." He pointed behind her. "Through the town. . . . You can easily walk it. Six or seven streets I think it is. . . ."

"Thank you," Alice said.

"*De nada, Señorita,*" the concierge said. His face went blank and he lowered his eyes.

Alice left the lobby and walked down the main gravel path. She followed the directions the concierge had given her and took out the piece of paper as she walked. Her legs felt tired suddenly, as though she had just come a very long way. She crossed the coast road and went up into the tourist town. The shops were all open until eight o'clock in the evening, but no one was in them except for the shop owners, and Alice had the street almost to herself. The autumn twilights were much shorter now and night had nearly come. It was not like the fading yellow of summer. The darkness settled like a fast shadow over the land. She passed a few women hurrying home with bundles, and in back of town she passed a burro standing in front of a cart, munching from a sack that was tied around its head. The back of town was empty and less well lit. It looked darker than ever where she was going. The cobblestone streets rose ahead of her and she could see a few bats flicking out from under the eaves of buildings, darting after the bugs that circled around the street lamps. The air was still. There were stray dogs too, and there were a few people sitting out on the balconies of their apartments enjoying the evening. Alice stopped under a street lamp and looked again at the directions on the piece of paper. She could feel the dry shadows of the bats slicing above her. The place she was going to

was on a street one block farther. When she found the
street she turned to her left and looked for the number.
It was a particularly dark street and she had to walk close
by the doors to read what was on them. Her legs were
beginning to ache now from the walking. She found the
number she was looking for in a dingy little building set
into a complex of cheap apartments. There was no bell,
and she knocked on the door. This time she did not have
to wait. The door swung back almost immediately and a
familiar big black shape stood looking down at her from
the stoop, like a piece of the night.

"I came to see you," Alice said.

Eugenia nodded. She did not appear surprised—she
looked as though she had been expecting the visit for some
time. Her black dress filled the doorway and she went on
looking below her.

"I'm tired," Alice said.

The old woman held her hand out. Alice hesitated only
a fraction of a second before stepping up.

The house was quiet. Eugenia set an arm around Alice's
shoulders as if she were wrapping her deep into the protective darkness.

Six days later the people who lived in Suelo took their
chairs in off their balconies. The autumn weather was starting and a faint chill had settled along the coast. The Hotel
Malage got ready for its winter season by general-cleaning
each empty villa and apartment. One by one the rooms
were vacuumed and the furniture oiled. All of the maids
were occupied. Eugenia was kept busy most of the day di-
recting the cleaning, but even so she broke free several
times to visit the blue villa. Alice had gone back there to
live for a few days. The thing was over with now. She was
in bed recuperating. Eugenia brought her soup or tea and
looked her over each time she came. By the fourth visit it
was apparent to the old woman that except for some minor
discomfort Alice was all right. There was no immediate
need for further attention. The thing had been a total
success.

In the blue villa the temperature was pleasant and the
air was drier and warmer than outside. For long hours Alice
lay doing nothing but staring up at the ceiling. She hardly
changed her position in the bed except during Eugenia's
visits. She had no desire to read or to listen to music. There
was a short-wave radio in her bedroom that she had given
to Will (he had forgotten it when he left the hotel) but the

radio sat in silence by her bed all day and she never turned
it on. A kind of gentle torpor had taken hold of her. The
sharp line between consciousness and unconsciousness melted
away and dreams drifted in and out of her mind as easily
as thoughts. The state of mind she was in had happened to
her just before the operation and it had never left her—
nothing was sharp at all and nothing was tense. She had
gone to Eugenia for the name of a doctor who would perform an abortion, and the old woman had taken things over
at her request. During the abortion itself Eugenia had stood
beside her and held her shoulders so that she would not
move. It had not been necessary. She had not wanted to
move. The doctor Eugenia had found was a nervous little
man who insisted on being paid beforehand, and he had
talked to Alice all during it, as though she wished to be in-
formed of what he was doing step by step. It had not taken
long. He had done it in his office and he had made it
clear that she could not stay there for more than an hour or
so; if it were ever known that he had done the abortion,
he would lose his license and be in for a possible twelve-year
jail sentence. Alice promised not to tell anybody. She had
already given the money to Eugenia. A thousand dollars
was the amount the old woman had asked for. It was a
large sum, but Spain was a Catholic country and aside
from being illegal, abortion was looked down upon by everyone.

It had taken Eugenia four days to make the arrangements.
The delay had been caused by the difficulty of finding a doctor who was not a quack, but who would take a bribe to
perform an illegal operation. Alice had not been surprised
when she had learned that this would take time. On her
visit to Lupe, after the main business between them had been
finished, she had told of her own plan, and Lupe had stopped
her at the door as she was leaving.

"You'll be going home, then," Lupe had said.

"I have no home."

Lupe had looked shocked. "But you can't do it in Spain."

"I want to tell him about it afterwards," Alice had said.

Of the thousand dollars Alice gave her, Eugenia had paid
the doctor eight hundred and fifty in pesetas. The rest she
had kept herself. Alice had known that the old woman would
keep some of the money. She had, in fact, expected her to
keep more than that. The doctor Eugenia had found—in a
neighboring town—was not the best, but the best did not do
abortions. Alice didn't remember much about the operation
except for the sound. The doctor gave her several drinks

first. The physical pain was brief, and it felt as though it were happening to someone else. Just the sound seemed to belong to her, and for long minutes she could hear the scraping as if it were taking place inside her skull. She knew that it was not possible to hear the scraping, but she heard it anyway. It was low and steady and she thought that nearly everything she had ever wanted to be was being methodically removed from her in neat little scratches. Then there was a quick spilling inside her and it was over. The worst part of it was seeing the doctor carry the thing in the basin and put it on the table next to her. He started to walk away from the basin and then he walked back to it and did something to it. After that he turned and looked at Eugenia. He made a few comic motions with his mouth, opening and closing it like a goldfish, and he giggled. He was a crude man and he was imitating the efforts of a fetus gasping for air. Alice turned her head away to the wall and closed her eyes. She did not look at the doctor again. Eugenia made her lie still for an hour and a half more, but there were no complications and Alice did not feel very sick. She did not feel anything but empty. She felt emptier than she had ever felt in her life and she kept her eyes shut and did not listen to the talking of the doctor or the traffic on the street. Eugenia had kept a taxi waiting and after she was sure there would be no further bleeding, she helped Alice to walk outside. Walking was not difficult and there was nothing at all but the emptiness. When they reached the curb Alice bent over and vomited into the gutter beneath her. Eugenia stood beside her while she vomited. Then Eugenia took her arm again and they got into the taxi and came to the hotel.

Hours later lying in bed in the blue villa Alice wondered if she would ever be anything but empty again. She did not feel sad. She did not even feel like weeping. On the day in Marrakesh when she had left Pepe Luis, she had wept for five minutes in Guzmán's arms without being able to stop. She had not had any real reason for weeping about that; but now that she had a reason, she did not feel like weeping. It occurred to her that there must be some meaning in the comparison between the two events, but she could not make herself see it. There was only the slow lazy drifting of dreams and thoughts and other things that seemed to pass above her on the ceiling of their own accord. A time of her childhood came to her that way, flowing gently through her mind as if it were accustomed to being there, though she had not thought about the event since it had happened. She could not have been more than about eight years old when it happened. It was before she left New Orleans, and she had been sitting out on the cement steps of Lake Pontchartrain with her mother. Her mother had been talking to some man (she did not remember who the man was or what he looked like) and a boy in his late teens had passed above them on a bicycle and had glanced down at Alice. Something about the way the boy looked at her caused her to feel strange and she had dropped the sandwich she was eating and jerked her skirt tight around her ankles. Her mother tried to give her something else to eat, but Alice would not take her hands off her skirt. Helen thought that she had a pain, but she shook her head. She had no pain. She was only trying to make herself invisible from the waist down. In the distance along the lakeshore drive she could see the same boy coming back on his bicycle. Then she knew that he was going to look at her again and all at once she had a crazy desire to wait until he was passing, to lift her skirt up and flap it over her head. She did not know where the desire to do that had come from, and she looked down into her lap suddenly and blushed purple. She kept her eyes on her lap and did not even look up at the boy, though she felt him pass on the road above her. That was the full extent of the memory. She could see on the ceiling the exact place where she had sat on the lakeside and the road where the boy on the bicycle had passed. Then her mind turned to other things.

For a while she thought about the summer guests who had left the hotel. There were none remaining that she knew of. The Donahues had gone to Germany—Sylvia was going to have her baby there; Mrs. Lawson had gone back to New York and the boy in the pink villa named Lepard had gone back to the States. Helen and Will were in Seville. The hotel was almost empty and the blue villa felt like the emptiest of all. She wondered whether the English woman named Sylvia Donahue wanted a baby or if she was having a baby for some other reason. Things were done for reasons, but the reasons for doing things became cloudy as soon as the things were done. Like herself, she thought. She had had the abortion because it had seemed the thing to do. Only now she could not remember exactly why she had thought that. She had not come to the decision from spite—though there might have been some spite in it. Yes, she thought, there's spite in most things. Only, her reason for having the abortion was not spiteful. All the walking she had done had jostled things into shape in her mind. She saw, on her

walks, that she had reduced Guzmán to his simplest definition as a man. He was a man with large dreams who had
never been able to do much about them. The truth was that
he had always symbolized more than he had ever accomplished. But if he had never done anyone much good, he had
certainly never done anyone any harm. You do not reduce
people just because they are reduceable. It was as if, like the
tree, Guzmán had been cut down to nothing so that everyone
was seeing him for less than he was. She had not meant to do
that at all. But she had done it, and it was for that reason
that she had no right to the baby in her mind. Only that
wasn't quite it either, she thought—that was too romantic
sounding. It was easier to say that things had not worked out
between them, and she had got an abortion. She had gone
for a long walk and the end of the walk had been this. She
had had it done in Spain, knowing that it would be dangerous; but it had worked. And now it was as if the reason
for the abortion had been aborted along with everything
else inside her. All she could remember was looking at
the hollow stump of the tree and knowing what she had to
do. Other than that, the event could have happened to another woman. She had expected that she would miss the
baby, but she did not miss it. She did not even miss seeing
Guzmán. She missed only the reason for getting rid of the
baby, and when she thought about Guzmán a strange unrea-
sonable anger filled her mind. The anger was as hollow and
rotten as the empty tree stump had been when she first saw
it, evil-smelling and awful, with things crawling about in its
roots. She did not think about Guzmán for long.

During the first ten hours her body felt ungainly and
heavy and that was why she lay there without moving.
The emptiness weighed more than anything else she had
ever carried inside her. She could not seem to lift her arm
without an effort, though there was no physical basis for
exhaustion—she had no pain. When she got up to go to the
bathroom she was able to walk easily without discomfort.
Her strength was returning and her color was good. Her
appetite was improving; Eugenia no longer bothered stopping in to see how she was feeling. There was nothing to
see. Physically she was fit. The trouble did not start until
more than forty hours after the operation and by then she
was feeling almost well.

The thing that happened then happened slowly. It happened without warning and there was no pain connected
with it so that she did not know in the beginning what
was wrong. At first it was only that the figures on the ceil-

ing began to change. The memory-shapes in her mind took
on a soft hot glow and some of the images began to have
melted edges. Her eyeballs felt warm and one of the shapes
on the ceiling was trying to scare her. It was a familiar
shape and for a time she could not remember where she
had seen it before. Then it came to her that it was only
her old nightmare—the shape of emptiness, the ugly thing
that used to come at her out of the sun—only it was different
now. It was trying to be frightening, but it couldn't. There
were other things around it and other memories in her head
—all with the same hot glow—as if her mind were trying to
burn up the past. After a while she got up and went to
the bathroom for a glass of water. Her face in the mirror
was flushed, and her eyes glittered sharply back at her.
They seemed to be telling her something. She decided that
her eyes were telling her not to go back to bed again and
not to waste any more time sleeping. It was nearly two days
and two nights now since the abortion and she did not feel
weak any more. Her skin tingled. She felt alive and her
body was electric with a new morbid energy. After she drank
the glass of water, she took a quick shower and put a dress
on; then she saw herself in the mirror over the dressing
table. Without the faint early swelling of the pregnancy, the
dress seemed wrong. She took it off and put on bluejeans
and a shirt and boots. Then she stood for a moment looking around her at the inside of the blue villa as though she
had forgotten something. After that, she went out onto the
porch. The air was unexpectedly cold and she shivered in
the night. The hotel looked deserted. Passing back through
the living room she grabbed a sweater from a drawer and
then went outside again.

She sat for a while in the front seat of the car wondering where she was going. She had had a destination in mind
when she got in, but after she slipped behind the wheel
she could not recall it. Then it came to her that she was
only going back to the Guzmán palace to tell him what
she had done. She started the motor and went down the
gravel path—but she did not take the road to Sanlúcar. When
she came to the coast road she turned right instead of left.
She did not want to go back to the palace for a while, she
decided. But she knew that she had only made the wrong
turn aimlessly, and that she had no other definite place to
go. The word *aimlessly* stuck in her mind and it occurred to
her now driving east along the coast that most of her life
had been connected with that same word. Aimlessness had
been as much a part of her, she thought, as anything. Now

for no reason she did not turn the car around; she kept going east. The road was straight for a long while. She did not stop when she got to the next town. The top was up and the convertible was warm. She could not think of anywhere to go. She drove all night.

In the morning she felt better and she stopped at a café on the coast road and had two cups of black coffee and a sweet roll. When she had washed her face and hands in the ladies' room she got back in the car and went on driving. She had seen a sign on the side of the road giving the number of kilometers to a town called Ronda. It was supposed to be a nice town. She had often heard about Ronda and she had always wanted to see it; a few hours after sunrise when she came to the turnoff she took it. The road to Ronda led inland. It was flat for a while and then it led up into the hills. It was a clear bright day without a cloud in the sky and the air was fresh and warm. Alice put the window down and let the breeze flow over her. Three times during the night she had begun to sweat violently and twice she had been so cold she had had to turn the heat on in the car. Now she drove for an hour in the winding hills before she began to be cold again. On either side of the car the drab colors of the hillside ranged from slate gray to rocky brown, and great sweeping vistas appeared around each turn, dead as places on the moon. Aside from some scrub brush there was hardly any vegetation. The earth was barren and dry. When she was cold again she stopped and put her sweater on, and started once more toward Ronda. She drove with care. After a while she was aware that she was sleepy and she pulled the car over to an open place and slept for an hour by the side of the road. When she woke up she was sweating again and she took off the sweater and put her dark glasses on. The light had begun to hurt her eyes and she sat for some time without starting the motor. She had not thought any more about the abortion. She did not connect anything with it. She felt as if she were coming down with the flu and the occasional chills and fever had convinced her of that. In Ronda, she decided, she would take a hotel room if she had to and get a bottle of aspirin and sit it out. Through her dark glasses and the windshield she could see a few birds flying over the gray hills. Then she saw her old shape of emptiness hovering over the hood of the car just in front of her in the heat waves. It was strange the way it used to frighten her so much in the old days, she thought. It was a friendly demon—it had eyes like Guzmán's, pale and icy, as expressionless as the eyes of God. Beyond it, the big black birds were sweeping up the sky. Alice got out and stretched, and then looked at the birds once more. They were mottled looking, as if they had spots of water between them. She took off her dark glasses and wiped them on her shirt. It was while she was cleaning them that she happened to glance down and see the stain on the bluejeans. It had spread out from her crotch and on one side it was about six inches above the knee. Only a part of it was blood; but there was something in it besides blood. When she realized what it was, she frowned for a moment looking at it. Then she put the dark glasses back on. She looked at the sky again over the hills: the birds were there all right. They were crows or vultures. They were scanning the countryside for something to circle over. No, she thought. Circle over something else. Just over something else. Not over me.

She turned the car around and drove easily back down through the hills to the coast road. Once along the coast, she felt much better, and she turned back toward Suelo. If she had to, she knew, she could always stop and see a doctor in one of the towns along the way. But she did not have to. The closer she got to Suelo, the better she felt, and there was still no pain. Once when she stopped in a gas station she looked down and saw that the discharge between her legs had spread a little. It was not spreading rapidly, and despite almost no sleep, she was not tired. The unnatural energy that filled the emptiness inside her was carrying her well. Besides, she liked driving. The emptiness weighed more than ever, and she wanted to stay in motion for as long as she could. The chances were that any doctor she saw would send her right back to bed for a week, and she did not relish the idea. It was Will she thought mostly about on the drive back; she had loved him better, and longer, she decided, than anyone. She needed to talk to him and she made up her mind to call him as soon as she got to the hotel. It was not until dusk, when she was about an hour outside of Suelo, that she even thought of the possibility of dying. The fever was high by then, and the chills were coming faster. During one of the peaks, when the shivering had stopped and her mind had reached an icelike state of clarity, she remembered that she had heard once that an infection of the uterus can become systemic in a matter of hours. Still she did not take the thought of dying very seriously. If she had been going to die, she would have died by now, she thought. It occurred to her that the doctor had not just been a crude man, but also a crude doctor, and that she had known it would have to be like that from the time she went to Eugenia. She had known how it would be and what might happen because of it. The moment of clarity left her as quickly as it had come and by the time she got to the hotel she felt as if her brain were on fire. The night air was thick and the pebbles of the gravel path in front of the car looked like a stream of individual boulders. When she stopped the car in front of the blue villa she felt not so much exhausted as suspended like a heavy weight between two terrible extremes. When she got out of the car to walk to the villa, she found herself lying flat on the lawn with a mouthful of grass. Her knees had given way only two steps from the car, and she had fallen. It made her chuckle at herself. After the amount of walking she had done in the last weeks, she couldn't seem to make it now the short distance from the carport to the blue villa. She picked herself up again and walked, rocking a little as she went. Her knees were like rubber and they seemed double-jointed, so that they bent as easily backward as they did forward. She pulled herself up by the porch railing and held onto the column on one side. After she had caught her breath, she pushed herself off the column and aimed her body at the villa door. She caught herself on it and leaned there while she fished in her purse for the key. Once inside the villa, she began to feel stronger. She sat down on the sofa and decided that she would not panic. She would do things slowly and well. First of all, she would take two aspirin for the fever. Then she would get the concierge to call a good doctor fast. Once having made that decision, she felt even more strong, and she got herself off the sofa and into the bathroom with hardly any trouble at all. When she was emptying the aspirin out of the bottle into her hand she caught a glimpse of her face again in the mirror. It was then that she knew. She dropped the bottle of aspirin on the floor.

When she got herself to the phone the comedy started. First she could not get the operator to answer her. Then she was told that Mr. Holtz had gone away for the month to one of his other hotels. She had to wait at least two minutes before she was connected to the concierge. She signaled the operator twice, but the concierge was away from his desk and there was no one there to answer the phone for him. When she finally heard him, the voice of the concierge sounded small and far away.

"I need a doctor," she said.

"Miss Littlejohn?"

"I need a doctor," she said, "I'm dying."

"You are what?" the concierge said.

"Dying."

"Excuse me? Could you spell it, Miss Littlejohn?"

"D-Y-I-N-G. Listen. . . . Oh, Christ, get a doctor," she said. "Get me a doctor."

"I will do what I can," the concierge said after a moment. He sounded confused.

After she had hung up it occurred to her that she could have said it in Spanish. She had forgotten for the moment that she spoke Spanish.

She opened the front door so that the doctor could let himself in, and then she got herself to the sofa and lay down flat. The emptiness in her body weighed so much now she could not move it any more. When she lay back and shut her eyes she saw two big things wheeling high in the air over her head. Then she knew that she was not on the sofa at all. The air was fresh and blue over her, and the sky was clear. She was still on the road to Ronda. She had only pretended to turn back; she had not really changed direction. She had only left the car and gone for a walk in the hills.

She was tired from the walking now, and her body was so heavy that it felt like sinking into the earth. She was walking as fast as she could, climbing all the time, and the car was already way below her. The sun was hot; then she remembered that when she first came to Spain she had been afraid of the sun. She moved step by step up the gray barren hill. She could see now what the two big things were that were wheeling in the air. They were only the crows. They were circling over her and waiting. A kind of panic swept over her seeing them and then she made up her mind not to let the panic get the best of her. It was better to go on climbing. The demon, the shape of emptiness, was leading the way. He was floating in the air just ahead. Then she saw him stop at a cliff on the edge of the high hill. He stood on the cliffside and looked back at her. Then he jumped off; but he did not fall. Instead, she saw him soar out delicately into space. She had not known that the demon could fly, but he could. He was as light as a whale in water or a bird in the air. He stayed there whipping back and forth in the wind. She saw that he was trying to tell her to jump too, but she was afraid; her body weighed more than lead now and she knew that she would surely be crushed on the ground below.

Then she looked behind her and saw that there was no

place else to move. A tree had grown in the earth where the hiil had been.

She broke a small branch of leaves off the tree and held it in one hand for luck. Then she jumped. All at once, with no effort, she was soaring. The heavy emptiness was gone from her body and she knew suddenly that everything was going to be better. A sharp long shiver of heat ran through her and her mind turned incandescent. She was even lighter in space than the specter shape had been. After she had left him behind, she went on rising straight into the sun.

EIGHT days after Alice Littlejohn walked out of the Guzmán palace in Sanlúcar, a strange thing happened in the town. The police captain's wife disappeared. The captain organized several search parties for her, but no one had any idea where she might have gone. For a time a story circulated that Lupe had been seen waiting in a neighboring town for one of the ferries that cross to Morocco—but the idea was ridiculous, and the rumor was soon forgotten. Besides, she never came back.

A day after her disappearance, the weather in most of the province took a turn for the better. There was a feel of autumn like a tinge of iron in the sky. Farther north the air was hard and alive. That afternoon, in a car, Will and his mother were driving in the outskirts of Seville. They had just come back from a weekend spent at a ranch outside of the city.

It was another week till school began in Madrid and Will's mother had taken him to visit one of her new friends for a house party. The friend was a widower who kept an apartment in Seville as well as a ranch in the country where he bred bulls for fighting. Will did not like bullfights and he had spent the weekend being polite about it. Helen's friend had taken it for granted that an American boy would be fascinated by bullfights and Will had had to lie solidly for two straight days. The second day he had been taken into a small private bullring and given a *muleta*, a fighter's cape, to play with, while Helen's new friend chased him around the ring holding a pair of horns. It had embarrassed him as well as annoyed him and if they had stayed another day in the country he would have had to tell the man the truth. Will did not like bullfights for a reason—it was not what happened to the bull that bothered him, but what happened to the crowd. The enjoyment at the sight of suffering was always visible in the faces of the people at a *corrida*, and it built to a high pitch when the pic entered the bull's body; it was that, the excitement of the audience at the sight of blood, that made Will dislike bullfights. If Helen was going to keep her new friend for any length of time, he would have to make clear to him sooner or later just what he thought of the subject. There is no telling to what lengths an aficionado of bullfights will go, and when they had left the ranch, Helen's friend had given Will two dried bull's ears and a bull's tail that had been won by a famous *torero* last year at one of the Holy Week *corridas*. The three objects, stiff with dried blood, had been presented to Will as a great gift; he had placed them on the floor of the car, and he had been trying to think during the drive of someone he could give them to who would get a kick out of them. Some tourists liked bull's ears. Him they made urp. Helen turned the car onto the broad tree-lined avenue that led to their hotel. They were staying at the Luna Verde, a brand-new high-rise hotel in the fashionable Macarena section of Seville. Helen was already planning a New Year's Eve party for the hotel owners. She pulled into the main driveway and gave her car up to the doorman. "Let's have a cup of tea," she said.

She led the way and Will went with her in the elevator up to the main terrace. The café of the Luna Verde was on the roof. They sat down and Helen ordered tea and pastry, and Will remembered that he had left the ears and the tail on the floor of the car. He did not mention it. While they were waiting for the tea he got up and went to the edge of the terrace to watch the river sixteen stories below. It was the same river the Guzmán palace overlooked a hundred miles south of here in Sanlúcar—the Guadalquiver—only from here the water looked thick and light chocolate, like a vein of the earth. At Sanlúcar the river was touched at the delta with green and white where it emptied into the sea. It was not as pretty from here, he decided, but it had a realer look. The sky above it rose like a big drop of dew. For a while he watched a couple of cargo boats snuggle after each other along the docks of the west bank. That side of the river was called Triana and much of it was a slum; it was where the poor folk and the gypsies lived. Sometimes if you walked through Triana in the evenings you could hear *cante jondo* in the courtyards or in the cheap bars. Will thought if he ever got to know enough of it he could get to like *cante jondo* as much as he disliked bullfights. In the luxurious Macarena section there was none of it, though. The houses were more like little estates. The hotel rose in the midst of them like a symbol of elegance, and the trees were like fur. Helen called Will back to the table and he went and sat down with her. The tea and pastry had arrived.

Sitting munching on an almond cake Will thought about some of the time that had passed since the party in Suelo. He had come a long way in his mind since then and he was not absolutely sure why. Nothing had happened. Maybe that was why. After he had run out of the Hotel Malage that morning he had sat down on the beach for several hours thinking and inside him a war had taken place. Several of his glands had shot down other glands with squirts of acid. Then he had got up and walked back. The thing he had seen in the pink villa had thrown him for a loop. It had made his scrotum feel like one of those glass bubbles with an imitation monument and snowflakes in it you shake up and watch. Only, when things had finally settled back down inside him, he knew that he had learned something. Except he did not know yet what he had learned. But somehow the faces on the wheel, and the mosaic of events— even the feeling of in-between—all had changed because of it.

The actual fact was that he hadn't had a whole lot of time to think about it because, apart from traveling and getting ready for school, he'd had something else on his mind. The something else was the same thing it had been all his life—Littlejohn. The disconnected way she had acted the last time he had seen her had got hold of Will's thinking like a cat with a stolen sardine. Since the beginning of the summer when she had taken off with Guzmán, Will had not really worried about her; but now that he could use the time to consider about his own problems, she was back in his head. It was like there was a clue missing in the way she had been behaving lately. All he had to do now was to take it out and look at it—only there were too many inconsequential facts in the way of the clue. Helen put another pastry on his plate and he cut into it with his fork and tried with his thinking to weed out his mind.

After they had finished the tea they went downstairs in the elevator to the main lobby. Helen wanted to bathe and change and Will was going to read for a while. He had this book, *Madame Bovary*, which he had already read once, and he was going back over the interesting parts. It was supposed to be too old for him, but one of the good things about Helen was she didn't consider anything too old for anybody to read. She got her key at the desk and Will asked for his. While he was waiting for it, he saw his mother's face change. The concierge had handed her a written message with her key. "What is it?" Will said.

"I want to put a call through to Suelo," Helen said looking at the note. "To the Hotel Malage."

The concierge spoke to the telephone operator through the window behind his desk. Then he turned to Helen again. "I'm sorry, Madame," he said, "we have a six-hour delay for calls to that part of the province. It is quite usual. The coastal provinces are often . . ."

"I know," Helen said, "I just came from there. To Cádiz then. Make it to the city. To the General Hospital in . . ."

"It's the same province, Madame," the concierge said.

Helen drew her breath in slowly and looked at the ceiling. She was something more than just angry. Her face had gone nearly white.

"I'm very sorry, Madame," the concierge said, "it's not our fault; the telephone lines . . ."

"Please," Helen said. "Have my car brought back."

The concierge took a look at her and gave the order rapidly to one of the bellboys.

"Call the garage yourself," Helen said without moving, "it's faster."

The concierge started to answer her and then thought better of it. He phoned the order down to the doorman. Will tried to see the note in Helen's hand but she had crumpled it into her fist. A little piece of it stuck out between two of her fingers like a leaf growing there.

"I told you where I'd be over the weekend," she said.

The concierge drew himself up with the innocence of an Andalusian who had been done an injustice. "This message came in only this morning," he said. "Your instructions were that you were coming back today. We . . ."

Helen had not waited for the answer but was already halfway to the elevator. Will followed her. He could see from his face what the concierge was going to say about Helen and about America in general once they were inside the elevator.

"Damn this country," Helen said when the doors had closed, "it's death."

Will looked at her. He had never in thirteen years known his mother to talk that way. She did not say anything further and Will saw from her face that there would be no use asking her any more questions for the moment.

When they were back inside the car and Helen had got directions from the doorman, Will settled back against the

right-hand door and studied her face. Helen swung out of
the hotel driveway and headed for the river.

"Will, don't stare at me," she said, "not when I'm driving."

Will looked ahead and smiled. Except for her tone, Helen
had sounded for a second exactly like Littlejohn.

Then he quit smiling. "It's her," he said, "isn't it?"

He saw Helen next to him nod without answering. He
did not like the look of her face. Something inside Will
seemed to catch at his stomach. "What's wrong?"

"I'll tell you in a second; help me find the signs to Cádiz.
The doorman said they were on the river road."

"There." Will pointed.

They had come to the east bank of the Guadalquivir;
Helen turned left down a broad avenue that was full of
traffic. The avenue led south like the river.

"I don't know what's wrong," she said. "The message
didn't say. I hope it's not a . . ."

She set her upper lip between her teeth.

Will could feel a chill settle slowly on the back of his
neck.

Helen was quiet for a few seconds.

"It's okay," Will said. "I know about the baby."

They drove for a while and Will felt a tight band con-
strict around his chest until it hurt.

Some of the thoughts were spinning now in his head and
he wanted to see the words that were written on the note
the concierge had given Helen. She still had it in her hand,
on the steering wheel. A piece of the note remained between the roots of two of her fingers. It was fluttering like a
leaf in the breeze from the open window. It reminded Will
of the note he had given Eugenia that day when he had got
on the bus with her; she had held the note in her hand
the same way.

"What's it say?" Will said.

". . . Say?"

"The note."

" 'Accident to Miss Littlejohn. Suggest you contact us or
General Hospital Cádiz.' In English. Signed by the concierge
of the Hotel Malage. Damn the concierge. Damn all hotels,"
Helen said. She turned right at a fork Will had indicated.

They did not talk again till they were out of the city.
The road south from Seville was wide at first and then it
narrowed. Watching it Will remembered suddenly that it
was this same road Littlejohn had taken the first day she
had come to Spain. The Fifth of June. The day he had

taken the bus up from Suelo and waited for her in a café in Jerez—she had been driving down from Seville.

He watched the flat land and the trees by the highway. Then he said something. Without knowing why he said it, as if the words formed of themselves in his mouth, he said, "I don't believe it was an accident."

At first he almost thought somebody else had said it. His mind had done a funny thing. It had gone from Littlejohn's face on the Fifth of June to a tree now on the side of the highway, to Littlejohn's face the last time he had seen her.

He felt Helen look at him. Then she looked back at the highway. "What does that mean?"

Will strained, but the thought in his mind was too tangled. They drove for another kilometer or so in silence.

Will's face had gone dark red from reaching after the thought and the cords in his neck were standing out. He could not talk. There was no sound between them in the car except for the wind where it came through the window and the note fluttering. The thought was just barely ahead of Will. It was hanging on the other side of the windshield like a carrot in front of a donkey.

But it was no use and they sat there for over an hour with Helen driving, her hands white on the wheel. She moved in and out of the cars and trucks, sliding their car up ahead when she could. The side of her face was white like her hands.

Will sat next to her in a kind of glaze. He felt as if they were approaching a place that they had all been coming to from the beginning, and he kept straining his eyes as if he wanted to see the place through the windshield. Ahead of them was nothing but flat country and one truck after another and Will thought that the place they were going was like the place that you get to from living your whole life on half-true things. He felt something on the floor of the car with his foot, and he looked down and saw the two bull's ears and the bull's tail lying where he had left them. His accepting them, too, had been just another half truth. He had been polite to Helen's new friend for a reason. The man was keeping Will's dog on his ranch for part of the first school semester—until Will found a *pensión* that would let him have the dog with him. So Will had had a reason for pampering the man about bullfights. There was a hidden reason for everything, and nothing was really what it looked like. That was why he couldn't name the place they were going.

It was a few minutes after they had passed Jerez, when they were crossing the low gray hills—the same hills he and Littlejohn had crossed in the car on the Fifth of June— that the first edge of the idea began to be visible to him Before he could say it, Helen pointed to a sign they were passing. The sign marked the Sanlúcar turnoff

"That's where he lives . . is it far from Cádiz?" she said "No."

"He might put some pressure on them; we may need a specialist sent down from Madrid if it's   " Helen coughed and got the word out ". . if it's serious."

"He's probably at the hospital with her."

"No," Helen said. "He can't be. He'd have sent a telegram himself or called, if he were. I told you It was signed by the concierge."

She took the turnoff and continued fast on the smaller highway that led to Sanlúcar. The road was bumpy Will kept getting little shivers in his back from nerves.

Helen said, "Has there been a fire?" She was looking at the fields on either side of the road. They were blackened and flat.

"The farmers," Will said, "they burn them in the fall then they plow under the roots." He was talking by rote, not thinking about what he was saying.

But Helen was not listening either and they went on along the narrow road through the black desolate fields.

Will showed her the way to the palace and she parked in the courtyard. She waited in the car while he ran up the steps. María answered the door. She seemed glad to see him and Will ran past her and then turned back.

"En la Sala del Loro," María said: "In the Parrot's Room "

Will ran through the Ambassador's Room into the other doorway. Guzmán was alone reading a book He looked up For a second Will could not speak.

"Listen," he said. Through the windows in the distance behind Guzmán he could see the big hollow stump of the tree. "You'd better come," he said

Guzmán stood up

"She's . .   it's about her." Will's throat tightened He turned around and ran back out After a moment Guzmán followed him more slowly They went out of the palace and down the steps, Will leading the way Guzmán stopped short when he saw who was in the car.

'Is Alice with you?"

'Please get in," Helen said

Guzmán bent slowly and looked at her Helen was still

watching straight ahead through the windshield. She didn't look at him.

Will slid in first and Guzmán got in frowning next to him. "What is it, please? Something about Alice?"

Without answering, Helen put the car into gear and drove out of the courtyard.

Will pointed the way back to the main highway. Guzmán waited for Helen to speak. When she was on a straight road, Helen held the crumpled note out across Will. Guzmán took it and opened it. He didn't say anything, but Will could feel him stiffen slightly in the seat.

"We don't know what it means," Helen said.

"Neither do I. I have not seen her since a good many days. Wasn't she with you?"

"Not since the night of the party."

"But where then?"

"The hotel, apparently."

They drove without speaking for a while.

"Did you have a fight?" Helen said.

"No. *I* had some personal trouble but . . . we had no fight."

"Then why the hotel?"

"I can't think of a reason."

"There has to be one. She hates the hotel," Helen said. "Don't you know she hates that hotel?"

"Yes," Guzmán said.

"Then why would she go there?"

Guzmán didn't answer.

"If she was in trouble," Helen said, her voice rising, "she'd have come to me. To one of us."

"Exactly," Guzmán said.

"No," Will said.

Neither of them looked at him for more than a second. Helen was watching the road. Guzmán had turned and was watching the coastline.

"It's the reasons. Like none of them are reasons. It's only half," Will said. "Don't you see? . . . It's just a bunch of half-true things. That's where it is."

"Where it is?"

"The place," he said. "We're going to the place of half-true things." He was talking in a feverish way and the words were not making the sense he had sent them out with.

"Half *true* things?" Helen said.

"Like Donahue. Like all of it. And the lies. I guess she found out too."

"Keep calm," Guzmán said gently.

"I *am* calm," Will said. "Don't you see? It was something about the Columbus tree. I saw her face when she looked at it. It's where we're going now. She knows . . ."

"William, control yourself."

"She knows," he said. "It's something about the Columbus tree. She knows."

He could hear his own voice getting louder. He was quiet then for a while. The two people sat in stony silence on either side of him. He knew they couldn't make sense of his words. It was like for the first time in his life he knew what he meant and he couldn't say it. They were driving along the coast now, with the sea on the right side and some low spare trees on the left that the wind had turned to big sticks. Will waited some more and then the words started again in his throat. The sound of his voice was even wilder.

"If she's dead . . ."

"She isn't dead. Stop that," Helen said sharply.

"She might be."

"She isn't. There's probably been some minor accident . . ."

"It wasn't an accident. She wouldn't go to anybody. Not if she was in trouble herself. Not if she didn't want the baby." Will said, "I think she wanted to get rid of the baby."

He felt Helen take her foot off the accelerator for an instant and the two people glanced at each other. When Helen put her foot back on the accelerator, she speeded up a little. Hillocks of bright green on the right were passing them, with patches of beach like white teeth between them. It looked as if the earth were smiling.

Then Will saw it through the windshield. It was a white fluttering thing like a ghost. All the other things were converging on it. It was the same vision he had had three times in the summer, the vision of the mosaic, only he knew what it was now. The white thing at the center was *her*. It was a reflection of the note Helen had given to Guzmán. Guzmán was holding it up, unnoticed, in his hand, and you could see the note in the glass. But it meant her. The white fluttering thing was Littlejohn. And all the other things trying to kill it.

"If she's dead . . ."

"She *can't* be dead," Helen said hard.

"Of course not," Guzmán said. Then there was a long silence.

Will said something in his mind. Let her be alive, he said; I'll do whatever. God let her and I'll do it now and for the rest of my life. I'll go to Madrid a week early. I'll do what she said. I'll go back to school. Whatever You want me to do, but let her be alive.

Then he decided that the way he was talking, God would only be angry. You can't insult Him by trying to make bargains. It would be like threatening Him, he thought. No, he said, all right, I'll do it anyway. So it's not a bargain. I'll go back to school. Only don't let her be dead. I don't care about anything else, but don't let her be dead. God please let her be alive.

Cádiz was a lollipop-shaped spit of land with a railroad trestle and a road running along the stick of the lollipop. The approach was a thin beach with water on either side. Then they were in the city. The traffic was bad. Guzmán asked a policeman the way to the hospital. They had to move slowly now because of the buses and they had to stop at a string of red lights one after the other. When they got to the hospital, there was no place to park. Helen drove around the block. Then she pulled into a bus stop in back. "They'll tow it away," Guzmán said. "Let them," Helen said.

They got out and ran to the back entrance of the hospital past a line of old trucks parked outside. The trucks were painted two or three different colors, and most of the colors had chipped or faded down to nothing. There were three new trucks. Just at the entrance, Helen came to a halt next to one of the new ones. Her face had gone ashen, but she was not looking at the hospital. She was looking at the new truck. It was directly in front of the door to the hospital. It was freshly painted and it sparkled in the sun. The truck was a bright nasty green.

"Come on," Will said. He reached for her hand but she did not seem able to move. Guzmán took her arm from the other side and they half pulled her away from the truck. They got her into the hospital and it was a long time before they found anybody. Somebody finally directed them to the emergency clinic. When they got there, the clinic was empty. It was a square white room with steel tables and an antiseptic smell. There was a glass partition at one end. Guzmán went to the partition and knocked on it.

A doctor who was smoking came out wearing a white smock and looked at them curiously.

"*Una señorita norteamericana,*" Guzmán said. "*Se llama Littlejohn. Lee-tay-jaw. Con ele.*" He spelled her name out and the doctor stared back at him.

"*Norteamericana?*" the doctor said. He looked puzzled.

He shrugged and went back to look at some files for her name.

It took them a long time to find her because she wasn't in that part of the hospital. She was in another part. Once he knew, Will stopped listening. His hands were shaking. He could not remember how they had got from the emergency clinic to the hospital morgue. But all his life he remembered being there with her. They sat in a white empty room with the concrete slab at one end, and he didn't want to look at her. He wanted to help Helen, but his hands were shaking badly. The top of the sheet was curled back and after a while he went and lifted it up and looked at her face. It didn't help him. She did not look like anything.

There was a stamp on the box saying that she had been dead on arrival.

He went outside in the sunlight and stood there for a while and watched the pigeons and listened to the sounds on the street. He knew what he had to do. Back in June he had first made her the promise. He had promised her he would get on the train and go back to school in Madrid no matter what. They had been standing in the salt field marshes and it had been a serious promise. He remembered too the last thing she had said to him all summer. "I'm a very standard girl, Will," she had said. He thought about both things. He did not know how dark it was getting until he saw the street lights come on. After a while he went back inside.

Helen and Guzmán were still there. They were sitting at opposite sides of the room like misplaced bookends, facing the same wall. "I have to go now," Will said. He didn't know who he said it to.

He walked out and went down the stairs and took a taxi to the station. The train was late and he got on it the way she had told him to and he took a compartment with a bed. He felt dizzy and he sat down on the bed. After a long time the train rattled and jerked forward. You could see a few street lights through the window. He didn't feel as if he were leaving her there. Something of himself had not got on the train.

Once they were out of the town, you could hear the engine.

THAT night was a bright one in Suelo and Eugenia could not sleep. At two in the morning she slipped out from beside Enrique and got dressed. She took fifty pesetas from her stash of petty cash in a shoebox, and went outside.

She stretched and then she walked to the bar that was open at the top of the town. She ordered a hard-roll sandwich filled with Italian salami and drank a glass of sweet *anís* while she was waiting for it. Then she had the waitress refill the glass and she took it and the roll out onto the back porch of the bar.

The hotel below her sparkled faintly in the night. She had not been able to sleep for thinking of what had happened to the American girl. But after a while she would be able to. There would be no problem about it—no one knew who had performed the operation. The girl's car had been seen quite far east along the coast the day before her death; the police would assume that she had stopped somewhere there for the abortion. Still, when Eugenia had time to think about it, she was sorry. She had had no grudge against the girl.

Those were the things that happened and that was the price you paid. The way the world went. *Pues allí 'stá:* So there it is. She bit into the roll and looked down over the town.

The wave of tourists had all left now; there would be another one starting in a few months. It was a shame, she thought, that everybody could not know how well she had done in the last weeks. Some people knew, but only the ones she had dealt with. The town was deserted looking and dark below her. Eugenia took another swallow of *anís*. It was beginning to work and soon she would go home to sleep.

The lap of the waves was even. She knew the edge of the sea was steady, though she could not see it from here. It was an average autumn night. Straight ahead and to the right, in the very pit of the darkness, a pale moon was rising.

Have You Read these Bestsellers from SIGNET?

☐ **THE CENTER by Charles Beardsley.** From the author of **The Motel** comes a torrid new novel of scorching sex and warped desires among therapists who cannot cure their own devastating lusts. (#Y5653—$1.25)

☐ **SEMI-TOUGH by Dan Jenkins.** This super bestseller is "funny . . . marvelous . . . outrageous. . . . Dan Jenkins has written a book about sports, but not about sports . . . it mocks contemporary American mores; it mocks Madison Avenue; it mocks racial attitudes; it mocks writers like me. . . . Women abound . . . I loved it."— David Halberstam, **New York Times Book Review**
(#E5598—$1.75)

☐ **THE SANTA CLAUS BANK ROBBERY by A. C. Greene.** A violent, ironic tale of nonstop killing in America's most bizarre bank holdup—the day that Santa decided to stuff his sack with all the dollars in the First National Bank. "Extraordinary power."—**Los Angeles Times**
(#Y5565—$1.25)

☐ **CARRIAGE TRADE by Robert Thomsen.** Not since **Gone With the Wind** has there been such a big, lusty, un-ashamedly romantic novel of love and war. "A book to be read . . . who can fail to find interest in a combination of prostitutes and Civil War soldiers."—**Newsday**
(#W5564—$1.50)

☐ **GENTLEMAN OF LEISURE: A Year in the Life of a Pimp,** text by Susan Hall; photographed by Bob Adelman. The pimp who makes more money than the president of the United States tells the shocking, intimate story of his profession—with explicit photographs of his world —and his women. (#J5524—$1.95)

Big Bestsellers from SIGNET

☐ **TO REACH A DREAM by Nathan C. Heard.** From the author of the bestselling **Howard Street** comes a seething new novel of streetcorner manhood at the bottom of a black ghetto. "Raw, brutal, memorable."—The New York Times (#Y5490—$1.25)

☐ **THE SEX SURROGATES by Michael Davidson.** The raw tapes of the sex clinic—a startling novel about the men and women—strangers—who find themselves partners in love. (#Y5410—$1.25)

☐ **AN OLD-FASHIONED DARLING by Charles Simmons.** Can a young man who works on a sex magazine and has a harem of sexually voracious ladies, break the sex habit? "Unrestrained delight."—The New York Times (#Q5355—95¢)

☐ **GETTING RID OF RICHARD by Joyce Elbert.** A saucy novel about a lovely young lady's sexual liberation by the smash author of **The Crazy Ladies.** (#Y5421—$1.25)

☐ **GOLDENROD by Herbert Harker.** Goldenrod is about love in its widest, deepest meaning, and like love, it is both funny and serious, joyous and sad, and very beautiful. "One of the most enchanting novels ever written. . . ."—Ross Macdonald, New York Times Book Review (#Y5487—$1.25)
